INCRIMINATING EVIDENCE

BANTAM BOOKS
New York Toronto London Sydney Auckland

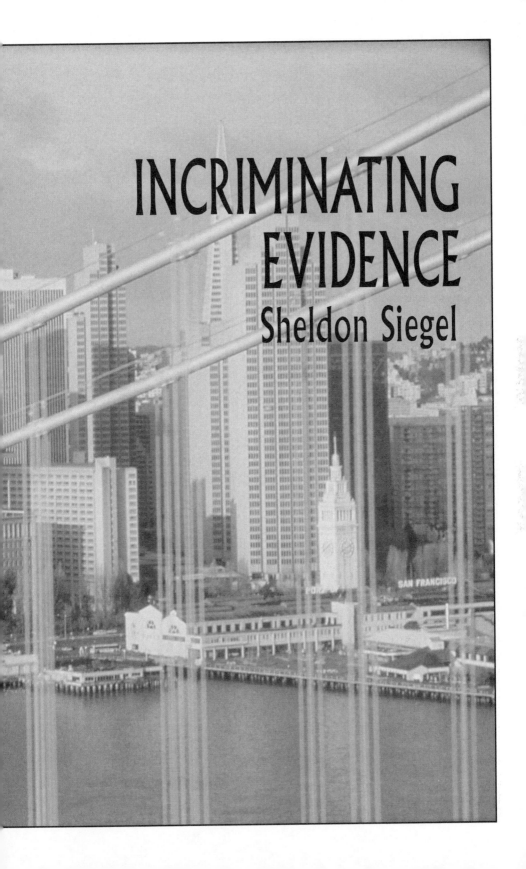

INCRIMINATING EVIDENCE

Sheldon Siegel

INCRIMINATING EVIDENCE

A Bantam Book / August 2001

Title page illustration courtesy of Index Stock Imagery

Library of Congress Cataloging-in-Publication Data

Siegel, Sheldon (Sheldon M.)
    Incriminating evidence / Sheldon Siegel.
      p. cm.
    ISBN 0-553-80144-9
    1. San Francisco (Calif.)—Fiction. 2. Public prosecutors—Fiction.
I. Title.

PS3569.I3823 I58 2001
813'.54—dc21

                                                            2001025473

Published simultaneously in the United States and Canada

PRINTED IN THE UNITED STATES OF AMERICA

BVG   10 9 8 7 6 5 4 3 2 1

For my dad

INCRIMINATING EVIDENCE

1

"WE HAVE A SITUATION"

"The attorney general is a law enforcement officer, not a social worker."
—Prentice Marshall Gates III, San Francisco district attorney
and candidate for California attorney general.
Monday, September 6.

Being a partner in a small criminal defense firm isn't all that it's cracked up to be. Oh, it's nice to see your name at the top of the letterhead, and there is a certain amount of ego gratification that goes along with having your own firm. Then again, you have to co-sign the line of credit and guarantee the lease. You also tend to get a lot of calls from collection agencies when cash flow is slow. In this business, founder's privilege extends only so far.

Unlike our well-heeled brethren in the high-rises that surround us, the attorneys in my firm, Fernandez and Daley, occupy cramped quarters around the corner from the Transbay bus terminal and next door to the Lucky Corner Number 2 Chinese restaurant. Our office is located on the second floor of a 1920s walk-up building at 553 Mission Street, on the only block of San Francisco's South of Market area that has not yet been gentrified by the sprawl of downtown. Although we haven't started remodeling yet, we recently took over the space from a now-defunct martial arts studio and moved upstairs from the basement. Our files sit in what used to be the men's locker room. Our firm has grown by a whopping fifty percent in the last two years. We're up to three lawyers.

"Rosie, I'm back," I sing out to my law partner and ex-wife as I stand in the doorway to her musty, sparsely furnished office at eight-thirty in the morning on the Tuesday after Labor Day. Somewhere behind four mountains of paper and three smiling pictures of our eight-year-old daughter, Grace, Rosita Fernandez is already working on her second Diet Coke and cradling the phone against her right ear. She gestures at me to come in and mouths the words "How was your trip?"

I just got back from Cabo, where I was searching for the perfect vacation and, if the stars lined up right, the perfect woman. Well, my tan is good. When you're forty-seven and divorced, your expectations tend to be pretty realistic.

Rosie runs her hand through her thick, dark hair. She's only forty-three, and the gray flecks annoy her. She holds a finger to her full lips and motions me to sit down. She gives me a conspiratorial wink and whispers the name Skipper as she points to the phone. "No, no," she says to him. "He'll be back this morning. I expect him any minute. I'll have him call you as soon as he gets in."

I sit down and look at the beat-up bookcases filled with oatmeal-colored legal volumes with embossed gold lettering that says *California Reporter*. I glance out the open window at the tops of the Muni buses that pass below us on Mission Street. This is an improvement over our view before we moved upstairs. When we were in the basement, we got to look at the bottoms of the very same buses.

On warm, sunny days like today, I'm glad we don't work in a hermetically sealed building. On the other hand, by noon, the smell of bus fumes will make me wish we had an air conditioner. Our mismatched used furniture is standard stock for those of us who swim in the lower tide pools of the legal profession.

Rosie and I used to work together at the San Francisco public defender's office. Then we made a serious tactical error and decided to get married. We are very good at being lawyers, but we were very bad at being married. We split up almost seven years ago, shortly after Grace's first birthday. Around the same time, I went to work for the tony Simpson and Gates law firm and Rosie went out on her own. Our professional lives were reunited about two years ago when I was fired by the Simpson firm because I didn't bring in enough high-paying clients. I started subleasing space from Rosie. On my last night at Simpson and Gates, two attorneys were gunned down in the office. I ended up representing the lawyer who was charged with the murders. That's when Rosie decided I was worthy of being her law partner.

I point to myself and whisper, "Does Skipper want to talk to me?"

She nods. She scribbles a note that says "Do you want to talk to him?"

Prentice Marshall Gates III, known as Skipper, is the San Francisco district attorney. We used to be partners at Simpson and Gates. His father was Gates. He's now running for California attorney general. His smiling mug appears on billboards all over town under the caption "Mr. Law and Order." Two years ago, he won the DA's race by spending three million dollars of his inheritance. I understand he's prepared to ante up five million this time around.

I whisper, "Tell him you just heard me come in and I'll call him back in a few minutes." I'm going to need a cup of coffee for this.

Skipper is, well, a complicated guy. To my former partners at Simpson and Gates, he was a self-righteous, condescending ass. To defense attorneys like me, he's an opportunistic egomaniac who spends most of his time padding his conviction statistics and preening for the media. To the citizens of the City and County of San Francisco, however, he's a charismatic local hero who vigorously prosecutes drug dealers and pimps. He takes full credit for the fact that violent crime in San Francisco has dropped by a third during his tenure. Even though he's a law-and-order Republican and a card-carrying member of the NRA, he has led the charge for greater regulation of handguns and sits on the board of directors of the Legal Community Against Violence, a local gun-control advocacy group. He's an astute politician. It's a foregone conclusion that he'll win the AG race. The only question is whether he'll be the next governor of California.

Rosie cups her hand over the mouthpiece. "He says it's urgent." Her eyes gleam as the sunlight hits her face.

With Skipper, *everything* is urgent. "If it's that important," I whisper, "it can wait."

She smiles and tells him I'll call as soon as I can. Then her grin disappears as she listens intently. She puts the chief law enforcement officer of the City and County of San Francisco on hold. "You may want to talk to him," she says.

"And why would I want to talk to Mr. Law and Order this fine morning?"

The little crow's-feet around her eyes crinkle. "It seems Mr. Law and Order just got himself arrested."

"I'll take it in my office."

My new office isn't much bigger than my old one downstairs. My window looks out on a large hole in the ground that will someday evolve into a high-rise office building across the alley. At least I don't have to walk up a flight of stairs to the bathroom.

I stop in our closet-sized kitchen on my way down the hall and pour coffee into a mug with Grace's picture on it. I glance at the little mirror over the sink, which is filled with empty cups. My full head of light brown hair is fighting a losing battle against the onslaught of the gray. The bags under my eyes are a little smaller than they were a week ago. I walk into my office, where my desk is littered with mail. I log on to my computer and start scrolling through e-mail messages. Finally I pick up the phone, punch the blinking red button, and say in my most authoritative tone, "Michael Daley speaking."

"Skipper Gates," says the familiar baritone. "I need your help ASAP. We have a situation."

I haven't heard the euphemism "We have a situation" since I left Simpson and Gates. We used to refer to this as Skipper speak. When somebody else screwed up, Skipper called it a fuck-up. When he screwed up, it was a situation.

I try to keep the tone measured. "What is it, Skipper?"

"I need to see you right away."

Nothing changes. I'm still glancing at my e-mails. We aren't the best of pals. He led the charge to get me tossed out of the Simpson firm and we've had our share of run-ins over the last couple of years. It comes with the territory when you make your living as a defense attorney. San Francisco is a small town. Everybody involved in the criminal justice system knows everybody else. We have long memories and un-limited capacity for holding grudges. "Where are you?" I ask.

"The Hall of Justice."

"Are you in your office?"

"No. The holding area. They're treating me like a prisoner."

"What happened?"

Silence.

"Skipper?"

I hear him clear his throat. "We had a campaign rally at the Fair-mont last night." Skipper tends to refer to himself in the royal we. He's one of the few people I know who can get away with it. "It ended late," he continues, "so I decided to stay at the hotel. When I woke up this morning, there was a dead body in my room."

"How do you suppose it got there?"

"I don't know."

"What do you mean, you don't know?"

"Just what I said. I don't know. It wasn't there when I went to sleep last night."

With Skipper, the imaginary line between reality and dreamland is often pretty fluid. He isn't exactly lying. Well, not on purpose, any-way. He spends a substantial part of his waking hours in a parallel real-ity. This is a very useful skill if you're a lawyer or a politician.

I ask, "Do you know who it was?"

"Uh, no."

"Did you call security?"

"Of course. They called the cops."

"What did they say?"

"They arrested me." He may as well have added the words "you idiot."

I stop to regroup. "Skipper," I say, "why did you call me?"

"We need somebody to deal with this right away. We have to start damage control. This isn't going to help me in the polls."

I'll say. A dead body is serious. "You know how the system works. You should hire somebody you trust. There are a lot of defense attor-neys around town. I may not be the right guy for you."

I hear him exhale heavily. "You *are* the right guy. Notwithstanding our history, I called you for a reason. You're a fighter. You have guts. You'll tell me what you really think." He pauses and then adds, "And unlike most of your contemporaries in the defense bar, you won't try to cut a fast deal or turn this case into a self-serving infomercial."

I'll be damned. A compliment from Skipper Gates. "All right," I say. "You're on." I ask him a few more questions and agree to meet him at the Hall.

I glance at my watch. Five to nine. Rosie walks in. "So, did you get lucky?" she asks.

"Maybe. Looks like we may have a new case."

"No, dummy. Mexico. Did you get lucky in Mexico?"

Rosie. Ever the pragmatist. First things first.

"No," I say. "I didn't get lucky." I'm probably the *only* guy at Club Med who didn't get lucky. "I'm still all yours."

She's pleased. "Well, then you *did* get lucky, didn't you?" She glances at the notes I've scribbled. "What's Skipper's story?"

I take a long drink of coffee. "Nothing out of the ordinary. A dead body wandered into his room in the middle of the night. The cops think he had something to do with it becoming dead."

She takes this news in stride. "Do they know who the victim is?"

"No ID yet. The cops told him it may have been a prostitute."

"How did she die?"

"They think it was suffocation." I arch my eyebrows and add, "By the way, it wasn't a she."

2
THE ASSHOLE PREMIUM

"The Hall of Justice isn't a big tourist attraction."
— SAN FRANCISCO POLICE CHIEF. *SAN FRANCISCO CHRONICLE.* TUESDAY,
SEPTEMBER 7.

In San Francisco, the wheels of justice grind at a snail's pace in the Hall of Justice, a monolithic six-story structure that rises above the 101 Freeway at the corner of Seventh and Bryant. The criminal courts, DA's office, chief medical examiner and county jail jockey for position in this crowded testimonial to industrial-strength urban architecture. A modernistic new jail wing that opened in the early nineties adds little to the overall ambiance of the original gray building, which dates to the late fifties and looks as if it could withstand a nuclear attack. I park my eleven-year-old Corolla in the pay lot next to the McDonald's and walk quickly through the throng of reporters who are already camped on the front steps of the Hall. The news is out.

I glare into the nearest camera and invoke Skipper speak. "We have a situation. This misunderstanding will be resolved shortly and Mr. Gates will return to his duties at the DA's office." I push through the heavy doors, nod to the guard as I pass through the metal detector and walk up the stairs to the sixth floor of the new jail wing, known as County Jail Number 9.

I present my state bar card and driver's license to Sergeant Jeff Dito, a mustached, olive-skinned sheriff's deputy who administers the intake center with a steady hand. He studies my bar card through deepset eyes. When I explain I'm here to see Skipper, he furrows his brow. " 'Mr. Law and Order' is in booking," he says. He punches some buttons on his computer keyboard and makes a phone call. "He'll be up in a few minutes."

It's early, but things are hopping. For historic bureaucratic reasons, the jail facility is run by the County Sheriff's Department. Deputies walk through the hallway. I nod to a couple of my former colleagues from the PD's office. I take a seat next to a man who is trying to persuade his parole officer that Jesus is talking to him. The parade of humanity resembles a flea market on a busy afternoon. Police, prosecutors, public defenders and criminals barter in the hallway. Instead of selling trinkets and other junk, the prosecutors sell trips to jail and probation terms. The defense attorneys do their clients' bidding. If you sit here long enough, it almost sounds as if you're listening in on a half dozen simultaneous time-share pitches for those condos in Mexico. When I was a PD, I used to make some of my best deals in the corridor just outside the old booking hub on the sixth floor of the Hall. That part of the facility is now used for hard-core prisoners. The new jail wing is a lot quieter.

Whenever I'm in the Hall, I think of my dad, who was a San Francisco cop. He died a few weeks after Grace's first birthday. He was beside himself when I decided to go to law school. He detested lawyers—even the prosecutors. He was appalled when I became a PD. He took it as a personal affront. Somehow, I still expect to see him walking down the corridor, chest out, cigarette in his hand.

Five minutes later, Sergeant Dito nods and a deputy leads me to an airless room just behind the intake desk, where I find Skipper pacing like a caged lion. Even unshaven and in an orange jumpsuit, he's impressively handsome, all trim six feet six of him. His charismatic public persona remains intact. Until now, I have never seen him dressed in anything other than a top-of-the-line Italian suit. He wags a menacing finger at me. "Somebody's ass is going to fry for this," he says.

Hopefully, it won't be yours.

"I'm going to kick the chief's butt all the way back to Northern Station for promoting McBride," he snaps. Inspector Elaine McBride made the arrest. She's only the second woman to make homicide inspector on the SFPD. She's tough. Her stellar reputation is well deserved. Skipper sits down in a heavy wooden chair. "This is preposterous," he says. "It's a publicity stunt."

This sort of thing just isn't supposed to happen to God-fearing Republicans. In many respects, getting arrested is society's great equalizer. Even a well-connected, rich white guy like Skipper has been strip-searched, showered with disinfectant, given a medical interview and placed in a holding cell. There isn't much dignity left after the process is completed. I place a pad of white paper in front of me on the table. Most lawyers have stopped using those ugly yellow pads because they can't be recycled. I look directly into his eyes. "You're the DA," I say. "You know the drill. Tell me what happened."

He's indignant. "Nothing happened," he replies, emphasizing each syllable. He looks at the drab walls. On Friday, he was sitting in his opulent office on the third floor of the old Hall. Now he's sharing space with murderers, child molesters and pimps. "We had a kickoff rally for my campaign in the grand ballroom at the Fairmont last night. Fifteen hundred people showed up. It was terrific."

Particularly if your idea of a good time is paying a thousand bucks a head to the Republican caucus to eat rubber chicken and kiss Skipper's ass.

"The program broke up around eleven," he continues. "Then we had a summit conference upstairs."

Skipper never attends garden-variety meetings. Every gathering rises to the level of a "summit conference." You would think they were talking about nuclear disarmament. Likewise, Skipper never serves on committees. Whenever he is with another person, they become a "task force." I decide to play along. "Who was at the summit conference?" I ask.

"A couple of people from Sherman's campaign. We were setting ground rules for our debates. They left around twelve-thirty."

Leslie Sherman is Skipper's worthy opponent. She's a state senator from L.A. She's a liberal Democrat. I don't mention it, but I'm planning to vote for her. Skipper can't stand her.

"Who showed up from her staff?" I ask.

"Dan Morris and one of his lackeys." His voice drips with contempt.

Morris is Sherman's campaign manager. He's the most successful political consultant on the West Coast. He's also the most vicious. Although he didn't invent the negative campaign ad, he may have perfected it. He makes the guys in Washington look like choirboys. He ran Skipper's campaign for DA two years ago. Then they had a little falling out. Seems Dan wanted to double his fee this time around. Skipper thought the four hundred thousand Dan charged for the DA's race was exorbitant, and he balked. True to form, Dan switched sides. He's already taken off the gloves. Although it's still early, the Sherman camp is running attack ads suggesting Skipper isn't morally qualified to be the chief law enforcement officer of the State of California.

I ask, "Was anybody else with you?"

"Turner was there." Turner Stanford is Skipper's confidant, campaign manager and former law partner. He lives around the corner from Skipper in Pacific Heights. They spend a lot of time hobnobbing in the rarified air of San Francisco's aristocracy.

"My daughter was there, too," he adds. Ann Huntington Gates is a one-woman wrecking crew in local government. A couple of years ago, Skipper convinced the mayor to appoint Ann to fill a vacancy on the Board of Supervisors. It's a decision the mayor has regretted ever since. She lobbies long and hard on behalf of the real estate developers and other big-business interests. By and large, the people from the neighborhoods hate her. She doesn't seem to care. When she isn't terrorizing the Board of Supervisors, she operates at the high end of the legal food chain. She's a partner at Williams and Perry, a big downtown firm. She's a tenacious commercial litigator. She'll remind you of it every chance she gets.

"What about Natalie?" I ask. Skipper's long-suffering wife. Serious old-line money. Her great-grandfather was a Crocker. Her mother's family used to own the *Chronicle*, where her name appears regularly in the society column.

"She stayed for a few minutes and went home. She was tired." He sighs and adds, "I have no idea how I'm going to explain all of this to her."

I guess even self-centered guys like Skipper have to answer to somebody from time to time. "So you decided to stay at the hotel?" I ask.

"I do it all the time," he replies. "I had a breakfast meeting this morning." His eyes wander over my left shoulder. "I didn't want to go all the way out to the house."

This is odd. He lives ten minutes from the hotel. "May I assume, Skipper, that the dead man wasn't there when everybody left?"

"That's right."

"And he wasn't in your room when you went to bed?"

He looks a little too solemn. "I was by myself."

Uh-huh. "And when you woke up this morning, the dead man was in your bed with you?"

"He was in the bed," he explains. "I fell asleep in the chair. I was watching TV. I woke up when the room service waiter knocked on the door. That's when we found the body."

"You didn't hear anything?"

"Nope."

"See anybody?"

"Nope."

He's a sound sleeper. "Did anyone else have a key to your room?"

"Just the hotel staff, I suppose."

There you have it. He fell asleep in the chair in front of the TV. In the middle of the night, a body wandered into his room and plopped itself into his bed. Same thing happened to me in Cabo last week. "Skipper," I say, "did you know the guy?"

His eyes dart toward the door. "I'd never seen him before."

"Do you know how he died?"

"It looked like he had suffocated. His face was covered with gray duct tape. He was handcuffed to the bedposts."

I can confirm this from the police reports. "Did you touch the body?"

"Of course. I checked for a pulse. I pulled the tape off his face in case he could still breathe. I tried to release the handcuffs, but I didn't have a key."

"Then you called the police?"

"I called the hotel operator, who put me through to security. I told them to call the cops."

"You realize your story sounds just a tiny bit odd, don't you?"

He looks right at me. "I didn't do it."

It's his story and he's sticking to it. "For some reason, the police seem to think you did."

His eyes narrow. "It's no big newsflash that I'm not going to win any popularity contests with the SFPD. I'm making the cops work harder than they have in a long time."

They hate his guts. Although the public perceives Skipper as a champion of law-and-order, the police aren't as easily impressed. They think he ducks the tough cases.

"I did the right thing," he says. "I gave them my statement. Next thing I know, McBride decides to be a big shot and arrests me."

"What are you leaving out?"

"Nothing." Even in an orange jumpsuit, he is capable of sounding condescending. "It's a setup. I'm ahead in the polls. My political enemies want to embarrass me. That's the only plausible explanation."

Another plausible explanation is that he did it. On its face, that would seem pretty far-fetched. Politicians call each other names, lie, cheat and run attack ads. By and large, they don't commit murders in hotel rooms. And it seems unlikely that a murderer would spend the night in the same room as the dead body and hang around until the cops showed up.

I ask if he's spoken to Natalie.

"I talked to her for a few minutes right before I called you. She's terribly upset. Ann went over to try to calm her down."

"I'll go talk to McBride and the DA," I say. "The arraignment will be later this week. I'll need you to sign a client retention letter and I'll need a fifty-thousand-dollar retainer."

"Fifty thousand?" he says. "Seems a little steep."

If this case goes to trial, he'll spend at least a quarter of a million dollars on legal fees and another hundred thousand for experts, jury consultants and investigators. He's well aware of this. "Grace has to eat," I say. "If you're out of here as soon as you think, your money will be cheerfully refunded."

"We're a little tight on cash. We've put a bunch of our liquid assets into the campaign war chest. You know how it is."

Actually, I don't. "If you want me to represent you, I'm going to need a fifty-thousand-dollar retainer. If that doesn't work for you, you'll have to find somebody else to handle your case."

I hear him sigh. "Okay," he says, "fifty thousand it is. Bring along the letter this afternoon. I'll sign whatever you want."

It's not like he's going to read it.

"I want to be able to pick co-counsel," he says. "I may want to bring in somebody else." He pauses and adds, "And I'm not sure I want to use your ex-wife."

Come again? "She's my partner. More important, she's one of the best criminal defense attorneys in San Francisco. If you hire me, you hire my firm. That includes Rosie. If you give her any gas, we'll withdraw. Understood?"

"Jesus, Mike," he says, "you have to let me pick my own team." He pauses. "And you can't expect me to use Carolyn."

Carolyn O'Malley is the third attorney in our firm. She's "of counsel," which means she isn't a partner but she shares office space with us and we pay her an hourly rate. She was a prosecutor in San Francisco for almost twenty years. She started out in misdemeanor court and worked her way up to the head of the sex crimes unit. She joined us about six months ago, after she was unceremoniously purged from the DA's office in one of Skipper's moments of uninspired judgment. In a characteristic fit of pique, she switched sides. Most of her vitriol has been directed at one person: Skipper.

"Rosie and Carolyn are essential members of my team," I say. "I won't work without them. Maybe it would be better if you find somebody else to handle your case." I stand and head toward the door.

As I reach for the handle, I hear Skipper's voice behind me. "Listen," he says, "I'm in a tight spot. I need your help."

I turn around and face him. "Rosie and Carolyn are part of the package. If you're smart, you'll hire the best defense attorneys your money can buy. Am I making myself clear?"

"Yes."

"If you still want me to represent you, I'll be back this afternoon with a retention letter. I'll let you pick co-counsel, but I'm going to make all the final decisions on strategy. Rosie sits at the defense table."

"Understood."

"Good. And I'm going to need a check for a hundred thousand dollars."

He's unhappy. "I thought you said it was fifty."

"It was. The price just went up." Rosie and I refer to this as charging the Asshole Premium. We reserve such special treatment for our more difficult clients. "Is there a problem?"

"No," he says through clenched teeth. "No problem."

The deputy knocks on the door. "We need to finish your client's paperwork," he says.

It's my turn to point a finger at Skipper. "Don't talk to anybody," I tell him. "I'll see if I can get this cleared up before things get out of hand."

"I didn't do it," he insists. "Somebody's going to pay for this."

I'm walking past the intake desk a moment later when I hear my name called out by an unmistakable velvet voice. "Michael, do you have a moment to chat?" Skipper's close friend and my former partner at Simpson and Gates, Turner Hamilton Stanford IV, doesn't speak to anyone. He chats.

I turn and look into the eyes of the man I once dubbed the Silver Fox. Everything about him is in muted tones of gray. The impeccably tailored Italian suit. The neatly pressed kerchief in his breast pocket. The full head of hair and meticulously trimmed beard. Turner may be the best-dressed man to have set foot in the Hall in thirty years. At sixty-one, he carries his slender six-foot-two-inch frame with the erect bearing of a former athlete. He and Skipper were teammates on the Stanford basketball team.

We shake hands. Turner's polished, soft-spoken demeanor and elegant air mask a vicious greedy streak. In legal circles, he's what's called a "juice" lawyer, which means he charges his clients exorbitant sums to manipulate the San Francisco planning commission and obtain building permits and zoning variances. Most people believe PacBell Park never would have been built without his influence. In his spare time, he dabbles in real estate development and political consulting.

He also owns an obscenely expensive French restaurant near Union Square.

Turner's earned millions from his law practice, but he made most of his money the old-fashioned way—he inherited it. Although I have never been able to trace his exact lineage, he claims he is a descendant of the family that founded the university in Palo Alto that bears his name. I've always had doubts about that.

He never raises his voice. "I got here as soon as I could," he says. "I stopped to see Natalie for a few minutes. Skipper told her he was going to call you." He pauses and adds, "This is a disaster."

I've never been able to read him. Although Turner is running Skipper's campaign and they're close, he's a registered Democrat. He manages to delude himself into believing the sixties never ended. It's difficult for self-righteous liberals like me to deal with limousine liberals like him, especially when they run political campaigns for fascists like Skipper. While I'm busy casting stones, I suppose I should point out that the lawyers of Fernandez and Daley are willing to represent Republicans as well as Democrats, as long as they are prepared to pay our very reasonable fees.

I explain that I have already spoken to Skipper. "He said you were there last night."

"I was."

I ask him if he knows what happened.

"The police won't tell me anything," he says. He glances at Sergeant Dito and lowers his voice. "We had a summit conference with Sherman's people."

Now he's doing Skipper speak.

"I left around twelve-thirty," he says. "Next thing I knew, there was a phone call from Skipper at seven-thirty this morning. By the time I got there, they had already arrested him." He says he had a conversation with Inspector McBride about the wisdom of her decision to arrest Skipper. Notwithstanding Turner's impassioned plea, McBride went ahead and hauled him in.

We decide the intake desk may not be the best place to talk about the events of last night. He says he's going to see Skipper. Then he's going to hold a press briefing.

———

I'm talking to Rosie from the pay phone in the lobby of the Hall. You aren't allowed to bring cell phones into the jail. "Did you really tell Skipper he was going to have to pay the Asshole Premium?" she asks.

"He *is* an asshole," I deadpan.

"Are you out of your mind? I'm surprised he didn't fire you on the spot." Rosie has never fully appreciated my rainmaking skills. It might be fair to say they are somewhat unconventional. She's also keenly aware of my rather lackadaisical attitude toward money.

I assure her that I did not use the term *asshole* when I told Skipper he was going to have to give us a larger retainer. I leave out any mention of the fact that Skipper isn't wild about including her or Carolyn on the defense team.

"Maybe you're starting to get the hang of private practice," she says.

I tell her about my conversation with Skipper. "He's adamant. He says he didn't do it."

"Do you believe him?"

I stare at the high ceiling for a second. "I find it very hard to picture him killing someone. Besides, he's very calculating. I can't imagine he would do anything that would jeopardize his political career."

She reflects for a moment and asks again, "Does that mean you believe him?"

I hesitate and say, "I'm not sure." I glance at the guard sitting by the metal detectors. "One other thing." Here goes. "We need to talk about whether we want to take on Skipper as a client."

"Not again," she says. I can hear the irritation in her tone. "What's there to talk about?"

"I don't trust him. It's too personal. There's too much history."

"I can think of about a hundred thousand reasons. That may be enough to pay for a year at Stanford when Grace gets there."

"She's going to Cal."

"Mike," she says, "let's take it from the top."

I hate this.

"What do we do at our firm?" she asks.

This little ritual reminds me of when we were married—and why we got divorced. "Criminal defense law."

"That means we represent criminals, right? You know, crooks?"

"Yeah. Crooks." I really hate this.

"And crooks do bad things, right? And they lie."

"Yes they do, Rosie."

"And we don't make moral judgments about our clients, do we?"

"No, we don't." Well, she doesn't. I do.

"That's right. So the fact that Skipper may be a manipulative liar makes him just about the same as all of our other clients, doesn't it?"

"It's not the same."

"It *is* the same, except for one thing."

I always lose these arguments. "What's that?" I ask.

"How much money does Skipper have?"

"Millions." If he runs short, we can get paid in campaign posters.

"Millions," she repeats. "I don't like him any more than you do. But he needs a criminal defense attorney and he can pay us. That's good enough for me."

I hate it when she's right.

"Get the retainer and we'll see what happens," she says. "One other thing. Natalie called. She wants to talk to you right away."

3
"HE REALLY DID IT THIS TIME"

> "Those of us who are more fortunate should try to set a good example and help those who are not."
> —NATALIE GATES. SAN FRANCISCO JUNIOR LEAGUE LUNCHEON.

A few minutes later, I'm getting nasty glares from the people in the line that has formed behind me at the pay phone in the lobby of the Hall. I dial the number Rosie just gave me. An unfamiliar female voice answers. The crackles indicate it's a cell phone. "It's Mike Daley," I say.

"Ann Gates." I've spoken to Skipper's daughter only once before, when one of my clients wanted her to intercede in a dispute over a building permit. It was not a pleasant conversation. "Mother needs to talk to you right away."

The phone goes silent before I can respond.

A moment later, the usually assured, cultivated voice of Natalie Gates sounds tenuous. "Mr. Daley—Michael—the police are here," she says. I can barely hear her. She doesn't sound anything like the woman who sits on the boards of the symphony and the DeYoung Museum.

Before I went to law school, I was a priest for three years. I summon the reserved tone I used when I listened to confessions. "Everything is going to be fine, Natalie. Let me talk to them."

The line goes silent again. The cops must be caucusing. Then their spokesperson comes on. "Inspector Elaine McBride here."

"It's Michael Daley."

"Yes?"

"I take it you want to search the house?"

"That's correct." She says she has a warrant.

"I'd like to look at it before you start. I'll come right over."

She's smart. She'll wait until I arrive. If we get to trial, she'll be able to say I approved the warrant. She says, "You have fifteen minutes."

I jog through the parking lot toward my Corolla. It's unseasonably hot and I'm sweating when I turn over the ignition. I punch the button to the air conditioner. Wishful thinking. A blast of hot air hits me in the face. The Freon gods are not smiling. I roll down my window and head toward the Civic Center. I make my way north on Van Ness past City Hall. Traffic is heavy.

My radio is tuned to KGO. "In local news," the announcer intones, "San Francisco District Attorney Prentice Marshall Gates the Third was arrested when a body was found in his room at the Fairmont this morning. Police are not releasing any additional details at this time. Informed sources say there is uncontroverted evidence linking Mr. Gates to the death of the victim, who has not been identified."

I wish the "informed sources" would give me a call so we can compare notes.

I turn left onto Pine and head west past the renovated Victorians in the old Jewish neighborhood that used to be called the Western Addition but was rechristened Lower Pacific Heights by the real estate developers in the eighties. I head north on Fillmore past the trendy coffee bars that have replaced the thrift shops in recent years. I hang a left at Broadway just before Fillmore plummets toward the bay. A mile to the west, two squad cars and two unmarked Plymouths are parked in front of the white walls and understated iron gateway to Skipper and Natalie's mansion on the north side of the street. Like many homes in this neighborhood, only a few small windows face the street. You'd never know there was a five-million-dollar house behind the unobtrusive gate. In this part of town, it's considered more desirable to live on the north side of Broadway, where the homes have clear views of the bay and the Golden Gate Bridge. The houses on the south side aren't quite as fashionable because their sight lines are obstructed.

A familiar round face greets me by name when I get out of my car. "I thought you criminal lawyers never left the Hall," says officer Rich Sullivan, a big kid from the old neighborhood. He knows that defense attorneys don't like being called criminal lawyers. I let it go. Rich is a good guy. We went to high school together. He married his sweetie and had four kids. They still live in the Sunset.

"They're expecting me, Rich," I say.

He turns serious. Except for some lines around his eyes, he looks the same as he did when he played offensive tackle at St. Ignatius thirty years ago. I used to run behind him. I was a halfback. He was also a pretty fair baseball player. He had a tryout with the Giants but blew out his throwing arm. He's been a beat cop ever since.

He escorts me through the carved wooden doors into a small foyer. I've never quite gotten used to the smell of affluence. I grew up in the flatlands of the outer Sunset. My dad never trusted the people who lived in the hills. He used to say the people up there took your money and you never knew it. We had respectable criminals down where we lived. They looked you in the eye when they stole your wallet. The wisdom of the late Thomas James Charles Daley, Sr.

The house hangs over the side of a cliff. The place doesn't exactly have a lived-in look. To my right is a hallway that probably leads to the servants' quarters. To my left is a three-story atrium with stained-glass windows and a skylight. A concert Steinway grand sits silently in the corner. I can picture Skipper and Natalie standing next to the piano and greeting their guests. At the moment, the only visitors are uniformed police officers and plainclothes evidence techs huddling by the piano.

Ann Gates approaches me from the atrium. Her features resemble her father's. She's a tall woman in her mid-thirties with highlighted blond hair and an athletic build. Her fair skin has a creamy texture. "Thank you for coming," she says perfunctorily. Her tone has the inflection of a woman who was educated in private schools and attended debutante balls. Unfortunately, her marriage to a carefully selected member of the cotillion set didn't work out. If you believe the gossip columnist in the *Chronicle*, Ann can be quite a handful. It made the papers last year when she and a dozen of her pals rented out a South-of-Market nightclub for an all-night party. Somebody called the cops when things got too noisy. Skipper had to intercede to get the charges dropped. The papers had a field day. It was a huge embarrassment for Skipper and the mayor. Rumor has it that Ann paid over a hundred thousand dollars to the owner of the club to fix the damage.

Whenever she's seen in public with a member of the male gender, it turns up in the *Chronicle* society column. At the moment, she's been linked romantically with a TV star whose nighttime soap opera is filmed in the city. She denies it, of course. Her alleged beau is still married to one of Ann's neighbors. So it goes in Pacific Heights.

"Mother is in the living room," she says. "She wanted you to be here before they started looking around the house."

Inspector McBride steps forward from the atrium and hands me a wrinkled piece of paper. I glance at a standard warrant, permitting the police to search the entire premises of the house and any vehicles in the garage.

"Thanks for waiting," I say. I hand the warrant back to her. "I'd appreciate it if you would tell your guys to take it easy on Mrs. Gates. She's been through a lot today." And try not to trash the house, either. Some of this stuff is pricey. "I'd like to have a word with her."

"Suit yourself. We'll start in a few minutes."

Ann is unhappy. "Is there anything you can do to prevent this?" she asks.

"It's legitimate. I can go to a judge, but they'll just come back with another warrant."

"If you are going to represent my father, you're going to have to do better than that."

Based upon my earlier experience with Ann, it seems that a confrontational tone is her standard manner of discourse. She's even more ambitious than Skipper, if that's possible, although her political views are at the opposite end of the spectrum—she's a Democrat. I realize it will not serve any useful purpose to initiate hand-to-hand combat with my client's daughter in front of the arresting officer. I assure her that the warrant is, in fact, valid.

She still isn't buying. "Mother is waiting," she says curtly.

We walk toward the living room, which is furnished with antique tables, Persian rugs, Louis the something chairs and large oil paintings. There is the obligatory picture-postcard view of the orange-gold towers of the Golden Gate Bridge, which is framed against a cloudless blue sky. Natalie has an eye for the exquisite and a checkbook to match. The room reeks of old money. The only item that appears out of place is a sleek laptop computer that is sitting on a table in an alcove near the windows. Nowadays, I guess even aristocrats surf the Web.

"Mother," Ann says, "Mr. Daley is here."

Natalie is sitting in one of the armchairs. To her credit, she has always played her role with style and eloquence. Her charitable work does seem to reflect a good heart. "It has been a long time, Michael," she says as she stands to shake my hand. Except perhaps for Ann, the people in this corner of town never seem to forget their manners.

Reading glasses hang from a gold chain around her neck. She's late fifties. Though she isn't classic beauty, she carries herself with graceful elegance, and like most of her peers in this part of the woods, I suspect she's had a few things tucked in here and there. I presume she has a personal trainer who runs her through her paces a couple of times a week. All things considered, she looks pretty good for a woman whose husband was arrested for murder three hours ago.

"I know this is very difficult, Natalie," I say.

She glances at an elderly servant who is standing nearby and asks me if I would like coffee. I decline.

We exchange small talk. Ann listens impatiently but doesn't say anything. I sense that she has seen her mother go through this social ritual countless times. She has the good judgment not to interrupt. Finally, I explain that the police have a search warrant and they have the right to look around.

Natalie doesn't fluster. Her great-grandfathers were among the founding fathers of San Francisco. She grew up three blocks from here. She's a Mount Holyoke graduate and the wife of the district attorney. She's been through political campaigns with Skipper and Ann. She does what she must. Rosie once said that Natalie reminded her of Pat Nixon. She looks over toward the uniformed officers in her atrium, her eyes signaling Elaine McBride. "Do what you have to do, Inspector," she says in a level tone. "Make it fast. And please be careful. Some of my belongings are quite fragile."

"Thank you for your cooperation, Mrs. Gates," McBride responds.

Natalie forces a polite smile. We watch the police fan out around the house. She turns to me and says, "He really did it this time, didn't he?"

Interesting choice of words. "All we know so far is that they found a body in his room," I say. "We shouldn't jump to any conclusions."

The corners of her mouth turn down slightly, but she doesn't say anything.

I say, "Maybe you can tell me what you saw last night."

She asks the servant to bring her a glass of water. She explains she went to Skipper's campaign rally. "Then we went upstairs for the strategy meeting."

At least she didn't call it a summit conference.

She says the meeting took place in adjoining rooms on the fifteenth floor at the Fairmont tower. There were refreshments in both rooms. "I went home around twelve-thirty," she continues. "The meeting was breaking up."

"How did you get home?"

"I drove her," Ann interjects.

"It was just a garden-variety political meeting," Natalie says. She clutches her glasses as she adds, "There was nothing extraordinary about it. They were discussing the ground rules for the debates." I sense an increased level of tension when she says, "I suppose the arraignment is going to be later this week."

"Thursday," I reply.

"You will need a retainer?"

"I told Skipper we'll need a hundred thousand dollars."

"I understand. And money for bail."

"It would help."

"Whatever it takes," she says.

"If they ask for special circumstances—" I begin.

She holds up her hand. "I know—no bail. It's the law."

I nod. In California legal lingo, special circumstances is the euphemism for a death penalty case.

She looks at Ann and then turns back to me. "Do what you can, Michael. Prentice has many political enemies." She pauses. "He has his faults. And like many couples who have been married for a long time, we have had our ups and downs. But he is a good and decent man. He has a good heart. He does what he thinks is right. You may not always agree with him, but he has principles. He loves this city. He has done a great deal to slow the distribution of guns. He donates time and money to charity. You never hear about the good side in the press."

"That's true," I say.

"Prentice is not a murderer."

My initial instinct is to agree with her. Murder isn't Skipper's style. He has people to handle everything. If he wanted to kill somebody, he would have hired someone to do it.

"Mother," Ann says, "there is that other issue we discussed."

Natalie turns to me. "Ann has expressed some reservations about your firm's ability to handle Prentice's case. She says you may not have the resources."

I glance at Ann, who doesn't look at me. "We handled the murder trial when those two attorneys were killed at the Simpson firm," I reply. "We represented the man who was accused of killing that drug lord down in the Mission last year—we got the charges dropped. We represented the mayor's niece when she was picked up for dealing cocaine. We got a member of the Board of Supervisors off from a bribery charge." I describe several other highly publicized crack cases that I have handled. "We aren't a big firm, but we're very good at what we do. Our track record speaks for itself. We fight these cases to the death, and we win." I realize I'm leaning forward in my chair.

"Prentice thinks very highly of you as a lawyer," Natalie says.

I suspect he may think somewhat less of me as a human being.

She casts a sharp glance at Ann and continues. "He and I think you are the right person to handle this matter."

Ann interrupts again. "But we may want to get you some help."

She works for a big law firm. She's used to calling out the troops. And perhaps she has some other agenda. You never know with Ann.

Natalie is irritated at her daughter. She addresses me. "I hope that will be all right with you."

"That's fine, Natalie. But if you want me to be lead trial counsel, I want it understood that I'll make all the final calls on strategy. I made this clear to Skipper."

Ann is not satisfied, but she doesn't say anything. Natalie nods.

After I leave Natalie, I stop at the Fairmont to find out what I can from the police officers who have secured the scene. You try to get as much information as you can as soon as possible. Memories tend to fade very quickly. I get as far as the elevators to the tower before I'm stopped by two uniforms. They explain that the field evidence technicians, the FETs, are still gathering evidence in Skipper's room and the adjoining room on the fifteenth floor, and that only police personnel are being allowed upstairs. I ask them for the names of the lead FET and the head of hotel security. It's all I'm able to do for the moment, so I head to the Hall and report to Skipper on my meeting with Natalie.

"How is she holding up?" he asks. He seems genuinely concerned.

"As well as can be expected in the circumstances. This isn't going to be easy."

"She's a fighter, Mike. We've been through a lot together. She's always there."

"Skipper," I say, "is this something we need to talk about?"

"We've been married for almost forty years. We've had mostly good days and a few bad days. Sometimes being married to a public figure takes its toll." He swallows hard and adds, "I want you to do everything you can to help her through this. That's very important to me."

"Understood." I ask if there's anything else I should know.

"No."

He's unhappy when I let him know the police are searching his house. He argues they have no right to do so. He's being unrealistic. I tell him that Ann has suggested that we may need some help with his case. He says she's just being protective. "She's my daughter. She's worried. She wants to be sure that we have the right team in place." There's a tension in his voice.

"Is there something else going on here?" I ask.

"She's just being cautious."

I'm not so sure.

My next stop is the homicide department for a fishing expedition with Elaine McBride's partner. I greet Roosevelt Johnson, who is squeezed into a heavy wooden chair at his desk in the crowded room he shares with the SFPD's homicide inspectors. His brown eyes are set back deeply in his ebony face. He's a pro.

"Seems like our friend the DA has found himself in a little trouble," I say.

He takes off his wire-rimmed glasses and sets them down next to his coffee cup. "You might say that," he replies. I've known Roosevelt since I was a kid. He's in his mid-sixties now. He was my father's first partner. He moved up the ranks and made homicide inspector. Dad stayed on the beat. "How's your mama?" he asks.

You have to let Roosevelt make the first move. The social part of our conversation will continue until he's ready to talk business. "Not so great," I say. "The Alzheimer's is getting worse. We have somebody staying with her now." My mother was diagnosed several years ago. She spends a part of each day in a state of disorientation. The best we can do is to hope it doesn't get worse very quickly. Although I make a decent living, a lot of my spare cash goes for my mom's treatment. Rosie says you know you're middle-aged when your kids and your parents are depending on you.

Time for business. "Elaine got there first," Roosevelt tells me. He was teamed with McBride a couple of months ago and they're learning each other's moves. "She's going to be very good," he adds. This means a great deal coming from an old warhorse like Roosevelt. He doesn't pass out compliments readily.

"I just saw her briefly at the house," I say. "We didn't have time to talk." In reality, I wanted to come see Roosevelt. He may be a homicide inspector, but he's family. "Besides," I say, "your feelings would have been hurt if I didn't come to you first."

He chuckles. "I'm too old and cranky to have my feelings hurt about anything." He gulps the rest of his coffee and wipes his mustache with a napkin. "Let's go for a walk," he says. "The walls in this room have ears."

We adjourn to the little Greek restaurant across Bryant Street, where we take a booth in the back. This has been Roosevelt's private office since the McDonald's down the block put the old cafeteria in the basement of the Hall out of business several years ago. I'm drinking a Diet Coke. Roosevelt nurses a cup of coffee. He asks, "Why the hell are you representing Skipper Gates?"

Don't sugarcoat it, Roosevelt. Tell me how you really feel.

I could give him the standard defense attorney line that every defendant is entitled to competent representation. He won't respect me if I do. "He called me. He needs a lawyer. He can afford to pay me. I don't have to love my clients, Roosevelt."

"He's an ass."

"He's no saint, but he's done some good things. Look at his record on gun control."

"He became a gun control advocate when he figured out he could get his name in the papers."

"After his predecessor, I would have thought you'd be happy about having a law-and-order guy." The man who occupied the DA's office immediately before Skipper had a background in social work. The cops thought he was soft.

Roosevelt points a finger at me and says, "Skipper isn't a prosecutor—he's a politician. He won't take on the close cases. He won't back up the cops. He's been running for governor since the day he was elected DA." He scowls as he adds, "I don't have much time. The room service waiter found them. The victim was handcuffed to the bedposts, face covered with tape. Skipper was asleep in the chair by the TV."

"It doesn't mean he killed him."

He cocks his head. Sometimes I get a little ahead of myself. He's doing me a favor. I shut up. "They found a roll of duct tape in his room," he says. "It looks like it's a match for the tape used to cover the guy's face."

"It could have been planted."

He gives me the "oh, come on" look.

"Have they been able to identify the victim?" I ask.

He looks at the picture of Willie Mays on the wall above our table. "Not yet." He's been a cop for four decades. He's seen everything. Even so, it's clear this case bothers him. "He was a kid," he says. "Maybe nineteen, twenty years old. We're guessing he was a prostitute.

If you believe Skipper, the victim beamed himself in and handcuffed and suffocated himself. It doesn't add up."

I ask him if they found anything else.

He says the FETs are still collecting evidence. "We're testing for prints. We've placed him at the scene. He had no credible explanation, so we went ahead and made the arrest."

I give him a skeptical look.

"Look," he says, "you find a guy in a hotel room with a dead hooker. He has no explanation, plausible or otherwise. He claims somebody must have brought the body into his room in the middle of the night. He says he didn't see anything. What would you have done?"

"I don't know." I would have made the arrest.

There are over twelve thousand felony arrests in San Francisco each year. Formal charges are filed in about half of those cases. Fewer than one percent of the arrests ever go to trial. The DA has forty-eight hours to file charges or turn him loose.

"Thanks for your help, Roosevelt," I say. He promises to call me if he hears anything.

When I get back to the office, Rosie's niece Rolanda, our secretary, office manager, computer technician and law clerk, hands me a stack of phone messages. She just started her second year of law school at Hastings. I can't wait for her to graduate so we can make her managing partner, a role she is already performing for the most part. I'm not much for administrative details, although Rosie gets me to do my time sheets every day under penalty of death. Rolanda is a petite woman in her late twenties. Her father is Rosie's older brother, Tony. "You looked good on the news," she says.

"Thanks. Could you page Pete? We're going to need him." My younger brother used to be a cop. He got into trouble a few years ago when he and some of his cohorts got a little heavy-handed when they broke up a gang fight. It cost him his badge. He's still bitter about it. Now he's a PI. I use him as the lead investigator on many of my cases. He's going through a tough time. He and his wife split up about a year ago. Their divorce was just finalized. He's bitter about that, too. I feel for him. I've survived an acrimonious divorce. It doesn't help that I introduced him to his ex-wife.

Rolanda hands me the phone. "He's holding," she says.

"Mick," Pete says, "you need some help with Skipper's case?"

"Absolutely."

"I'll be there as soon as I can." He says he has to take a few more pictures of a man who is going to pay a lot of alimony to his soon-to-be ex-wife. If you live in San Francisco and you decide to cheat on your spouse, you would be well advised to keep a close eye out for Pete.

I walk into Rosie's office. She's on the phone. "No," she says, "he hasn't come back from the Hall of Justice." A small white lie. "I'll have him call you." She hangs up and looks at me. "Turner Stanford. He says he's issuing a blanket denial of any wrongdoing by Skipper. He expects you to do the same."

"Sounds like a good idea. Any other messages?"

"Ann called. She expects you to get the charges dropped by the close of business tomorrow."

"I'll take care of it," I say with a grin.

"I knew you would. Did you find out anything from Roosevelt?"

"Not much." I pause and say, "I may need a little help with the case. Are you busy for the next six or eight months?"

"I'll check my calendar," she tells me.

4
FERNANDEZ AND DALEY

"Fernandez and Daley specializes in criminal defense in federal and state courts. The firm offers personalized service at competitive rates. For immediate assistance twenty-four hours a day, dial 1-800-CRIM-LAW."

— SAN FRANCISCO YELLOW PAGES.

When I worked at Simpson and Gates, we had a conference room that was about a hundred feet long and housed a polished rosewood table and eighty chairs. At Fernandez and Daley, our "conference room" consists of two card tables pushed together in the middle of the exercise mats in the old martial arts studio. Rosie and I are sitting there on folding chairs at five o'clock the same day. Bruce Lee glares at me from a faded poster.

Our third lawyer, Carolyn O'Malley, walks in through the doorway from the old women's locker room. "You two look like something the cat brought in," she chortles. I've known her since we were kids. As with most aspects of my life, we have some baggage. We dated for a couple of years when we were in college. We almost got married. *Almost* is the operative word. We split up when Carolyn decided to go to law school in L.A. More precisely, Carolyn broke up with me. Although I concluded long ago that our relationship was little more than a youthful infatuation, she was, in fact, the first woman who ever broke my heart. When Carolyn came to work for us, Rosie expressed some concerns that I still had feelings for her. I reassured her that I had no intention of trying to reheat that soufflé. Carolyn has been divorced twice and is the single mother of a rebellious teenage son. Still, I do wonder sometimes how things would have worked out if we had stayed together.

"We have a new case," Rosie begins.

Carolyn's green eyes light up. She's a small woman, five one and barely a hundred pounds, but she has unlimited energy. "We aren't really going to represent Skipper, are we?" she asks.

"Looks like it," I say.

She smiles. "This is too good. Maybe we can get him a plea bargain for the death penalty."

Rosie chuckles. "It looks like we may need to refresh your memory on the role of the criminal defense attorney," she says.

"I'm a pretty quick study," Carolyn replies. She turns to me and says, "You seem to have stumbled into another big case."

"Marketing," I deadpan. "I told you those coupons in the Sunday paper would pay off big someday."

I look around the table: my ex-wife, my ex-girlfriend and me. We aren't a law firm—we're a support group. Somebody will probably name a 12-step program after us.

"Let's get started," I say. I describe my conversations with Skipper and Roosevelt. "The arraignment is at ten o'clock on Thursday."

"What do we know about the victim?" Rosie asks. You always start with the victim.

"We don't even know his name. Just a kid. May have been a prostitute."

Rosie is perplexed. "Does this seem a little odd to you?" she asks. "Let's assume for a minute the victim was, in fact, a male prostitute. What was he doing in Skipper's room?"

Dead silence.

After a moment, Rosie looks at me and says, "Let me try again. I know this group is about as PC as they come, so forgive me for saying this bluntly. Is Skipper gay?"

I expect everybody to shout in unison the line from the old Seinfeld episode, "*Not that there's anything wrong with that!*"

I look to Bruce Lee for guidance. He remains silent. "As far as I know," I say, "Skipper is straight. It's possible that there may be sides to his personality that we don't know anything about."

Carolyn snaps, "I'm only familiar with the side that's a pig."

At least we're starting on an even keel. I steal a glance at Rosie, who says, "Just so we avoid any surprises, it might be a good idea to confirm that he does, in fact, like women."

"Oh, he definitely likes women," Carolyn says. "At least when I was sleeping with him, he seemed to be enjoying himself."

Oh Christ.

I clear my throat. "When was this?"

"Last year," Carolyn says. She has a knack for dating men who are unsuited for her. I give her a sideways look and she adds, "He asked me, okay? I said yes. For the record, he was a perfect gentleman."

Well, as perfect as a gentleman can be when he's cheating on his wife.

Rosie whispers something to Carolyn, who wiggles her fingers and says, "Not bad." Then she reconsiders and adds, "Pretty good." I surmise that they are discussing our client's sexual prowess and perhaps technique.

"Are you still seeing him?" I ask.

"No. It happened just twice." Carolyn acknowledges it was a mistake but then adds, "We're adults, Mike."

"I recognize that."

"You don't expect me to apologize, do you?"

"Nope. It's none of my business." I don't want to get into a discussion of whether her relationship with Skipper had anything to do with the fact that he fired her. Carolyn had told us it was the result of office politics. I'm beginning to understand what she meant.

"Damn right it's none of your business," she says. "Before we get too far down the garden path here, I'd like to raise a fundamental issue. With all the baggage, maybe it isn't such a good idea that we accept this case." She then adds, "You have some history with him, too."

This is true. It doesn't seem like a particularly opportune time to revisit Skipper's role in getting my petard hoisted from Simpson and Gates.

Rosie takes all of this in without saying a word. Then she folds her hands and addresses Carolyn. "In fairness, Mike expressed some of the same reservations that you did. I can also tell you Skipper has agreed to give us a one-hundred-thousand-dollar retainer that would look very nice on our bottom line."

Carolyn glances at me.

"Look," Rosie continues, "this case will be good for the reputation of our firm. But I'm not going to take it on if you don't want to do it. Everybody in this room has some history with Skipper."

"Not you, too," I say.

She gives me the "get real" expression and casts a judgmental eye at Carolyn. "I don't sleep with married men. Besides, he's not my type. And, if you must know, he asked me only once. I turned him down."

Is there anybody he hasn't propositioned?

Rosie looks at each of us in turn. "I'm going to let you decide," she says. "If you say yes, we'll take the case. Otherwise, we won't. Let me know." She heads toward the door.

Carolyn and I sit in silence. Her jaw tightens. I couldn't read her mind years ago. There's no reason to believe I'll be able to do so now.

I say, "We don't have to take this on."

Her chin juts forward. "Is it true you didn't want to represent him?"

"I'm not crazy about it, but I still think we should do it."

"I have a problem with it."

"Don't you think he's entitled to representation?" I ask.

"This isn't a legal issue. This is personal. He treated me like dirt. Then he fired me."

"You could have filed a claim."

"Get a clue. We might have settled five years later." She points her finger at me. "I agree that he's entitled to a lawyer, but it doesn't have to be me. Why should I do it?"

"Maybe because it's the right thing to do?"

Rosie isn't the only one in our office who invokes guilt from time to time.

Carolyn throws up her hands. "You and Rosie decide. It's your firm. If you want to do it, I'll help you. I'll do the research. I'll do whatever you want. But I won't talk to the bastard."

"If you're uncomfortable because of your past relationship with him, we don't have to do it."

"The fact that I slept with him has nothing to do with this," she says. "It was two meaningless dates."

I'm not entirely convinced, but I don't respond.

"My problem," she continues, "is that he has no respect for any-body. I wasn't the only person he treated badly."

I ask her what she wants to do.

She pauses to consider. "Look," she says, "we've represented ass-holes before, right?"

"All the time." I'm pleased by her attempts to be conciliatory. More important, if I can't persuade Carolyn to help us with this case, Rosie will kill me.

"Are you guys getting tight on money again?"

"Yep."

"I won't have to spend any time with Skipper, will I?"

"Nope. And I'll make him promise he won't hit on you again until after the trial is over."

I get just the hint of a grin. "All right. I'm in."

I can't begin to imagine how much more successful we might be if we didn't have to do an hour of group therapy every time we wanted to bring in a new client.

"Was I too hard on Carolyn?" Rosie asks later that night. We're watch-ing the news with the sound off in her bedroom in her rented bunga-low across the street from the Twin Cities Little League Field in Larkspur, a modest suburb just north of the Golden Gate Bridge in Marin County. I live two blocks away in an apartment behind the fire station. We'll never be able to afford a house without a subsidy from the California state lottery. On the other hand, the neighborhood is safe and the public schools are good. Parenthood imposes certain con-straints upon your domestic choices. Grace is asleep.

"What would you do if I said yes?" I ask.

"Nothing," she says with a smile. "I was just asking."

I lean over and peck her on the cheek. About a year ago, we agreed that all of our partners' meetings would be held in her bed. As a result, we tend to dispose of firm issues quickly and then we get down to serious business. I took a fairly substantial bath last year when it was time to decide my compensation. In the vernacular of our daughter, you might say I got "pantsed." It was worth it. We impose a moratorium on the recreational aspects of our partners' meetings in the all-too-infrequent circumstances where either of us is involved in a serious relationship with someone else. At our stage in life, a serious relationship is defined as one that lasts longer than two weeks. We have not been required to call a cease-fire for about a year, since Rosie broke up with her last boyfriend. While we're both willing to admit that the current state of our domestic situation is somewhat less than optimal, everyone gets lonely. Rosie says that sleeping with your ex-husband beats sleeping alone, but not by much.

"That's why you're such an effective managing partner," I say. "You got us to do exactly what you wanted, and you let us think we were making the decision ourselves."

"It's all in my new book," she says. "*Management by Guilt.*"

"It's going to be a best-seller."

She brushes her lips against mine. Her warm breath smells like Merlot. I have been kissed by fewer women than your average forty-seven-year-old. In my limited experience, Rosie is still the best. "You seem to have found a hot case," she says. "How do you do it?"

"Networking. It's all going into *my* new book on rainmaking for lawyers. I think I'll call it *Networking—A Way of Life.*"

Her eyes gleam. "It's going to be a best-seller, too. Mind if I ask you something?"

"Sure."

"When you were a priest, people used to come to you to make confessions, right?"

"Yes."

"And you used to do marriage counseling, too, right?"

I see where this is going. "Occasionally."

"What made you think you were the least bit qualified to dispense advice to married people? You weren't even allowed to *do it.*"

I grin. "I trust this is a rhetorical question."

"Indeed."

"That's good."

"Now let me ask you one that isn't rhetorical."

"Okay."

"Pretend you're still a priest. A divorced couple comes to you and says they're still sleeping together. They still love each other, but they can't figure out a way to live together. What would you tell them?"

I try to dodge the question. "I would tell them that their situation isn't ideal."

"I could tell them that much. Would you tell them to stop?"

"Not necessarily. It depends on the circumstances."

"That's still an evasion."

"Yes it is. I don't give that kind of advice anymore. I got out of that line of work."

She won't let it go. "What if they ask you for a real answer?"

I pause to consider and say, "I would tell them they should take as much time as they need to work out their feelings for each other. I certainly would say they shouldn't rule out the possibility of a reconciliation."

"Now, that's a pretty good answer."

"I was a pretty good priest." I was also a very sad priest. I loved it at first. I thought I was helping people and making a difference. Then I became frustrated by church politics. I spent more time by myself. I became lonely. The loneliness led to sadness, the sadness led to depression. I was a wreck. I couldn't eat. I couldn't sleep. I couldn't provide any guidance or comfort to anyone. I was just going through the motions. Finally, I got some counseling. Luckily, a forward-looking colleague convinced me it was okay to get out before the depression consumed me.

I glance at the TV. It shows footage of Skipper making a campaign speech, followed by a shot of him being led into the Hall. I catch a glimpse of myself proclaiming his innocence. The scene shifts to the front steps of the Hall, where Turner Stanford is making an impassioned plea for justice. "Turner's spinning," I observe.

A handsome reporter with windblown hair looks into the camera. He's standing on the steps of a church. Rosie sits up. "What is he doing at St. Peter's?" she asks.

I'm puzzled, too. St. Peter's Catholic Church has been a center of worship at the south end of the crowded Mission District for more than a century. It rises above the modest bungalows and the two-story apartment buildings on Alabama Street, between Twenty-fourth and

Twenty-fifth. It isn't a particularly impressive structure, but it reflects the working-class community it has served for many years. What it has to do with Skipper or a dead body in the Fairmont I can't fathom. I turn on the sound.

The reporter pretends he's addressing his remarks directly to the anchorman. "A makeshift memorial has been established in the Mission District for the young man who was found dead earlier today at the Fairmont Hotel."

The Mission District is one of San Francisco's oldest and most complex neighborhoods. It sits on a sunny plain just south of downtown. Its main artery is Mission Street, which is home to businesses, residential hotels and restaurants. Like many inner-city neighborhoods, it has undergone several evolutions. Fifty years ago, it was working-class Irish. My mom and dad grew up on opposite sides of Garfield Square and were married at St. Peter's. We lived in an apartment at Twenty-first and Alabama when I was little. We moved to the Sunset when I was nine and my dad had saved up enough money for a down payment on a house. About the same time, many of the Irish residents moved to other parts of the city and out to the suburbs. When they moved out, the Hispanics moved in. Rosie's parents were among the new arrivals. Her mom still lives at Twenty-fourth and Bryant, three blocks from our apartment when I was a kid. Small world.

"The name of the victim is John Paul Garcia," the reporter says.

At least we now know his name. The camera pans toward the door to the church, where a small pile of flowers sits beneath a hand-lettered sign that says "Justice for Johnny."

The phone rings and Rosie answers. It's her older brother, Tony, whose produce market is around the corner from St. Peter's. "Yes," I hear her say, "I just saw it." I watch her face turn ashen. She says "Uh-huh" a couple of times. She says she'll make some calls and hangs up.

I grab the remote and turn the TV off. Rosie is sitting in stone-cold silence, her right hand covering her mouth, her eyes open wide.

"What is it?" I ask.

"It's Johnny Garcia," she whispers in a broken voice.

"Did you know him?"

"He's from the neighborhood." She bites her lip. "We knew his mother."

5

"THE DA IS SUBJECT TO THE SAME LAWS AS EVERYBODY ELSE"

"The district attorney's office will conduct business as usual during Mr. Gates's leave of absence."

—CHIEF DEPUTY DISTRICT ATTORNEY WILLIAM McNULTY. WEDNESDAY, SEPTEMBER 8.

Rosie is on the phone right away. She is pulling on a Cal sweatshirt as she talks in Spanish to her mother. Sylvia Fernandez is always available to her children. She stays with Grace when Rosie is in trial. We couldn't practice law without her help. After Rosie hangs up, she says, "She's going to ask around."

This may help. Sylvia has known everybody who's lived within a one-mile radius of St. Peter's for the last forty years.

"How did you know Johnny Garcia's mother?" I ask.

Rosie is sitting up in bed. "She lived down the street."

I ask if they were close.

"Pretty close."

"Do you know how to reach her?"

"Theresa's dead, Mike," she says. "She died about five years ago. Johnny and his older brother Carlos were kids. Johnny couldn't have been much older than twelve when she died."

"What about the father?"

"That's a long story."

"I have plenty of time."

Rosie stands and says, "Let's make coffee."

Rosie has brewed a pot of Peet's. She explains that Theresa Lopez Garcia was a pretty girl who tried to please. "She was a cheerleader. Very sweet," Rosie says. "Not very forceful or independent, though. She married her high school sweetheart when she turned eighteen. Her parents weren't happy about it. They wanted her to go to college. They didn't like her husband, Roberto, who was a football player at Mission High. He wasn't interested in school. He thought he was going to get a football scholarship. He didn't." She says Theresa worked at one of the produce markets on Mission. She and Roberto had two kids: Carlos and Johnny. Then things went to hell.

"Roberto had a temper," Rosie goes on. "He couldn't hold a job. He drove a forklift. He worked at a hardware store. He tried to sell cars. When the money got tight, he'd come home late and drunk. That's when he used to hit her. You can guess how it ended. When Johnny was little, Theresa told Roberto that she'd leave him if he didn't stop drinking. A week later, he was gone. We heard he died in an armed robbery in L.A. a few years later. Theresa and the kids moved in with her parents, but they were elderly. When they died, they moved into Valencia Gardens."

In contrast to the working-class Hispanic enclave near St. Peter's, much of the north end of the Mission is a blighted, crime- and drug-ridden ghetto. There is nothing garden-like about the decaying, low-rise Valencia Gardens housing projects. Likewise, the broken-down residential hotels in the immediate vicinity of the BART station around the corner at Sixteenth and Mission are a depressing cesspool of drugs, prostitution and homelessness.

"She went back to her job at the market," Rosie says. "Then she got into drugs. She ended up on welfare. She worked as a prostitute." She takes a drink of her coffee and glances toward Grace's room. I know this look. Even during our divorce, Rosie made sure that Grace had everything she needed. It's hot-wired into Rosie's psyche—and mine. Your kids don't ask to be born. You can screw up your own life but not theirs. You can't send them back.

I ask her how Theresa died.

Rosie swallows hard. "Overdose. She was only thirty-four."

"And the kids?"

"Carlos died in a gang fight. Johnny moved in with a great-aunt in the projects and I remember hearing it didn't work out. He was tough to handle. Last I heard, he was out on his own. I'd guess he must have been about seventeen by now. Tony didn't know what Johnny had been doing for the last couple of years. We lost contact with the family when Theresa died."

We sit in silence, finishing our coffee. Rosie looks right at me and says, "I want to find out what happened."

"I do, too." I pause. "Rosie," I say, "Skipper is our client."

"Understood."

"We can't personalize this case. Skipper is entitled to a defense."

"Which we will give him. That's our job." She points her finger at me and adds, "I can't help it that this case is already personal."

I lean forward and take her hand. "Are you going to be able to deal with this?"

"For one thing, we shouldn't assume he did anything wrong. For another, we defend evil people every day. We've represented murderers, rapists and pornographers." She draws the line at accused child molesters. She got one off when she was a PD. He turned around and tortured and killed the girl next door. She vowed she'd never let that happen again. She adds, "We don't have to love our clients."

"Even Skipper?" I already know the answer.

"Even Skipper. I want to know the truth. We'd better get down to the Mission first thing in the morning."

At seven-thirty in the morning, I'm back at Rosie's, eating a bagel in her small kitchen. Grace is sitting at the counter eating Froot Loops and speculating on when she'll get her first homework assignment. She explains that third grade is much harder than second.

The TV is turned to the news. Three times a week, an aging criminal defense attorney named Mort Goldberg holds court on Channel 4. "Mort the Sport" was a fixture in the corridors of the Hall for four decades before he found a new career as a TV legal analyst a couple of years ago. His segment is known as "Mort's Torts." Although he once taught criminal procedure at Hastings, his TV spot isn't scholarly. On the other hand, it's wildly entertaining. He's sort of a short, bald, Jewish Rush Limbaugh. Theoretically, he is supposed to discuss legal issues, but on a given day, he'll cover everything from world politics to the state of the Giants' pitching staff. His producers admit they never know what he is going to say. His ratings are almost as high as those of the attractive young woman who reads the traffic reports and has every male in the nine-county Bay Area sending her marriage proposals.

An anchorman whose blow-dried hair makes him resemble a middle-aged Leonardo DiCaprio lobs the first softball. "Well, Mort," he says through a wide grin, "what do you think about our district attorney?"

Mort makes a valiant attempt at looking serious. He stares through thick Coke-bottle-bottom glasses. His puffy face looks a little like the late Harry Caray. He sounds like him, too. "Well, Sam," he lisps, "District Attorney Gates has a substantial problem."

There's insight for you.

Mort squints into the camera. "My sources tell me that the police have evidence placing him at the scene and tying him to the commission of the crime."

His "sources" are the night custodial staff at the Hall and the bail bondsmen across the street. He takes a drink of coffee from an oversized mug with the Channel 4 logo on it. It took him six months to learn to hold the cup with the logo facing the camera. The blond guy asks him about Skipper's defense team.

Mort wags his index finger toward the camera. "I know Michael Daley," he tells us. "He's a first-rate lawyer." He nods to reassure himself that he's still conscious. "Solid reputation."

It's great to get a ringing endorsement from a guy who stepped off the curb twenty years ago.

At nine o'clock that morning, Deputy District Attorney William McNulty is sitting behind the mahogany desk in Skipper's ceremonial office, which was remodeled at his expense when he became DA. The sculptured carpeting, oak paneling and heavy furniture lend an air of authority to the formerly austere chamber. The only hint of tackiness is the picture of Skipper shaking hands with the governor that hangs behind his desk, just between the Stars and Stripes and the California state flag.

Bill McNulty is a grouch. His perpetual frown contrasts with the smiling, silver-haired Skipper in the picture behind him. Skipper wears the accoutrements of power far more elegantly than Bill does. McNulty is a career prosecutor whose dour manner and combative nature have earned him the not-unwarranted nickname McNasty. He's fifty now, and two years ago he thought his number had come up for the top spot at the DA's office. Then he got hit by a freight train. Skipper outspent him by ten to one and clobbered him in the election. It's too bad. McNulty is a solid guy who plays by the rules and puts away the bad guys. It isn't his fault he was born without a personality. You don't get to choose your gene pool.

Rosie sits to my immediate left. Ann Gates is standing next to the credenza. She's decided we could use a hand this morning. Turner Stanford is here, too. At any moment I expect him to proclaim that we are all participating in a summit conference.

McNulty takes a drink of coffee from a paper cup and scowls. He looks toward a petite woman with stylish red hair and an icy expression who is standing near the windows. Her St. John Knit suit and pearl earrings suggest she has spent some time with one of those personal shoppers at Nordstorm. "I'm sure you've met Hillary Payne," he says. "She's the ADA assigned to this case."

Payne glares at me through hostile green eyes but doesn't say anything.

"Nice to see you again," I lie. I've been on the other side of two contentious crack cases with her. Some people think she hates men on general principles. I disagree. I think she hates everybody.

Her lips form a tight line across her pale face. If she smiled once in a while, she would be pretty. "Likewise," she snaps through clenched jaws. Like her mentor, McNasty, she is a person of few words, most of which are delivered in a strident tone intended to put you on the defensive. When she gets in front of a jury, however, she's all sugar and honey.

McNulty's expression never changes. "The arraignment is at ten tomorrow before Judge Mandel," he says. "We're going first degree."

I try not to show any emotion. "You can't be serious," I say.

McNasty doesn't blink. "We're serious."

Ann decides to add her two cents. "You'll never get past the arraignment."

McNasty assures her, "We'll get past the arraignment."

"Mind telling us what you've found out so far?" Rosie asks.

"You know everything we know," McNulty replies.

I ask if the chief medical examiner has determined how Johnny Garcia died.

"We don't know for sure," he says. "We won't have the autopsy report for a few days."

Payne is more forthcoming. "Off the record," she says, "it's almost certain it was suffocation."

Turner casts his vote. "You don't know it was Skipper. You aren't even close to probable cause. You'll never get to the prelim."

We zoomed past probable cause around seven o'clock yesterday morning.

"It's a setup," Turner insists.

Payne's catlike eyes gleam. "No way," she says. "It was a crowded hotel. How the hell could somebody get a body up there without anybody seeing it?" She looks at McNulty for an instant and adds, "We're going to ask for special circumstances."

I look back toward McNasty and ask, "Do you really intend to make this a death penalty case?"

"You bet."

Ann says, "This is San Francisco. You don't get death penalty verdicts in this town."

"The DA is subject to the same laws as everybody else," McNulty replies.

I wonder if he already sees his name on campaign posters for the top job at the DA's office.

Ann, Turner and I are in the consultation room at the Hall with Skipper. Rosie has gone down to the Mission to check in with her brother. Skipper's confident public facade is showing its first signs of peeling. He is pacing. "The first thing I'm going to do after the charges are dropped is to fire McNulty," he says.

I'm glad he isn't vindictive. I try to keep the tone measured. "McNulty assigned Hillary Payne as the ADA on this case," I say. I tell Skipper about my experiences with her. "What else can you tell me about her?" It helps to know your enemy.

He stops walking and says, "It's her first big case. She's inexperienced, but she's smart. She's fearless. She relates well to the jury, especially the male jurors. She's been with our office for about a year and a half. Before that, she worked for a big firm. Then she left, or got fired. She had trouble finding a job. She can be opinionated. She was out of work for about six months. Then she was working at Macy's for a while. Small leather goods, I think. That's when her uncle called me and asked if I could help her out."

"Who is her uncle?"

"The mayor."

How very San Francisco. Rosie calls it affirmative action for the upper class. "So you decided to help your buddy out?"

"Happens all the time. It's just politics. I'd help your kid if I could."

Especially if I donated a couple of hundred thousand to his campaign. "Why do you suppose McNasty chose her to work on your case?"

"They're soul mates. He likes her. She's tough. She's thorough. She's on a mission from God." He pauses and adds, "There's something else you should know about her."

Uh-oh. "What's that?"

He looks at Turner, then he sets his jaw. "She doesn't like me."

"Why?"

"She was bucking for a promotion to head of narcotics. I told her she hadn't been with the office long enough and she got mad."

"People get passed over for promotions all the time. It shouldn't be a big deal."

"It may be in this case," he says. "She was very upset about it."

Swell. The prosecuting DA has a personal vendetta against him. "How pissed off is she?"

"Very."

"We can get her disqualified."

"On what grounds?"

"Conflict of interest. You don't want your case tried by somebody who has a personal ax to grind." More important, she may be unreceptive to a plea bargain if we have to cross that bridge. I see why Mc-Nulty chose her. She certainly has motivation. "We'll get her removed."

"No, we won't. You can't get a prosecutor removed because she's pissed off at the defendant. There's nothing on that subject in the California Rules of Professional Conduct."

"We'll find another reason."

He isn't budging. "You can't take her off the case. It would look terrible for my campaign."

"This isn't about politics."

"*Everything* is about politics. Campaign politics. Office politics. It's important for you to know about her, but you can't take her off the case," he repeats.

"This case has to take priority over your political ambitions," I say.

"This case better be over by the end of this week. I can't have my history with Hillary Payne become a matter of public record. End—of—story."

"I want to think about it," I say. "We can move to have the attorney general's office step in."

Turner answers for him. "There's nothing to think about."

Skipper agrees. "I'm calling the shots here," he says. "I'm the client. I'm in charge."

Great. Now I'm representing a guy who thinks he's Alexander Haig. I try to return to the matter at hand. "Skipper," I say, "do you know anything about Johnny Garcia?"

"Nothing."

"Never met him?"

His eyes wander in Turner's direction. "Nope."

"Do you know where we might find anybody who knew him?"

He's indignant. "I know nothing about this guy."

I keep probing. "Skipper," I say, "are you sure?" In other words, are you telling me the truth or lying through your teeth?

Ann answers for him. "He's already told you he didn't know him."

I lean back in my chair without saying a word. Skipper folds his arms and says, "How many times do I have to say this? I know *nothing* about this guy."

It's as far as I can go for the moment. "I'll see you at the arraignment," I say.

Noon. Rosie and I are eating turkey sandwiches in her mother's kitchen. The little wooden bungalow could use a coat of paint and some new carpet. Rosie's mom won't hear of it. She says the next owner of the house will pay for the new paint job. Our repeated suggestions that she treat herself to a few new appliances have gone unheeded. Handmade curtains adorn the small windows that look out upon a paved backyard. I can see the steeple of St. Peter's. The house has hardly changed since I first met Rosie. I suspect it looked about the same when her parents moved in almost forty years ago, except there's a small color TV in the corner of the kitchen and an old laptop computer on the dining room table. Sylvia uses the computer to e-mail Grace. The TV is always tuned to CNN. Black-and-white pictures of Rosie and her brother and sister when they were kids hang on the kitchen wall.

Sylvia is a shorter, chunkier, older version of Rosie. She has been widowed for twenty years but has managed to get by. She always seems to have a few extra dollars when Grace wants a special toy. She is cleaning vegetables at the sink. She's wearing a blue housedress and, in a modest concession to the twenty-first century, Nikes. Her shoulder-length silver hair is pulled into a ball at the nape of her neck. She celebrated her seventieth birthday last year.

Rosie takes in my account of my conversation with Skipper without a word. She reports that Johnny Garcia's mother had no relatives still living in San Francisco. Sylvia nods.

The doorbell rings. Rosie's brother, Tony, comes in and gives his mom and Rosie a hug. He carries a large brown paper bag containing tomatoes, mushrooms, onions, strawberries and limes. He's a good guy. He started working at the produce market that he now owns when he was in high school. About ten years ago, he'd saved up enough money to buy it. He works hard and he knows how to run his business. He's had to deal with some very tough stuff. About a year after he bought the market, his wife contracted leukemia. She died a short time later and he's never been the same. He's as friendly as always, but there is a profound sadness about him that wasn't there when Perlita was alive, and he hasn't shown any real interest in women since then.

"I'm going to talk to the neighbors," Rosie says. She asks Tony to check with the business owners on Twenty-fourth about Johnny.

I finish my sandwich. "There's something else we may need to think about," I say to her. "I think there may have been something going on between Skipper and Hillary Payne."

Sylvia stops cleaning the vegetables.

Rosie asks, "What did Skipper tell you about her?"

"She's pissed off at him because he didn't give her a promotion."

Rosie smiles. "She's pissed off about a whole lot more than that. They were sleeping together. Carolyn told me."

I guess this shouldn't surprise me. "And?"

"He dumped her." She pauses and adds, "She hates his guts."

The Fairmont Hotel sits majestically atop Nob Hill at the corner of California and Mason. It is a grand old hotel that was once used as the setting for a TV series. The old wing was designed by Julia Morgan and built of heavy dark stones after the 1906 earthquake. An ornate array of flags greets visitors who arrive at the elegant circular driveway on Mason. An unimaginative high-rise tower was added about thirty years ago.

I walk through the main entrance later the same afternoon. The crowded lobby is the size of a football field. The old maroon carpet and velvet chairs were replaced a few years ago by more modern trappings. The marble pillars and the stairway to the Venetian Room add an elegant touch. A group of Japanese businessmen wait by the door, their name tags conspicuous. People are lined up five deep at the check-in desk. A string quartet is playing classical music in the lobby bar. Not much has changed in the last hundred years, except that the hotel is now part of an international chain.

I walk past the concierge desk and head down the corridor on the

California Street side. Just past the health club and the sundries shop, I see a plain white door that is marked Private. A man wearing a blue suit opens the door to my knock. He's expecting me. A wire extends from the walkie-talkie on his belt to his right ear. If he had dark glasses, he could pass for a secret service agent. "Are you Mr. Daley?" he asks.

"Yes."

"Dave Evans. Director of building security." His delivery is crisp. He looks like he's in his early fifties. He invites me into his tidy suite. In one of the inner offices, I can see another man in a dark suit watching an array of television monitors. We go into Evans's windowless office. He tells me he's worked at the Fairmont for five years. I was right. He used to work for the FBI.

"How many cameras monitor the building?" I ask.

"A couple of dozen. We have a camera on the main entrances, the parking garage, the loading dock and the lobby. There's a camera in the corridor leading to the tower."

"Are all the entrances covered?"

"Yes."

I ask whether there's a camera in the tower elevator.

"No. It's too expensive to rig up cameras in all the elevators. And, frankly, there isn't much crime in the elevators. It's too tough to get away."

"What about the stairways?"

He hesitates and says, "We have cameras in most of them."

"But not all of them?"

"Correct." He says there are no cameras in the stairways that are open only to staff.

"Is it possible to get into the building without being detected by a camera?"

"Our system is state-of-the-art. It is virtually impossible to enter or leave this building without being detected."

"I understand. But virtually impossible isn't one hundred percent foolproof, right?"

"No system is one hundred percent foolproof."

Exactly the answer I wanted to hear. "Were you here on Tuesday morning?"

"Yes. I was the first security person on the scene. I took Mr. Gates's call. I called the police."

"What time was that?"

"Seven-oh-five. I went upstairs as soon as I called the police."

"Are there security videos?" I ask.

"We've already provided them to the police." He hands me a shopping bag containing about a dozen videotapes. "Inspector Johnson asked us to make copies for you."

"Did you see the victim in any of the videos?"

"We're still reviewing them."

"But you haven't found him yet."

"Correct."

"How is that possible? I thought you said your system is state-of-the-art."

He backpedals. "This is a hotel, not a maximum security prison. Our cameras cover all of the public entrances but not every conceivable entry. If somebody wanted to get in without being detected, it's possible they could have done so."

That's what I wanted to know. "Did you ever see the victim around here?"

"No."

"Can you show me the room?"

"Sure. The police gave us the go-ahead to clean it up this morning."

He takes me through a basement corridor to a stairway on the Sacramento Street side, which leads to the entrance to the tower. Although the Fairmont is no longer considered a crime scene, a police officer is sitting by the elevator. He nods to Evans. We enter the elevator and Evans punches the button to the fifteenth floor. "We aren't going to let guests stay in the room until things calm down a bit," he says.

"How else can you access the fifteenth floor?" I ask.

"There are two stairways on each floor." He adds there is also a small service elevator.

The door opens at fifteen and I survey the corridor. There are about a dozen rooms in all. Evans tells me Skipper was staying in Room 1504, which has a southern view. The summit conference with

Sherman's people took place in Room 1504 and the room next door, 1502. He says the two rooms are connected by an internal door and the participants were able to circulate between them. Hotel room service provided drinks and hors d'oeuvres in both rooms.

Room 1504 has been cleaned and all traces of the events of earlier this week have been removed. It smells of disinfectant. There is a queen-sized four-poster, a desk, an armchair and a TV. The carpet has been shampooed. The bed has been stripped of linens. He points out where Skipper was sitting when the waiter walked in. I ask him whether there were any police or security guards on the floor that night.

"No. A security guard and a police officer were stationed at the elevator on the ground floor. The politicians didn't want a bunch of cops upstairs."

"Was anybody else staying on the fifteenth floor?"

"No."

"Realistically," I say, "how difficult would it have been for somebody to have gotten upstairs without being detected?"

"The last thing we needed was an incident while the DA was staying at our hotel."

True, but not exactly the answer to my question. He shows me the closed internal door that connects Room 1504 with Room 1502. I ask whether it was open when he arrived.

"Yes."

I ask him to open the door that leads to Room 1502. Like most hotels, the connecting door consists of back-to-back doors, one facing Room 1504 and one facing Room 1502. Evans uses his master key to unlock the door that opens into 1504. Then he pushes open the door on the 1502 side, which is not locked. The room is identical to 1504 but is furnished with tables and armchairs—no bed. Evans explains that 1502 is often used as a hospitality room for social events.

I say, "So somebody could have gotten into 1504 by going through 1502."

"That's true."

I've started to look around the room, when we hear the toilet in the bathroom flush.

Evans gives me a puzzled look. "It must be a member of the maintenance crew," he says.

The bathroom door opens. "Hi guys," says Pete.

Evans reaches for his walkie-talkie. "Who are you?"

"He's my brother," I say.

"Nice to meet you," Pete says.

Evans clears his throat. "Dave Evans. Building security. What the hell are you doing here?"

"Taking a look around."

"You're trespassing."

"He's a PI," I say. "He works for me."

"That doesn't give him the right to break into one of our rooms."

"I didn't break in," Pete says. "The door was open." Pete produces his license for Evans to study. Then he turns to me and says, "So what are you guys doing here?"

I glance at Evans and say, "Dave was just showing me their security system and telling me how hard it would be to get to this room without being detected."

Pete grins. "It isn't that hard."

6
HANGING AL

"And how *did* you get in here?" Dave Evans asks Pete a moment later. We're still in Room 1502.

"I walked in the front door."

Evans isn't amused. "The hell you did."

"You're the one with all the fancy surveillance equipment."

Evans glares at me. "I don't have time for this nonsense," he says.

"Suit yourself," Pete says. "I'm not telling."

"Pete," I say, "let's try to be cooperative."

"Fine. I came in through the catering kitchen," he says to Evans. "I took the tunnel under the grand ballroom to the service stairs. I jimmied the door and walked up to the fifteenth floor. That's when I got lucky. The door to this room was open. I suppose the cleaning people left it that way. I'll bet you dinner at that fancy restaurant downstairs that you won't find me in your security video."

"We'll find you," Evans says.

"No, you won't."

Evans turns to me. "I don't care if he's a PI. I don't appreciate the fact that you sent him to break into my building."

"Mike had nothing to do with this," Pete says. "I got up here on my own."

This isn't entirely true. I did ask Pete to check out the security system. I didn't ask him to see if he could beat it.

Pete adds, "We did you a favor. We found a hole in your system. Now you can fix it."

Evans snaps, "This doesn't have anything to do with what happened the other night."

"Maybe not," I say. On the other hand, if this case moves forward, we will put Evans on the stand to admit there are ways to get into this hotel that cannot be detected by his security cameras.

"Bless me, Father, for I have sinned," I recite. I'm sitting in a confessional near the back of St. Peter's later the same evening. The church is quiet. A dozen votive candles flicker.

· St. Peter's was first dedicated on July 4, 1886, when San Francisco was still young and the Mission was a stronghold of Irish immigrants. It has been and always will be a symbol of our neighborhood. It rose like a phoenix after it was gutted by fire a few years ago. Although it has been completely refurbished, the feeling I have for the church that I attended when I was a kid is still there. To me, St. Peter's will always be much like the Mission itself: ordinary-looking on the outside but special within.

"How long has it been since your last confession, Mike?" a familiar voice responds. Nowadays, there aren't too many churches where you can recite your confession to a priest who knows you by name. For the last twenty years or so, St. Peter's has been the sanctuary of Father Ramon Aguirre, a strong-willed priest who grew up a few blocks from here and was a classmate of mine at the seminary. When we were in school, Ramon once told me that he didn't just want to become a priest; he wanted to become the priest at St. Peter's. He has brought a modern perspective and unlimited energy to a once-demoralized parish. He's known as the "rock-and-roll reverend" because he allows rock bands to play at youth functions in the social hall on Saturday nights. From time to time, he's been known to pick up a guitar and take the microphone. He's the first to admit that he must bring political as well as spiritual capital to hold the parish together. He is worthy of the legacy of the legendary Reverend Peter Yorke, a pastor who plied his trade in this very building over a century ago. Yorke fought for labor unions, edited his own newspaper and supported Irish revolutionaries. He once sat in this very confessional booth.

"It's been a long time, Ramon," I reply. "At least a year or so."

"You should try to set a better example for Grace."

"I know." We go to church when we can. I find it difficult to make Grace go into a little chamber by herself to confess some alleged sins that don't seem particularly sinful to me. I worry about the effect of this. I want her to like herself. "It's the old story," I say. "It's hard to get the kids interested. They'd rather be home playing with their computers."

"Tell me about it. Last week I had a nine-year-old ask me if she could just log on to God's Web site and submit her confession by e-mail."

"What did you tell her?"

"God isn't online yet."

I can't resist. "And what did she say?"

"If God is so almighty, how come God doesn't have a Web site?"

It's a fair point. "What was your answer?"

"Same thing we always say. Sometimes there are no easy answers and you have to take it on faith." He chuckles and adds, "I told her she could e-mail her sins to me in a pinch and I would see what I could do."

There are some things they just don't teach you at the seminary.

"So," he says, "I understand that you're representing Mr. Gates."

"It's true."

"What's that like?"

"Challenging."

He grins and asks, "Did he do it?"

I shake my head and say, "I don't think so."

"It's a sin to lie to a priest."

"Very funny. It's also a sin if I violate the attorney-client privilege.

Actually, I was hoping you might be able to give me some information about the boy who died at the Fairmont. I understand he was from the neighborhood."

His interest is piqued. "He was, but I think we have some business to attend to first."

"Business?"

"Yes. This is a confessional and I'm a priest. You haven't been here for a year. You're going to have to confess to something while you're here."

Every time I go to confession, it seems I have to tell my deepest, darkest secrets to a priest who thinks he's David Letterman. "Can I e-mail you?"

"No."

"Fine. Have it your way. I have slept with a woman who is not my wife."

His head drops. "Oh, Mike."

"Wait," I say. "There are mitigating circumstances."

"There are no mitigating circumstances when it comes to this."

"Hear me out."

"I'm listening."

"I'm sleeping with a woman who *used* to be my wife."

He sighs. "You're still at it with Rosie?"

"Uh-huh."

"Jesus, Mike, you've been divorced for what, five years?"

"Seven."

"When are you going to start acting like divorced people? Maybe you should get some counseling."

"We're doing the best we can, Ramon."

"I can't just give you a pass on this."

"I understand."

The penalty is lenient. He tells me I have to do my Hail Marys. Then he says he'll ask around to see if there are any available single women who might be interested in meeting me.

"Thanks, Ramon." He's certainly a full-service priest.

I do my penance and we take a seat in the dark wood pews in the third row of the sanctuary. Ramon's restored church looks better than it did when I was a kid. It was made of painted redwood in an era of

Victorian-style construction in northern California. The interior is an example of an architectural style known as Carpenter Gothic, full of geegaws and elaborate fretwork. The ceilings are painted to resemble Gothic stone tracery in a manner called trompe l'oeil. The huge stained-glass window above the altar has been painstakingly restored to its original splendor. The smaller stained-glass windows along the sides of the church were remade from scratch. A new organ sits in the loft behind us.

I look at the ceiling and remember the words of Isaiah that are inscribed at the highest arch of the church: "I have loved, O Lord, the beauty of thy house and the place where thy glory dwelleth." My mother still recites these words every time she enters this building.

"How are you doing?" Ramon asks me.

"Fair," I say. "When you're still sleeping with your ex-wife seven years after your divorce, I think you'd agree that things aren't perfect."

"I suppose that's true enough. I take it you aren't seeing anyone else?"

"Not at the moment. Rosie and I have gone out with other people from time to time. Nothing has worked out for either of us. Somehow, we end up back with each other. It isn't a great situation."

"No, it isn't." We sit quietly for a moment and he asks, "Do you ever regret your decision to leave the church?"

"Sometimes. The church has answers for everything. Out there in the real world, there seem to be none. I thought I had a lot more answers twenty years ago."

"So did I." He looks at the altar and says, "Life is complicated. You were a good priest."

"I was a frustrated priest, Ramon. I tried so damned hard. I wanted to make a difference. I thought I was going to help people. By the end, it seemed I couldn't help anybody."

"You were too hard on yourself. People have difficult problems. You should have accepted the fact that you couldn't solve all of them. You took everything personally."

"How can you not take it personally? That's what being a priest is all about. That's why I became so frustrated. I couldn't solve the problems of my parish. I couldn't deal with the church politics. There was nothing sacred by the time I left." I look at him and say, "*You're* a good priest."

"Thanks. I'm a good priest, but I'm a great politician. In fact, I'm more of a politician and a fund-raiser than a priest these days. God's work takes money. Our parish is poor. Sometimes I feel as if I spend all my time asking for money. It's just part of the job now." He reflects for a moment and asks, "Are you happier as a criminal defense attorney?"

"I don't know. It's a tough job, too. I still believe that I am doing something important—that what I do really matters. That's why I do it, Ramon. On the other hand, sometimes I get disillusioned. Most of my clients aren't nice people. They're guilty of something. The system is imperfect. The process is unpredictable. Nobody is concerned about serving justice. The prosecutors want to get high conviction statistics. The judges want to keep their calendars moving efficiently."

"And the defense attorneys?"

I smile. "We're just trying to get our clients off—or get them the best deal we can. In that respect, this job is a lot easier than my old one."

"How's that?"

"You're still in the business of saving souls. I just try to keep my clients out of jail. In the cases where I manage to succeed, I can turn them over to you to see what you can do about their eternal rewards."

"I wouldn't trade places with you."

"That doesn't surprise me. Now it's my turn to ask you something. Do you ever regret you've stayed in the church?"

"Not for a moment."

"You could have made a zillion dollars on the Internet." Ramon has a master's in electrical engineering from Berkeley.

"I'm not interested."

"And you don't ever get the urge to meet an attractive woman and go out on a date?"

"Never." He winks at me and adds, "Well, almost never."

"Can I confess to something else? I'm jealous of anybody who has such a passion for his work."

"You seem to have a passion for yours."

"I'm still committed to the cause, but I've lost some of my enthusiasm for it. I used to think I could change the world. Now I just try to get the best result for each client. The system wears you down."

We sit in silence. Ramon closes his eyes. I look up at the majestic archways at the top of the church. A few minutes later, he turns to me and says, "I presume you came down for something other than to assuage your guilt for the fact that you haven't been to confession for a year."

"That's true."

"How can I help you?"

"I'm looking for information about Johnny Garcia. Do you know anything about him?"

He gives me a circumspect look. "Not a lot. He lived in the neighborhood. After his mother died, he was on the street for a while, but I'm told he'd found a job. I used to see him from time to time on Thursday nights."

Ramon opens the parish house every Thursday night to feed the homeless. Much to the chagrin of some of the yuppies who are moving into the area, the line often extends down Florida all the way around the corner to Twenty-fifth.

"Did you get to know him well?"

"No. In fact, I'm trying to find out as much as I can about him in the next couple of days. I've been asked to officiate at his funeral. It's going to be here in the church on Friday."

"I would appreciate any information that you might be able to provide," I say.

"Sure—I'll call you. I should know more in the next day or so."

The following morning, Rosie and I push our way through the throng of reporters at the front steps of the Hall. I look into the nearest camera and deliver my standard lines about the fundamental weaknesses in the prosecution's case. "We are shocked and dismayed that Mr. Mc-Nulty has chosen to pursue these unsubstantiated charges," I insist. "We expect Mr. Gates to be exonerated." I turn and walk inside. I've never liked playing the shill. Then again, you have to take every opportunity to make points with what's referred to as the "potential juror pool."

Ann and Natalie are waiting just inside the door. Natalie is wearing dark glasses and a stoic expression. Ann looks angry. We walk through the metal detectors and head for the fourth floor. Inside the stuffy courtroom, McNulty nods at us. Payne doesn't acknowledge our presence. Natalie and Ann take seats in the front row of the gallery. Turner Stanford sits next to them. Rosie and I head for the defense table. Skipper is brought in a moment later, clad in an orange jump-suit.

Most arraignments look more like a cattle charge than a legal pro-ceeding. On a typical day, the defendants and their lawyers sit in the courtroom and wait until they're called, then take turns trotting up to the lectern. Each one enters a plea and heads right back out the door. The fortunate get out on bail. The unlucky return to their cells. The lawyers mill around, waiting to make their thirty-second speeches to the judge. Defense attorneys often have several cases to plead on the same day. Sometimes it feels as though you're waiting in line to place an order for a sandwich at the deli counter at Safeway.

Today is unusual. The gallery is filled with reporters instead of de-fense attorneys. If my guess is right, the back of the house will be empty within two minutes after Skipper enters his plea. Then the cus-tomary parade of felons will have the courtroom back to themselves.

Most days don't start very well for Judge Albert Mandel, a superior-court veteran who oversees criminal arraignments and bail hearings. Today is no exception. It's seventy-five degrees outside and he's in court instead of on the golf course. He's also a champion squash player. Thirty years ago, Al Mandel was an up-and-comer at the Jack-son law firm. He's been trying to figure out a way to move to the more grandiose trappings of the federal courts ever since. A member of a prominent San Francisco family and a political conservative, he was appointed to the bench at the age of thirty-six. He had the requisite po-litical connections, but the stars have never lined up his way. His bit-terness is reflected in his demeanor. He looks a little like Ross Perot. He acts like him, too. He administers expedient justice from the seat of his pants. He's known around the Hall as Hanging Al. Skipper's ar-raignment won't take long.

"The People versus Prentice Marshall Gates the Third," an-nounces Mandel's bailiff. Arraignments are a news director's dream. They last only five minutes and they look great on TV. The ultimate sound bite. What could be better than a prominent, jumpsuit-clad defendant looking guilty as hell in a packed courtroom before a judge with a Napoleon complex?

Judge Mandel glances at Hillary Payne and then at me. "You aren't the only people on my dance card this morning," he snaps. He's even more abrupt in the afternoon. Payne and I state our names for the record. We agree to waive a formal reading of the charges.

"Mr. Gates," Mandel says to Skipper in the same condescending tone he uses for pimps, drug dealers and other equally esteemed members of society who pass through his temple of justice each day, "do you understand the charges?" Nobody can accuse Hanging Al of giving Skipper special treatment.

Skipper stands, his six-six frame erect. Although Mandel is sitting on the bench, Skipper is looking at him at eye level. "Yes, Your Honor."

The judge looks at his notes. He doesn't acknowledge the packed courtroom. "On the count of murder in the first degree with special circumstances, how do you plead?"

"Not guilty, Your Honor."

Mandel confers with his clerk. "Preliminary hearing one week from Wednesday on September twenty-second," he says. He raises his gavel.

"Your Honor," I say, "we'd like to discuss bail."

Payne leaps to her feet. She manages to get out the words "Your Honor" before he cuts her off with a wave of his hand.

Judge Mandel takes off his reading glasses and points them in my direction. "Mr. Daley," he says, "you haven't had a case before me in quite some time, have you?"

"That's true."

"And it appears you haven't spent a lot of time reading the penal code either, have you?"

"Excuse me?"

"I trust you've heard of section twelve seventy-five point five of the California penal code?"

"Yes, Your Honor."

"And what does it say?"

I knew this was going to happen. "It says that in a capital case, the judge cannot set bail when the proof of guilt is evident or the presumption is great."

He flashes a sarcastic grin. "That's right, Mr. Daley." He puts on his glasses, opens his bench book and begins reading. "Section twelve seventy-five point five says that 'a defendant charged with an offense punishable with death cannot be admitted to bail when the proof of his or her guilt is evident or the presumption thereof great.' " The glasses come off. "This is a capital case, isn't it?"

"But, Your Honor," I say, "the proof is not evident. The judge always has discretion—"

He slams his gavel. "This is a capital case, Mr. Daley. True?"

I try again. "But, Your Honor—"

"True?"

"Yes, Your Honor." McNulty and Payne are standing at the prosecution table. They should be enjoying this.

"So, Mr. Daley," Mandel continues, "you know full well I don't have the authority to set bail in this case, don't you?"

"Your Honor," I say, "you do have the authority."

He holds up his hand. "Don't you, Mr. Daley?" he repeats. A stream of saliva flies out of his mouth as he spits out my name.

I pause for an instant and then say in my most respectful tone, "The judge always has the discretion, Your Honor. The judge can make an independent determination."

He gestures with the glasses again. "Duly noted, Mr. Daley. It is my view, however, that your argument was nothing more than a waste of this court's time. I'll say it again for the record. No bail. The preliminary hearing will be on September twenty-second. We're done." He practically knocks the head off the gavel when he slams it on the little wooden base.

"That didn't go very well, did it?" Skipper says when we return to the consultation room behind Mandel's courtroom. Ann has joined us to give him moral support and to begin the second-guessing of my ability as a lawyer. Rosie stands by the door.

"You knew he wouldn't grant bail," I reply. "It's a capital case and it's bad politics."

Ann says, "He could have found a way if he wanted to."

Thanks, Ann.

"I'm losing too much time," Skipper says. He stares at the drab walls. "I'm going to need more firepower for this case."

"Look, Skipper," I say, "if you want to hire somebody else, it's fine with me. We'll substitute in anybody you'd like." And we'll cheerfully refund your money right after Rosie is finished ripping my internal organs out with her bare hands.

"No," he says, "we'll need you if this thing goes to trial."

This is a positive sign. At least he recognizes the realistic possibility that the case will move forward.

He regains his composure. "I want to bring somebody else in," he says. "I need somebody to get this resolved before things get out of control."

"Who did you have in mind?"

"I'm going to set up a meeting with Ed Molinari."

Hell. "Fast Eddie" Molinari is a local institution. He's lived in North Beach his entire life. His ancestors were among the early merchants in San Francisco and his family is well connected. He's in his late fifties and started his career as a small-time personal injury attorney. Then he made a name for himself when he was one of the first lawyers to file class-action lawsuits on behalf of individuals who were exposed to asbestos. It's lucrative work. Some people think such cases are just a form of organized extortion. Guys like Fast Eddie milk the system until the insurance companies agree to settle. Then the lawyers collect big fees and the victims get what's left. Fast Eddie pulls down seven figures a year.

When he isn't shaking down the insurance companies, he handles criminal defense matters from time to time. He gained some notoriety twenty years ago when he defended a member of a Chinatown gang who was accused of participating in a shoot-out in a restaurant on Grant Avenue. The other gang members got jail time. Fast Eddie's client walked. To this day, some people think Fast Eddie was able to put in the fix with the judge. His client ended up at San Quentin on other charges.

"Skipper," I say, "Ed hasn't handled a criminal trial in a long time."

"He's smart. He's tenacious. He's good at strategy."

He's a self-centered, egotistical asshole. We worked on a case together about fifteen years ago, when I was a PD. He handled a death
penalty appeal for a case I had tried and lost. The guy was guilty as
hell. He had kidnapped and raped two high school girls and then
stabbed them to death with an ice pick. He rejected my recommendation that he accept a plea bargain. Fast Eddie was brought in at the last
minute. He lost the appeal. It was the only time I've ever had to watch
a client die. Fast Eddie went on TV and blamed me. I learned an important lesson from that case: I will never give another attorney the authority to make strategy decisions in a death penalty case.

Skipper's eyes narrow. "Make the phone call. Set up the meeting."

"Christ—Fast Eddie, of all people," I say to Rosie as we're driving back
to the office.

"Skipper is pissed off because he didn't get bail."

"Mandel was never going to grant bail. It's a capital case. He
knows that."

"He figured the judge would make an exception."

"Why's that?"

Rosie smiles and says, "Because he's Skipper Fucking Gates."

"I'm not sure I recall seeing that exception anywhere in the penal
code."

Rosie pauses to reflect and says, "He's scared, Mike."

"I know. I'd be scared if I were in his shoes."

"And what do we do about Molinari?"

"Deal with it," I say. "We have no choice."

Pete is triumphant. "I won my bet," he says to me as we're sitting in my
office a short time later.

"Your bet?"

"With Dave Evans. The uptight security guy at the Fairmont. I bet
him that he wouldn't find me in their security videos. I just talked to
him. He owes me dinner."

"Congratulations. Did you have a chance to look at the videotapes?"

"Briefly."

"And?"

"Skipper was there that night."

"Tell me what I don't know. Who else did you see?"

He rattles off the names of Natalie, Ann, Turner. "And Dan Morris," he adds.

"So?" I ask.

"So what?"

"Did you find Johnny Garcia in the videotapes?"

"I figured you were going to ask me that."

"What's the answer?"

"What's it worth to you?"

"Dinner next door. What's the answer?"

Pete's grin widens. "Nope. He wasn't in the security videos."

I decide the head of security at the Fairmont may be having a career-interruption event in the near future.

"MAKES YOU WANT TO CRY"

"A funeral mass for John Paul Garcia will be held this afternoon at St. Peter's Catholic Church. In lieu of flowers, donations should be made to the Mission Youth Center."

— SAN FRANCISCO EXAMINER. FRIDAY, SEPTEMBER 10.

The next morning, Rosie and I are sitting about ten rows from the front in St. Peter's. We're here for Johnny Garcia's funeral. We have had an unspoken understanding for years. If either of us has to go to a funeral, the other one goes, too. We observed this rule even during the darkest days of our divorce and our custody battle. There are times when you just have to set aside your differences for a few hours.

The first two pews of the large church are half full. The next thirty are almost empty. Unlike the balmy weather outside, it's cool here. Elaine McBride and Roosevelt Johnson are sitting two rows behind us. It's customary for homicide detectives to attend the funeral of the victim. We've stationed Pete outside the church to see who else shows up.

Ramon Aguirre walks to a small lectern, brushing his flowing hair away from his eyes. The sanctuary becomes silent. He shuffles some notes. "We are here today to celebrate the life of one of our companions," he begins. "Johnny Garcia has gone to a kinder place. His youthful spirit will always be with us. From this we can take comfort."

He looks at the small group of mourners as he describes Johnny's troubled life.

When I was a priest, I did a lot of funerals. I used to give the standard eulogy about five times a week. Most of the time, I didn't know the deceased. I found it very difficult to muster the conviction that Ramon conveys. I listen as he tells us Johnny lived in the projects with his great-aunt after his mother died. By the time he was fifteen, he was living on the streets. "That's when Johnny got into drugs," he says.

Rosie takes my hand. If I'm guessing right, she's thinking about Grace. I gaze at the empty pews and remember the Sunday mornings when I sat there next to my mom and dad. I recall watching my older brother Tommy when he was an altar boy. Some of my earliest and fondest memories were of this church. I still get the chills when I'm here.

Ramon asks us to rise. He calls on a woman to lead us in a hymn. Then he nods to a heavyset middle-aged man with a bald head and a thick mustache, who strides to the lectern. The church becomes silent. "My name is Ernesto Clemente," he says. "I am the executive director of the Mission Youth Center."

I've known Ernie Clemente for years. A native of the Mission and a leader of the Hispanic community, he used to work for the San Francisco Redevelopment Agency. About fifteen years ago, he decided to attack the problems of San Francisco's urban youth head-on. He personally raised the money to start the Mission Youth Center, a combination dormitory, social hall, halfway house and drug counseling center for the poor kids of the Mission, Bay View and Hunters Point neighborhoods. When I worked at Simpson and Gates, I used to do pro bono work for him. My former partners were never happy about it. Except for a few enlightened souls, they thought law firms were formed for the sole purpose of making money. I'm embarrassed to realize I haven't done any free work for him since I moved to Rosie's office. I guess it's easier to give your services away when somebody else is footing the tab.

Clemente scans the faces of the scattered mourners. "We lost a good friend," he says. "We worked with Johnny Garcia. We had his life back on track." He pauses. "At least I thought we did. We found him a place to live. We helped him get off drugs. And then . . ." His voice trails off. "We lost him. It is a great tragedy."

He takes a deep breath. "Johnny Garcia came to us two years ago," he says. "He had no home. No family. So we gave Johnny a home. We became his family."

There are a couple of kids in the front row whom I presume are from the Mission Youth Center. If it weren't for guys like Ernie Clemente, boys like these wouldn't have a chance. My eyes catch those of Dan Morris, Leslie Sherman's campaign manager, who is looking back over his shoulder and surveying the empty church. Rosie sees him, too. "I can't believe he showed up here today," she whispers.

Turner Stanford is no better. He's sitting on the other side of the aisle. I squeeze Rosie's hand.

Clemente continues his eulogy. "It isn't easy being young and poor and homeless." He pauses. "And gay. Johnny Garcia lived his entire life alone and scared. We let this one get away from us, my friends. We let Johnny Garcia slip through the cracks. We let him down. And when we did, we let ourselves down. We mustn't let it happen again."

Ramon Aguirre escorts Clemente from the lectern, then introduces a clean-cut man in his mid-twenties. Kevin Anderson works for the mayor's office. I've seen him on TV from time to time. He's the mayor's adviser on youth issues and has political aspirations of his own.

Anderson looks solemnly over the podium at the small crowd. He adjusts his paisley tie and buttons his navy blazer. "I knew Johnny Garcia," he says. "I was his social worker. I thought we had a chance with Johnny," he says. "Obviously, we didn't do enough." He fills in some of the blanks in Johnny's short life. Heroin addiction. Prostitution. He describes how they found Johnny a job at a local restaurant. He says Johnny was self-sufficient and was living on his own. "And now this," he says. He turns and walks away. Ramon Aguirre puts his arm around his shoulder.

At the conclusion of the service, we file out of the church into the warm afternoon sun. Before my eyes can adjust, I'm bombarded by microphones. I stand tall next to Rosie and we push them aside. "No comment," I say. The cameras swarm around Turner Stanford and Dan Morris. They stand on the top step of St. Peter's, trying to look solemn while they argue about which of their respective clients is more sorry about Johnny Garcia's death. Political consultants are never off duty.

Rosie is offended.

A moment later, we see Ernesto Clemente saying good-bye to Father Aguirre. Clemente nods in our direction. He comes over and we exchange small talk. I ask him how well he knew Johnny Garcia.

"Pretty well," he says, sounding sad.

Rosie takes his hand. They were seeing each other for a short time a few years ago. It didn't work out, but they have remained friends. "Ernie," she says, "you don't want to go back to work, do you? You look like you could use a bite to eat."

He smiles.

I look back and see Kevin Anderson heading for his limo. "Rosie," I say, "I'll meet you down at La Victoria in a few minutes. I want to talk to somebody."

"I'm sorry, Mr. Daley," Anderson says as he gets into his waiting car. "I'm on my way to the airport." He says he's going to London, where his father is buying an office building.

He tries to close the door and I grab the handle. "I was hoping you might be able to give me a little information about Johnny Garcia."

"I'll call you when I get back."

Not good enough. I keep my grip on the door. "I need just thirty seconds of your time. How long were you his social worker?"

"About a year."

"When was the last time you saw him?"

"A couple of weeks ago."

"Do you know where he lived?"

"He was living in a place on Capp Street for a while. Then he moved into a room at a hotel near the BART station. I don't recall the name of it."

Some social worker.

"Mr. Daley," he says, "I don't work with a lot of kids. I wish I had more time for them."

I ask whether Garcia had any friends.

"He had a job at a restaurant on Sixteenth. I don't know the name. He had a roommate, but they weren't getting along very well. He wanted his own place."

"Do you know the name of the roommate?"

"Andy Holton."

"Any idea where we might find him?"

He shrugs. "I'll call you when I'm back in town."

La Victoria is a hole in the wall at the corner of Twenty-fourth and Alabama. It's a bakery and small grocery store and it's been there since I was a kid. The sweet smell of freshly baked cakes and cookies surrounds you. Handmade piñatas line the ceiling. We come here every year just before Grace's birthday to pick out a special decoration. When you walk in the door, the women behind the small counter hand you a metal tray and tongs. You select baked goods from the racks in the window and along the wall. A long counter runs the length of the store and there's a small refrigerator in the rear that holds drinks. There are a few seats near the back. It will never make the *Chronicle*'s list of the fifty best restaurants in San Francisco. On the other hand, it's reliable and cheap.

La Victoria sits in the heart of what was once the Irish enclave at the south end of the Mission, and my mom and dad passed by this corner thousands of times. But that's long gone. The business district on Twenty-fourth now caters to the Hispanic neighborhood. Tony's produce market is across the street. When you're at the corner of Twenty-fourth and Alabama, you can smell the mesmerizing aroma of baked goods, burritos and ripe fruit.

The neighborhood is changing again. Affluent new arrivals are moving down the hill from Noe Valley to the west into the traditional working-class area. As a result, rents are on the rise. Longtime residents are feeling the squeeze and they're fighting back. Community organizers are trying to retain the Mission's character, but sometimes things get a little out of hand. Every now and then, there's a story on the news about tires being slashed on a BMW. Rosie's mom insists that the Hispanic community won't give up its neighborhood without a fight.

Ernie, Rosie and I sit in a semicricle of mismatched chairs at the back of the store. We're the only people here. I'm eating a piece of pound cake. Rosie nibbles on a sweet roll. I ask Clemente how he got to know Johnny Garcia.

He takes a bite of his pastry and says, "I found him about two years ago," he says. "He was living in the streets near the projects." He looks away. I suspect he's thinking back to the place where he first saw Johnny. "He was only fifteen. Like a lot of kids, he'd ended up on the street."

My turn for a long drink of coffee.

"He came to live at the center," he continues. "He stayed with us for almost a year. He was already addicted to heroin. We got him into treatment—they gave him methadone and it seemed to be working. We found him a room and a job at a restaurant. It wasn't much, but it was something."

I ask whether he had any friends.

He leans back in his chair. "I don't know. We got him a volunteer social worker named Kevin Anderson, the guy who spoke at the funeral."

"I just talked to him," I say. "He wasn't particularly forthcoming. What's his story?"

"Kevin is a good guy. He works in the mayor's office and he's helped us raise money for the center. He's a little full of himself at times, but his heart is in the right place. His father is a big wheel in the real estate business. Some people think he's trying to run the working-class folks out of the neighborhood. He bought a couple of buildings on Guerrero Street and has converted them into expensive lofts, and the neighbors weren't happy about it. But he's from Visitacion Valley and he's never forgotten his roots. He's donated millions over the years to many neighborhood causes. He made a seven-figure contribution to St. Peter's to help pay for the refurbishing of the building after the fire."

A cynic might also suggest that Anderson and his father make large donations to neighborhood charities to keep the neighbors from contesting their development projects. I'm inclined to be cynical.

I ask Ernie whether he knows anything about Andy Holton, Garcia's roommate.

"He's another kid who was on the street," Ernie replies. "A little older than Johnny but a very different background. His father runs a biotech company. The family disowned him when he became addicted to heroin. He came through the center a few years ago. He worked at the same restaurant that Johnny did."

"Could you find out where they lived?"

"Sure."

"Any idea where we could find this guy Andy?" I ask.

He shakes his head. "I haven't seen him in a couple of months."

We finish our pastries and head out the door. Under the beat-up sign that reads "La Victoria Abardotes y Reposteria," Rosie takes Clemente's hand. "I'll call you, Ernie," she says.

"I'd like that," he replies.

Rosie's brother, Tony, always reminds me of Sylvester Stallone. There isn't an ounce of fat on him. He's a lot blunter about Johnny Garcia than Ernie. "He was trouble," he says. "It's a wonder he didn't die a couple of years ago." It's later the same afternoon and Tony is sweeping the floor of his overflowing produce market. He lives in an apartment around the corner and he's worked by himself since his last employee quit a year ago. He hasn't taken a vacation in five years.

"What kind of trouble?" I ask.

"You name it," he says. "Booze. Pills. Dope. He got in with the wrong crowd."

"Did the business owners know anything about him?" Rosie asks. "Did you find out where he lived?"

Tony holds up his hands. "Somewhere over near the projects," he says. "A guy I know is looking into it."

"Does your guy have a name?" I ask.

"Like I told you," he says, "a guy is looking into it."

It is not uncommon in this part of town for the businesses to pay some protection money to the local gangs. Tony undoubtedly participates in the program; he wouldn't have a choice. He runs a cash operation. He's never been robbed. "My source promised to get back to me in the next few days," he says.

———

Rosie and I are driving toward the office. "I wonder who paid for the funeral," she says.

"Ramon probably figured out a way," I say. "He's resourceful and he probably has some discretionary funds tucked away for situations like this." I shrug and add, "Maybe he found somebody to make a donation."

"Maybe." She reflects for a moment and says, "Did you ever preside at a funeral where there was such a small crowd?"

"Many times."

"What was it like seeing an empty church in front of you? Could you imagine being so alone in the world that nobody came to your funeral?"

I remember presiding over dozens of funerals where nobody showed up. It made me profoundly sad. "There are a lot of very lonely people out there, Rosie."

"Yes, there are." She swallows and asks, "What do you think about Johnny Garcia?"

"Makes you want to cry."

8

FAST EDDIE

"We're lawyers. We sell bullshit. Trial work is ninety percent theater."
— Edward Molinari, continuing legal education seminar.

Fast Eddie Molinari is all smiles when I arrive at his office in a flat on the second floor of a renovated two-story building overlooking Washington Square later that afternoon. The place looks like an Italian villa and smells of North Beach Pizza, which is just down the street. Instead of traditional artwork, the walls are adorned with enlarged newspaper clippings about Fast Eddie's legal conquests. Right above his antique rolltop desk is a blown-up headline that reads "Molinari Wins Stay of Execution—Client Avoids Death Penalty." Fast Eddie has a nose for publicity.

I can't think of a better way to end my week. I get to spend some quality time with the man whose grandstanding and sloppiness resulted in the execution of one of my clients. "Nice to see you again, Mike," he lies.

I take a seat and admire the view of St. Peter and Paul across the park. The hardwood floors are a nice touch. A state-of-the-art laptop sits like a trophy on the corner of his cluttered desk next to a fashionable humidor. Not surprisingly, there are no pictures of a spouse or children.

Fast Eddie plays pretty loose with women. He's been married five times. His divorces always make the gossip column in the *Chronicle*.

Molinari got the moniker Fast Eddie because he once pulled a gun on a former client who came to his office with a baseball bat and threatened to kill him. He's a short, wiry man who can't sit still. His most distinctive features are the wild eyebrows that sit above his beady eyes. In his spare time, he's an amateur boxer. The combative element of his personality seems to extend to all aspects of his life. He may not be likable, but if you're looking for a lawyer with unlimited capacity for war, he's your guy. Today, the avuncular Ed greets me. This means he wants something. If he doesn't get what he wants, the pit bull will appear.

I shake his thin hand. He smiles and says, "Looks like we're going to have a chance to work together again."

Yeah. Just like old times.

He opens his arms in a gesture of welcome. "Look, Mike," he says, "I know we've had some hard feelings in the past."

Tell me about it. It wasn't only the day he announced on Channel 4 that our client had been executed because I wasn't adequately prepared for trial. There was also the time he told the judge in open court that the San Francisco public defender's office was a cesspool of corruption. That didn't do much for morale around the PD's office. "Are you still seeing Jill?" I ask. Ed was going out with the ex-wife of one of my former partners from Simpson and Gates a few years ago.

"It didn't work out," he says.

No big surprise. He talks about business for a few minutes. He tells me he's just handled a matter for a man who was exposed to asbestos forty years ago. As always, Fast Eddie is the hero of his own story. "The defendant settled for five million bucks," he boasts. "My client's estate is going to get a nice piece of change."

So are you. Fast Eddie will collect one third of the money as his fee. Too bad his client died seven years ago and won't have a chance to enjoy his newfound wealth.

"Mike," he says, "I hope we can put our differences behind us and handle Skipper's case in a professional manner." Grandpa Ed is here to make everything all better.

"Of course," I reply.

The lizard grin broadens. "That's just what I was hoping you would say." He slides into the ergonomically correct leather chair that looks as though it was borrowed from the space shuttle. It doesn't jibe with the rolltop desk. He offers me coffee and buzzes his secretary. It's a warm day. You would think he would be more comfortable if he took off his jacket. No chance. His navy suit seems to be surgically attached to his body.

A moment later, his secretary appears with two small bone-china coffee cups. She looks as if she were taken intact from a feature article in *Cosmo*. I take a drink of the scalding espresso. It's tastier than the Maxwell House we pour over at Fernandez and Daley. Ed takes out a gold fountain pen, removes the cap and pulls a white pad of paper out of the top drawer of his desk. He's all set to go. "What have you found out so far?" he asks.

"Not much more than you've read in the papers."

He leans back in his chair, takes off his glasses and says, "Skipper wants me to take a significant role in the case. He wants my input on strategy and all major decisions." He replaces the cap on his pen. "If it goes to trial, you'll sit first chair and try the case. I'll be Keenan counsel."

In California, death penalty cases are divided into two parts. First there is a determination of guilt or innocence. If the defendant is found guilty, the trial proceeds to the penalty phase. The penalty phase attorney, known as Keenan counsel, is almost always different from the trial attorney. It's good to show the jury a fresh face, and the penalty phase attorney often argues that the trial attorney was incompetent. If the same lawyer handles both parts of the case, the lawyer might have to argue that he or she screwed up.

"I want to address one other issue," I say. "The only way I'm going to represent Skipper is if I have full authority to make all final decisions on strategy. I have told him this. Is that clear?"

"I was thinking we'd make it more of a partnership."

"Not good enough. I get to make the final calls on strategy or I'm walking."

"Let me talk to Skipper about it," he replies.

"There is nothing to discuss. I make the final calls on strategy or I'm out."

He pauses for just a moment and says, "I understand."

I decide to change the subject. "How well do you know him?" I ask.

"We see each other socially. We're both members of the P.U. Club and the Calamari Club." The Pacific Union Club is housed in the old Flood mansion across the street from the Fairmont. It takes decades to get in unless you're well connected. People from my old neighborhood don't get in at all. The old-moneyed gentry of San Francisco gather there to play dominoes. The Calamari Club is even more exclusive. It's a group of about two dozen politicians, labor leaders, businesspeople and lawyers who meet for lunch at a restaurant at the Wharf every Friday and decide who's who and what's what. Its existence isn't exactly a secret, but it certainly isn't well publicized. You can buy your way into the P.U. Club, but you have to wait for somebody to die before you can get a seat at the table at the Calamari Club. Fast Eddie may be a hothead and his ancestors may have been of modest means, but the fact that he has been able to gain entrance into the P.U. Club and the Calamari Club is conclusive evidence that he's a player. He reflects for a moment and then adds, "You could describe us as friends."

Not an especially enthusiastic response. "Do you believe his story?" I ask. Might as well see where he's coming from.

He pulls a long Cuban cigar from the humidor. "I think so," he says.

"But?"

"You never know with Skipper."

I give him a puzzled look. "How does a dead male prostitute fit in?" I ask.

"I'm not sure."

"Ed," I say, "Skipper is straight, isn't he?"

"As far as I know," he answers. I'm inclined to think he's right.

"We need to talk," I tell Skipper. I've come by myself. It's time to clear the air.

"What do you want to talk about?" he asks.

"The composition of the defense team."

"There's nothing to talk about. You're in charge. Ed is Keenan counsel. That's it."

"Ed has other ideas."

"He's mistaken."

"I want you to make that very clear to him."

"I will."

Good. "There's another issue I want to discuss."

"What else?"

"Your daughter."

He sighs. "You certainly play your cards faceup, don't you?"

"It's the way I'm wired."

He asks me what I want to talk about.

"I am having issues with Ann."

"What sorts of issues?"

She's bitchy. "She's hostile. She second-guesses everything I do. I don't understand her agenda."

"She's concerned," he says. "And she's entitled to her opinions."

"Which she is more than willing to express."

"She's opinionated. She's very independent. I can't help that. That's the way *she's* wired."

"I understand," I say, "but we're all on the same side in this case. I'm worried that she may say something to the press that will come back to bite us."

His response surprises me. "Frankly, so am I." He reflects and adds, "She simply hasn't been the same since her divorce. She's become very unpredictable."

I'll say. "Skipper, this stays in this room. Maybe it would help if you'd tell me what happened."

He holds up his palms. "She was married to Richard Stanford, Turner's nephew. The marriage lasted only a couple of years. It seemed like a great idea at the time. He's from a good family and he had a job as an investment banker." He sighs. "It all came apart in a hurry. They were very young. We encouraged them to have counseling, but it didn't work. Ann blamed Natalie for pushing her into marrying Richard. And she blamed me, of course. She became terribly strident. She said she'd never let us interfere with her personal life again." He gets a faraway look in his eyes. "Mike," he says, "she's my only daughter. I know she can be difficult, but this is a very hard time for her. My current situation hasn't helped. I hope you'll take her as she is and help us deal with everything."

"I can deal with almost anything, and I'll do the best I can," I say, "but I don't want her to do something that might interfere with our defense."

"I'll talk to her," he promises.

Rosie and I are sitting on the sofa in her living room. The TV is tuned to the late news, but the sound is turned down. I brief her about my meeting with Skipper. She's worried about Ann, too, but is pleased that I was firm about being the one in charge. "Molinari's an asshole," she says, "but he's smart and at least we know where he's coming from. I try not to worry about things I can't control."

I grin and ask, "Do you still worry about me?"

"All the time."

"I thought you said you don't worry about things you *can't* control."

Her eyes gleam. "Oh, I can control you when I want to."

"How do you figure?"

"You're a man."

"So?"

"Men can be controlled. Not all the time, of course, but most of the time. You can control a man when he's hard up. In my experience, most men are hard up about ninety percent of the time. In your case, the percentage is a little higher."

"You still want to do this case?" I ask.

"Of course," she says. "We're only a week into it and we've already got a client we can't stand and a co-counsel we detest. Sounds pretty good so far. Besides, you're going to need me."

That's true. I look at the TV and see Skipper's picture. I turn up the volume. "There has been a startling new development in the case of District Attorney Prentice Marshall Gates the Third," the anchor tells us. They replay footage of Skipper being led into the Hall. They show me proclaiming his innocence. Leslie Sherman gives a brief statement that the criminal justice system must take its course. A few days ago, she was fifteen points down in the polls. Today, they're dead even. Elaine McBride recites the party line that the police have important, compelling evidence tying Skipper to the crime. She says she'll have no further comment.

The scene shifts to the front of Skipper's house. Reading from a prepared statement, Ann says that her father is innocent and she strides back inside. The camera then turns to the man who was standing next to her on the front step of the house. It's Fast Eddie.

"What's he up to?" Rosie asks, startled.

I put a finger to my lips. Molinari looks into the camera and says that he's been retained by Skipper's family. "We expect Mr. Gates to be released early next week," he says. He spends another minute pleading Skipper's case.

I turn down the sound and I dial Fast Eddie's cell phone number. I get a recording. "Ed," I say, "I just saw you on TV. We need to have an understanding about the press. I don't want you talking to the media without telling me first." I slam down the phone. I turn back to Rosie and say, "This is going to get ugly."

She doesn't answer. She points at the TV. A frightened-looking young woman with long blond hair has appeared on the screen. She is standing in front of a BART station at Sixteenth and Mission. I turn up the volume again. We hear her identified only as Candy.

The reporter asks, "Did Mr. Gates pay you?"

"Yes."

"And did you and Mr. Gates engage in rough sex?"

Her glassy eyes water. "Yes," she says. She glances away from the camera. The reporter says that Candy may be a witness at Skipper's trial.

"Looks like we may have another problem," Rosie whispers.

9

"THEY'LL NEVER CALL HER AS A WITNESS"

"Hooker Says DA Made Her Have Kinky Sex."
— SAN FRANCISCO CHRONICLE. SATURDAY, SEPTEMBER 11.

I'm jolted out of an uneasy sleep by the ringing phone the next morning, Saturday. The first thing I hear is Ann's strident tone. She's furious. "Who is this prostitute that they interviewed on the news last night? You don't seriously think Father is sleeping with hookers, do you?"

"It was the first we knew of it, too," I tell her. "We'll talk to her, Ann. We'll get her story as soon as possible."

"Damn right we will. I'll meet you at the Hall. Somehow we're going to have to try to explain this to Father."

Skipper is indignant. "That prostitute is lying," he says. "She's a plant." He paces in the consultation room. Turner, Fast Eddie and Ann are here with Rosie and me. Skipper is going to tell his story to the entire team today. "It's a setup," he insists as he points a finger in my direction. "This proves it."

I'm not so sure. "Who's setting you up?" I ask.

"Sherman's people. Dan Morris. It's politics."

"Have you ever seen this woman?" Turner asks. He shows him the morning *Chronicle*. It's a front-page story.

"Of course not."

Ann asks, "Where did they find her?"

Skipper takes a drink of water from a paper cup. "I haven't the slightest idea," he says. "Probably on the street." He points to her picture. Her eyes are glazed. "She's a junkie. She's looking for publicity and drug money. They'll never call her as a witness."

I wish. Still, she doesn't have a commanding look of authority.

Molinari is surprisingly reserved. He takes off his glasses and fixes his eyes on Skipper. "Are they going to find anybody else out there who is going to make these accusations?" he asks.

Skipper's eyes dart. "If you're asking whether I sleep around with hookers, the answer is no."

Ann looks at me triumphantly.

I'm having lunch with Roosevelt Johnson at Tommy's Joynt, a bar and hofbrau on Van Ness and Geary. We'd set this up yesterday; I wanted an update on the police findings. Tommy's isn't the most politically correct restaurant in the Bay Area. Moose heads hang from the walls. A long cafeteria-style counter where burly men cut brisket, turkey, roast beef and even buffalo extends the length of the restaurant. It smells like a cross between a deli and a gymnasium. People from all walks of life show up here. You stand in line and tell them what to carve for you. Except for an occasional paint job, the place hasn't changed much in the last forty years.

Roosevelt picks at his turkey sandwich. "I called your mama last night," he says. He wipes his mouth with his napkin. "She didn't sound too good."

The doctors are trying to control her Alzheimer's with medication. The disease is winning. "She's having more bad days than she used to."

"Getting old is no fun," he says.

The proprietors of Tommy's boast that they serve over a hundred different beers. Roosevelt and I drink coffee. He looks around the busy restaurant. A gruff busboy who looks as if he's been working here since the place opened asks Roosevelt if he wants more coffee. He accepts. This is a good sign. If he didn't want to talk, he would be standing up. "They found some interesting things at the Fairmont," he begins. "Skipper's fingerprints were on the handcuffs."

I nod. This isn't news. We'll argue he got his fingerprints on the handcuffs when he tried to release them.

He takes off his glasses and wipes them with a napkin. "We still can't figure out how the victim got there," he says.

I don't want to tell Roosevelt about Pete's triumph over the Fairmont's security system. "Were there any signs of a struggle?"

"Not as far as we can tell."

I ask what else they found in the room.

He takes out a pad from his breast pocket and consults his notes. "Two empty champagne flutes. The lab techs are testing them to see if they can find traces of any chemicals."

I ask about fingerprints on the flutes.

"Skipper's prints were on both of them. The victim's fingerprints were on one." He finishes his sandwich and adds, "The room service waiter and your client told us the victim's eyes, nose and mouth were covered with duct tape. The kid couldn't breathe."

My chest tightens. I can visualize Johnny Garcia pulling against the handcuffs and struggling to find air. I wonder how long it took for him to die. "Did you find anything at the house?"

"They're still sorting out the evidence. They took Skipper's computer. One of our tech guys is looking at it. We found a gun in the bedroom safe. It was registered to Skipper. We found a storage locker key. We're getting a court order to open it."

We'll fight the court order and lose. I make a note to ask Skipper what's in the locker. "None of this adds up to much of a case," I say.

He lets that pass. "Our guys searched his study. They found two pairs of handcuffs in his desk that match the ones we found at the scene."

"He was the DA. I'm sure he kept a couple of extra pairs of handcuffs."

Roosevelt gives me the I've-heard-it-all-a-million-times look. "Could be," he says. "For now, we just have a bunch of coincidences, a death involving suspicious circumstances and some incriminating evidence. McNulty and Payne are going to have to tie this all together very soon."

Which is precisely what they will do. "Any chance the victim was dead or drugged before he got to the Fairmont?"

"I don't know. We're still waiting to receive the final autopsy report. You'll have to ask the medical examiner."

I ask if he's interviewed the prostitute who appeared on the news last night.

"Not yet. The vice cops who found her say she's articulate and credible. We're going to talk to her later today. We are very interested in hearing what she has to say."

10

"HE DIED OF ASPHYXIATION"

"It's like putting a puzzle together. You have to be patient and it helps if you have an insatiable curiosity."
— SAN FRANCISCO MEDICAL EXAMINER RODERICK BECKERT. SAN FRANCISCO CHRONICLE. SATURDAY, SEPTEMBER 11.

Two o'clock the same afternoon. I'm in the basement of the Hall, in the antiseptic office of Dr. Roderick Beckert, the chief medical examiner of the City and County of San Francisco. He's in his early sixties and is a leading expert on pathology and forensics. He eyes me through aviator-style bifocals and forces a polite smile. "Good afternoon, Mr. Daley," he says. His trim beard has grown more gray than brown in the last few years.

He wears a white lab coat and a striped tie. A thin gold pen sits in his breast pocket. Books on forensics and pathology are arranged in alphabetical order on his matching bookshelves. There isn't a speck of dust or a piece of paper on his desk. A model of a skeleton grins at me from the corner of the cold room. In what passes for whimsy in this part of the Hall, the skeleton is wearing a black Giants baseball cap.

"Thanks for coming in on a Saturday," I say.

We shake hands. His grip is firm, his manner businesslike. He pushes his glasses to the top of his bald head. "In my line of work, you can't keep regular hours," he says. He isn't the kind of doctor you'd call if you're sick. He is, however, the kind of doctor you'd call if you're dead. He teaches at UCSF in his spare time. He's big on the pathology lecture circuit.

He hands me a photocopy of his autopsy report and gives me a few minutes to scan it. "I just finished it," he says. "I wanted to get you a copy as soon as possible."

I would have preferred to have seen it before we met. I realize, however, that it isn't an ideal world and he has no obligation to talk to me. He is doing me a favor by fitting me into his schedule. I'll study the report in detail after we're finished. For the moment, I'll take what I can get from him.

Every time we've met, I've told him he can call me Mike, but Rod Beckert's not a first-name guy. When you talk to him, the protocol dictates that you ask him questions with mannerly restraint. "I was hoping you could tell me a little about your autopsy," I say. I figure I'll start with an open-ended question to see if I can draw him out.

"It's in my report," he says. This is his standard answer for almost every question, delivered in a clinical tone with a hint of a New York accent. Ninety-nine times out of a hundred, the information *is*, in fact, in his report. This doesn't deter me. He's going to testify at the preliminary hearing and I want to hear everything he's going to say. More important, I want to hear how emphatically he's going to say it.

"I haven't had a chance to study it. I was hoping you'd give me the highlights."

"Of course, Mr. Daley." We've done this dance many times. He knows I'm fishing for information. To his credit, he plays his role without irritation. "Where would you like to start?"

"How about time of death?"

He flips through his report, pausing to moisten his finger every page or two. "Page three," he says. "Time of death between one and four A.M." He says he determines time of death by looking at body temperature, discoloration and the state of rigor mortis. Then he recites the standard caveat that he always gives himself at least a three-hour window. I'm not going to make an issue of it. Beckert is one of the most respected coroners in the country. He's going to get it right.

I ask about the cause of death.

"He died of asphyxiation," he says. "The room service waiter reported that the eyes, nose and mouth were covered with duct tape. We found traces of adhesive chemicals on the victim's face that were consistent with the conclusion that the nose and mouth had been covered."

"Any chance he died before his face was covered with tape?"

"No."

"Could you tell whether he died in the hotel room?"

The first hint of impatience. "That's in my report, too." He pulls out three enlarged photos of Johnny Garcia's naked body lying on his stomach on the bed in the hotel room. I've been through this ritual before, too. I don't enjoy it. He thumbtacks them to a bulletin board next to his desk. He moves his glasses from the top of his head down to his eyes and studies the pictures. He gestures with the pen toward a side view of the body. He points toward Garcia's stomach. "You see this area here, Mr. Daley? There is discoloration. We call that lividity." I listen to him explain that when a person dies, the heart stops pumping and gravity causes the blood to rush to the lowest point in the body. "The victim was found lying on his stomach," he says. "The discoloration in that area indicates to me that he was lying on his stomach when he died."

I ask whether it is possible he may have been killed someplace else and moved into this bed.

He gives me the not-in-this-lifetime look. "I suppose," he says, "it is theoretically possible that he could have been killed somewhere else while lying on his stomach and then carefully moved to the defendant's room and placed in the same position. You would lose a great deal of credibility if you make that argument to a jury. In addition, urine stains were found on the bed." When you die, your muscles relax and there is often a discharge. "The stains confirm that the victim was lying on his stomach on the bed when he died." He says they will do DNA tests to be sure that the urine stains came from Garcia. They will also ask for a DNA sample from Skipper.

I ask him if he found any evidence of a struggle.

"No. No bruises or contusions on his body. No bruises on his wrists or ankles from the handcuffs. Nothing under his fingernails evincing a fight."

This seems odd. Even if Johnny Garcia was unconscious, I would think he might have struggled or begun to convulse in his desperate attempts to find air. It's hard to believe there wouldn't have been some reflexive effort to free himself. I ask about food in his stomach.

"A partially digested tuna sandwich and some potato chips. It looks like he had a late dinner."

"Any alcohol?"

"Traces in the stomach and urinary tract." He pretends to study his report. It's all for show. He could recite every word verbatim. "A glass of wine late in the evening."

"Or perhaps a glass of champagne?"

"Perhaps."

"What about drugs?"

"We found traces of heroin in his bloodstream." He pauses. "And traces of gamma hydroxy butyrate."

This is curious. GHB is a date-rape drug. It's a clear liquid that knocks you out almost immediately. It can kill you if you take enough of it. "How much GHB?"

"Enough to have rendered the victim unconscious."

"Or to kill him?"

"No."

"Is it possible that the combination of heroin and GHB caused an overdose?"

He's adamant. "No, Mr. Daley. The victim died of asphyxiation."

We'll need our own medical expert on this. We may try to argue that he OD'd. Of course, if Skipper gave him the GHB, and if an overdose is what killed him, Skipper could still be responsible. "Doctor," I say, "your report indicated that the victim may have engaged in sexual activity before he died."

"He did. We found traces of semen on the bed and on his body. We're going to do DNA tests on that, too."

I didn't really expect Beckert to help us.

A short time later, I'm in the second-floor office of Sandra Wilson, a meticulous African American woman who is recognized as the SFPD's best field evidence technician. She turns her brown eyes toward me and forces a smile. She's six months pregnant with her second child. A picture of her five-year-old son grins at me from the top of her computer. It must be hard on a pregnant woman with a small child to be working on a Saturday. She's a trooper. She takes a drink of water. "My doctor won't let me drink coffee," she complains. "The best I can do is pretend."

I like her. She doesn't play games. I assure her that I'll get out of her hair as soon as I can. "Have you found anything that might cast some doubt on my client's guilt?" I ask with a smile.

"Of course," she says. "The fact that he admits he was found in a hotel room with a man who was suffocated shouldn't suggest that he did anything wrong. I'm sure it was all just a coincidence." She gives me a sly grin. "Or, as Skipper likes to say, it was all just a big misunderstanding."

Tell that to Johnny Garcia.

She opens a manila envelope and starts spreading crime-scene photos across the top of her desk. The same pictures that Beckert showed me of Johnny Garcia's body handcuffed to the bedposts. Sheets and blankets strewn about the floor. Close-ups of the handcuffs. A handcuff key. A roll of duct tape on the nightstand. An overnight bag that I surmise belongs to Skipper. Two champagne flutes and an empty bottle. An ice bucket.

I point toward the handcuff key. "Where did you find that?"

"In the toilet."

That's odd. "Did you find any fingerprints on it?"

"Nothing identifiable. It's too small. We found Skipper's fingerprints on the duct tape, the handcuffs, the champagne bottle and the two glasses," she adds. "And, of course, the telephone."

I remind myself that Skipper told me he called building security. "How about Garcia's fingerprints?"

"On the champagne bottle, one of the glasses, the doorknob and the phone."

Why would Garcia have touched the phone? "What about phone records?"

"We're still looking into it."

I leave Sandra Wilson and head toward the lockup in the new wing of the Hall. As I walk toward the intake desk, I see Natalie, who's coming toward the elevator. She's wearing sunglasses and she almost bumps into me in the crowded corridor.

"Are you all right?" I ask.

She stops but doesn't take off her sunglasses. Her voice cracks as she says, "I needed to talk to Prentice." Her hands are shaking. "Is there any chance the judge will reconsider his decision on bail?"

"The chances aren't good."

"I didn't think so."

I ask if there is anything that I can do.

There is a look of anguish on her face. "This is all terribly unfair," she says, and heads to the elevator.

When I arrive in the lockup, I find Skipper in the consultation room, talking with Turner about the campaign. Turner says it might be appropriate to run some ads claiming that Leslie Sherman lacks the experience to be the chief law enforcement officer of the State of California.

I bring Skipper up-to-date on the evidence and autopsy findings. "How did Johnny Garcia's fingerprints get on the champagne glass?" I ask him.

He keeps his eyes on the drab green wall of the cramped consultation room. "I don't know," he says. "Whoever killed him must have pressed his fingers on the glass."

That's a stretch. "And the phone?"

"I don't know."

"And how did GHB get into his bloodstream?"

"I don't know that, either."

"Who ordered the champagne?"

Turner says, "I did. It was part of the order to room service."

"Only one bottle?" I ask.

"Yes." He says the order also included wine, soft drinks and hors d'oeuvres. Except for the champagne, the food and drinks were removed by room service around twelve-thirty.

"Why did they bring only two champagne glasses?"

Turner holds up his hands. "They were supposed to bring more."

Seems decidedly odd. "And there were refreshments in Room 1504 and in 1502?"

"Yes," Turner says. "We needed two rooms because we wanted each side to have a place to meet separately from the larger group. There was a door in between."

Something doesn't quite add up. "Help me here, Skipper," I implore him. "They put the first team on this case. Rod Beckert is going to get it right. So is Sandra Wilson. Johnson and McBride are the best homicide team on the force. We'll play whatever cards we have, but I don't want to get sandbagged."

His handsome face rearranges itself into a confident smile. He stands and holds up the index finger on his right hand, lecture-style. "There was a meeting. It broke up around twelve-thirty. I was by myself in my room after that. I fell asleep in the chair. When I woke up, there was a dead body in the bed. That's it."

At least his story has remained consistent. I shift gears and ask about Natalie. "I saw her a few minutes ago in the hallway," I say.

The confident look disappears. "I wish there were something I could do to make this easier for her."

"She's very strong," Turner adds, "but she's been through some very difficult times."

"Look," Skipper says, "there's something I think you should know. This information is highly confidential and must stay in this room."

I glance at Turner, who strokes his beard but doesn't say anything. We both nod.

"Natalie has been on medication since Ann's divorce," Skipper says. "The dosage had to be increased when Ann got in trouble at the nightclub last year. You'd never know it, but she's been fighting depression for many years."

I glance at Turner, who nods almost imperceptibly. "We'll do everything we can to help her get through this," I say.

"I would be very grateful," Skipper replies.

"There's more going on between Natalie and Skipper than meets the eye," I say to Rosie. We're in her mother's living room that evening. Sylvia and Grace are playing computer games. Rosie and I are sitting on the sofa.

"Depression's a serious problem," Rosie says.

"Yes, and she's not in good shape now. In some respects, Skipper's terribly callous toward her, yet he's also very protective—that seems genuine. And she's always the first to come to his defense."

"It's a more complex relationship than their public personas would suggest," Rosie says. "He's less of an asshole than I thought he was."

I agree with her, though I point out his blanket denials about how Johnny Garcia's body got onto his bed do sound pretty strained. "But you're right," I add. "Underneath that incessant politician mode there's a guy with feelings I didn't think he had. He genuinely cares about Natalie. That's for real."

"And she about him," Rosie says. "That's pretty amazing when you consider his compulsive womanizing over the years. In her place I'd be depressed myself. She's got to have known about it—after all, the whole world does—yet she's kept up the dignified society matron front. I don't think she's ever lost her composure."

"Until now." I'm thinking about the anguish on Natalie's face when I encountered her in the Hall a few hours ago, and those shaking hands. "You know, it's not the public disgrace—it's Skipper's plight itself that's hit her so hard."

"I think you're right," Rosie says. "And it's worse when you don't have anyone you can share your feelings with. I suspect she was never good at that, and now—Jesus, what a burden to carry all by yourself. If only Ann . . ."

Ann. It's hard to see her mother accepting her as confidante—there's too much past there. And Ann's still a powder keg as far as I'm concerned—I doubt that Skipper's talking to her is going to make any difference. "Where do you suppose she fits into this?" I ask.

"That's a tough one. She seems to run hot and cold. It's clear she worships her father—at least on a professional level. She's every bit as ambitious as he is. I can see some affection for her mother, but they don't seem to be close. It's a dysfunctional situation."

Families, families. "Were we ever as dysfunctional?" I ask.

I think I glimpse a quizzical expression on her mother's face.

"Pretty close," Rosie says, "but when issues came up, we laid them all out on the line. Maybe that was part of our problem. Sometimes, you have to learn to pick your spots. We never did."

Zingo. It occurs to me that whenever we're working on a case together, we learn as much about ourselves as we do about our clients.

"In Pacific Heights," Rosie points out, "you aren't allowed to have knock-down-drag-out fights like normal people do. Skipper seems to get it all out of his system by sleeping around and running political campaigns. I don't think Natalie has any similar outlets."

"Which means that there's a woman ready to explode behind the polite facade."

"It wouldn't surprise me," Rosie says. "She's a tormented soul."

"Are you guys ready?" Pete asks.

Rosie and I nod.

It's the next morning, Sunday. A shroud of fog is beginning to lift. We are standing at the corner of Fifteenth and Valencia in front of the cast-iron fence near the entrance to the Valencia Gardens housing projects, a series of faded pink three-story buildings with a dozen or so apartments in each. They were built back in the fifties, when urban renewal meant tearing down the old ghetto structures and housing the poor in new ones. Although the Valencia projects are not as notorious as those in Bay View or the back side of Potrero Hill, they're a mean place, too. The politicians are talking about starting over yet again. Kevin Anderson's father is trying to get permits to raze them and put up a mixed-use project with some low-income housing and some expensive lofts. He's hired Turner Stanford to help him get the approvals from the city. We'll see.

A few kids are playing in the concrete courtyard. A family dressed in their Sunday best passes us on their way to church. There's a bearded homeless man wearing an overcoat sitting next to his shopping cart on the corner. I slip him a couple of dollars and tell him to find something to eat. He thanks me and begins pushing his cart down the sidewalk toward Sixteenth.

"He'll just go buy some booze with that," Pete says. He isn't being harsh. He's being realistic. "Apartment 17B," he says. "Let's be careful. They don't know we're coming."

Apartment 17B is the address that appeared on Johnny Garcia's driver's license. The current residents may know something about him. There is also a chance that we'll get our brains blown out when we knock on the door.

We approach the second-floor apartment with caution. Pete motions us to stand back. If my guess is correct, there is a small-caliber gun in his pocket. He's licensed to carry one. He stands to one side and knocks firmly on the door three times. No answer. He knocks again. Still no answer. He frowns. He knocks once more and we hear movement inside. Rosie and I step back. Pete inches forward. I hear the locks turn. The door opens about six inches, but a chain prevents it from opening further. We make out a heavyset Hispanic woman in the gap. "Sí?" she asks hesitantly.

Pete shows her his detective permit. "We'd like to ask you a few questions," he says.

The woman looks at the permit blankly. "Police?" she asks.

Pete shakes his head. "No," he assures her.

When the woman begins to close the door, Rosie calls out to her in Spanish. She responds. They talk for a moment, and the woman unfastens the chain and opens the door. She motions us into the small living room. A beat-up sofa sits against one wall. There's an eleven-inch TV on a folding chair and a table covered with crayon drawings. I can see a tiny kitchen with a sink full of dishes. We hear a TV in the bedroom tuned to a Spanish-language channel. There are photos of three small children on a table. A huge man with a dark complexion appears in the doorway leading to the bedroom. He's wearing jeans and a white T-shirt and he's holding a baseball bat. The woman motions to him to remain calm. He glares at us but doesn't say anything.

Rosie shows the woman a picture of Johnny Garcia. She shakes her head. Then she shows the picture to the man. He shrugs but doesn't respond. Pete is studying every move. From the woman's body language, I sense that she doesn't know the whereabouts of Johnny Garcia's family.

Time to go. Rosie extends her hand to the woman. She shakes it.

Rosie offers her hand to the man, but he ignores it. She hands him a business card that he accepts reluctantly, then glances around the room and sees a brown paper bag with a familiar logo on it. "You ever shop at Tony's Produce?" she asks him.

"Sometimes."

"Do you know Tony?"

"Yeah."

"He's my brother."

There's a crack in the facade at last. He gives us the tiniest hint of a grin. "Everybody knows Tony. I deliver vegetables to him."

"What's your name?" Rosie asks.

"Hector Ramirez."

"Hector," Rosie says, "do you think you might be able to help us get some information about Johnny Garcia and his family?"

The grin broadens into a full-blown smile. "Tell your brother I'll make a few calls and see what I can find out," he says. "And tell him he owes me."

11

"YOU REALLY NEED TO TALK TO HIM"

"With the preliminary hearing for District Attorney Gates less than ten days away, his defense team is scrambling to refute mounting evidence of his guilt."

—NewsCenter 4 Legal Analyst Mort Goldberg. Monday, September 13.

I've arrived in the office early Monday morning to prepare for a meeting with Bill McNulty and Hillary Payne. Ann was standing by the door when I got here. It's always nice to find an uninvited guest waiting for you first thing in the morning.

"We spent yesterday down in the Mission," I tell her. "We found somebody in the apartment where Johnny Garcia used to live."

"That's it?"

"This case is six days old, Ann. We've been going door-to-door in the area around the projects and near St. Peter's. We'll find more."

"I'm not sure you have the resources to do this."

"We'll find out what happened, Ann," I repeat.

"What time is your meeting with McNulty and Payne?"

"In an hour."

"I'm coming with you."

Damn. "I think they want to meet with your father's lawyers."

"I'm a lawyer."

"But you're not representing him."

"That may change. I'm coming to the meeting."

I have no choice. "I'll see you there."

McNulty and Payne look like twins who were separated at birth as they sit on one side of the conference table in the corner of Skipper's office later the same morning. There are papers and manila envelopes on the table in front of her.

Ed Molinari is at my right. His breathing is heavy. He has placed a legal pad on the table in front of him. He glares alternately at McNasty and at Payne. Ed's ready for war. I've assigned him the role of the bad cop. He's a natural.

Rosie pours herself a cup of coffee and takes the seat to my left. She's prepared to cast doubt on every piece of evidence that we've been told about so far. We may not be able to stop the freight train, but we may be able to slow it down.

Ann is standing by the window. She hasn't said a word since she walked in. Skipper has assured me that he has asked her to be discreet. I'm still concerned that she'll disrupt this meeting.

We discuss the autopsy report and Sandra Wilson's findings. Then I decide it's time to see their cards. I ask, "Why did you ask us to come down here, Bill?"

"Your client is in extraordinarily serious trouble," McNasty says.

Tell me. I try not to react.

"The police found some very disturbing evidence at the house," he continues. "You really need to talk to him."

"What's the new evidence, Bill?"

He signals to Payne. Her eyes never leave the legal pad on the table in front of her as she says, "We found two sets of handcuffs in his study. They match the handcuffs found at the scene."

I already knew about the handcuffs, but I don't want to let on that I've been talking to Roosevelt. "Skipper is the DA," I say. "He's a law enforcement officer. He carries handcuffs from time to time. You guys must have them, too."

Payne's lips form a frown. She picks up a manila envelope and removes three copies of *Hustler* magazine wrapped in a clear plastic evidence bag. "We found these in his study, too," she says. "And just so we're clear on this, we law enforcement officers don't keep *Hustler* around the house."

Molinari jumps in. "You have no evidence to prove those magazines are relevant to this case," he says. "There's nothing illegal about having copies of *Hustler*. He may have had them to work on a pornography case. You'll never get these into evidence." He glares at her, as if to say "So there."

Notwithstanding Ed's heavy-handedness, it's a legitimate point. His bulldog persona may prove useful.

Payne doesn't even acknowledge him. She turns back to her notes and says, "We found a key to a storage locker at the Public Storage on Geary. We're getting a search warrant."

I knew about this from Roosevelt, too. "Suit yourself," I reply. Hopefully, they won't find a bunch of back issues of *Hustler*.

"You may want to check with your client to see what's in the locker," McNulty says.

I assure him that I will. I ask if they have any other information.

Payne holds up the index finger on her right hand and says, "One more thing." She opens another manila envelope and removes three Polaroids that are enclosed in clear plastic bags. "Look at these," she says as she hands them to me.

I place them on the table between Rosie and myself. They're pictures of three young women, all of whom are naked and handcuffed to the posts of a bed, eyes and mouth covered with duct tape. "Where did you get these?" I ask.

McNasty says, "The top right drawer of the desk in your client's study."

Rosie says, "Those pictures have nothing to do with this case. They could have come from a case file or an investigation." Or they could have been from Skipper's personal pornography gallery.

Molinari leans forward and adds, "They could have been planted. This doesn't prove anything."

Payne is indignant. "They weren't planted, Ed," she says.

I eye the pictures. Without looking up, I say, "Did you find any fingerprints on the pictures?"

"None that we can identify," Payne says. "The prints were smudged."

Good. "Do you know anything about these women?"

McNulty points to one of the photos and says, "This is the same woman who was on the news the other night. She's prepared to testify that Skipper used to pay her to tie her up and have sex." He pauses. "The same way he tied up and had sex with Johnny Garcia."

"You can't be serious about building your entire case around this woman," I say. "She's a drug addict. You can tell from her eyes."

Payne answers for him. "She's in protective custody. She's going to be clean by the preliminary hearing. She's very bright. College degree. Just down on her luck."

"We want to talk to her," I say.

"Right away," Rosie adds.

"We'll make the arrangements," Payne says.

"Mike," McNasty says, "I want you to go back to your client and tell him about this conversation." He hands me a duplicate set of the photos. "I want you to show him these pictures and I want you to take him a message. I'm willing to offer him a deal. We'll take the death penalty off the table right now if he'll plead guilty to second degree."

Molinari says, "You're out of your mind."

McNulty taps his index finger on the table. "Look at the pictures, Ed. Think about how they'll play in front of a jury. Think about this woman's testimony."

"We'll tear her apart on cross," I say.

"Maybe," Payne says. "But if you do, the jury may become even more sympathetic."

"It's a good deal," McNulty tells me, "and I'll take a lot of heat if I settle for second degree."

"He'll never go for it," I reply.

"Maybe not," he says. "But you have a duty to take our proposal to him."

Skipper's response to McNulty's proposal is succinct. "Second degree?" he says. "No way!"

We're all in the small consultation room in the jail wing. We've just sat through five minutes of invective from our client. We let him vent. It's better to let him get it out of his system.

I ask about the handcuffs in his study.

"I'm a law enforcement officer," he says. "I keep a few extra sets at the house and a couple of sets at the office. So does McNulty. So does Payne."

Ed joins in. "What about the copies of *Hustler*?" he asks.

"I'm the district attorney. I have a unit that investigates pornography. I had a couple of copies of *Hustler* to study their advertisements."

So Molinari had pointed out. It's plausible if not persuasive. "What about the storage locker?" I ask.

"Just some old records from my law practice."

"So we shouldn't object if they want to search it?"

"Tell them to be my guest."

"What about the pictures of the women?" I ask. "How did they find their way into your desk?"

We wait. Skipper holds up his hands. "I have no idea," he says at last.

I try to give him an out. "You didn't need them for a case, did you?"

"No."

"Who else has access to your study?"

"Just Natalie and the servants."

Molinari looks him right in the eye. "Skipper," he says, "if there's something you need to get off your chest, now would be a good time to do it."

"I've never seen those women in my life."

"He's lying." Ed Molinari is sharing his views on Skipper's credibility on our way back downtown. "I've listened to his bullshit for thirty years. If you're going to be a successful defense attorney, you have to develop some instincts for whether your client is telling the truth."

Thanks for bringing that to my attention.

He continues to lecture. "The bullshit has gotten thicker in recent years," he says. "He's convinced those *Hustler* magazines were in his desk because he was working on a case. I'm sure he believes he's never seen the pictures they found in his desk. When Skipper becomes adamant or indignant, nine times out of ten he's lying. It's very natural for him. In fact, he believes what he's saying at the time. It's part of his persona."

"Why didn't you call him on it?"

"You have to catch him red-handed," he replies. "That's the only time he'll level with you."

"I talked to Joseph Wong, the room service waiter at the Fairmont," Pete says. We're sitting in the dining room in my mother's house at Twenty-third and Kirkham the same evening. The fog shrouds the Sunset district. I can barely see the wall of the house next door through the small window.

My sixty-nine-year-old mother walks in with a platter of roast chicken. Margaret Murphy Daley is about four foot ten, with short gray hair and hazel eyes. Her full-time attendant, a young British woman in her early twenties, follows right behind her. "Eat your chicken, Tommy," my mom tells me. About half the time she confuses me with my older brother, who died in Vietnam. I glance at Tommy's picture on the mantel in the living room. He's been frozen in time at the age of twenty-one. He was a star quarterback at Cal before he volunteered for the Marines.

"It looks real good, Mama," I say as I take a piece of chicken and pass the platter to Pete. She and her attendant adjourn to the kitchen. I turn to him. "What did you find out from the waiter?"

"Very discreet. Didn't want to talk. Been working at the Fairmont his entire life. Started as a kid. Straight out of Chinatown. Lives in the Richmond now." Pete still talks like a cop. "Skipper had ordered breakfast the night before. Wong knocked at seven. When there was no answer, he opened the door and began to wheel in the cart. He found Skipper sleeping in the chair. Garcia was in the bed. He woke up Skipper, who called downstairs right away. Skipper tried to revive Garcia, but he couldn't. Then the security guards, the cops and the paramedics arrived."

"Did he see anybody else or hear anything?"

"Nope."

This whole business is fishy. Pete says what I've been thinking all along: "None of this adds up. If you had just killed a guy, you wouldn't go to sleep in the same room. You'd get the hell out."

12

THE HEART OF THE MISSION

"We are attempting to balance the economic needs of the Mission District while still retaining its character. We are proud of our community."
—FATHER RAMON AGUIRRE. SAN FRANCISCO CHRONICLE. TUESDAY, SEPTEMBER 14.

Ernie Clemente calls me at the office the next morning. "I found out where Johnny Garcia lived," he says.

"Where?"

"The Jerry Hotel."

I don't recognize the name. "Where is it?"

"Sixteenth and Mission. Across the street from the BART station. It's a dive."

So is every residential hotel in the immediate vicinity. "What about Andy Holton?"

"He lived there, too."

"Do you know where we can find him?"

"Not yet. I'm still checking."

"I take it you aren't prepared to reveal your sources."

"That would be correct."

I hit the End button on my cellular and punch in Rosie's cell number. When she answers, I tell her about my call from Ernie.

"Do you plan to call the police?" she asks.

"Absolutely. That's my next call. Do you think I'd go there by my-self and let Hillary Payne claim I tampered with the evidence? Where are you?"

"Tony's market."

"Can you meet me at the hotel in twenty minutes?"

"You bet."

The area around the BART station on the corner of Sixteenth and Mission is a mixture of run-down two- and three-story buildings hous-ing burrito shops, produce stands, fast-food restaurants and seedy ho-tels. According to a recent article in the *Chronicle*'s magazine section, there are fifty-six residential hotels within walking distance of the BART station. Most of them are on Mission and the surrounding num-bered streets and alleys.

Sixteenth and Mission is the center of San Francisco's heroin trade. It isn't something neighborhood residents are proud of. They understand the problem and they don't try to hide it. They acknowl-edge it can't be fixed easily. The J. C. Decaux public toilet next to the BART station has become a center of commerce and is known as the Green Monster. People hop off the BART trains, buy their stuff and get back on. It gives new meaning to the term "one-stop shopping." The Mission police station is just around the corner on Valencia. It doesn't seem to deter the dealers. The area gained notoriety a few years ago when the son of a local rock star died of an overdose in one of the residential hotels on Valencia.

The sun hits my face as I come up the escalator from the under-ground BART station and look around the familiar red brick plaza, which is dotted with sad-looking palm trees and fenced-in shrubs. A Wells Fargo bank branch greets me as I reach ground level. At least ten people are lined up at the automated teller machine. Two young men ask me for money as I step off the escalator and turn toward Sixteenth. I glance behind me toward Mission, a busy street with a colorful array of small stores, restaurants and produce markets. Tired banners hang-ing from the streetlights proclaim that we are standing in the "Heart of the Mission." Cars and orange Muni buses sit bumper to bumper on Mission in front of the BART station. The street is too narrow to have any hope of keeping up with the volume of traffic. It's a lively corner, but the assortment of homeless people, prostitutes and drug dealers would be intimidating to those who are unfamiliar with the territory. Things have changed a lot since I was a kid.

A large man wearing a dirt-covered windbreaker stands next to the Green Monster. He's chatting with a middle-aged prostitute who is dressed in a short green skirt, a halter top and high heels. She's been around the block a few times. Up Sixteenth, I see a bar called the Skylark, which used to be a transgender and gay Latino bar called La India Bonita. Now it's a hangout for the young professionals who are moving into the neighborhood. Farther up Sixteenth, just past Valencia, is another popular yuppie hangout called Ti Couz. They line up on Friday night to eat crepes. It's common knowledge among those of us who spend time down here that people in the hotels across the street are shooting up. The Mission has something for everybody.

The police have moved quickly. Four squad cars are already parked on Sixteenth, directly across the street from the BART station. A hand-lettered sign above a black metal door denotes the entrance to the Jerry Hotel, which occupies the top two floors of a decaying three-story building. El Pollo Supremo, one of those fast-food chicken places, is on the ground floor. Pete and Rosie are standing just outside the hotel entrance, talking to one of the five police officers who are cordoning off the area. I dodge the cars on Sixteenth and head toward them.

"They won't let us in," Rosie says. "Roosevelt and Elaine are upstairs. They're searching the room. The evidence techs are on the way. They won't be finished for a while."

From all outward appearances, it's hard to imagine that the Jerry was ever a decent hotel. I glance inside the open metal door at the steep staircase beyond. There is no lobby. The ceiling light over the entrance area reveals a urine-stained linoleum floor and flocked red wallpaper that must date back to the Eisenhower administration. I can make out two uniformed officers guarding the stairs.

Pete nods toward an African American man with a tattoo of a St. Bernard on his arm. "This is Ellis," he says. "He lives upstairs."

Ellis eyes me with suspicion. "Johnny was a nice kid," he says. "It shouldn't have happened to him. He was starting to get his life together." His voice is an octave too high for a guy who weighs over three hundred pounds.

"How long did he live here?" I ask.

"A few months." He says that Johnny worked at the Pancho Villa, the taqueria across the street. I know the place myself. It's a hole in the wall with a long counter, industrial-strength Formica tables and chairs and zero ambiance, but I'm one of the aficionados who think it serves the best burritos in town.

"Did you see Johnny the night he died?"

"I saw him leave."

"Do you know where he was going?"

"He didn't say."

"Was he by himself?"

"Yes."

Ellis isn't the forthcoming type. I ask him whether Garcia was walking or driving.

"Somebody picked him up in a car."

"Do you know what kind of car it was?"

He holds up his hands and says, "No. I didn't really see it. I was coming in as he was leaving. I said hello to him as he walked by. We didn't stop to talk."

"Would you be able to identify the driver or the car?"

"Nope."

I'm not going to get any more about that, so I ask him to tell us about Andy Holton.

"Andy worked at the Pancho Villa, too," he says.

Pete glances up the street toward the restaurant and asks, "What happened to him?"

"Don't know. I haven't seen him in weeks," he replies. He tells us that Holton is early twenties, brown hair and eyes, slim build. "I barely knew him," he adds.

"Any idea where we might find him?" I ask.

He shrugs. "You might ask over at the Pancho Villa."

"Is there any chance he may have been driving the car that night?"

"I don't know. I told you I didn't see the driver."

"Did Johnny have any other friends?"

"He used to spend some time with a social worker—the guy from the mayor's office." He adds, "I saw him on TV at the funeral."

Pete ponders. "Did you ever see the district attorney around here?" he asks.

This produces a chuckle. "Not in this part of town." He tells us the Mission doesn't attract a lot of attention from the DA's office or City Hall. "The guys over at Mission Station do the best they can, but they've got their hands full just trying to deal with all the crack and the heroin."

"Were Johnny and Andy lovers?" Rosie asks.

Ellis exhales. "I don't know," he says.

I ask if there is anybody else who knew Holton or Garcia.

"I didn't know them very well. In this neighborhood, it's better not to ask too many questions."

A police officer interrupts us and says he wants to talk to Ellis. He tells Pete, Rosie and me that he has to clear the area in front of the hotel. Pete used to work out of Mission Station. He still knows most of the beat cops. He nods to the officer and asks, "Did you guys find anything, Jim?"

The officer's nameplate says "Meeker." He shrugs and says, "I'm just trying to seal the area."

Pete nods. "Mind if we talk to some of the other residents of the hotel?"

"You can talk to anybody you want, but you can't go inside until I say so."

I hand Ellis a business card. "Call us if you recognize anybody else who knew Garcia or Holton," I say.

Later the same afternoon, we're eating burritos with Pete at the Pancho Villa. The lunch crowd has left and the place is quiet. It didn't take long to interview the residents of the Jerry Hotel once the police let us inside. All we learned was that Johnny Garcia and Andy Holton kept to themselves. Many of the residents have drug problems of their own. All of them were reluctant to take any role in a police investigation.

Pete takes a bite of his *carne asada.* "I'll make the rounds of the businesses in the vicinity," he says.

Rosie glances around the restaurant and motions to the young man behind the counter. He's slim, with two earrings in his left ear. She asks him in Spanish if he can take a break for a moment. He comes around the counter and stands next to our table. She asks him if he's seen Holton.

We see him freeze for a moment. "I don't want any trouble," he says in English.

"Neither do we," she replies.

"Are you guys cops?" he asks.

"No," I reply. "I'm a lawyer."

"Even worse."

Over the years, I've learned it's better to let people take their shots at members of my esteemed profession. "We're looking for Andy," I tell him.

"Why?"

I don't want to say much to him. "We think he may have some information."

"I haven't seen him since Johnny died," he says.

Pete asks whether Johnny appeared upset in the weeks before he died.

"Yeah. He and Andy weren't getting along very well. They were fighting."

"About what?" I ask.

"I don't know."

"Does Andy still work here?"

"He quit about three weeks ago."

I ask why.

"He didn't say. He just left. I haven't seen him since then."

"Is he a nice guy?"

He takes a moment before he answers, "He's an operator."

"Is he involved in drugs?"

"He's involved in a lot of stuff."

"Do you have any idea where we might find him?" I ask.

"Ask around the BART station," he says. A customer enters the restaurant. "I have to get back to work," he says, sounding relieved.

I thank him for his time. "If Holton had anything to do with this, he's probably left town," I say to Rosie and Pete.

"Maybe he's hiding," Pete says. "Maybe he's scared."

Rosie crumples the tinfoil from her wrapper into a tight ball, tosses it across the restaurant into the trash can and says, "Maybe he's dead."

13

THE CHAMELEON

"Unlike many political consultants, I believe that there is still a place for ethics and values in politics. I am very proud of my work."
—Political Consultant Daniel R. Morris. *San Francisco Daily Legal Journal*. Wednesday, September 15.

Early the next morning, we're in Hillary Payne's office, where the prostitute known as Candy is telling her story to Rosie and me. Her eyes are dull. "He paid me for sex," she says. "He liked to handcuff me to the bed and put duct tape on my face." Her dirty-blond hair cascades into her eyes. She's wearing jeans and a white blouse. Her skin has a pallor you often see in drug users.

Payne is sitting in the corner. She's giving us some leeway. The fact that she's letting us talk to Candy indicates she believes her story.

"How long were you involved with Mr. Gates?" Rosie asks Candy.

"About a year."

"How much did he pay you?"

"Five hundred dollars a night." Her eyes never leave Rosie's.

"Why did you stop seeing him?"

Candy dabs at her eyes. "He got rougher and rougher. I was afraid he was going to kill me."

A few minutes later, Payne intercedes and says, "I think you get the gist of Candy's story. That's it for now."

The Mission Youth Center is housed in a fortress-like building that used to be a high school around the corner from St. Peter's. Fifty boys between the ages of thirteen and eighteen call the center home. Ernie Clemente's staff provides counseling and services for over three hundred other kids. The facility has grown substantially over the years. Every penny that Ernie raises goes into the programs. A couple of years ago, he was able to purchase two of the adjoining apartment buildings, which he has converted into dormitory space.

Ernie's small office is just inside the main entrance. His beat-up wooden desk is covered with piles of papers, books and magazines. He has an open-door policy. In fact, he has no door at all. He told me that he never wanted a needy kid to see a closed door.

In the ten minutes we've been sitting here, Rosie and I have watched dozens of teenagers walk past toward the dining room and the dorm. Although the place seems chaotic, Ernie runs a tight ship. He knows every kid by name. A tall boy with wisp of a mustache pokes his head inside the office and says, "Everything's ready for the basketball tournament."

Ernie smiles. "Thanks, Rick." He asks whether Rick was able to get enough food to feed the teams.

"You bet." Rick heads down the hall.

Ernie's pleased. He says, "He just turned eighteen. He was a heroin addict two years ago. He's going to finish up at Mission High this year. He wants to go to college." He gets a faraway look in his eyes and adds, "You get a small victory every once in a while. That's why I do this."

"That's why you do the job of three people," Rosie says. Ernie's overloaded schedule became a significant issue when he and Rosie were seeing each other last year. He works twenty-four hours a day and he takes no vacations. It's difficult to sustain a relationship in such circumstances.

"Somebody has to do it," Ernie says. "If I didn't, somebody else would."

"Do you ever worry about what will happen to the center when you retire?" I ask.

"I can't retire. And I certainly can't die or get sick. It would help if I could find a couple of clones of myself to help run the place. I know that. I'm fifty-eight. I'll need to pass the torch in the next few years. The center could use some renovations. We're running at a deficit. I spend most of my time raising money. Ramon Aguirre has the same problems. St. Peter's needs a lot of work and the archdiocese is willing to put up only so much money. We commiserate from time to time."

Rosie and I glance at each other, thinking the same thing: What a huge difference Ernie and Ramon make. They save lives. They get very little thanks. When I talk to guys like Ernie, I wonder sometimes if I might have done more when I was a priest. I worked for a couple of years at a small church in the Sunset. It wasn't an affluent community, but it was stable. Although there were drug and alcohol issues, they never rose to the level that Ernie and Ramon see every day.

"We should have kept a closer eye on Johnny Garcia," he says. "We let him out on the street too soon. He was too young."

"You can't fix everything," I say.

"We can try."

Rosie says, "It's really urgent that we find Andy Holton. We don't know whether the police turned up anything at the Jerry, but it does look as if he's the real connection to what happened to Johnny."

Clemente clears his throat. He knows everybody in the neighborhood. "If he's anywhere around here," he assures us, "we'll find him for you. I promise."

"How would you like Ernie's job?" I ask Rosie as we're leaving the center.

"No thanks."

I agree with her. "Could you imagine being responsible for three hundred kids?"

"Nope. We have enough on our hands dealing with one. And we have to handle only a few cases at a time. That's plenty for me."

"He loves it," I say.

"Yes, he does. Ernie takes on the problems of the entire community."

"I stopped doing that a long time ago. I couldn't do it anymore. Do you ever think about trying to heat things up again with him?"

She shakes her head. "He doesn't have time for a relationship, Mike. I need more than he can give. It's not his fault. He has a full plate." She reflects for a moment and adds, "You're very different from Ernie. He cares about the kids, but he doesn't personalize all of their problems. He looks at the big picture much more than you do."

This is true. I couldn't let anything go when I was a priest. Then again, I can't let anything go in my law practice, either. "He's very effective at what he does, Rosie."

"Yes, he is—terrifically so."

"But he's starting to burn out," I say.

"So are you."

I'm not the only one who's been thinking about relationships. Tony's had it on his mind, too. The first thing he asks me when I stop by the market a little later is whether I've been seeing anybody.

"You mean a woman?" I ask.

He hands me a bag filled with Fuji apples and says, "Yeah."

"You mean somebody other than your sister?"

"Yeah."

"No."

"You know," he says, "if you don't mind my saying, it seems you and Rosie aren't real clear on the concept of being divorced."

"People have pointed that out to us from time to time."

He smiles. "One of my suppliers has a sister. She's single. Late thirties. New in town. Works for an insurance company. Are you interested?"

"I'm always interested." I stop for a moment and ask, "Are you?"

"She isn't my type."

"Have you met her?"

"I've seen pictures. Definitely not my type."

I put my bag on the counter and say, "Tony, it's been almost ten years. It's okay for you to go out on a date every once in a while."

"She really isn't my type," he repeats.

We've had this discussion from time to time. "Tell you what," I say. "Why don't you ask her out? If she says no or you don't hit it off, then you can send her over to me."

He winks. "You're willing to take my leftovers?"

"Absolutely." I wonder if he'll actually ask her. I decide to shift gears. "Has that source of yours been able to provide any information about Andy Holton?"

"I asked."

"And?"

"He wasn't real happy when I mentioned Holton's name."

"Any inkling why?"

"Nope."

"I don't suppose your source might be willing to talk to me?"

"Don't think so."

"Is he, well, in a reputable line of business?"

"Yes."

"Does his business comply with the customary rules of law of the State of California?"

"For the most part," Tony answers. "What is it you lawyers always say? His business complies with the spirit of the law, if not the letter."

The following morning, Thursday, begins on something less than a high note when I pay a visit to the office of Dan Morris, political consultant to the stars. The paunchy, fiftyish redhead is dressed in a charcoal Wilkes Bashford suit with a blinding white shirt and a tie that has a picture of a mule on it. "I'm running a campaign for a Democrat these days," he says through a wide grin. "For the next few months, I have to wear my Democrat wardrobe." He laughs at his own joke. "We're all whores, Mike. You're a lawyer. I'm a consultant. You know what I'm talking about."

In some respects, I admire his honesty. As far as I can tell, he has no political agenda of his own. He's the ultimate political chameleon. I don't know if he's a Republican or a Democrat. He's up front about it. He's in it for the money. He'll represent Republicans, Democrats, Independents, Communists and former professional wrestlers if they can come up with the eight hundred thousand dollars he charges to run a campaign.

Dan is sitting in his memorabilia-filled office on the ground floor of a refurbished gold rush–era building on Montgomery, just north of the Transamerica Pyramid. The space was formerly occupied by a flamboyant personal injury attorney. The desk is covered with souvenirs from his political triumphs. Coffee mugs. Buttons. Banners. Straw hats. One wall is full of political posters. Another has an array of photos of Dan's favorite person—himself. You can walk up Montgomery and look right into his office. It is a privilege to watch him work.

I ask him how Leslie Sherman's campaign is going.

The freckles on his forehead seem to get brighter right before my eyes. "Great," he says. "Your client did us a tremendous favor by murdering that hooker." His smarmy grin broadens. "Not that I'd ever say that to the media, of course. For the time being, we're going to stick with the party line. We're going to look very serious and say that we have great faith in the justice system and we are sure Mr. Gates will have his day in court." He beams. "On behalf of everybody involved in Leslie's campaign, I'd like to express our eternal thanks."

I underestimated him. I thought he was just a garden-variety jerk.

"Let me tell you a story," he says. Before I can stop him, he recounts the tale of a well-known politician in a southern state who had a big lead. The night before the election, he told reporters that the only way he could lose was if he was found in bed the next morning "with a dead girl or a live boy." He cackles. "Your client is trying to take this one step further. He's trying to see whether he can still win after they've found a dead boy in his bed."

I manage to restrain myself. "I understand you were there that night."

"I was."

"Who else was there?"

He leans back and names Skipper, Turner, Natalie and Ann. "Kevin Anderson was there, too."

It strikes me as a bit odd that the mayor's aide and Garcia's social worker happened to be at the hotel that night. "Why was he there?" I ask.

"The mayor asked him to help with the arrangements for the debate."

Interesting. Young Kevin has more influence with the mayor than I thought.

He adds, "Bill McNulty and Hillary Payne were there."

Really. "Why?"

"A show of support from the rank and file."

I'll be sure to ask them about it. "I understand your associate was there with you."

"Jason was there, too." Morris's toady is a young man named Jason Parnelli, who looks and talks a little bit like George Stephanopoulos but has the brain of George of the Jungle. His job consists of agreeing with everything Morris says and shilling for whatever candidate they are currently representing.

"I'd like to talk to him."

"I can tell you what happened."

"Let me just ask him a few questions."

He pauses and says, "Sure." He punches a button on his speaker-phone and summons Parnelli. I swear he arrives before Morris has hung up his phone.

Parnelli is late thirties but appears younger. He looks like he sprang to life from a Dockers ad. He's sort of a political toady-in-training. His grandfather was a United States senator and his aunt is on the Board of Supervisors. Dan hired him because of his family connections. Parnelli can't hold back a grin. "Looks like your client is in some trouble," he says.

"I understand both of you were there that night," I reply.

Dan answers. "We had a meeting with Skipper and his people about the debates."

Parnelli interrupts him. "Of course, in light of the events of the last few days, it's unclear whether the debates will ever happen." He's pleased with himself.

Morris reddens and he glares at Parnelli, whose smile disappears. He slinks down in his chair. He won't have another speaking part in this little drama.

"What time did you leave?" I ask.

They glance at each other. "The meeting broke up around twelve-thirty," Morris says.

Not quite the answer to my question. "Did you go home?"

Another look at Parnelli. "Yes," Morris says.

Parnelli starts to squirm. "Dan," he begins.

Morris stares daggers at him. "We went home around twelve-thirty."

This will need pursuing. I study Parnelli. He's uncomfortable. "Yeah," he says. "I got home around one. My wife can confirm it if you'd like."

Morris is triumphant. "As I said, we'd like to thank your client for his great contributions to Leslie's campaign."

I'm glad to leave.

I have a visitor when I return to the office. "I apologize for not making an appointment," Natalie says. "I didn't want Ann to know I was coming down to see you."

"You can see me whenever you want," I say. "You're always welcome."

She fingers the reading glasses. "Do you have to tell Ann that I was here?"

"Of course not."

She looks relieved.

I ask her how she is holding up.

She swallows. "All things considered, not bad." She leans back in her chair and adds, "I'm hopeful that things will be resolved before too long."

"Natalie," I say, "I know the situation is very difficult—"

"We are going to get through it, Michael," she says. "We've been through difficult situations in the past. We will get through this one, too."

I ask, "Is there something between you and Ann that I should know about?"

She says a touch hesitantly, "I expect you've noticed that Ann and I don't always communicate very effectively. I love her more than she'll ever know, but I haven't always agreed with some of her choices."

"What sorts of choices?"

"Career choices. Choices about the company she keeps, how she lives her life. She's very ambitious and talented, but she exercises bad judgment from time to time. She seems so—so angry. She's never been the same since her divorce. She blamed her husband and she blamed Prentice and me. She said we manipulated her into marrying Richard and then she said we weren't supportive when they had difficulties." There are tears in her eyes. "It wasn't true, Michael," she protests. "It was terribly unfair. We did everything we could to help them."

"You never want your children to hurt, Natalie."

She doesn't respond, but I can see the pain in her eyes.

I search for my calming priest-voice. "I don't mean to pry, and I realize this is very painful for you. Then again, it may help me to know a little more. Did the situation with Ann affect your relationship with Skipper?"

"Prentice and I began to drift apart many years ago," she says, "but Ann's divorce exacerbated the situation. Prentice immersed himself in his work." Her voice breaks as she says, "I feel as though I've lost my daughter and my husband."

I thank her for explaining. "It helps me to understand," I tell her.

"I don't mean to burden you, and it does help me to talk about it," she says. "But I really came down here to see if I could help. I didn't know what else to do."

"We'll take care of the legal maneuvering. It will help if you provide whatever support you can for your husband. I need you to be strong for your daughter, too. The entire situation has been very difficult for her."

"I'm glad you realize that, Michael," she says. "I know Ann has been hard on you."

"She cares," I reply. In spite of the vitriol, I mean this.

"Yes, she does. She has always admired Prentice."

"We'll do our best for him. You have to take care of yourself, too. This can be a painful process—the justice system doesn't work very quickly."

"My family is falling apart, Michael," she says, her composure beginning to break. Prentice is not a murderer. If the charges aren't dropped, I won't have a family."

"Natalie," I say, "if there's anything I can do to make things easier for you . . ."

She stops me. "You've done enough. Thank you for listening."

I'm studying police photos when Rosie walks in and takes her favorite spot on the corner of my desk, her usual Diet Coke in her hand. "I understand Natalie stopped by," she says.

"Yep." I summarize the highlights of our conversation.

Rosie nods. "Just because you're rich doesn't mean you get a free pass from the issues we all have to deal with," she says, looking thoughtful. "She and her husband grew apart. It happens. So did we. She has issues with her daughter. You can bet we will, too. And it's going to get even more complicated when she's a teenager."

Tell me about it. "Wait until Grace brings home her first boyfriend."

"Wait until Grace announces she's getting married. The guy better be pretty impressive."

I don't say it out loud, but I cringe when I think that maybe Grace, too, will come home someday and announce she's getting divorced.

The phone rings and I punch the button on the speaker. "I'm out at Public Storage on Geary," Pete says. "The police just opened Skipper's locker."

"And?"

I can hear voices behind him. "There were some files in it, but there was also some disturbing stuff, too. More copies of *Hustler*. And some—well—photos."

"Of what?" Pete has this irritating propensity for playing cat and mouse.

"Women," he says. "Naked women."

My head starts to throb. "How many?"

"Three. They were each handcuffed, spread-eagle to a bed. Eyes and mouths covered with tape."

"Did you recognize any of them?"

"Just one. The woman who was on the news the other night."

Terrific.

"Not good," Rosie says when I hang up.

"Not good at all." I pick up the phone and punch Carolyn's extension. "Can I talk to you for a minute?" I ask. "Something's come up."

Carolyn sits down and eyes me warily. Rosie is still perched on the corner of my desk. "Look," I say, "I know this is none of my business—"

Carolyn stops me. "You're damn right it's none of your business."

Rosie interjects. "We have a problem," she says. "We need your help."

"It's still none of your business."

Rosie tries again. "What we talk about here today will never be repeated outside this room." She leans forward. "The police found pictures of naked women at Skipper's house. They found more pictures in his storage locker."

Carolyn closes her eyes.

Rosie continues. "The women were handcuffed, gagged and blindfolded in a manner that is similar to the way Johnny Garcia was found."

Carolyn opens her eyes and looks at Rosie, then at me. "Are you asking me if he ever did anything kinky with me?"

"Yes."

"This isn't in my job description, you know."

"I know," I say.

"And I'll never testify about this in court."

"Understood."

She takes a deep breath. "The second time we did it, he asked me if I would try something exotic. I asked him what he meant and he asked me whether I would mind if he tied me up." She takes off her glasses. "I told him I wasn't into that stuff," she says in a voice that is barely a whisper.

We sit in silence for a moment. Then Rosie puts her hand on her shoulder. "What happened?"

"We did it the . . . uh . . . conventional way. That was the last time we slept together. Anything else you need to know?"

"No," Rosie says.

Carolyn heads for the door.

"Thanks," I say to her back.

"Well," Rosie says, "that didn't go very well, did it?"

"Nope. I don't suppose it could have. Maybe it was a mistake to ask her about it."

"Maybe. She's been through a lot, you know."

I'm kind of surprised to hear this. Rosie was dead set against bringing Carolyn into the firm when she approached us. Carolyn was a career prosecutor. Rosie was skeptical about her ability to work on the other side of the street. She was also aware of my past relationship with Carolyn, but she finally agreed we should hire her and acknowledges that Carolyn pulls her weight. "Sounds like you know her better than I do," I reply.

"Maybe. Women do," she says. "She's had a lot of bad luck with men."

That much I knew. Her first ex-husband is a tax attorney. He is also a condescending jerk. I have no idea why she married him. Her second ex-husband is an investment banker. He's an egomaniac and an ass. He walked out a couple of years after their son was born. "You would have made a better priest than I did," I say. "You have a knack for getting people to tell you things."

"You know," Rosie says, "what Carolyn needs is to find herself a good, stable guy like my brother."

"Do you think they'd be interested in each other?"

"Oh, no," Rosie says. "I didn't mean to suggest that Tony would be right for her. Their interests are too different. But I wish she could find a solid guy like him." She pauses and then adds, "And I'd like to see Tony find somebody, too."

"Tony's still reluctant to test the waters," I say. I tell her about his attempt to fix me up.

"Perlita was the only woman he ever dated," she says. "It takes some people a very long time to heal." She reflects for a moment and adds, "Some people never do."

"Natalie should be home by now," I say. "I guess I'd better call her and tell her about the storage locker."

"And Ann and Turner," Rosie says. "Ann will be beside herself. Turner is going to throw a fit."

And Natalie will feel more pain.

14

"A BLANKET DENIAL IS THE APPROPRIATE RESPONSE"

"This case will not be tried in the media."
— MICHAEL DALEY. NEWSCENTER 4. FRIDAY, SEPTEMBER 17.

Natalie and Ann react as we expected when I call each of them. Natalie greets the news with silence, and I can barely hear her response when I ask her who else had access to the locker. "Just Prentice," she says, clearly shaken. "He had the key."

When I call Ann and describe the contents of the locker, her first reaction is that her father is going to be furious. I'll bet. But she agrees to tell him about the findings, so when I meet with him first thing the next morning in the consultation room at the Hall, I'm able to focus on my worry about Natalie. "This is becoming more difficult for her," I say to him.

"This is becoming very difficult for both of us," he says. His eyes turn to steel. "I don't engage the services of prostitutes. I'm not into kinky sex. I have no idea how a bunch of pornographic pictures found their way into my storage locker."

I say firmly, "We're going to have to provide an explanation for it."

He folds his arms. "I just gave you the explanation."

"Can you give me anything more than a blanket denial?"

"In the circumstances, a blanket denial is the appropriate response."

Christ. "Okay," I say, "let's take this one step at a time. Maybe we can discredit the prostitute. She's an addict. But how do you expect us to explain the stuff in your locker?"

"Somebody must have planted it."

"Who? How?"

"I don't know."

"Nobody is going to believe that, Skipper."

"It's the truth, dammit."

He's back to the setup defense, so I switch gears. "Natalie came to see me yesterday."

His eyebrows go up. "Why?"

"Because she's concerned about you." I tell him about her comments about Ann.

"Ann's a complicated soul," he says. He thinks about it and adds, "In many respects, she's a great deal like me." He's more perceptive than I thought. "What else did she say?" he asks.

"She mentioned that you have grown apart over the years."

"Anything else?"

"Just that she's worried."

"I know. So am I." He remains silent for a moment and asks, "Is that it?"

"That's it."

He reflects and adds, "We're not the only couple in the world with an imperfect marriage."

That's for damn sure.

"But we still care for each other. We both care for Ann. I would never do anything to hurt either of them."

His concern seems genuine, yet I know he's cheated on Natalie. I decide to push just a little more. "We have reason to believe that there may be others who might come out of the woodwork who will say that you slept with them."

He tenses. "Who?"

I won't betray Carolyn's confidence—not even to Skipper. "Just rumors. I don't want anything else to come out of left field." I look straight into his eyes. "Are we going to hear from anyone else who will accuse you of engaging in kinky sex?"

"Absolutely not."

Ernie, Rosie, Pete, Tony and I are in the industrial-strength kitchen at the Mission Youth Center that afternoon. We've been joined by Ramon Aguirre and Sergeant Ron Morales of Mission Station, who used to be Pete's partner. He and Pete help each other out from time to time, and his appearance today is off the record. The place smells of soap and disinfectant. We are sitting amid the stainless steel tables and the restaurant-sized ovens while a few stragglers finish their lunches. The large dishwashers roar behind us. The topic of our discussion is the whereabouts of Andy Holton. Clemente is filling us in.

"We've been trying to find him for the last couple of days," he tells us. "Nobody in the neighborhood has seen him. He had a lot of big ideas. He was always hustling."

Morales interjects, "Hustling is the right word. He was working the street." He hands out a list of the residential hotels around the BART station. There are red check marks next to most of them. "For the last four days, I've had six officers talking to people in the flophouses. Nobody's seen him, but we're going to get to the rest of the hotels in the next day or two." In addition to prostitution, Morales says Holton was also known as a small-time drug dealer. "He wasn't particularly successful," he says.

Pete says to Morales, "I'll go door-to-door around the BART station."

"I'll take the businesses on Valencia Street," I say.

"I've already put up some flyers at St. Peter's," Ramon says. "I'll mention it at mass."

Rosie and Tony volunteer to knock on doors around St. Peter's.

I realize the search for Andy Holton rests squarely on our shoulders. The DA won't help us—they have already concluded that Skipper killed Garcia and they think Holton is irrelevant to this matter. It will only complicate their case if we locate him. "We have to find him," I say, "or we have to find out what happened to him." Andy Holton may have been the last person who saw Johnny Garcia alive.

Monday, September twentieth, two days before the preliminary hearing. We've been pounding the pavements of Mission and Valencia from Sixteenth to Twenty-fourth since Saturday in search of Andy Holton. Nothing. A couple of people recognized his picture. One guy told me he thought he saw him on Valencia a few days ago. When I probed, the man walked away. When I started to follow him, he flashed a knife. I found the guy's photo in a mug book at Mission Station and Ron Morales picked him up for questioning an hour later. It turns out he's a well-known small-time thief. He clammed up as soon as they hauled him in. They kept him overnight and let him go.

Ernie hasn't gotten anything from the kids at the center. The police report from the search of Johnny Garcia and Andy Holton's room at the Jerry provided very little new information. The phone had been disconnected two weeks before Garcia died. The phone records revealed almost no calls had been made from it. There were no cell phones registered in either name. If Andy Holton was dealing drugs, he was conducting business from a pay phone or a cell phone under another name. Johnny Garcia's personal effects included a couple of changes of clothes, a backpack and a Bible. Roosevelt told me it looked as though Holton had cleaned out all of his belongings except for his clothes. There was no indication that either had a bank account.

At ten o'clock in the morning, Rosie, Molinari and I sit in Judge Louise Vanden Heuvel's stuffy chambers on the fourth floor of the Hall. The walls are lined with tan legal volumes. McNulty and Payne have joined us for the morning's festivities.

The first item on our agenda is to try to get the judge to slow down the flow of information to the media. The contents of the storage locker were described in prurient detail on the news last night. Somebody gave them the skinny—and it wasn't us. "Your Honor," I begin, "we have a very serious problem."

Judge Vanden Heuvel studies our standard motion requesting a gag order. She's in her mid-fifties, a former prosecutor with a pale complexion, a willowy frame and a stoic air, and she's been listening to motions like ours for the last twenty years. "What's the problem, Mr. Daley?" she asks. Although I have never heard her raise her voice, her tone is nonetheless commanding.

"The prosecutor's office is leaking damaging and highly prejudicial evidence to the media. It will be impossible for Mr. Gates to get a fair trial. I have no choice but to ask you to dismiss the charges."

There is no chance she'll do this, but it can't hurt to ask.

Payne starts to stand and Vanden Heuvel raises her hand. "Ms. Payne," she says, "we'll hear from you in a moment." She turns back to me and chuckles. "Mr. Daley," she says, "you don't seriously believe that I will dismiss the charges, do you?"

I will seriously believe you have lost your mind if you do. "Yes, Your Honor," I reply. "My client's rights have been damaged, if not ignored in their entirety."

Admittedly, this is total bullshit.

Payne pops up again. She's starting to look like a pogo stick. Vanden Heuvel motions her to sit down and gives me a bemused look. "With all due respect to your client and his rights," she says, "I'm not going to dismiss the charges."

"At the very least, Your Honor," I say, "we request that you impose a gag order on all parties. We are reaching a point where the prosecution's irresponsible leaks are making it extremely difficult for my client to have any chance of empaneling an impartial jury."

Judge Vanden Heuvel glances at Payne. "Now it's your turn, Ms. Payne," she says.

Even though we're in chambers, Payne decides to stand when she speaks. "Your Honor," she says, "may it please the court."

Judge Vanden Heuvel is losing her patience. "Get on with it, Ms. Payne," she says.

"Your Honor," Payne says, "the prosecution has not leaked any evidence to the media. Mr. Daley is blowing this issue out of proportion."

The hell I am. "Your Honor—" I begin.

She cuts me off. "Not yet, Mr. Daley." She turns to Payne. "Ms.

Payne," she says, "I watch TV just like everyone else. How do you explain the reports on the news last night that all sorts of X-rated materials were found in Mr. Gates's storage locker?"

"It didn't come from our office," she replies.

Ed Molinari decides to chime in. "Where did it come from?" he bellows. "You can't possibly believe that we would have given this inflammatory, questionable evidence to the media. It's absurd."

Judge Vanden Heuvel points two fingers at Molinari and then at me. "Gentlemen," she says, "I need you to elect a spokesman. I don't want to hear from both of you. Now, who's going to talk?"

I say, "I will, Your Honor."

We get the hint of a grin.

Payne fires back. "The evidence is not questionable," she snaps. "We found it in his storage locker. A representative from the defense was there."

This is true. Pete was there.

Judge Vanden Heuvel is unimpressed. "I don't care who found it," she says. "I don't care how good the evidence is. We'll talk about that at the prelim. For the moment, all that matters is that the evidence was leaked to the press. I'm going to make this very simple for all of you. I don't want anybody involved in this case talking to the press. If anything is leaked, I will hold the people in this room personally responsible. I will sanction you. And I will make you spend some time in our lovely jail. Do you understand?"

We nod in unison. "Your Honor," I persist, "I think the prosecution should be sanctioned for the reckless leaks that occurred yesterday." She'll never go for it. I'm trying to goad Hillary to see if she'll piss off the judge.

"Your Honor," Payne says, "I resent the suggestion that information was leaked from our office. That simply isn't the case." If she had half a brain, she'd shut up right now.

Vanden Heuvel stops her. "I'm not going to sanction anybody this morning. I will say this only one more time." She holds up a menacing index finger to each of us in turn. "I am issuing a total gag order. I don't want anybody talking to the press. If you violate this order, I'll throw you in jail."

We nod again.

"Good," Vanden Heuvel says. "I'll see you Wednesday. Every-body out."

"I have a little information for you," Tony says. It's five o'clock the same day. I'm sitting behind the counter at the produce market. Grace is helping Tony rearrange a stack of oranges near the front of the store. She's doing a very careful job. Rosie is eating an apple. "My source tells me that Holton was looking for funding for a new business," Tony says.

"Drugs?" I ask.

"I don't know."

"Was your source interested in providing funding?"

"No."

"Did the business ever get off the ground?"

"I'm trying to find out," Tony says.

That evening, I go off to have dinner with our other family member on the investigative team, Pete, at my favorite Chinese restaurant, which isn't in Chinatown. It isn't in the new Chinatown in the Richmond District, either. It's a hole in the wall on Polk, just south of Broadway, called Tai Chi. People line up out the door and down the block for the house specialty, General Tsou's Chicken, a heart attack on a plate made of nuggets of deep-fried, batter-covered chicken in a flaming sweet and sour sauce that could burn a hole in the stomachs of mere mortals. Pete and I come here every couple of weeks for our fill. Then we go home and drink water until the sun comes up.

Pete and I are sitting in a red booth in the back room of the tiny restaurant. I ask him, "Did you find out anything else from the people who work at the Fairmont?"

"Not a thing," Pete says. "I talked to Dave Evans again. I inter-viewed everybody I could find who was working at the hotel that night. Andy Holton seems to have dropped off the face of the earth. Ron Morales thinks Holton quit his job so he could spend more time on his pharmaceutical business."

"What type of medication was he selling?"

"Heroin."

"And was Johnny Garcia one of his customers?"

"Yes, but he was also one of Holton's subcontractors. Andy supplied the drugs. Johnny sold them. And Andy got a substantial cut of Johnny's action."

"Have you heard anything about a new business that Holton was trying to start?"

"Ron said they'd heard rumors, but they haven't found anything yet."

I glance at the old man with a pair of clip-on sunglasses who stands by the cash register. Nobody else in the restaurant is permitted to touch the money. It strikes me that it is likely Andy Holton performed a similar role in his business dealings, too.

15

"WHY WOULD HE LIE?"

"With the preliminary hearing only one day away, it is a virtual certainty that San Francisco District Attorney Prentice Marshall Gates the Third will be held over for trial."

— CNN's *Burden of Proof*. Tuesday, September 21.

The preliminary hearing is tomorrow and I have been summoned to Bill McNulty's office at nine o'clock for a last-minute meeting. He's drinking coffee from a paper cup when I arrive. Hillary Payne is standing by the window. She seems to suffer from a terminal case of ants in her pants. I've brought Molinari and Rosie along for moral support.

Payne gets right to it. "We have some new information that may be of interest to you," she says. "We got the phone records from Skipper's room. There were two calls. The first was at one-ten, the second at one-fifteen."

I hold up my hands. "And?"

"The calls were placed to Kevin Anderson's phone."

"So?"

"We talked to Anderson a little while ago. He just returned from London. He said Johnny Garcia called him and left messages on his voice mail saying he'd made a terrible mistake. He wanted Anderson to come get him at the Fairmont."

"Did Anderson call him back?" Rosie asks.

"No. He didn't pick up his messages until the following morning."

"And this is the first you learned about the calls?" I ask.

"Of course. We just got the phone records."

Rosie decides to probe a little deeper. "That means he didn't call and tell you about this until you confronted him."

"We didn't confront him," Payne responds. "We asked him a question. He answered it."

"Nonetheless, Anderson has been withholding material information ever since Garcia's death," Molinari snaps.

I add, "And you guys have left it at that. You are affirmatively choosing not to pursue it."

Payne glares at me. "There is nothing to pursue," she says. "Johnny Garcia was a prostitute. He came to Skipper's room. He was high on heroin. He realized he had made a mistake. He called his social worker to try to bail him out."

"How do you know what Garcia said to Anderson?" I ask. "All you have is his version."

McNasty chimes in. "Frankly, I find Hillary's version of the events a lot more plausible than Skipper's. We have a witness now who can attest to the fact that Johnny Garcia went to the hotel. We've wiped out any arguments you may want to make that he was killed someplace else and taken to the Fairmont."

Not so fast. "You're assuming that Anderson is telling you the truth," I interject.

"Why would he lie?" Payne says.

"How should I know? Maybe he was involved. Maybe he's got something to hide. Did he save the messages?"

McNasty and Payne glance at each other. "No," she replies.

What? "So you have no confirmation of what was said. He could be lying."

"We have the phone records," Payne says. "We have Anderson's testimony."

"Which you have conveniently chosen to believe because it helps your case. It doesn't prove anything. It shows that two calls were made from the phone in Skipper's room around the time Garcia died. That's it. You had better prepare young Mr. Anderson for a lot of questions about those voice-mail messages. The news of Garcia's death broke early that morning. He must have known by the time he got the messages that Garcia had been murdered and Skipper had been arrested—I can't believe he erased them. He destroyed evidence and then kept silent. You've simply taken his word for it. You aren't going to do a thing about it, are you?"

"Come on, Mike," McNulty says, trying to sound reasonable. "It's staring you right in the face."

"It's staring *you* right in the face, Bill. You guys should be following up on this."

McNulty doesn't answer me. One thing is for damn sure: I need to talk to Kevin Anderson right away.

"We have some issues to discuss before the prelim," I say to Skipper a few minutes later. "If this case moves forward, we're going to want to move for a change in venue. Everybody in town has heard about this matter. I would suggest that we try to get this case moved somewhere up north. Maybe Sacramento."

Skipper disagrees. "We aren't moving this trial," he says.

"Can we talk about it?" I say.

"We can talk about it all you want. Bottom line, we're staying."

"May I ask why?"

"This is my hometown. I'm the district attorney. I'm not afraid to be tried by a jury of my peers."

In this case, his "peers" will consist of students, retirees and those who can't otherwise come up with a decent excuse to get off jury duty. I try to keep my tone measured. "Skipper," I say, "as your attorney, I would strongly urge you to reconsider. This isn't the time to make a political statement. Your freedom and your life are at stake. You should be tried in a place where you have the best chance of prevailing."

He sets his jaw. "I am not afraid to stand trial in San Francisco," he says. "We're not moving. That's final."

I glance at Molinari, who is tapping his pen on his pad of paper.

"You're the boss," I say. Actually, in some respects, we may be better off staying here. San Francisco juries are generally pretty liberal and fairly well educated. More important, they almost never impose the death penalty.

Molinari looks up and says, "There's something else we need to discuss. We need to tell the judge that we plan to waive time." Section thirteen eighty-two of the penal code says that criminal defendants are entitled to a trial within sixty days after their arraignment. In murder trials, ninety-nine times out of a hundred, the defendant "waives time," which means that the trial is delayed to give the defense a longer time to prepare its case.

"That's easy, too," Skipper says. "We're not waiving time."

Come again? "Excuse me?" I say. "You know how the system works. You know we're going to need more than sixty days to interview all the witnesses to put together your defense."

Molinari agrees with me. Skipper doesn't. He's adamant. "It isn't a topic for discussion," he says. "This case doesn't involve a complicated analysis. We don't need a lot of experts. I've already been in jail for two weeks longer than I should have. I'm not going to rot in here for the next six months. I am not waiving time."

"That settles that," Molinari says succinctly when we brief Carolyn, Pete and Rosie a little later. "He's nuts."

But Rosie sees it a little differently. "He's stubborn," she observes. "He's scared. Just because you're the DA doesn't mean you're exempt from normal human emotions. Put yourself in his shoes. You're sitting in jail. The only thing on your mind is getting out. He wants this to end. I don't blame him."

My cell phone rings as I'm driving north on the Golden Gate Bridge on the way home late that night. It's Ernie Clemente. "I got a call from Andy Holton," he says. "He heard I was trying to reach him."

Yes! He's alive! "Where is he?"

"He wouldn't say—I don't know if he's still in the area."

My heart pounds. "What did you find out?"

"Not much," Ernie says. "He was too scared, Mike—he thinks the cops will connect him to Johnny's murder and arrest him if they can get their hands on him. There was no way I could get him to tell me anything more."

I tell Ernie I've got to talk to him. "There must be some way I can reach him," I plead.

There isn't. Ernie says he was adamant. "The best I could do was get him to agree he'd call me again, but that was it. And he wouldn't say when; he hung up on me."

Christ—so close, and yet so useless. I want to scream.

16

THE PRELIMINARY HEARING

"You look at all the evidence and then you make the best call you can."
— JUDGE LOUISE VANDEN HEUVEL, CONTINUING LEGAL EDUCATION
SEMINAR.

"All rise." Judge Louise Vanden Heuvel's bailiff recites the customary call to order at ten o'clock in the morning on Wednesday, September twenty-second. The small courtroom is packed. Reporters jockey for position. The five rows of pews behind us are full. Natalie is in the first row, her eyes concealed behind sunglasses, sitting between her daughter and Turner.

It's almost eighty degrees outside and ninety inside. It smells like the locker room at the Embarcadero YMCA. Air-conditioning may find its way into the city's budget in another millennium or two. Bill McNulty and Hillary Payne shuffle papers at the prosecution table to my right, next to the jury box. McNasty has chatted up the reporters. He told the press he intends to let Payne take the lead. Per my instruction, Skipper is dressed in a navy business suit. I've asked him to keep his clothing understated. Armani doesn't play very well to judges who live on a civil servant's salary. Ed Molinari sits at the end of the defense table, fondling his Mont Blanc pen. He's promised to put it away before the judge walks in. Ed understands that every nuance matters.

Designer pens may send the wrong message. Rosie is sitting next to me.

Judge Vanden Heuvel glides to the bench, her black robe trailing behind her. She hauls a heavy bench book in one hand and a calendar in the other. She takes her seat under the Great Seal of the State of California. She puts on her reading glasses and studies the calendar. She's trying to pretend this is just another case. She doesn't look up when she says, "Are counsel prepared to proceed?"

Payne and I say yes almost simultaneously. We state our names for the record.

"First up this morning," Vanden Heuvel says, "we have a preliminary hearing for Mr. Gates." She asks her clerk to recite the case name and number for the record.

"The People versus Prentice Marshall Gates the Third."

Judge Vanden Heuvel reminds us that Skipper has entered a plea of not guilty, and that the case carries the possibility of the death penalty. For the benefit of the rookie reporters in the gallery, she explains that we are about to conduct a preliminary hearing to determine whether there is sufficient evidence to hold Skipper over for trial. She doesn't mention that the standard of proof is very low. The prosecution must simply show there is a reasonable possibility that Skipper committed the crime in question. Preliminary hearings usually have as much suspense as the ceremonial throwing out of the first pitch at a baseball game. Judge Vanden Heuvel points her gavel at Hillary Payne. "You may proceed, Ms. Payne."

Payne stands and says, "Thank you, Your Honor." The preliminary hearing is the prosecution's show. A smart prosecutor like Payne will show just enough to get the case pushed over to trial, but nothing more. You don't get convictions at the prelim. "May it please the court," she begins. She launches into her opening statement. She says they'll show that Skipper was present at the hotel room that night and that he had direct contact with the victim. They'll show that the victim died of suffocation after Skipper put duct tape on his eyes, nose and mouth. "The defendant had opportunity, motive and means, and there is no doubt that the defendant lured the victim to his room, engaged in bizarre sexual activity and then killed him." Her opening lasts less than five minutes. McNasty has coached her well. Just the essentials.

Judge Vanden Heuvel is pleased when Payne sits down. With a little luck, her part in this case will be over by the end of the day. With a lot of luck, she'll be able to get out the door and onto the freeway before the traffic gets heavy. "Thank you for your concise presentation," she says to Payne. She turns to me. "Mr. Daley, it's your turn."

Skipper leans over and whispers, "Keep it short."

"Your Honor," I begin, "the evidence will show that the prosecution's case rests on highly suspect circumstantial evidence. Mr. Gates was, in fact, in the hotel room at the Fairmont that night. As we will demonstrate, the prosecution simply cannot prove that Mr. Gates committed any of the acts of which he is accused."

Vanden Heuvel raises her eyebrows. The reporters stir.

"Your Honor," I continue, "this case is a setup. The prosecution knows it." I assure her that we will punch so many holes in Payne's case that by the end of the day, she'll have no choice but to dismiss the charges. She isn't buying a word of this, of course. I try to cast doubt on every piece of evidence. I litter my remarks with generous use of the words "contrived," "shaky" and "unsubstantiated." Judge Vanden Heuvel takes it all in. Five minutes later, I sit down.

Judge Vanden Heuvel asks Payne to call her first witness.

"The people call Inspector Elaine McBride," she says.

Solid choice. They're leading with their strength. McBride strides to the front of the courtroom. Her bearing is professional, her expression stern. She acknowledges the judge. Her gray pantsuit is freshly pressed, her white blouse starched. She's sworn in and takes her seat in the witness box. She adjusts the microphone with the confidence of a woman who has testified at hundreds of trials. She states her name for the record and nods to Payne, as if to say "Let's get this show on the road."

Payne approaches her. "Inspector McBride," she begins, "how long have you been with the SFPD?"

She tugs at the microphone. "Eighteen years."

"And how long have you been a homicide inspector?"

"Eight months. I was the head of the sex crimes unit for six years before I was promoted to homicide inspector." Payne begins to walk her through her résumé. I stop her after a moment and stipulate to her credentials. We aren't going to win any points by trying to attack her experience.

"And you are the homicide inspector assigned to investigate the death of the victim in this case, Johnny Garcia?"

"That's correct." She confirms that she was the first homicide inspector to arrive at the Fairmont. She describes the scene. Garcia's body. The handcuffs. The duct tape. The champagne bottle and glasses. "The police officers had secured the area," she says. "The paramedics had arrived. A team from the coroner's office was on the way."

Payne turns and looks at Skipper. "And did you have an opportunity to interview the defendant?" She's using one of McNulty's favorite tricks. She'll never refer to Skipper by name. Neither will McBride.

"Yes. The defendant admitted that he had been present in the hotel room the entire night."

The first score goes to the prosecution. She's placed Skipper at the scene.

"And did the defendant offer any explanation for what happened?"

"No. He said he fell asleep in front of the television."

"Did he hear anything?"

"No."

"See anybody come in?"

"No."

"Hear anybody knock on the door?"

Enough. "Objection, Your Honor. We get the idea."

"Sustained. Move along, Ms. Payne."

"Just so we're clear on this, Inspector, when you arrived, there was a dead body in the bed and the defendant admitted he had been there the entire night."

"Objection. Asked and answered." I'm trying to break up her rhythm.

"Sustained."

Payne takes this in stride. "Inspector, did the defendant offer any explanation for how the body got there?"

"No. He had no explanation, plausible or otherwise."

I think I see the hint of a smile on Payne's impassive face. "Let's talk about something else for a moment," she says. She takes out an enlarged photo of Johnny Garcia handcuffed to the bedposts. She points to the handcuffs. "Inspector," she says, "did the defendant have any explanation for how the victim became handcuffed?"

"Objection. Asked and answered. The witness has already testified that Mr. Gates did not offer an explanation with respect to this issue."

"Sustained."

Payne pouts. She leads McBride through an explanation of how Skipper's fingerprints were found on the handcuffs. McBride cannot account for the handcuff key found in the toilet. Payne takes her through a description of the duct tape found on Garcia's eyes, nose and mouth. She has her describe the search of Skipper's house. Finally, she takes her through an item-by-item inventory of the photos and *Hustler* magazines they found in Skipper's study. I object sporadically and inconsequentially. McBride is on the stand for more than an hour.

At eleven-fifteen, Skipper jots a note that says "Can you stop this?" I shake my head. I can slow her down, but I can't stop her.

Finally, Payne decides she's extracted everything that she can from McBride. "No further questions for this witness," she says. She got what she needed, and then some.

I stand, button my jacket and approach McBride. I look at the picture of Johnny Garcia's body. "Inspector," I say, "you have testified that Mr. Gates's fingerprints were found on the handcuffs and the duct tape."

"That's correct." The voice of authority.

"Did Mr. Gates offer an explanation as to how his fingerprints found their way onto the handcuffs and the duct tape?"

"Mr. Gates indicated that he had tried to remove the handcuffs and did, in fact, remove the duct tape."

Just what I wanted. "I see. Isn't it therefore logical to conclude that Mr. Gates got his fingerprints on the duct tape when he removed it from the victim's face? And isn't it also logical to conclude that he got his fingerprints on the handcuffs when he attempted to remove them?"

"Objection. Leading."

Right objection, wrong grounds. On cross-exam, you can lead the witness. In fact, you're supposed to do it. She should have objected because it was a speculative question. That's a no-no.

Vanden Heuvel makes the right call. "Overruled. The witness will answer." She glances at Payne. "Next time, Ms. Payne, when Mr. Daley asks a speculative question, you might try objecting on those grounds."

A small victory. Payne's fair skin reddens.

McBride says, "Anything is possible, Mr. Daley. And it still doesn't explain the key that was found in the toilet."

It's a fair point. "But you didn't find any fingerprints on that key, did you, Inspector?"

"No. It was too small to show any prints."

Time for one more quick trip through the looking glass. "Inspector, is it possible that the person who brought Mr. Garcia's body into Mr. Gates's room may have pressed the handcuffs against Mr. Gates's fingers while he was asleep?"

McBride looks at Payne, who gets the message. "Objection. Speculative."

"Sustained."

"Isn't it possible, Inspector, that somebody who wanted to set up Mr. Gates may have drugged him and brought Johnny Garcia's body into the room? And isn't it possible that the same person may have caused Mr. Gates's fingerprints to have been placed on the handcuffs?"

Before Payne can object, McBride says, "That's preposterous, Your Honor. Mr. Daley is trying to concoct a scenario where anybody in the world could have framed Mr. Gates that night."

That's exactly what I'm trying to do. "Your Honor," I say, "would you please ask the witness to answer the question?"

"Objection," Payne shouts. "Speculative."

Murmurs in the gallery. Vanden Heuvel pounds her gavel. She points it toward the reporters in the jury box. "The objection is sustained. There will be order in my courtroom." She turns back to me. "Any further questions for this witness, Mr. Daley?"

"No, Your Honor."

Judge Vanden Heuvel slams her gavel and recesses court for lunch.

———

"Jesus Christ, Mike, you should have taken McBride apart." Ed Molinari is offering some helpful suggestions on my courtroom technique in the consultation room behind Judge Vanden Heuvel's courtroom. At the same time, he slides into one of the heavy wood chairs and unwraps a pastrami sandwich.

Skipper ignores the bag with his lunch and paces. He's been nervous all morning. "Dammit, Mike," he says, "you've got to be more aggressive. You should have taken McBride by the balls and squeezed."

Such a delicate way with words. "What did you think I was going to prove today? McBride was up there to place you at the scene and to confirm that your fingerprints were on the handcuffs. Those are the facts. You were at the scene. Your fingerprints were on the handcuffs. We'll go to war about how your fingerprints got there at the trial. For the moment, all they need to show is that you were there and that you had contact with the body. And it doesn't help that they found the photos and magazines in your study."

He looks right through me and doesn't respond. Then he takes the white bag that contains his sandwich and soda and hurls it across the room into the trash can.

The afternoon session doesn't improve when Rod Beckert takes the stand. Payne hands him a copy of his autopsy report, which he holds as though it is the Super Bowl trophy. I stipulate to his expertise in pathology as soon as he takes his seat in the witness box. There's no sense in giving him twenty minutes to read his résumé into the record. He testifies that Johnny Garcia died of asphyxiation sometime between one and four A.M.

"Was it a painful death?" Payne asks.

I could object because it is a speculative question. I would look like an idiot if I did.

Beckert strokes his beard. "Initially, it would have been quite painful," he says. "After a few moments, the victim would have lost consciousness. At that time, it is very difficult to determine what, if anything, the victim is feeling."

"Dr. Beckert," Payne says, "are you absolutely sure Johnny Garcia died of suffocation?"

"Yes."

She turns away and heads toward her chair. She's about to sit down, when she turns back to him. "Doctor," she says, "did you find traces of any drugs in the victim's bloodstream?"

He acts as if he didn't expect the question. He flips through his report. He pushes his glasses down to the tip of his nose. "Yes, Ms. Payne," he says. "We found traces of heroin."

"A substantial amount?" She's trying to undercut the argument I'm about to make that he may have OD'd.

"Not enough to kill a young, healthy male."

"Did you find any other drugs?"

"Yes. We found traces of gamma hydroxy butyrate in his bloodstream, commonly known on the street as GHB."

"What happens when you take GHB, Doctor?"

"It induces unconsciousness," he replies. "It's frequently seen in date-rape cases."

"So, Doctor, in addition to being bound and gagged, the victim was high on heroin and was rendered unconscious by a date-rape drug."

"That's true."

"But it is your conclusion that he died of asphyxiation."

"That is my conclusion, Ms. Payne."

"No further questions."

Beckert is still clutching his report when I approach him. "Dr. Beckert," I begin, "I would like to direct you to page thirteen, which indicates that you found heroin in the victim's bloodstream."

"That's true, Mr. Daley."

"And, in fact, there was a substantial amount of heroin in his bloodstream, wasn't there?"

"No, Mr. Daley. I said there were traces of heroin in his bloodstream. I also said that there wasn't enough to kill a young, healthy male."

"And you understand, of course, that the exact amount of heroin in a person's bloodstream would determine whether a person has over-dosed."

"Yes."

Here goes. "Isn't it possible that Johnny Garcia died of an over-dose?"

"No, Mr. Daley, it isn't possible. There simply wasn't enough heroin in his system to cause an overdose. The victim died of asphyxi-ation." He nods as if to say "That's all there is to it."

We joust over the level of heroin in Garcia's bloodstream. He doesn't give an inch, although I do get him to acknowledge that other highly qualified pathologists may disagree with his conclusions. We go through a similar exercise over the level of GHB in Garcia's system. Beckert acknowledges that GHB can kill you if you take enough of it but insists that Garcia ingested only a trace of that substance, too. I de-cide to try one more end run. "Doctor, isn't it possible that the combi-nation of the heroin and the GHB created a reaction that caused Johnny Garcia's death?"

"No, Mr. Daley. It didn't happen that way. He simply didn't have enough heroin or GHB in his system to cause the reaction that you suggested."

It's the best I can do for now. "No further questions, Your Honor."

Payne trots out Sandra Wilson to confirm that all of the evidence was gathered in accordance with proper police procedure. I elect not to cross-examine her.

Payne finishes up with Roosevelt Johnson, who describes the con-tents of the storage locker in persuasive detail. Photos of handcuffed, nude women. *Hustler* magazines. The reporters in the jury box seem to be enjoying themselves. I catch the police beat reporter from the *Chronicle* winking at his counterpart at the *Oakland Tribune*. I can al-ready picture the headlines in tomorrow's paper.

At a quarter to three, Payne asks Roosevelt whether he believed there was any connection between the pictures and the items found in the storage locker and Johnny Garcia's case. The judge overrules my objection.

"Yes," Roosevelt says. "I believe Mr. Gates needs help. I believe he likes to engage in alternative forms of sexual stimulation. I believe he likes to tie up and drug his victims. Then he has sex with them."

"Is that what happened in this case?"

"Objection. Speculative."

"Sustained."

"I'll rephrase. Do you have a theory about what happened in this case, Inspector?"

"One of the sexual encounters got out of hand. Unfortunately, Johnny Garcia was in the wrong place at the wrong time. He paid for his mistake with his life."

Payne says she has no further questions. My cross-examination lasts for only a few minutes. I can demonstrate that Roosevelt's conclusions are speculative. However, there's no way I can discredit his testimony.

Payne and I make our perfunctory closing arguments. She says it is a simple case of an evil man who lured in a teenager for sex and then killed him. I argue it's all a setup.

Judge Vanden Heuvel doesn't hesitate. "I have concluded that there is sufficient evidence to bind the defendant over for trial."

Skipper doesn't move.

Vanden Heuvel consults with her bailiff. "May we assume," she says to me, "that Mr. Gates will waive time?"

"No, Your Honor," I say.

Vanden Heuvel gives me a puzzled look. "Are you sure about this, Mr. Daley?"

"Yes, Your Honor."

"May we assume that you'll be asking for a change of venue?"

"No, Your Honor," I say. "Mr. Gates would like to have his case heard in San Francisco. As DA, he has come to respect the fairness and judgment of San Francisco juries."

I swear my nose is getting longer as I say these words.

Vanden Heuvel studies her calendar. I'd bet almost anything she figured this case was heading out of town. Now we've gone and gummed up the works. She confers with her bailiff. Finally, she says, "Judge Joanne O'Donnell Kelly is supposed to finish a jury trial two weeks from Friday. Her calendar should be free on Monday, October eleventh. I am setting a trial in her courtroom on that date."

"That's two weeks from Monday," I say.

"That's right, Mr. Daley. You asked for an early trial date, and now you're going to get it."

I glance at Skipper. The judge says, "Is there a problem, Mr. Daley?"

"One moment, Your Honor." Two and a half weeks to prepare for a murder trial is a very short period of time. Judge Kelly is a veteran of at least thirty years on the bench. She was one of the first women appointed to the San Francisco superior court. She's another former prosecutor who speaks her mind and spends most of her time trying to negotiate plea bargains. She prides herself in keeping a clear docket. She isn't the most thoughtful jurist on the San Francisco bench, but things move along very quickly in her courtroom. I ask the judge for a moment and I confer with Skipper. "Are you sure about this?" I ask.

"It's perfect," he says without hesitation. "Go for it."

I turn back to the judge and say, "We'll be ready, Your Honor."

"You don't look great," Rosie observes after we've returned to the office. I feel much worse than I look.

"On top of everything else," I say, "Ann read me the riot act."

"You were expecting some other reaction from her?"

"It's a god-awful case," I say.

She shrugs. "You've known that from the start. The evidence is stacked against us. It's a case we can't win for a client we can't stand."

"That pretty well covers it."

"And how is this different from most of our cases?"

"It isn't." I reflect for a moment and add, "You know, Rosie, there is something very odd about Skipper's demeanor."

"How's that?"

"Most of the evidence cuts against him, but he isn't acting like a guilty man. Not a bit. He hasn't changed his story. He's adamant about a plea bargain."

"I've noticed the same thing," she says. "Guilty people waver. They keep adjusting their story to make it a little better each time. He isn't doing that. He's indignant—even angry at times. That's more likely to be a sign of someone who's been wrongly accused."

"Or someone who is a terrific liar," I say.

Rosie's lips turn up slightly. "Well, do *you* think he's innocent?"

"Something certainly happened at the Fairmont that night, but I'm not convinced he killed Johnny Garcia. What about you?"

"I don't know."

"Oh, no, you don't. I'm not letting you off easy. I told you what I thought—now it's your turn. Turn your cards up. What do you think? Did he do it?"

Rosie gets a faraway look in her eyes. "Fair enough," she says. "Something very bad happened at the Fairmont and I think Skipper was involved somehow. But no, I don't think he killed Johnny Garcia, either—at least not on purpose."

"You won't change your mind, will you?"

She breaks into a wide grin. "I might." She looks at the stack of phone messages in my hand and asks, "So, what are you up to tonight?"

"I thought I would treat myself to a nice dinner."

"Got a hot date?"

"Not exactly. I'm having dinner with Kevin Anderson."

17
"WHAT CAN YOU TELL ME ABOUT JOHNNY GARCIA?"

"Police are still searching for the mysterious roommate in the Garcia slaying."
—SAN FRANCISCO CHRONICLE. WEDNESDAY, SEPTEMBER 22.

Kevin Anderson and I are sitting in the back of Mike's Chinese Cuisine, an inconspicuous two-story restaurant in the middle of the block on Geary, between Fifteenth and Sixteenth Avenues. Many people believe the muckity-mucks who run San Francisco dine only in places like Postrio, Boulevard and Aqua. Not true. On a given day, our resident United States senator, our congresswoman and half the Board of Supervisors will stop by Mike's. I'm amazed the paparazzi haven't figured this out yet. Then again, maybe they have. I'll bet they eat here, too.

"What can you tell me about Johnny Garcia?" I ask Kevin as he takes a bite out of a pot sticker. No sense beating around the bush. He has made it clear he has only half an hour to talk to me. Then he and Turner Stanford are off to work their magic at a planning commission meeting; his dad wants to convert some old industrial space down by the ballpark into lofts. He is wearing a business suit for the occasion. He's an unpretentious lad for a millionaire.

"Not much," he replies. "He was from the Mission. Raised in the projects. No father. Mother was an addict. We found him in the BART station plaza a couple of years ago."

This squares with the accounts of Ernie Clemente and Ramon Aguirre.

He glances around the crowded restaurant. He says he was able to convince Garcia to come to the Mission Youth Center. They cleaned him up and gave him a place to live. They got him into rehab. They found him a room and a job.

I ask about his drug problems.

"Heroin. He was in bad shape when we found him. He would have been dead within a month or two. He was selling his body to pay for drugs. He was the poster child for everything that could have gone wrong. I thought we had him straightened out." He wipes his hands on the white cloth napkin. "I guess not. I hear they found heroin in his system when he died. I should have watched him more closely. I have only so much time to work with the kids."

I pick up a spring roll and dip it into the sweet sauce. Then I add a touch of hot mustard. It's easy to see why the bigwigs eat here. "Kevin, you seem to have a pretty full plate. What brought you to social work?"

"It comes from my father, Mr. Daley. He came from a poor family. He caught a few breaks when he was growing up—some people helped him out when he was short on money, and one of the guys at the YMCA gave him a job so he could work his way through State. He's never forgotten it. He donates a lot of money to charity. He insists that everybody in the company give something back to the community. I like to work with kids."

He seems like a solid citizen, yet there is something in his tone that sounds a bit too slick for me. I change the subject. "Can you tell me anything about Andy Holton?"

"Not much."

It's a circumspect answer. I'm not surprised, given the word of mouth about Holton. He has political ambitions. The mayor has taught him to be cautious. He motions to the waiter to bring us more tea. "I met him a couple of times," he says. "Andy was a street kid, too. He went through the Mission center about five years ago. He was on amphetamines. Ernie got him off drugs and found him a place to live and a job. We used to bring him back to the center to talk to the kids. He was one of our success stories."

Now he's a missing person.

"He took Johnny under his wing," he says. "He showed him the ropes and helped him get the job at the Pancho Villa."

"Do you have any idea where he may have gone?"

"Nope." It seems to me the answer comes a little too quickly. "I expect he's scared. I'm sure he figures the cops will want to talk to him."

No doubt. "Does he have anything to hide?"

"Not that I'm aware of," he says. He looks across the room and nods to the mayor, who has just entered the restaurant. Then he leans forward. "You know," he says, "Johnny and Andy weren't getting along very well."

"I've heard."

"Johnny said they had an argument at the restaurant a couple of weeks before he died."

"About what?" I'm getting annoyed. He mentioned this once before but didn't provide any details. He's too damned coy.

"The usual. The room. The rent."

"That's it?"

"As far as I know."

"We heard they may have been lovers."

He takes a fortune cookie. "I don't know."

"We heard Holton was a drug dealer."

This time he's emphatic. "I don't know anything about that."

"We've also heard he was trying to start a new business."

I seem to have his attention now. "What kind of business?" he asks. It's my turn to say, "I don't know."

He shrugs. "Sorry, Mr. Daley. I wasn't Andy's social worker. I don't know anything about that, either."

Let's try something else. "I understand Johnny called you the night he died."

"Twice," he answers, feigning nonchalance. "I reported it to the police." His expression changes to one of concern. "If I had been home when he called, I might have been able to do something. I didn't get the messages until morning." He's being very sincere, but it doesn't ring true.

I ask if he saved them.

He hesitates. "No."

"Why not?"

"I don't know—no special reason. I just hit the delete button."

"You may have destroyed some valuable evidence."

He holds his hands up. "Hey, calm down. I didn't mean to do any-thing."

I'm not giving in yet. "What did he say in the messages?"

"He was at the Fairmont. He said he'd made a terrible mistake. He asked me to come pick him up."

"Did you do anything about it?"

"There was nothing I could do. It was the next morning when I got the messages. It was too late. I'd already heard about it on the news by then."

"I'd like to talk to Holton. Any idea how to find him?"

"Not really. Before he went to work at the Pancho Villa, he used to work at another restaurant around the corner. I suppose you might ask around down there."

"You happen to know the name of the place?"

"LaCumbre Taqueria."

It's a start. "Thanks for your help." The boy millionaire with the trust fund graciously lets me pick up the check.

Pete and I survey Sixteenth Street from the BART station plaza the next morning. The activities around the Green Monster have already started. Heroin addicts wake up early and try to get their daily fix. The plaza has a busy ambiance, almost festive if you didn't know what was going on. A homeless man with a shopping cart asks us for money. Pete obliges with a quarter.

We head up Sixteenth past the residential hotels and the Pancho Villa toward Valencia, where we turn left. We see a dangling sign over the entrance to LaCumbre. It's early for lunch, so the modest taco stand is quiet. The sweet aroma of burritos and beans fills the small room. There's a young Hispanic man behind the counter. We order two cups of coffee.

"Busy day?" Pete asks him.

The young man nods but doesn't say anything.

Pete tries again. "You from the neighborhood?"

Still no response. I notice an economics book sticking out of a beat-up backpack on the end of the counter. "You in school?" I ask.

"You guys cops?" He says it without expression.

Pete smiles. "I used to be." The kid shows the hint of a grin. "My brother here is even worse. He's a lawyer."

That gets a full grin. "I was thinking maybe I could be a lawyer," he says. "I'm at State."

"Stick with it," I say.

He studies me. "You're the guy on TV. You're representing the DA."

So much for anonymity. "Yeah."

"Did he do it?"

"No."

"He looks pretty guilty to me."

"A lot of people think so. They're wrong."

"Whatever you say. Why are you guys here in the low-rent district? I thought you fancy lawyers worked downtown."

I'm not a fancy lawyer, but I don't want to burst his bubble. "We're looking for information," I say.

"Really? I didn't know the DA spent any time down here."

"He didn't, but the victim had a friend who used to work here."

Pete shows him pictures of Andy Holton and Johnny Garcia. "Recognize these guys?" he asks.

He studies the photos. "Yeah. They used to live at the Jerry. That's Andy Holton. He worked here for a short time. Then he got a job at the Pancho Villa."

"We've already been there," I say. "Did you know him?"

"Not really. He kept to himself." He points toward Valencia. "You might ask over at the Royan. He used to live there before he moved to the Jerry. Ask for Mario."

I leave my business card and a twenty on the counter. "Thanks," I say.

Pete and I walk past the small markets until we reach the corner of Fifteenth and Valencia, where a faded sign on the marquee of a dilapidated five-story building says "Hotel Royan, daily, weekly and monthly." A burnt-out cheese steak shop sits behind metal bars on one side of the entrance. A boarded-up currency exchange is on the other side. Next door is an empty lot. It's been a long time since the Royan has seen better days. It's a pit. The entrance has a heavy steel mesh door. It's open, and there's a hand-lettered sign on it saying "No visitors between 7 P.M and 7 A.M." The lobby, if you can call it that, consists of a folding chair on a black tile floor. It's acrid with the smell of urine.

A wiry Hispanic man with a gold earring and a neatly trimmed goatee is sitting inside the old cheese steak shop. I presume he lives here. He's reading the paper. He ignores a small black-and-white TV that's tuned to a talk show. A cigarette smolders on a broken plate next to him. He doesn't look up when we walk in.

Pete doesn't wait for him to acknowledge us. "Are you the manager?" he asks.

"We're full," he replies without lifting his eyes from the sports section.

This doesn't deter Pete. "Are you Mario?"

"Maybe. Who's asking?"

"Pete."

"Pete who?"

"Just Pete."

Mario looks up. "You a cop?"

"Nope."

"I don't know anything."

"I haven't asked you anything yet."

"Doesn't matter. Whatever you're asking, I don't know anything. I don't talk to guys named Pete."

Pete looks at me. "This is my brother, Mike."

This brings an eye roll. "So?"

"He isn't named Pete. So you can talk to him. We're trying to find somebody. If you don't know him, you don't know him. We'll leave you alone."

"I don't know him."

"I haven't even shown you his picture."

"I still don't know him."

Pete lowers his voice. "Humor me, Mario. I have a few friends over at Mission Station. They'll pay you a visit if I ask them."

I cringe. Somewhere behind the sports section and the TV, Mario undoubtedly has a gun that could blow my head clear out to Valencia Street. For that matter, I'm certain Pete is carrying a gun, too. I don't want to start my day with a shoot-out at the Royan. I begin to question my brother's judgment and my sanity.

"I don't want any trouble," Mario says.

"Neither do we," I reply. "We're just looking for information." I show him the pictures of Johnny Garcia and Andy Holton.

He points to the picture of Garcia. "I've seen his picture on the news."

"He's dead," I say. "The DA is accused of killing him."

"I saw him around here a few times," Mario says. "I think he was a hooker."

I point to the picture of Holton. "Ever seen him?"

"I don't think so."

"You sure?"

"I'm sure."

Pete leans on the counter. "He used to live here. You know him, don't you?"

"No," he says.

Pete glares right into his eyes. "If your memory clears up," he says, "give me a call." He hands him a business card. "You might save his life."

The Mission police station is a modern low-rise building that takes up half a block on Valencia, between Seventeenth and Eighteenth. Pete and I are sitting at the desk of Sergeant Ron Morales. His face looks younger than forty-two, but his hair is almost completely white. The day-to-day life of a cop tends to age you. "Still no luck on Holton," he tells us. "We've been going door-to-door looking for the last week. Nobody has seen him since the night Garcia was killed. We want to find him as much as you do."

We keep hitting dead ends. I ask him whether he thinks Holton is still in the area.

"He could be. It would be pretty easy for him to blend in, but no one's talking."

"It's still worth looking," Pete says. "If he needs money, he may be back to look up some of his old customers."

We spend the afternoon and the early evening going up and down Mission and Valencia, still hoping to find somebody who might have seen Andy Holton. One guy thought he had seen him delivering pizzas. A woman says he may have been near the BART station. No IDs. No real leads.

Eventually, we head back to Twenty-fourth and meet Rosie and Tony at the produce market. Rosie's mother is staying with Grace. I take an apple and Pete sips a beer. Tony is counting today's receipts. The evening rush is over. Rosie is sitting on the counter and drinking a Diet Coke. She asks, "Any luck?"

"Nothing," I say. "We're striking out so far."

She has news for us. "To make your day complete," she says, "we have another problem. They found another prostitute."

Hell. "Male or female?"

"Female. She says she's prepared to testify that Skipper paid her for sex."

"I understand that's the usual procedure."

"And she's prepared to testify that he liked to handcuff her to a bed in a room in the Fairmont."

"Where did you hear about this?" I ask.

"The producer of the Jade Warner show called. They wanted me to comment. I didn't."

Jade Warner is a former housewife who was married to a heavy hitter in one of the high-tech companies in Palo Alto. Her husband left her for a younger woman. She found the nastiest divorce lawyer in Silicon Valley and took the guy to the cleaners. After the dust settled, she had time on her hands and she started giving advice on a local cable access station. She developed a cult following when the president of a dot-com said she thought Jade's tough-love approach was the wave of the future. That was two years ago. Now she's considered a marriage guru and has her own show on Channel 4. She's running head to head against Oprah in the Bay Area.

"When is she going to be on?" I ask.

"Tomorrow."

"Great. What else?"

"We got more phone records."

"I thought we had them all. The police already gave us the records for the phone in Skipper's room."

"They did. Now they have provided the records for Skipper's cell phone. At one-twenty, there was a call placed to Turner's house. It lasted about five minutes."

Turner never mentioned it. For that matter, neither did Skipper. More unanswered questions. I ask, "Any other good news?"

"Nope. We've got enough. But it might be a good idea for one of us to go down and watch the taping of the Jade Warner show."

An excellent thought. "I'll go," I say.

"That might not be such a good idea," Rosie says. "They'll recognize you. For that matter, they'll probably recognize me."

That's true. I pick up my cell phone and punch in Carolyn's number. When she answers, I ask, "What are you doing tomorrow afternoon?"

18

"HOW LONG HAVE YOU BEEN WORKING AT THE FAIRMONT?"

"The evidence against District Attorney Gates continues to mount."
—CNN's BURDEN OF PROOF. THURSDAY, SEPTEMBER 23.

Later that night, I'm with Joseph Wong, who is sitting in an armchair in his modest apartment. A small, dignified man in his late fifties with tired eyes, he tells me with pride that one of his two daughters went to Cal, the other to UCLA. His wife is sitting in the rocking chair in the corner. A picture of their daughters sits on the top of the TV, which is tuned to the Chinese newscast on Channel 26. The sound is off.

"How long have you been working at the Fairmont?" I ask.

"Almost forty years." His manner is forthright, his deportment professional. You don't get to work at the Fairmont for as long as he has without being competent—and discreet. I'm certain he has found guests in compromising positions from time to time. The sticky situations have been resolved expeditiously through the payment of modest gratuities.

"I understand you found Mr. Gates and Mr. Garcia."

"Yes." He explains that he was delivering a continental breakfast at seven o'clock that morning. "Coffee, muffins and fruit," he says.

In Joseph Wong's world, it's important to get the orders right.

"I knocked on the door," he continues, "but there was no answer." I ask him what he is expected to do in such circumstances.

"Knock again. If there's still no answer, I'm supposed to open the door with my key and leave the food. I'm supposed to be careful not to wake anybody."

"And if you do?"

"I'm supposed to apologize and leave as soon as possible."

Sounds right. I ask him what he saw when he first opened the door.

"Mr. Gates was asleep in his chair. Mr. Garcia was on the bed." He's been trained to refer to guests this way. "I woke Mr. Gates and he called security. I believe security called the police. Mr. Evans came upstairs right away. Then Mr. Gates tried to wake Mr. Garcia."

"Did you see Mr. Gates touch Mr. Garcia's body?"

He glances at his wife. "He tried to remove the handcuffs. He removed the tape from Mr. Garcia's face."

So far, he's confirming Skipper's version of the story. "Did Mr. Gates have a key to the handcuffs?"

He looks around. "Yes."

Bad answer. Skipper said he didn't. "And did he use the key to open the handcuffs?"

"He tried. It didn't work."

"Did you see what he did with the key?"

"No."

I decide to change the subject. "Was Mr. Gates helpful when you woke him?"

"He was confused."

"Was he helpful when the police arrived?"

"Yes." He tells me about the arrivals of the paramedics and the police. He talks about his interview with Elaine McBride and Roosevelt Johnson. He describes Skipper's arrest. His delivery is credible.

I thank him for his time and leave. He'll be a strong witness.

It's going to be a long night. At ten-thirty, Pete and Carolyn are sitting in front of the TV that we keep in the martial arts studio. "What are you guys watching?" I ask.

"The Giants," Carolyn says with a grin.

I glance at the black-and-white footage. "It doesn't look like a baseball game to me."

Pete smiles. "It's a rain delay, so we decided to look at something a little more interesting."

I ask him what that would be.

"The security tapes from the Fairmont. I'm like a football coach. I can't tell you what happened until I study the videotapes."

I pull up a folding chair and join them. We watch the grainy videos for twenty minutes without saying a word. "We haven't seen Johnny Garcia," Pete says. "We've been trying. We've gone through the tapes a couple of times."

We stare at the TV screen for an hour. Then another. We see dozens of unrecognizable faces. We rewind several times when we think we might have spotted Johnny. I hear the clock on the ferry building chime two A.M. An hour later, we are looking at footage from three o'clock in the morning. The Fairmont lobby was quiet but not deserted. The camera flashes to the California Street entrance to the hotel. "There!" Pete says.

I'm startled. "What?"

Carolyn rewinds the tape. Pete walks toward the TV. "Run it in super slo-mo," he says. He studies the videotape for a moment and then says, "Stop!" He points to the doorway. A bearded, well-dressed young man is entering the building behind an attractive couple. He heads inside. The white numerals in the lower left corner of the tape indicate that the footage was shot at three-oh-two A.M. Then the tape shifts to an entrance in another part of the hotel. "That's Andy Holton," Pete says.

We rewind the tape three more times and run it in slow motion. "You're right," I say. "He's wearing a baseball cap, but that's him."

"What do you suppose he was doing there at three in the morning?" Carolyn asks.

"Maybe he came to pick up Johnny Garcia," Pete suggests.

"Or maybe he came to kill him," I say.

19

THE JADE WARNER SHOW

"Today, Jade Warner will interview two women who claim they were forced to
have kinky sex with a prominent Bay Area politician."
— COMMERCIAL FOR THE JADE WARNER SHOW. FRIDAY, SEPTEMBER 24.

I'm meeting with Skipper early the next morning, Friday. I inform
him that a second prostitute has surfaced and I tell him about the Jade
Warner show. He reiterates his denial of any contact with the prostitutes. He's adamant.

"Skipper," I say, "the room service waiter at the Fairmont says you
had a key to the handcuffs."

He begs to differ. "I had a key to *my* handcuffs," he insists. "I didn't
have a key to the handcuffs that were on Garcia. My key didn't work."

I find this explanation glib. "And was it your key that ended up in
the toilet?"

"Yes."

"How did that happen?"

"I went into the bathroom to get a drink of water. I must have
dropped it."

How very convenient. "You're sure that key didn't fit the handcuffs
they found on Garcia?"

"I couldn't get them open." He pauses. "It was a key for standard-issue SFPD handcuffs. You'd better be careful. They may be able to get somebody to open the handcuffs with my key."

That would be bad.

The Jade Warner show hits the air at four o'clock. The star is a statuesque blonde in her late forties. Her public confessional every afternoon is a combination of Phil Donahue, Oprah, Jerry Springer, Howard Stern and Doctor Laura, with a dash of Judge Judy thrown in. She has a knack for finding people who want to tell their deepest, most sordid secrets to a syndicated audience. Her show is the highest-rated afternoon talk fest in any local market in the country.

Rosie and I are sitting on the sofa in Natalie's living room. Ed Molinari is pacing behind us. Ann is standing near the TV. Natalie nurses a glass of water. She looks distant. I told her about the Jade Warner show right away—Ann has made it clear that there are to be no surprises. On the other hand, I did suggest to her that she might not want to watch—the embarrassment might be unendurable—but she insisted. I'd have preferred to have watched the show with Skipper, but he was adamant that we be with Natalie to provide support. Turner is here, too, in a chair next to her. He seems to be in a trance.

Jade Warner's theme song is a synthesizer-enhanced disco version of "I Am Woman." The music plays and the announcer intones that Jade will be visiting today with two women who have been involved in destructive relationships with a prominent local politician. Jade never meets with anybody—she visits. And everybody she visits with is involved in a destructive relationship.

Jade makes her grand entrance from behind the red curtains. She's at least six feet tall and model lean. She has admitted on the air that she had her hips, breasts, ankles and nose altered in an effort to please her evil ex-husband. It didn't save her marriage, but she looks terrific. Her radiant smile lights up the studio. She's dressed in a light beige pantsuit. She claps for her predominantly female audience, and they howl their approval.

"Who are we?" she shouts.

"We are individuals!" the audience shouts in unison.

"How are we?"

"We are strong!"

"What are we?"

"We are independent!"

Jade pumps her right fist. The audience roars.

Rosie shakes her head. She thinks Jade Warner portrays all of her guests as victims. It doesn't advance the cause.

Jade's set consists of three armchairs placed in front of the curtains. She begins every show with a brief monologue. She sounds a little bit like Joan Rivers but looks like Heather Locklear. "Ladies and gentlemen," she says, repeating the announcer's lead-in, "our guests are here to discuss their destructive relationships with a well-known politician."

The audience hisses. In Jade Warner's world, the men are always the bad guys. In all fairness, the men she talks about on her show are usually pretty bad hombres.

Jade holds up her hand. "I want to remind the women in the audience in particular that you do not have to continue in abusive relationships."

Ann nods. "I'll give her points on that," she says.

Ed Molinari harrumphs, "Is this for real?"

It certainly is, Ed. Every day. Four o'clock. Channel 4.

Jade introduces the two women who will tell their stories today. They enter the set from behind the curtains and take their seats in the armchairs. The camera zooms in on the first woman. "This is Candy," Jade intones. "She has been involved in a destructive relationship with the district attorney of the City and County of San Francisco."

"How can they *do* this?" Ann asks. "How can they get on TV and make these wild accusations?"

"We tried to get the judge to issue an injunction this morning," Ed replies. "She ruled in favor of free speech."

"There are some things that are more important than the First Amendment rights of a couple of publicity-seeking drug addicts and a nutcase like Jade Warner."

Natalie closes her eyes. Turner takes her hand reassuringly.

The camera shifts to the other woman, who has short dark hair.

"Roberta," Jade says, "is only nineteen years old. She's been involved in a destructive relationship with the same man."

Jade is cupping her chin in her hands when she asks Candy to tell the audience what she does for a living.

Her tone is flat. "I've been a prostitute for six years," she says. She says she's twenty-three.

"How did you meet Mr. Gates?"

"I was working on Post, near the theaters. He asked me if I wanted to have sex with him."

"And did you?"

"Yes." Candy describes her first six months with Skipper. She says he started out as a gentleman, but then he asked her to do more unusual things. "He liked to handcuff me to the bed," she says. "I didn't want to do it at first, but he convinced me." She adds that for five hundred dollars a night, she was pretty accommodating.

"So," Jade says, "you engaged in consensual sex with overtones of bondage for about six months. He paid you for the sex." Her tone is rather clinical.

"That's right."

"Then things started to get abusive?"

I turn to Rosie and shake my head. Does she mean to suggest that six months of paid sex where he handcuffs her to the bed weren't abusive?

Candy's eyes begin to wander. "He started to get rough with me."

"Did he hit you?"

"Not exactly. He used to like to pin me to the bed very hard when he put the handcuffs on me." She pauses and begins to tear up. "Then he started to cover my eyes and mouth with tape."

Natalie's eyes are closed.

"One night, things got out of control. We were doing our usual ritual, when he covered my nose with tape, too." She's starting to cry. "It turned him on. I couldn't breathe. I blacked out."

Turner rubs his temples.

Jade asks her what happened next.

"He became more abusive. He kept making the handcuffs tighter and tighter. He kept my eyes and mouth taped shut for longer periods of time. The highlight seemed to be when he covered my nose with tape and I couldn't breathe. That's when he used to come."

"You mean he used to penetrate you when you were handcuffed to the bed and your eyes, nose and mouth were covered with tape?"

"Yes." She wipes away her tears. "It stimulated him."

"When did you finally put an end to this?"

"He practically killed me one night. I lost consciousness. I thought I was going to die. If the truth be told, Jade, I think I wanted to die." She's sobbing now. "That's when I told him I wouldn't see him again no matter how much he paid me."

Jade pauses to let her get her bearings. "Candy," she says, "you're a college graduate. You're a bright young woman. Why did you let this man take advantage of you?"

"I'm addicted to heroin. I needed the money. He is an important and powerful man. I couldn't say no."

Jade remains composed as she looks into the camera. "When we come back, we'll hear the story of another young woman who succumbed to the powers of the same man."

Natalie opens her eyes and whispers, "Prentice is going to be furious."

It doesn't get any better after the commercial break. The second prostitute is younger and more vulnerable-looking than Candy. And more articulate. "He made it clear from the beginning," she says, "that he was interested in me only for a particular kind of sex." She says Skipper handcuffed her to the bed and taped her eyes and mouth shut. "It was humiliating."

Jade asks, "Why did you remain in this abusive relationship for so many months?"

"I have a drug habit. I have a child to support. I had no choice."

I think of Grace.

"I finally broke things off," Roberta says, "when he almost killed me." She says Skipper almost suffocated her one night. And he hit her in the face and broke her cheekbone.

Add physical abuse to the list.

———

After another commercial break, Jade takes her cordless microphone into the audience and asks for questions. An older woman in the blue dress asks whether either of the women was in therapy. They both say yes. Candy says that she's also in drug rehab and has been suicidal.

A young man with a buzz cut suggests that Candy and Roberta were willing participants. "After all," he says, "it takes two people to engage in sex. Even kinky sex."

The audience hisses. Rosie explains to us that the man is a regular audience member who is there to stir things up. I have no idea where she gets information like this, unless she's taping the show and watching it late at night.

"Ladies," Jade says, "is there any message you'd like to give Mr. Gates if he's able to see this program?"

Candy responds first. "Tell him to get some help."

Roberta is blunter. "Tell him he's an animal."

"Time for one more question," Jade says. She points the microphone.

"Isn't it true," a familiar female voice says, "that both of you are being paid a large amount of money to appear on this program today? And isn't it also true that you came forward only when you were offered money to tell your story?"

I'm stunned. It's Carolyn.

Jade says, "We don't pay our guests, young lady."

Carolyn doesn't back off. "I'm not saying you do. But somebody paid these women twenty-five thousand dollars each to tell these lies on your program. You've been used."

Jade takes the offensive. "Do you have any proof of this?" she asks.

Carolyn doesn't flinch. "We're prepared to provide it to the newspapers. Unless, of course, these women are prepared to issue a full retraction."

Jade looks into the camera. Then she turns to Candy and Roberta. "Well," she says to them, "what do you have to say about that?"

"She's lying," Candy says. Roberta agrees.

Jade turns back to Carolyn. "What do you have to say, Ms. . . . ."

"O'Malley." She pulls out a copy of a computer printout. "This is a copy of Candy's bank account," she says. "There was a twenty-five-thousand-dollar deposit on Tuesday." She pulls out another sheet of paper. "A similar deposit was made into Roberta's account on the same day."

"Who are you?" Jade asks.

"I'm Mr. Gates's attorney. It is irresponsible of you to let these two women on your show."

The audience is stunned. We see Candy and Roberta consult with each other for a moment. Candy acts as spokesperson. "We have no idea where that money came from," she says. "We are telling the truth."

Molinari is speechless. I see the hint of a smile on Ann's face. "When did they get the bank records?" she asks.

Rosie beams. "This morning. Pete's very resourceful."

All hell breaks loose when the Jade Warner show ends. We convene an impromptu press conference in front of Natalie's house. Ann proclaims her father's innocence and promises to bring swift legal action against the two women who soiled his name, as well as Jade Warner and her production company. I tell the world that we plan to ask the judge to drop the charges.

We're back inside at five-fifteen, when Jade Warner gives Channel 4 an exclusive interview. She's ready for the onslaught. "We screen our guests," she insists. She pushes her flowing bangs out of her eyes. "We believe they were telling the truth and we stand by their stories."

A cynic might suggest that she is playing this for all the free publicity she can get.

The media frenzy is fully engaged. Carolyn appears on Channel 4 with her computer printouts. "We felt we had a responsibility to tell Mr. Gates's side of the story," she says. "In our media-driven society, we think it is still important that somebody tell the truth." She is clutching the documents that show the deposits into the two bank accounts.

"Ms. O'Malley," the anchorwoman asks, "do you have any idea who paid these women all that money?"

"We have no idea, Jessica. We're pretty sure it wasn't Jade Warner."

Right on, Carolyn.

Carolyn is waiting for us when Rosie and I get back to the office. Rosie gives her a high-five. "Nice work," she says.

"I think we've done a decent job of discrediting those two women," Carolyn says, looking pleased.

"At least good enough for now," Rosie replies.

"I don't want to break up the celebration," I say, "but we might want to keep this in some perspective. Did it occur to you that they may have been telling the truth? After all, they did find those pictures of Candy in Skipper's study and in the storage locker."

We look at each other and we stop cold.

I'm in my office when the phone rings a little while later. "That was a very interesting discovery you made about the two prostitutes," Roosevelt says.

"That's true."

"It still doesn't explain the pictures of the prostitutes that we found in his desk."

"No, it doesn't." I pause. "Roosevelt," I say, "why didn't you tell me Andy Holton was at the hotel that night? We found him in the security videos."

"We weren't sure it was him."

I believe him. I don't think Roosevelt would sandbag me. I'm not so sure about his partner, though. "Is there anything else you haven't told me?"

Silence. "No," he says. Then he clears his throat and goes on. "I want to ask you a favor."

"Sure."

"It is possible that your little stunt on the Jade Warner show may make victims of abuse more reluctant to come forward. I would ask you to soft-pedal this a little, Mike. For those of us who are in the trenches every day, I don't want to set the cause back twenty years."

His point is well taken. "You have my word, Roosevelt."

"Thanks. There's one other thing I wanted to mention," he says. "One of our men thought he saw Andy Holton not far from the Mission Youth Center yesterday. We're checking it out."

"We'll do the same." I pause. "Roosevelt?"

"Yes."

"Thanks."

My phone rings again. "Mike, it's Ernie Clemente. Can you meet me down at my office at the center around eleven o'clock tonight?"

"I'll be there."

"Come by yourself, okay? And use the side entrance."

"Sure." My heart is pounding. "What's up?"

"There's somebody who wants to talk to you."

20

"HE'S GOING TO NEED PROTECTION"

> "In local news, the daughter of District Attorney Prentice Marshall Gates the Third is threatening legal action against two women who accused her father of soliciting sexual favors."
>
> —KGO RADIO. FRIDAY, SEPTEMBER 24, 9:30 P.M.

A single lightbulb illuminates the alley that leads to the side entrance of the Mission Youth Center at eleven o'clock. There's nobody around. I approach the heavy steel door to the kitchen. I can hear Ernie Clemente's voice inside. Just as I'm about to knock, the talking stops and the door opens. Ernie looks grim. "Come in," he says.

The kitchen smells like cleaning solvent. "Did you find Andy Holton?" I ask.

"Maybe." He escorts me to a table just inside the large dining room where Kevin Anderson is sitting. The mayor's little helper is dressed in blue jeans and a maroon sweater. His face is serious. The only illumination comes from the night-light in the kitchen. I can make out the long steel tables and the trays stacked by the door.

I remain silent. I want them to make the first move.

Ernie takes the lead. "I got another call from Andy," he says.

"When?"

"At eight o'clock."

"Where is he?"

"Nearby. That's all I know; he wouldn't say where. He's scared. He said he was at the Fairmont the night Johnny died, but he doesn't know what to do. He's afraid the police will arrest him."

I remind him that they've already arrested Skipper.

"I understand. But he can't afford a lawyer and he's afraid they'll haul him in on drug charges."

They will. I look at Anderson. "Why are you here?" I ask.

"He called me right after he talked to Ernie. I told him the cops wanted to talk to him and I promised him I'd find him a lawyer. Then I called Ernie."

"Andy needs a lawyer," Ernie says. "You're the first one who came to mind."

"That's fine, except I'm representing Skipper. If Holton was involved in Garcia's death, I have a conflict of interest. I can't represent him."

"I figured you'd say that," Ernie replies, "but I was hoping that at least you'd talk to him and convince him to talk to the police. I couldn't. Then we'll figure out what to do next."

"Why didn't you call the cops?"

"I gave him my word I wouldn't."

"You know other defense attorneys."

"You're the only one I trust."

Great. I stop to think for a moment. Criminal defense attorneys face this unpleasant dilemma all the time. As far as I know, Holton is not a suspect in Johnny Garcia's murder. On the other hand, he is a material witness in Skipper's case. If I find him and I don't tell the cops, I could open myself up to a charge of obstruction of justice — not a pleasant thought. In addition, the cops will claim that they want to talk to him about his alleged drug dealings, which means he may be charged with one or more felonies. If I don't talk to him, I'll be guilty of not vigorously pursuing a material witness in Skipper's case. No matter what I do, I'm going to have a problem. There can be a fine line between fulfilling your obligations under the California Rules of Professional Conduct and harboring a fugitive. "I'll talk to him," I say, "but I won't represent him. And we may need him to be a witness at Skipper's trial."

Anderson shakes his head and says, "He'll never go for it."

"We saw him in the Fairmont security tapes at three in the morning. He must have been there for a reason."

Anderson frowns. "He said he took Johnny to the Fairmont that night. Johnny was working for Andy."

"Andy was his pimp?"

"Yeah."

What? Anderson never mentioned this before. This confirms my suspicions about the relationship between Garcia and Holton. It also confirms my suspicions about Anderson—the sleazy bastard. If he's known about it all along, what else has he been holding back? After all the silence and evasion, he's become strangely forthcoming. I need to know why. It's time to press him further. "How long have you known about this?"

He answers too quickly. "I just found out about it tonight," he says.

Bullshit. "What was he doing at the Fairmont at that hour?"

"He had arranged to pick up Johnny at three A.M. and take him home."

And collect his cut. "What happened?"

"He went upstairs and knocked on the door. There was no answer, so he left. He didn't want to draw attention to himself."

"He never got into the room?"

"No."

So he says. "Did he know if Garcia was still alive?"

"He told me there was no answer," he repeats.

On the other hand, Holton could have gone into the room, found Skipper and Garcia unconscious and killed Garcia, leaving Skipper to take the blame. But why would he kill Garcia? "Kevin, you told me the other night that Holton and Garcia were fighting."

"That's true."

"What were they fighting about?" I'm sure it wasn't the room and the rent.

He's hesitant. "I'm not sure."

"Was Garcia taking Holton's action? Did he stiff his pimp?"

"I don't know."

"Was Holton mad enough at Johnny Garcia to kill him?"

"I don't know."

The hell he doesn't. I'm sure there was a lot more between them than he's letting on, but he's a slippery character. I ask why Holton called him; after all, he was Johnny Garcia's social worker, not Andy's. But no surprise—I get more of the same. "I'm not sure," he says. "I guess because he knew me a little through Johnny and he knows I have connections."

That he does. I'm certain there's more to it than that, but I decide to save it for later—I'm not going to get any more from him tonight. I turn to Ernie. "I've got to talk to Holton," I say.

"And he wants to talk to you. But it has to be confidential."

"I can't make any promises," I say.

"He's supposed to call me back at midnight about a lawyer," Anderson says. "He wants to set up a meeting. I'll tell him to call you; give me your cell phone number. He'll expect you to come alone. And he's going to need protection."

That's for sure. I go home and wait for the phone to ring. It doesn't.

21

"YOU AREN'T HEARING THIS FROM ME"

"Evidence against district attorney continues to mount."
— SAN FRANCISCO EXAMINER. SATURDAY, SEPTEMBER 25.

Rosie is sitting in my office the next morning. "Did you hear from Andy Holton?" she asks.

"Not yet," I say. I reflect for a moment and add, "But I did hear from Kevin Anderson again. He called a little while ago."

"Why?"

"I'm not sure. Maybe he's worried because he erased the messages from Garcia. It looks suspicious, and he must realize we'll call him as a witness to explain it at the trial. He hadn't heard from Holton. He's persistent all of a sudden. It seems to me he's fishing. At first he didn't want to talk to us at all—now he wants to know everything."

"I don't trust him," Rosie says. "He's always trying to sound so virtuous. It's hard to mix this with the rest of him. When you cut through it, he's still a rich guy who spends a lot of time sucking up to the mayor and pushing his father's development projects. Not my type. I like people who really mean it—guys like Ernie and Ramon."

So do I. I've never dealt well with sanctimony. Pete saunters in, wearing a bomber jacket. He looks at the enlarged crime-scene photos propped up against the walls of my office and says, "We went through the security videos again. We noticed a couple of unusual things this time."

"Like what?"

"Dan Morris and Jason Parnelli left at one-thirty."

I'll be damned. "They said they left right after the meeting broke up at twelve-thirty. Did they show up in the video at twelve-thirty?"

"No. They lied."

So they did. "What the hell were they doing up there for another hour?"

"We'll find out. And there's something else," he adds. "Turner came back to the hotel at three twenty-five in the morning."

"Turner? He came back? Did he go upstairs?"

"I would presume he did. The video showed him heading for the elevators. We spotted him heading back out the door ten minutes later."

I wonder how Turner's presence at the Fairmont ties to the fact that there was a phone call to him from Skipper's cell phone at one-twenty. "Anything else?" I ask.

"Maybe. I've had somebody watching your buddy Dan Morris for the last few days."

I think we're wasting our time watching Morris, but Skipper insisted on it. I suspect he's hoping we'll find something that will embarrass—or, better yet, humiliate—Morris. In San Francisco politics, grudges, revenge and retribution frequently play a much larger role than garden-variety issues such as the economy, transportation and the homeless problem. "And how is our favorite attack dog?" I ask.

"He's great. Looks like his candidate for attorney general is going to win, and it seems that he may be getting ready to begin working on another campaign." He says a member of the Board of Supervisors has been spending a lot of time at Morris's office. In and of itself, this isn't news. Morris is a political consultant. The fact that a local official has come to see him is hardly noteworthy. Then again, like it or not, over the years I have learned that my brother is going to tell his stories at his own pace. When you make your living as a PI, you don't have many opportunities to be the center of attention.

I play along. "How interesting," I say. "And which board member would that be?"

"That would be Ann Gates."

This *is* getting interesting.

"There's a little more to the story," he continues. "My associate was watching Dan's house last night. You'll never guess who came over around eleven-thirty."

"The mayor?"

"Nope." He gives me a sly grin. "Ann."

"Really? And may I ask when she left?"

"About nine o'clock this morning."

Rosie cuts to the chase and asks, "Is Ann boinking Dan Morris?"

"Looks that way."

"You aren't mistaken, are you?" I ask.

"I don't make mistakes about that sort of thing."

Rosie glances at me and says, "Fascinating. It gives new meaning to the concept of sleeping with the enemy."

"You have to help us, Skipper," I say. Rosie, Molinari and I are in the consultation room at the Hall at nine o'clock Sunday morning.

"Mike's right," Ed says. "We need some plausible explanation. They're going to say you drugged Johnny Garcia. You have to give us something more than 'I don't know.' "

Skipper remains defiant. "I don't know," he repeats. "I didn't do it."

I point out that the records showed that two outside calls were made to Kevin Anderson from the phone in his room. "If you didn't make the calls," I say, "who did?"

"It must have been Garcia."

"Bullshit. He was unconscious. He was doped up with GHB."

Skipper doesn't reply. I ask him whether he called Turner on his cell phone.

"Yes. I wanted to talk to him about scheduling for the debates."

"At one o'clock in the morning?"

"He had just left. I knew he hadn't gone to sleep yet."

"Turner came back to the hotel at three twenty-five in the morning."

"He did?" He sounds genuinely surprised.

"Yes. Did you see him?"

"No."

"Do you know why he was there?"

"No. Ask him."

I drum my fingers on the table. I look at Molinari, who nods to me. "There's one other thing we need to talk about," I say. "It involves your daughter."

Skipper's eyes light up. "What about her?"

"It seems she's been spending some time with Dan Morris."

He's indignant. "You had my daughter followed?"

"We had Morris followed." I add, "You told us to watch him, Skipper. Ann has been meeting with him at his office every day this week."

"She's thinking about running for mayor next year," he says.

"I know. Last night, she went to his house." I look right at him. "She spent the night."

He stops for a moment. Then he says, "They're adults. Ann is divorced. They've known each other for a long time."

"It's bad form," Ed says. "And it doesn't help our case."

"Skipper," I say, "you told me when I took this case that you wanted me to be completely open with you. I have to ask. Is Ann on our side?"

He doesn't hesitate. "She's family. She's on my side." He swallows hard and adds, "I'll talk to her about it, but I don't want you to say anything to her. Her private life is none of your business."

"It is now," Rosie says.

"You aren't hearing this from me," Tony says to Rosie and me. I'm sitting on the counter at the produce market later the same afternoon. Rosie is showing Grace how to work Tony's cash register. Grace loves being here. There's always something interesting for her to do.

"We understand," Rosie says. "What did you find out?"

"Remember Hector Ramirez, the guy you met in the projects who lived at Johnny Garcia's address? He was in today. He's a delivery guy for my main wholesaler. He's been working in the neighborhood for a long time. He knows everybody. He's tuned in and, for lack of a better term, he's a bit of a gossip. I figured it was worth asking him about Andy Holton."

Rosie asks, "Did Ramirez know him?"

"Yes, but not well."

I ask where he met Holton.

"Hector met him when Holton was working at the Pancho Villa. Hector makes deliveries to the restaurant."

As far as I can tell, the fact that Ramirez knew Holton has nothing to do with Skipper's case. I ask Tony whether there is any possible connection.

He shrugs. "I don't know. I'm just telling you what he said. Holton was an operator. He was looking for money to fund a new business. He asked Hector about it."

That's odd. "Tony," I say, "I know you and Hector are friends, but he's a driver for a produce business. He lives in the projects. Why would Holton think Hector might be a funding source?"

"Because his boss is Donald Martinez. He has a lot of money."

I'll say. Everybody knows about Donald Martinez. On a given day, you'll find his name in the paper for any number of reasons. He runs one of the biggest produce wholesalers in the city and owns a majority interest in a large construction contracting firm. He has a lot of pull downtown. He's in tight with the mayor. He is also the head of the Mission Redevelopment Fund, a local nonprofit that provides start-up capital to neighborhood businesses. Still, it seems unlikely to me. "I don't get it," I say. "Why would a player like Martinez invest in a business run by a pimp like Andy Holton? And why would Holton think Hector could help him? He's just a low-level guy."

"The way he figured, Holton was looking for an introduction to Martinez—any introduction. Hector knew it was a long shot, but he's been working for Martinez for a long time and he's smart—he knows a lot about his operation. I guess Holton picked up on that. Martinez likes to pretend he's still one of the guys from the neighborhood. He lets it be known that he spends some time every week down at the loading dock with the drivers—he takes great pride in it. It's all for show, but he does know most of his employees by name, including Hector. It's damn near impossible to get a small-business loan from a bank in this part of town, and Martinez has provided the community with an alternate source of funds. For a guy like Holton, it must have seemed worth a try."

I'm still not buying this. It's too much of a stretch. "What kind of business was Holton starting?" I ask. "A restaurant? A fruit and vegetable business?"

"No," Tony says. "An Internet business."

Right. A guy who worked at the Pancho Villa who is also a pimp is now a high-tech entrepreneur. I ask what kind of Internet business.

"Cyberporn."

I suppose this shouldn't surprise me. "And where did Hector get this information? I presume he didn't wander up to Martinez's office and ask him about it."

Tony frowns. "Of course not. He wouldn't tell me his source, but I'd bet somebody at the Pancho Villa told him about it. Apparently, Holton was looking for funding and showed some of his stuff to a couple of people at the restaurant. When the manager got wind of it, he fired Holton."

This is a plausible explanation for Holton's rather sudden departure from the Pancho Villa a few weeks ago. Nevertheless, if Martinez is legit, there isn't a chance he would have funded anything like that. "Did Holton actually approach Martinez?" I ask.

"Hector didn't know. And he has no idea whether Martinez provided any funding to him."

It seems unlikely. "And Hector shared this with you out of the goodness of his heart?"

"Hector's a good guy, Mike. And he's a talker." He smiles and adds, "And I'm a good listener." This is true. Rosie says that Tony has a sympathetic face. Complete strangers tell him their deepest and darkest secrets when they come to the market. Tony's expression changes to one of concern. "Mike?" he says.

"Yes?"

"Martinez is my main supplier. If he gets pissed off at me, I'm out of business."

"Don't worry," I say. "I doubt this ever happened—and if we do decide to talk to him, we'll tell you first and we'll keep you out of it."

Rosie and I are sitting on the sofa in her living room. A candle flickers on the mantel. We're hugging. "Your brother is a good guy," I whisper to her.

Her hands gravitate to the middle of my back. Rosie knows how to push all the right buttons. She kisses me and says, "The people who work in the produce business can be very nasty. Donald Martinez didn't become a player by being a nice guy. I don't want Tony to get in the middle of this case."

"I know. I promise we'll be careful."

She gets a faraway look in her eyes. "I wish Tony would find somebody," she says. "Of all of us, he had the only successful marriage."

"My dad used to say that the toughest things to deal with in life are those that you can't control."

"He was a wise man."

"Yes, he was." Although we weren't always close, I still miss him.

She smiles and pulls me to her. She cups my cheek in her hand. "Why don't we take a couple of minutes and try to deal with something we *can* control?"

I'm asleep in my apartment when the ringing phone jolts me awake. It's still dark. I stab for the phone. The digital clock next to my bed says it's four forty-five.

"Hello?" I say.

"It's Andy Holton."

I'm completely awake in an instant. I flip on the light and grab a pencil. "Where are you, Andy?"

"Nearby."

"How can I help you?"

"I think I need to talk to a lawyer."

"I think you're right," I say.

"I'd like to meet with you."

"When?"

"Eleven o'clock tonight. The Jerry Hotel. Room Four."

"I'll be there."

"Mr. Daley?"

"Yes?"

"Come by yourself. I'll have some people watching you."

22
THE JERRY HOTEL

"Please flush toilets after each use."
— SIGN INSIDE THE DOORWAY TO THE JERRY HOTEL.

"I don't like it," Tony says. A single light is on in the back of his produce market at ten o'clock the next night. He's talking. "It's a bad idea. You should let the cops handle this."

In an hour I'm going to be a mile up Mission Street at the Jerry Hotel. Rosie is quiet, but Pete agrees with Tony.

"I've got to talk to him first," I insist.

"You're going to get yourself killed," Pete says.

"We're supposed to talk to our clients before we call the cops to arrest them."

"He isn't your client," Tony points out.

True, nor will he be. "I'm not crazy about the idea, either," I acknowledge. "On the other hand, he called me for advice. I agreed to listen to him. I can't just call the cops and have him picked up."

Tony asks, "Why do you have to meet him at a seedy hotel?"

Rosie answers for me. "We're criminal defense attorneys. Sometimes we have no choice. We can't always meet clients and witnesses at Starbucks."

Tony says, "You're bringing reinforcements, right?"

"I'm going with him," Pete says.

"Pete will cover the entrance when I've gone in," I say. "I'll meet with Holton. If I don't return in five minutes, Pete will call the cops."

Tony glances at Rosie and says, "I'm coming, too."

"This isn't your fight, Tony," I say.

"It is now. You're still family, even when you act like an idiot." He puts his broom down and picks up his cell phone. He walks to the front of the market and returns wearing a beat-up denim jacket. I'd bet almost anything he's carrying the gun that he keeps behind the counter. "I'm coming with you," he says again. "If you geniuses get delusions of grandeur, I'm going to call the cops myself."

Rosie puts on her own jacket and folds her arms. "I'm coming, too," she says.

I argue with her for a few minutes. Inevitably, I lose. "All right," I say. "You're in. You can watch the back of the hotel. But you and Tony stay together. And you've got to stay out of sight—Holton said I'd be watched."

Rosie exhales. "If you go and get yourself killed, I'm going to be really pissed off at you," she says to me. And then, a little tremulously, "Be careful, Mike."

At ten-forty, I'm standing in the BART plaza across Sixteenth from the Jerry Hotel. Pete is somewhere in the immediate vicinity where he can't be seen. We arrived separately. Rosie and Tony are supposed to be in the alley in the back of the building. It's a warm evening. The smell of burritos fills the plaza. A young entrepreneur is transacting pharmaceutical business next to the Green Monster. This is a cash-only enterprise. In the five minutes I've been standing here, he's made about two thousand dollars. A police car drives up Mission but doesn't stop.

I'm watching the entrance to the Jerry. It's about as far as you can get from the Ritz. A female prostitute has opened the heavy steel door and gone upstairs. A young Hispanic man comes and goes in short order, presumably to deliver drugs. He darts up Sixteenth after making the drop. My eyes are working at a hundred miles per hour.

The drug dealer walks up to me and asks, "Can I interest you in some high-quality products?"

"What do you have?" I ask.

"Anything you want."

"Not interested tonight," I say. "Maybe another time."

"Suit yourself," he replies, and heads back toward the Green Monster. A group of people are coming up the escalator from the BART station. A train must have just arrived. New customers are on their way.

The door of the Jerry is covered with graffiti. The restaurant on the ground floor is dark. Some of the windows on the second and third floors are boarded up. I repeat the plan to myself once more. If I'm not back within five minutes, Pete will call the cops and come upstairs with the cavalry. At least I hope so.

The door to the Jerry is ajar when I push on it at eleven o'clock. It opens grudgingly and I head in. In front of me is a dimly lit stairway. The banister has been ripped from the wall. It's stuffy. A single lightbulb halfway up the stairs provides the only illumination. It's dark at the top. A man with a long beard is sitting just under the lightbulb, drinking malt liquor from a tall can. In the murky light his olive-colored skin has a pasty pall. His clothes are tattered and filthy. I smell him as I climb past him. He ignores me.

It's grimmer at the top of the stairs. There's a strung-out prostitute sitting on the linoleum floor as I turn the corner. Her halter top is wrapped around her neck and her bare breasts hang lifelessly. She moans as I walk past her. My heart is pounding. I'm sweating. There's another bare lightbulb halfway down the short corridor. I see four rooms on each side. There's a number on each, and I hear groaning from behind the closed door to Room One. The door to Room Two is open. Two men are shooting up just inside. They slam the door when I walk by.

A well-dressed man hurries out of Room Three and walks past me. "What the fuck do you want?" he mutters as he goes by. He jams his nightly fix under his coat.

Room Four is at the end of the hallway, so it must face the back of the building. I can hear myself breathing. I derive little comfort knowing that my guys are outside waiting for me. I put my ear up to the door and listen. Not a sound. I make a fist and knock twice. No answer. I try the handle. The door isn't locked. I push it open. The room is dark except for the light coming through the window from the alley. It opens onto a fire escape. I can make out a mattress on the floor and a wooden chair. There is a dark spot in the corner that may have held a sink. Now it's just a hole in the floor. The smell of urine permeates the room.

I step inside and my eyes begin to adjust. "Andy? Andy Holton?" I ask.

There's a clicking sound to my left, and I feel cold metal against my left ear. "Don't move," a male voice whispers. It sounds familiar, but I can't place it.

Panic. My stomach churns. I feel the sweat in my armpits. I think of Grace. I think of Rosie. I think I'm going to die tonight in the Jerry Hotel.

The voice asks, "Are you by yourself?"

"Yes."

"Put your hands on top of your head."

I do as I'm told. Hands frisk me. My heart pounds. I don't respond well to terror.

"Are you Daley?" he asks.

"Yeah."

He asks for my wallet. I pass it back to him. He looks at it and hands it back.

"Are you Holton?" I ask.

"No. He sent me to get you."

"Is he here?"

"No."

Shit.

He's still standing behind me. The barrel of the pistol moves to my back. "We're going for a walk," he says. "If you turn around and try to look at me, I'll kill you."

I believe him. "Where are we going?"

"Not far."

I begin to turn toward the door, and he pokes me in the kidney.

"No," he says. "We're not using the front door. We're taking the fire escape."

Christ. We're going out the back of the building. Pete won't see me, but maybe Rosie and Tony will. He pushes me toward the window. I climb out onto the fire escape and start making my way down the iron stairs. I'm afraid of heights. He warns me again not to look at him. He jostles me in the back with his pistol. I question my sanity.

We reach the ground and begin walking up the alley toward Valencia. I try not to move my head as I dart helpless glances for Rosie and Tony. I come to the hard realization that I may be flying solo. When we reach Valencia, I don't feel the gun anymore. I presume this means he's hidden it under his jacket. He tells me to turn right. I'm tempted to try to make a break for it or to stop one of the cars on Valencia, but I don't have the guts. We walk about fifty paces north. The looming presence of the Hotel Royan casts a shadow on the street. I recall my visit with the man in the old cheese steak shop. I'm sweating right through my clothes.

The mystery man pushes me toward the door under the dilapidated marquee. "Room 201," he says.

I think about trying to go back and find Rosie and Tony. Not a chance.

"He wants to see you right now," the voice says. He shoves me through the steel mesh door. I have no choice.

The Royan is even worse at night than it is in the daytime. It's dark. It stinks of urine and vomit. I hear muffled screaming from above. A crack addict is shooting up just inside the door. A man is passed out on the lobby floor.

I want to turn back but the barrel of the gun presses against my back again. If I make a break for it, I'm dead. If I go upstairs and look for Holton, I may be dead anyway. There is a rickety stairway at the end of the hall. The gun nudges me forward. We head up the stairs.

The hallway on the second floor is dark. The door to the bathroom is open. A man is sitting on the toilet, injecting something into his left arm. The only illumination is from the streetlights on Valencia that shine through an open window at the end of the hall.

I find Room 201 and knock on the door. There is no answer. The man standing behind me tells me to try the handle. I do. It's unlocked. I open the door. "Andy Holton?" I ask.

I hear screams from the room next door. I jump. Inside the dark room, I can make out a sagging bed. I can see a dresser and a sink in the corner. The tile floor is sticky underfoot. There's a naked man lying in the bed. "Andy?" I ask again.

No response.

I feel the pressure of the gun against my back. I walk into the room toward the figure on the bed. I can smell the breath of the man with the gun. I hear him utter the word "Shit." As I'm about to reach for the man in the bed, I hear a loud crack. Something cold and heavy has hit the back of my head. I think I see a flash of light. Time slows down. I see Grace's face. I see my mom's face. An instant later, everything goes black. I don't feel it when I hit the floor.

23
"YOU FOUND HIM"

"Police continue the search for Johnny Garcia's roommate."
—NEWSCENTER 4 DAYBREAK. TUESDAY, SEPTEMBER 28.

My head hurts. A lot. My body aches. My throat is dry. It's dark. My right cheek is sticking to something hard. A second later I realize it's the floor. I make out a black shoe in front of me.

"Mick?" A familiar voice. My brain begins to engage. I can't talk. "Mick? You okay?"

I try to lift my head, but I can't. I think my eyes are open. I begin to focus. I feel a hand patting my left cheek.

"Mick, it's Pete."

I finally regain some sense of place. My relief is overwhelmed by the pain in the back of my head. Pete gets right in front of my face. "You're okay, Mick," he says. "Somebody whacked you on the head."

I move my head slowly. The pain is excruciating. I try to rub the back of my head, but my hand isn't working yet. "Where the hell am I?" I ask.

Another familiar voice answers. "The Royan." It's Rosie. Her face comes into sight next to Pete. Tony is standing behind her.

"What time is it?"

"A few minutes after midnight," Rosie says. "You've been out for about half an hour."

My head starts to clear through the throbbing pain. I realize the room is full of people. I see two uniformed police officers. I recognize Roosevelt Johnson, who is talking to Elaine McBride. I wonder what the homicide team is doing here. Two paramedics examine my head, neck and back. They're concerned about concussions and possible neck and spinal injuries. I'm glad they're being cautious. I tell them that my head hurts but insist I'm otherwise okay. They check my eyes, test my reflexes and put an ice pack against the bump on the back of my head. Then they carefully help me up to a sitting position. The room whirls around me for a moment, then settles down.

I look at Rosie. "I'm glad you came."

"It's a good thing we were there," she says. "We followed you here."

"Did you get a look at the guy?" I ask.

"Yeah," Rosie replies. "I'll be able to identify him if we can find him."

Great.

"Mike," Pete says, "next time I want you to stick with the plan."

There won't be a next time. "Sure, Pete." I look around the crowded room. I wave a shaky hand to Roosevelt. "Glad you guys could make it," I say.

Roosevelt is annoyed. "Next time you decide to play Dirty Harry, I want you to call me first."

"No problem. I was trying to find Andy Holton."

He nods toward the bed. "Congratulations," he says. "You found him."

Holton's naked body rests faceup with his eyes and mouth open. He had fair skin and light hair. I see a syringe on the floor next to the bed, about a foot from where I'm sitting. A team from the coroner's office is setting up just outside the door. I hear one of them murmur, "Looks like he OD'd."

Roosevelt surveys the room. "Who else knew you were coming?" he asks.

"Just Pete, Rosie and Tony."

He asks if I caught a glimpse of the guy who hit me.

"Nope."

Roosevelt asks whether Holton was already dead when I arrived.

"I'm not sure. I think so. I only saw him for an instant."

"Can you think of any reason why somebody might want to scare you?"

"I don't know." I'm glad he said "scare" instead of "kill."

"Are you missing anything?"

I take inventory. My watch and my wallet are gone. He says he'll get my statement after they check me in at San Francisco General.

The paramedics lift me onto a gurney. I turn to Rosie and Pete and say, "Thanks."

Pete says, "You're the only brother I've got left. I'm coming with you in the ambulance."

San Francisco General Hospital is a huge brick complex on Potrero Avenue next to the 101 Freeway, just west of Hospital Curve on the eastern boundary of the Mission. I was born here. The facility is a small city that somehow manages to handle everything from gunshot wounds to drug addiction to insect bites. It has one of the largest AIDS wards in the country. The doctors live on the front lines of the urban medical war. They win most of the battles.

The emergency room is like a giant assembly line. Even at this hour, it's busy. A young resident named Dr. Chu takes a close look at the golf-ball-sized bump on the back of my head right away. She says it looks like a concussion, but orders an X ray and a CAT scan to check for fractures or brain injury. In an abundance of caution, she decides to admit me for twenty-four hours of observation. She tells me that I should try to stay awake for a few hours to reduce the possibility that I will slip into a coma. She lacks a certain degree of bedside manner, but she seems to know what she's talking about.

I'm escorted back to the waiting area until the CAT scan equipment becomes available. It is depressing to watch shooting victims and unconscious drug overdoses being wheeled past me. I take a seat between Pete and Rosie. Tony's across from me. I recall sitting in almost the same spot over thirty years ago, when my dad got shot in the leg. Cops get the royal treatment. My mom was stoic. I'll never forget the look on her face.

Pete scans an ancient copy of *Cosmo*. Tony leans his head back and tries to sleep. Rosie is talking to her mom on her cell phone. She's staying at Rosie's house with Grace. "Mike is okay," she says. "Don't wake up Grace. I don't know when I'll be home." After she switches off the phone, she turns to me and says, "So we found Andy Holton."

"Yep. Too late—he's terminally dead."

Pete interjects, "You'd be dead, too, if Rosie and Tony hadn't been there."

I glance at Tony, who is dozing in his chair. "I'll have to thank him when he wakes up," I say.

Rosie asks me, "How's your head now?"

"I'm okay."

"You damn well better be." She leans over and whispers in my ear, "This isn't going to interfere with your performance in bed, is it?"

I can't help myself and I start to laugh. It makes my head hurt even more. "No, Rosie. The guy hit me in the head. I should function fine elsewhere."

"That's good," she says. She considers for a moment and asks, "Doesn't that depend on which head he hit?"

I'm caked in dirt. My clothes stink. I'm sitting in the emergency room of one of the biggest public hospitals in the country. I won't be able to get an X ray or a CAT scan for at least another hour because they have too many other patients with more serious injuries. And I'm laughing so hard, my head throbs.

I'm resting in my double room on the third floor of the south wing of San Francisco General later that day. I'm doing better than the man in the next bed, who had a bullet removed from his right leg earlier. I've taken a shower and I'm wearing my Cal sweats. Rosie brought them over. I'm watching TV with the sound turned off. Things could be worse. My head is still throbbing, but the aches in the other parts of my body are starting to subside. I've been given enough Advil to dull the pain a little. I took a nap, but they want me to stay awake most of the time. A nurse comes in every twenty minutes to poke me or take some blood. Dr. Chu assured me that I'll get to go home tomorrow.

Rosie hasn't left. She's on the phone with Grace at the moment. "Yes, sweetie," she's saying. "I'll be home later tonight. Daddy gets to come home tomorrow. You'll have to be good and do what Grandma says, okay?" She says "Uh-huh" a couple of times and smiles. Then she turns to me and says, "I just promised her that we'd buy her that fancy new bike for being such a good girl while Daddy was in the hospital."

Sounds fine to me. Give Grace credit. She knows when to hit us up. In my current condition, I would have agreed to buy her a new Ferrari.

A little later, we watch the early evening news. The jovial anchorman reports that a young man named Andrew Holton was found dead of an apparent overdose at the Hotel Royan. "In what may be a related matter," he says, "Attorney Michael Daley was attacked at the same hotel." My smiling face pops up just behind him. I look a lot better on TV than I feel in person. He tosses the ball to a reporter who is standing under the marquee of the Royan.

I turn off the tube. My head is starting to ache again. I look at Rosie. "Did you talk to Roosevelt again?" I ask.

She tugs at her hair, which is hanging down to her shoulders. She's had a long eighteen hours, too. I may be doped up, but I recognize her for what she is—the most beautiful woman I've ever known. "Yes," she says. "He called while you were asleep. Rod Beckert did the autopsy on Holton. He died of a heroin overdose."

"Any signs of a struggle?"

"Nope. They haven't ruled out foul play entirely, but he definitely died of an overdose."

"And the guy who hit me?"

"Nothing. They talked to everybody at the Royan. Nobody saw anything."

This doesn't surprise me. Most of the residents of the Royan are involved in drugs in one way or another. It is unlikely that any of them would want to become involved in a police investigation. We're back to square one.

24
"MOTHER IS VERY UPSET"

> "Police continue investigation of attack on attorney at Mission hotel."
>
> —NEWSCENTER 4. WEDNESDAY, SEPTEMBER 29.

We regroup first thing Wednesday morning in the martial arts studio. It's September twenty-ninth—less than two weeks until we begin jury selection. I've asked Ann and Turner to come in for a debriefing on the events at the Royan. Molinari is pacing. Rosie is sitting with her arms folded. After I describe the events that led up to my discovery of Andy Holton's body, Ann and Turner waste no time berating us. They tell us that Skipper and Natalie are both upset at not having been told about our hearing from Holton. Then they get to the real point—our competence. Turner says Skipper is thinking about making a change. He doesn't think we're being aggressive enough.

Support comes from an unexpected source. "It's not as if Mike killed Holton," Molinari says. "He was just trying to do something that might have helped."

Especially if Holton hadn't been dead and I hadn't been knocked unconscious.

Ann is unimpressed. "Why the hell didn't you tell us he had called you?"

"He asked me to keep it confidential," I reply. "I simply wanted to try to talk to him."

Turner picks up on Ann's statement. It's obvious they've discussed this and rehearsed their lines. "Skipper wants Ed to play a bigger role in the defense," he says. "He doesn't like the direction the case is taking."

Rosie lights up. "And what, pray tell, would *you* have done differently?" she snaps.

They exchange uncomfortable glances. Turner says, "Skipper wants Ed to take the lead."

I don't respond. I have already taken a physical beating. I will not give them the satisfaction of seeing me take an emotional one as well.

Turner says that I will sit first chair at the trial and Molinari will act as Keenan counsel as before. However, all decisions on strategy will run through Ed. In other words, I'll get to try the case, but Molinari gets to pull the strings.

"And if that's not acceptable to us?" I ask.

Ann doesn't hesitate. "Father will terminate your services immediately."

Rosie looks straight at Ann and sets her jaw. "If that's the way our client wants it, that's the way we'll play it."

I begin to interrupt, and she holds up her hand. "If that's the way our client wants it," she repeats, "that's the way it will be."

Ann is triumphant. She looks at Ed, Rosie and then me in turn and says, "There is something else. I want to be kept fully informed of all developments in Father's case. I don't want to hear about anything on the news. I don't want to get phone calls from the press about something I haven't been told about. Above all, I don't want to have to explain to Mother that she wasn't kept fully apprised. Understood?"

We nod in unison.

"I expect you to call on Mother this afternoon to straighten this mess out."

My turn. "Ann, there's something we need to ask you about."

"What?"

I keep my face impassive and I say, "We've been keeping a close eye on Dan Morris. While we were watching him, we couldn't help but notice that you've been spending some time together."

She tenses. "It's just business."

"Really? What type of business? Political or personal?"

She's annoyed. "I'm thinking about running for mayor in the next election. That shouldn't be a great news flash. I went to ask Dan if he might be interested in helping me with my campaign."

"You realize that he may be a key witness in your father's trial and may conceivably be considered a suspect."

"I suppose that's possible."

"Yet you're thinking of hiring him as your campaign manager?"

Icy stare. "I'm considering it. It's business," she repeats. "It's politics. Father understands."

"Ann, are you and Dan involved?" I ask.

"Involved?"

"Romantically. Are you and Dan seeing each other socially?"

"I won't dignify that question with an answer," she says.

I won't let it go this time. "If we are going to defend your father, we need to understand *all* the facts surrounding his case. We need to know if you're involved with Dan Morris. Our private investigator has seen the two of you together at his house."

She fires back, "And what would that have to do with Father's case?"

"Maybe nothing. But it is widely known that Dan and your father had a falling-out."

Her creamy skin reddens. Her lips purse. "I've known Dan for many years," she says. "We enjoy each other's company. We're seeing each other. Are you happy?"

"Thank you, Ann. You might try to be discreet about your relationship until the trial is over."

She stalks out of the room. Turner follows.

After she's gone, Fast Eddie unwraps a cigar and holds it like a trophy. "I thought Ann's reaction to your question about Dan Morris was pretty interesting," he says. He seems to be enjoying this.

"It's hard to figure out what game she's playing," I say. "I don't think she's capable of loyalty to anyone but herself. The only thing that seems to drive her is ambition. You don't really think she'd set up her own father, do you?"

He gestures with the cigar. "She used to admire him. Now she hates him. She didn't like the way he handled her divorce. She resents the way he's cheated on her mother. She thinks he's a hypocrite and a liar."

"You seem to know her pretty well," I say.

"I've known her for a long time," he says. "We were involved for a few months."

Add yet another notch to Ed's list of conquests. The fact that he was sleeping with Skipper's daughter doesn't seem to faze him.

"It didn't last very long," he adds. "No chemistry."

I can see that. There was a chance for a nuclear meltdown. "Come on, Ed," I say. "It's hard to imagine she was involved in Garcia's death. It would have been impossible for her to orchestrate, and there's no evidence she returned to the Fairmont that night. And he *is* her father, after all."

He shrugs. "Maybe you're right," he says. He pauses and adds, "Listen, do me a favor. Don't talk to any more witnesses without telling me first, okay?"

Join the chorus, Ed. "No problem," I say.

"And while you're at it, try not to get yourself killed."

Thanks. That's very sound advice.

"You don't look good," Rosie says to me after Ed leaves.

"I don't feel good."

"Does your head hurt?"

"Yeah, along with my ego. I hate the idea of Fast Eddie taking over the lead in this case."

"Clients change their minds all the time," Rosie says.

"It's a mistake to do it so close to the beginning of trial." Then I add, "It's a mistake to let Ed Molinari run this case."

She leans back. "I didn't think we had any choice if we wanted to stay in the case."

"We didn't."

"You *do* want to stay in the case, don't you?"

"Absolutely." I look at the picture of Grace on Rosie's desk. I've taken abuse from our client, his daughter and our co-counsel. I've been physically and emotionally attacked. Yet I do accept that when you're this close to trial, you cannot afford to start second-guessing your decision to accept a case. This isn't the time for questions like that. Or for others that I find I ask myself more often as I get older. Like why am I doing this at all? When I decided to become a lawyer, I had all the familiar motivations that come with being young and sure you can make an impact. I guess I still carried a lot of the baggage that had brought me to the seminary. I'd wanted to be a good priest and I wanted to be a good lawyer—justice and all that. I know "the system" has become a mocking word, but I believed in it. I suppose I still do, but it's hard to keep that up when you have to deal every day with all the grief and corruption around you. I want to do a good job, but I'm so tired a lot of the time. I think I've forgotten how to have fun. I wish I had more time for Grace. I wish I knew how to fall in love. I wish— hell, I wish I knew how to be happy. I look at Rosie, beautiful Rosie, and wonder yet again why I—we—couldn't make it work.

And then I shake myself back to reality. This is not the time to tear myself apart. I've got a client who's relying on me for the outcome. That's my job. Doing a good job comes with the territory, and I chose the territory. I turn to Rosie and say, "We're taking this to the finish line."

"Are you sure?" she asks.

"Yeah. We owe it to Skipper. Anyway, it's too late to bring in another trial lawyer."

"It's never too late," she points out. "The judge would grant a continuance. This isn't about our client. This is about you."

She's right. But I've got my pride and it's right up front. "If we quit, they'll win," I say. "I won't give them the satisfaction."

She knows me. "You shouldn't put your pride above the interests of our client."

I don't answer for a moment. "If I didn't think I was the best person to try this case," I say, "then I would let them bring in somebody else. I am the right person. I'm going the distance." Then I add, "And it isn't only pride, Rosie. I'm stubborn. There's a difference."

She smiles at me.

"And when this is all done," I say, "I think we should take some time off."

"Agreed." She always knows where I've been.

We return to the matters at hand. "Ann was in full force, wasn't she?" Rosie says.

"Par for the course," I reply. "We work our tails off, go chasing all over town trying to find witnesses, get smacked on the head and end up in the hospital. You didn't expect her to thank us, did you?"

"I noticed you didn't mention anything about Andy Holton and his Internet porn business," Rosie says.

"I'll get in trouble for that, too. Pete's checking out Donald Martinez. If he finds something, we'll tell them about it. If he doesn't, we won't."

"You're protecting Tony, aren't you?"

"Damn right. He did us a favor by giving us the information. He was there when I went to find Andy Holton. It's the least I can do."

"You're a good man, Michael Daley," she tells me.

We pay our promised visit to Natalie at two o'clock. Her servant shows us to the living room. She's becoming more remote as the case moves forward. Today, I see the screen on her laptop is on. She turns around to greet us, saying she monitors the progress of the case on the Internet. I realize this may be less brutal than facing the newspaper stories or the television set every day. She keeps up with her charity work that way, too. This seems to be how she connects with the outside world. Turner has joined us. He's standing by the windows. To his credit, he has been spending a lot of time at Natalie's house, giving her moral support. I suspect a lot of her friends have vanished.

"Thank you for coming," Natalie says, courteous as always. She asks how I am feeling. I tell her I'm on the mend. Truthfully, my head still feels like it is going to split in two.

"Natalie," I say, "we wanted to assure you that we will keep you fully informed of developments in Skipper's case."

"I need to know you will keep your promises," she answers. "An important witness is dead. I wasn't informed that you had heard from him until after the fact. I don't want that to happen again."

"It won't."

She sighs. "It keeps getting worse. They keep reporting these terrible lies about Prentice. Surely, there must be something you can do to stop them."

I sense this is the real reason she wanted to see us, but the truthful answer is we can't. "I know how distressing they are," I say, "but the most urgent priority is to continue to prepare for trial. I wish we could stop them, but that's beyond our control."

Rosie decides to push in a different direction. "Natalie," she says, "is it possible that somebody could have gotten into Skipper's study?"

She pauses. "The room is at the back of the house. It would have been very difficult for anyone other than the servants to get in." This jibes with what Skipper's told us.

"But not impossible, right?" Rosie persists.

"Yes," she says reluctantly.

Turner is annoyed. "What is this leading to, Rosie?" he asks.

"We may need Natalie to testify that somebody may have had access to the study. It may be the only way to establish a credible argument that somebody planted the photos and the magazines there."

"Why Natalie?"

"Because she would be a very sympathetic witness," I interject. I leave out the fact that she would be a much more sympathetic witness than Skipper, the other possible choice. He isn't going up on the stand unless things are hopeless.

Natalie is not pleased about the prospect. "I have never been a witness at a trial," she says.

Rosie tries to reassure her. "If it should become necessary, we'll be there to help you," she says, but Natalie is not persuaded.

A few minutes later, Turner escorts us out. "Listen," he says as we're standing in front of the house, "I would appreciate it if you would take it easy on Natalie. She's been through a lot."

I assure him that we'll do everything we can. Actually, I'm glad to have encountered him. "Turner," I say, "there is one other issue that has come up."

His eyes question me.

"We had a chance to look at the records for Skipper's cell phone. It seems that a phone call was placed to you at about one-twenty."

He freezes for just a second. "He called me about scheduling."

"At one-twenty in the morning?"

"I told him I'd be up late. He wanted to be sure we had enough lead time to schedule debates in both Los Angeles and San Francisco."

Of course. "The police found out about it through the phone records. You never mentioned it until they asked, did you?"

"I don't recall. I know I told them about it."

Not a particularly convincing dodge. "Did Skipper sound agitated?"

"He sounded fine. All business. Nothing out of the ordinary."

"And there was nothing unusual about his tone or manner?"

"It was after one in the morning. He sounded tired. Otherwise, he was just fine."

"Turner," I say, "you were seen in the security videos in the lobby of the hotel at three twenty-five A.M. What were you doing there?"

He acts as if he expected the question. "I was concerned. We were told he might be under surveillance. A friend of mine at the *Chronicle* told me he thought Sherman's people had hired a private eye to try to dig up some dirt. I came back to check things out."

"What did you find?"

"Nothing. I went upstairs, but there was no sign of a private eye, and I didn't see or hear anything at his door. I didn't knock. I figured he was asleep, so I went back home."

Right.

"He's lying through his teeth," Rosie says. We're in my car, heading downtown. "What do you think he's up to?"

Damned if I know; he's slippery. "Maybe he's protecting Skipper?" I suggest, though as I say it I realize loyalty has never been a Turner trait.

Rosie is skeptical, too. "No way," she says. "But I can see him covering for somebody else."

"Like who?"

"Like himself," she answers. "Or Ann. Or Natalie."

My cell phone rings. It's Pete. "Mama fell down," he says. "She hit her head."

Christ. I ask him where he is.

"I'm on my way to San Francisco General."

"We'll meet you there," I say, and drive like hell.

25
"IT DOESN'T LOOK GOOD"

"Please respect the needs of our patients."
—SAN FRANCISCO GENERAL HOSPITAL.

The drab walls and plastic chairs provide little comfort to those of us who are sitting in the waiting room of the intensive care unit at San Francisco General. A TV is attached to the wall. A local news-magazine show is playing. The sound is turned down and nobody's looking at it. We're waiting for word on my mom. She's in surgery. She fell down in the kitchen. The broken hip may mend. The blow to her head is much more worrisome. The nurse came by about an hour ago and said Mama's in a coma. There's fluid on the brain. They're going to try to relieve the pressure. My head aches.

Pete's always been the closest to my mom. He's talking on his cell phone to our sister in L.A. I can make out the words "It doesn't look good."

Rosie is next to me. She licks her lips from time to time. It seems we're spending a lot of time at San Francisco General. Our memories of this hospital are mixed. Grace was born here. Rosie's dad died here. So did mine. We don't need to speak. There's nothing to say. I can't imagine being here without her.

I pretend to be looking at a copy of *Time*. In reality, I'm replaying in my mind the highlight reel of the life and times of Margaret Murphy Daley. Born in San Francisco. Grew up in the outer Mission. Married my father when she was twenty. Moved to the Sunset. Raised four kids. Watched them all go to college. Lost one of them in Vietnam. Lost her husband too soon. Watched us get married. Celebrated when Grace was born and again when my sister's son was born in L.A. Was there for us when we got divorced. Took care of my father when he got sick. Loved us all. Worried for sixty-nine years.

I glance at Pete. He nods toward a doctor and a nurse who are approaching us and swallows hard. "This isn't good," he whispers. "They always come together when it isn't good."

We stand. The young internist tells us the inevitable. I barely hear the words, "There was nothing we could do for her." The trauma to her brain was too severe. The internal pressure was too extreme. She never regained consciousness.

"We'd like to see her," I say.

The nurse says she'll return in a few minutes to escort us to see Mama. She asks us if there is anybody we would like to call.

We sit in the waiting area with each other and our memories. Pete calls our sister. Tears are streaming down his face.

Rosie calls her mom to tell her, then asks to talk to Grace. I hear her say, "It's going to be all right, honey. I know you're sad, but Grandma is in heaven with Grandpa now. They're together again with Uncle Tommy." She turns back to me, tears in her eyes. I ask her how Grace sounded. "Fair," she replies, her voice cracking. She takes my hand. "I'm so sorry, Mike," she whispers.

"I didn't even have a chance to say good-bye." I bury my head in her shoulder and sob.

Sylvia Fernandez says, "Margaret was a very special lady."

We're sitting in her kitchen a few hours later. I've been on the phone making funeral arrangements and calling friends and family.

"Thanks, Sylvia."

"You know, we didn't always see eye to eye on everything."

I am well aware of this. Sylvia and my mom were not pleased

when Rosie and I told them we were getting married. Sylvia thought Rosie could do better. My mom expected me to marry a nice Irish woman. The two of them were similar in many ways. They were both fiercely independent and very protective of their children. I smile at Sylvia and say, "We had an inkling about that."

Rosie chuckles and says, "You guys seemed to get along a lot better once Mike and I split up."

This is true. When we separated, they pooled their resources. They thought our custody fight was going to ruin Grace's life. They were right. I dropped the battle after they interceded. It isn't hard to figure out where Rosie got her independent streak.

"Looks like I'm the last one of this generation left," Sylvia says.

"It isn't easy when you outlive your immediate family," Rosie says.

"And many of your friends," Sylvia adds. She lifts her teacup and says, "Here's to my wonderful friend, Margaret Daley. I'll miss you, my dear. I'll do my best to keep an eye on everybody for as long as I can."

The obituary for Margaret Murphy Daley says she lived to the age of sixty-nine. It says she was married to Thomas James Charles Daley, Sr. for forty-two years. It says she had four children and two grandchildren. It doesn't say that she gave everything she had to us. It doesn't note that she made all of us feel special every time we saw her. It can't begin to describe the sparkle in her eyes every time she saw her grandchildren.

The gatherings for the wake and the funeral are small. The priest from our old parish in the Sunset delivers a beautiful eulogy. He talks about family. He conveys the essence of her life when he says, "She was always there when anyone needed her."

On Friday, October first, Margaret Murphy Daley is laid to rest between my dad and my brother in the old Irish cemetery in Colma. Grace places flowers on the casket. Pete stands next to Rosie and me. My baby sister, Mary, holds hands with her husband and her son. I watch the casket being lowered and think how small the grave looks.

I'll miss you, Mama.

26
A RAT IS STILL A RAT

"It is unfortunate that we must take time away from the important issues to address the legal problems that concern Mr. Gates."
—DAN MORRIS. NEWSCENTER 4 DAYBREAK. MONDAY, OCTOBER 4.

Monday, October fourth. There's been little time to mourn; we have a trial starting in two weeks. Skipper vetoed the possibility of asking for a continuance. He expects the trial to be completed before election day in the first week of November. We've hired an attorney to handle Mama's small estate. Pete and I sorted out her personal belongings. We've decided to hold off putting the house up for sale until after the first of the year.

I saw Roosevelt at the funeral. He told me the police had no new leads on the man who slugged me at the Royan. Rod Beckert has declared Andy Holton's death an accidental heroin overdose. I'm not surprised and I'm not convinced.

Skipper is subdued when I see him. The gravity of his situation seems to be sinking in at last. He's changing from belligerent to modestly helpful, though he has nothing new to say. Unfortunately, the same is not true of his daughter. Ann is becoming even more contentious, if that's possible. I don't understand it. She tells me she plans to announce her candidacy for mayor after the first of the year. She isn't letting her father's murder trial get in the way of her political ambitions.

At ten o'clock this morning, I've managed to get an appointment with Ann's boyfriend, Dan Morris. Ann told us it's official: He's her new campaign manager. He gives me a lukewarm greeting as we sit in his memorabilia-filled office. It's overcast outside.

He leads off. "I don't get it, Mike," he says. "It's staring you right in the face." His cuff links are in the shape of little gold American flags. The stars are made of diamond chips.

"What's that, Dan?" I try to sound innocent.

"Your client. Everybody can see it. He's guilty as hell. He should withdraw from the race. You guys should stop wasting everybody's time and see if McNulty will go for a plea bargain."

They can wear designer clothes. They can wear diamond-studded cuff links. They can sit in a fancy office. Any way you cut it, a rat is still a rat. It also strikes me that Ann may not be sharing all the details of her father's case with her new squeeze. Unless he's sandbagging me, it seems she hasn't mentioned McNulty's overtures about a plea bargain to him.

I decide to approach from another angle. "Dan," I say, "we were looking at the security tapes."

His face is expressionless. "So?"

"We saw you leave the building at one-thirty."

"So?"

How do I say this politely? I hate this guy. "So, you told me a while back that you and Jason left around twelve-thirty, right after the meeting ended."

He feigns exasperation. "What difference does it make? We left shortly after the summit conference broke up."

Bullshit. An hour later is not "shortly." "What were you doing there?"

"Talking about logistics for the debates." He glances up at the wall of campaign posters as if he's trying to remember. "We met in the room next door to Skipper's."

"How long were you there?"

"I guess it must have been about an hour, if that's what the security tapes show."

I ask him who else was there.

"Just Jason." He says he didn't hear anything in Skipper's room.

"You didn't happen to see Johnny Garcia?"

"Of course not."

Damn. "And you went straight home?"

"Yes."

I take a deep breath. "Dan," I say, "I understand you've been asked to run Ann's campaign for mayor."

"She's hired me," he says. "We're going to hold off on the announcement of her candidacy until after the first of the year. We want to get her father's trial out of the way."

Right. "Does any of this strike you as a little odd?" I ask.

"What do you mean?"

"I mean you're running a vicious negative campaign against her father. Now you're going to run Ann's campaign. Isn't that kind of like switching sides?"

"It's business. You know that. I run campaigns. She needs a manager. I'm good. She knows it. So she hired me."

There I go again—turning every tiny issue into some sort of morality play. "You realize that you may be called as a witness at Skipper's trial?"

"I have nothing to hide."

"Some gossipmongers around town have suggested that you and Ann may be seeing each other socially."

"We're friends."

"Some people have suggested that you're more than just friends."

His tone remains measured. "What if we are?"

"You're a suspect in the murder for which her father has been accused."

"That's absurd."

I point out that everybody in town knows that he and Skipper had a big falling-out.

"Are you really suggesting I killed Johnny Garcia?"

"Maybe."

"I didn't. Forget it. And for the record, Ann and I are seeing each other."

"Mind if I ask Jason a few questions?"

"Be my guest." He starts to pick up the phone.

I stop him. "Dan, I'd like to talk to him alone."

"Suit yourself."

Jason Parnelli is on the phone when I take a seat in his office down the hall. Evidently, political lackeys-in-training work in small, windowless rooms. He's wearing one of those headsets that used to be the sole province of telephone operators. Now everybody has them. It's the status symbol of the electronic age. I suspect he spends most of his life working the phones, trying to raise money for the candidate of the week. At the moment, he's refilling Leslie Sherman's campaign tank. In politics, the fund-raising never stops.

Parnelli and his headset sit behind a small teak desk. There's a poster of Leslie Sherman thumbtacked to the wall behind him. He punches a button on his phone console and grins at me. His boyish good looks are beginning to show some signs of wear and tear. It happens to the best of us, I guess. There are a few crow's-feet around his eyes. "Raising money is the toughest part of this job," he says.

I agree with him. Then I ask him to tell me what happened after the summit conference ended. I have to see what I can get as fast as I can. He'll start dialing for dollars in a moment.

"Did you talk to Dan?" he asks.

"Yes."

He glances toward the door. He doesn't want to contradict his boss. It would ruin a not terribly promising political career before it ever gets off the ground. "What did he tell you?"

No way I'm going to give him the answers. I decide to lob a softball to him to see if he'll start talking. "He said you guys stuck around for a while and had a meeting next door."

"That's true."

I try again. "What were you talking about?"

"Strategy."

I mask my irritation. I ask him how long they stayed.

"Not long," he replies. He may as well have added "Dan told me not to say anything to you."

I spend fifteen minutes trying to draw him out. It's a tedious exercise. He responds to my open-ended questions with one-word answers. Finally, I ask, "What time did you leave?" I'm curious to see how his story jibes with Dan's.

"Around one-thirty. I went straight home."

He's more forthright than his boss—and his story accords with the security tapes. "Was anybody still there when you left?"

"No." He reaches for his phone.

I'm losing him. "Jason, did you guys have anybody watching Skipper?"

He pauses and takes off his headset. "What do you mean?"

"Did you hire anybody to follow him around to try to dig up some dirt? Maybe a PI?"

"Of course. It's a standard part of politics these days. You try to find out anything you can." He shrugs. "Usually the press does most of the legwork for you."

This is true. "Did your PI find anything?"

He looks uneasy. "Yes."

Uh-oh. "What?"

"He caught Skipper sleeping around with hookers."

"Male or female?"

"Just female, as far as I know."

We knew about the hookers. The fact that they were women is little consolation. I ask him why they didn't make the information available to the public.

He gives me a knowing grin. "We didn't need to. Your client was kind enough to get himself arrested for murder. That was more than enough to kill any chance he had in the election."

True enough.

"Of course," he adds, "if the charges are dropped, we're prepared to make the information available to the public."

And they say lawyers play dirty. "Did you report this information to the police?"

"Yes. We gave them some of the pictures." He pauses and adds, "By the way, those two prostitutes who appeared on the Jade Warner show were telling the truth. We have the pictures to prove it."

"Has your PI talked to the cops?"

"Yes."

I'm troubled that Roosevelt didn't mention this to me. "Mind telling me his name?"

"Sure. You may know him. He's the little guy who works out of North Beach. His name is Nick Hanson."

We're dead.

"Nick the Dick?" Rosie shouts. "They hired Nick the Dick to watch Skipper?"

Rosie, Molinari and I are meeting in the martial arts studio. I have just reported on my conversations with Morris and Parnelli. Rosie sits in disbelief. Molinari is stone-cold silent. His neighbor, "Nick the Dick" Hanson, has been working as a private investigator in North Beach for more than sixty years. Now in his mid-eighties, he started out as the lead investigator for a flamboyant criminal defense attorney named Nunzio Della Ventura, who was the law partner of Ed Molinari's father. All of Nick's children and a couple of his grandchildren work for him. He's a natty, pint-sized man-about-town who writes mystery novels in his spare time and relishes publicity.

Molinari is as concerned as we are. "Did he find anything on Skipper?"

"He found Skipper in bed with a couple of prostitutes. The good news, if you can call it that, is that they were female. He has photos of them."   ·

Molinari drums his fingers on the table. "The fact that Skipper was sleeping around isn't necessarily relevant to this case. Or news. We'll try to get the pictures excluded. He'll have nothing to talk about."

Rosie is more realistic. "He'll kill us if they put him on the stand," she says.

For the first time, Ed agrees with her. "We'd better find out what he knows," he says.

"I'm planning to."

After weeks of dead ends, we're beginning to have more trails to follow than we can handle. Pete's briefing us on Donald Martinez. He says

Martinez's influence extends far beyond his produce and construction businesses. "He owns a couple of car dealerships and several apartment buildings and hotels," he says. "When we ran his name through the SEC's database, we found that he has some significant investments in a couple of big high-tech firms. He owns controlling interests in a small investment bank and pension adviser. He's a player—and not just down here in the Mission."

We're all sitting in the living room of Tony's three-room apartment on Alabama, around the corner from his market. Tony is drinking a beer. Rosie is nursing a Diet Coke.

"He's also an important member of the community," Pete continues. "It's not only the Mission Redevelopment Fund—he donates a lot of money to the Mission Youth Center. He paid for the remodeling of the social hall at St. Peter's."

"He's done a lot for the neighborhood over the years," Tony agrees.

"That's true," Pete says, "but there's a darker side to him. The wholesale produce business has some shady players. It's controlled by a couple of operators, of which Martinez is the largest. It's not unusual for substantial amounts of cash to change hands in order to keep the lines of distribution working smoothly."

That's one way to put it. I see Tony nod, but he doesn't say anything.

Pete says, "He's been indicted a dozen times for everything from bribery to fixing contracts to tax evasion, but none of the charges have stuck. Ron Morales showed me his file. He said the feds were after him, too. They haven't caught him in the act yet."

That's news to me. I remind myself that Martinez is Tony's wholesaler. His livelihood depends upon his ability to deal with Martinez.

"He has friends in high places," Pete says. "He has good lawyers. Some people think he can put in the fix at the Hall of Justice."

That's easier said than done. The San Francisco legal community is very small and our press is very aggressive. Although the system is far from perfect and there are some cops and judges suspected to be on the take, it would be difficult to fix a case—especially one involving someone as prominent as Martinez—without somebody finding out and making a stink. "How does Martinez fit in with Johnny Garcia?" I ask.

"We haven't found any direct link. We did, however, find a connection between Martinez and Holton." He says Holton approached Martinez for money. "Martinez is the president of the Mission Redevelopment Fund. As far as I can tell, it's a perfectly legitimate nonprofit organization that provides subsidies to neighborhood businesses to encourage them to hire people from the community. Nobody has ever filed a complaint with the attorney general, and it's in good standing with the secretary of state. Its filings with the IRS and the California franchise tax board are up-to-date. Because it's a nonprofit, it has to disclose a lot of information to the public, including the names of the businesses that request funding. I asked for the list of proposals submitted to the fund in the last year. The office administrator was happy to provide it."

This is all very useful information, and it confirms what Hector Ramirez told Tony, but I find it hard to believe that even an unsophisticated guy like Andy Holton would have had the gall to ask a reputable charity for money to start a cyberporn site. I say, "You can't possibly think the Fund would have made a grant to Holton's porn business, do you?"

"I looked at his proposal. He didn't ask for money for a porn business. He asked for funding for a business that was supposed to develop proprietary software for cash and inventory management for companies in the food and produce industries. The software might have been useful to Martinez."

I'm skeptical. So is Rosie. "So," she says, "you're saying Andy Holton, a known prostitute, drug dealer and pimp, had somehow managed to develop sophisticated Web-related software that would streamline the operations of Donald Martinez's business? How do you suppose he managed to do that? Where would he get the expertise and the programming experience?"

"Look," Pete says, "I'm not saying he actually developed any software. For that matter, I'd be willing to bet you anything that he didn't. All he did was submit a proposal. It was only a couple of pages long. The fund's staff reviews them and submits the most promising to Martinez, who makes the final call. Holton's proposal made the first cut and he got an interview with Martinez. I don't know what they talked about. Maybe Holton made a pitch for his porn business. The only person who knows the answer is Martinez. In any event, the fund didn't give Holton the money. They turned him down a few weeks after his interview."

"Do you have any idea whether the cyberporn site ever got off the ground?"

"I don't know. Not surprisingly, it wasn't mentioned in the documents Holton submitted to the fund."

I call Roosevelt later the same evening. "Why didn't you tell me Nick Hanson was involved in this case?" I ask him.

"We aren't sure that he will be involved. We aren't certain his information will be relevant to your client's case. He provided photos of Skipper and several prostitutes."

"The judge will never let you introduce the pictures into evidence. They're irrelevant."

"Perhaps. We found pictures of one of the prostitutes in Skipper's study and in his storage locker. It shows a pattern of predatory sexual behavior. It may be relevant."

He's holding something back. "Are you planning to call him as a witness?"

"Not at this time."

Not exactly what I asked. "But it's possible?"

"Perhaps. We're going to spend a little more time with him. We want to find out what else he knows. Then we'll decide if he can shed any light on your client's case."

He hangs up. It is unusual for Roosevelt to give me circumspect answers. He's sending me a signal: I'd better talk to Nick Hanson right away.

27

THE INFORMATION SUPERHIGHWAY

"D-Day for DA is less than a week away."
— *San Francisco Chronicle.* Tuesday, October 5.

Hillary Payne is sullen as she sits behind the gunmetal-gray desk in her cramped office Tuesday morning. The defense team has been summoned for a private audience. The vibes aren't good. Payne tells us McNasty wanted to be here, but had a prior commitment. She passes along his regards with an ironic smile. "You know," she says, "we don't have to share this information with you."

I have no idea what she's about to share, but I have no choice. "What did you find, Hillary?" I ask.

She gestures toward Ed and asks him to turn off the lights. "You guys are going to have to come around back here to see this," she says. We crowd behind her desk. Ed's wiry body is jammed into my side. Rosie is looking over his shoulder. She's half a head taller than he is. I squeeze against Hillary's chair. The place feels like a meat locker with the refrigeration turned off.

Hillary's computer is on. She logs on to the Internet and pulls up Netscape. She moves her mouse to hit the word Home at the top of the screen. Slowly, her Yahoo! home page begins to materialize. "Someday," she mutters, "we'll get real computers."

Ed is bewildered. "What's this all about?" he asks.

If I'm guessing right, this is his first ride on the information super-highway. I don't want to ask him in front of Hillary whether he's ever heard of the Internet. A more pertinent question would be to inquire about whether he's ever figured out how to turn on the computer that sits like a trophy on the corner of his own desk.

Rosie interjects, "It will take her just a few seconds to pull up her browser." She says it in a way that suggests Ed may have some idea of what she's talking about.

Ed nods. I'll explain later.

Hillary maneuvers her mouse with her right hand. I smell her perfume. She has to reboot her computer. Ed is becoming impatient. Finally, Yahoo! appears. She doesn't turn around when she says, "Our tech guys went through your client's computer. They were able to pull up his Internet browser. They found some interesting stuff." Hillary holds up a sheet with a list of Internet addresses. She says they were able to find the sites that Skipper bookmarked. I explain to Ed that this means Skipper had tagged the sites so that he could access them without having to type in the long Internet addresses.

Hillary types in the first address. "We found a bunch of porno-graphic sites," she says. "Most involved nudity. Some involved bondage." The computer starts working. At the bottom of the screen, there is an indication of how many seconds must still elapse before the images will be clear. It takes about forty-five seconds for the first Web site to come up. A message indicates it is available only to those who are over the age of eighteen. She clicks in the appropriate place to confirm that she qualifies.

The results aren't pretty. "This one is called 'Boys from Brazil,' " Hillary says. She gestures toward the screen. "It's mostly gay sex." There are photos of naked young men. Some are bound with hand-cuffs. As my mother used to say, they don't leave anything to the imag-ination.

Hillary takes us through a quick tour of "Boys from Brazil." Then she opens another site, called "Girls of the West Coast." Once again, she goes through the screening process and pulls up a directory of the types of pictures she wants to show us. She chooses the category Bondage, and the subcategory Naked Sex.

The menu shows an array of about a dozen photos of nude women who are bound with rope, handcuffs and tape. Hillary clicks on one photo in particular. The enlarged picture begins to materialize on the screen. It's a woman who has been handcuffed spread-eagle to a four-poster, her eyes and mouth covered with duct tape.

Ed, Rosie and I stand in silence. Hillary turns toward us and says, "This is where we think Skipper got his inspiration." She points to the screen and asks, "Do you recognize this woman?"

"No," we reply in unison.

"Look closer," Hillary says. "It's Roberta, the dark-haired prostitute who appeared on the Jade Warner show."

We remain silent.

Hillary loads up another sex gallery. This one is called "Boys of the Bay Area." "We think it's produced locally," she says. She pulls up a page with tiny pictures of each of the male models who appear in the site. She clicks on the fourth picture in the third row from the top. "Recognize this man?" she asks.

It's Johnny Garcia.

She clicks on his picture. It invites us to view a montage of photos of Johnny Garcia. She clicks on a photo of Garcia handcuffed to a four-poster. His eyes and mouth are covered with duct tape.

"Do you know who put this Web site together?" I ask.

"We're going to find out."

She takes us for an endless tour of the site and a dozen other Web sites bookmarked on Skipper's computer. After almost two hours of this torture, she finally turns her computer off. She is triumphant.

I'm not about to let her see my concern. "Anything else you want to show us?" I ask.

"Nope."

"This doesn't prove anything, you know," Ed says. "It just showed somebody was able to load up a bunch of pornographic pictures on his computer."

"He had a password," she snaps. "He knew these sites were there."

I decide it may not be a good idea to let Molinari act as our spokesman on technology issues. "He may have been monitoring them for work," I say. "Maybe he was keeping them under surveillance."

I get the not-in-this-lifetime look. "We're going to introduce this material into evidence," she says. "We're going to show that he was watching pornographic sites on a regular basis. You'd better be prepared to come up with an explanation."

I assure her that we will.

I go see Skipper right away. He claims he was keeping the Web sites under surveillance. He insists the DA's office was merely trying to stem the flow of pornography in San Francisco. He insists the head of the sex crimes unit can corroborate his story. He says he did not know that the prostitute who appeared on the Jade Warner show also showed up in one of the Web sites.

His denials are getting tedious. I'm becoming frustrated when I ask him, "Were you aware that Johnny Garcia appeared in one of the Web sites? And that he was bound with handcuffs and his eyes and mouth were taped shut?"

He's indignant. "Of course not. Do you think I would recognize any of the people in those sites?"

"I don't know. Would you?"

"No. It's a coincidence. Nothing more."

There are a hell of a lot of coincidences in this case.

"Hi, Mike," Ramon Aguirre says. I am sitting next to him in the front row of St. Peter's. The church is quiet. "Are you still engaging in the same acts with your ex-wife that we discussed the last time I saw you?" he asks.

"I didn't come here to confess."

"Follow-up is part of my job. Are you and Rosie still at it?"

"I'm afraid so."

He motions toward the altar. "You know the drill."

I walk to the front of the church and say my Hail Marys. Then I return and ask Ramon, "Do you know anything about a man named Donald Martinez?"

"Sure. I know a lot about him. He's been coming to St. Peter's his entire life. We couldn't have rebuilt our church after the fire without his help. Let me show you something." He leads me out the doors and across the courtyard to the social hall in the adjacent building. The large white structure has a fresh coat of paint. He shows me a plaque next to the entrance that says "Donald Martinez Community Center." We walk inside to see the newly refurbished auditorium. A group of high school students are rehearsing a production in Spanish. "We have a new kitchen, lights, sound system and a complete retrofit," he says. "All compliments of a million-dollar donation from Donald Martinez."

Impressive. "I'm reluctant to ask," I say, "but we think Mr. Martinez may have been involved in some questionable activities."

"That's nothing new, Mike—it's been in the papers. He's been indicted a couple of times. The feds were after him for a few years because he supposedly put in the fix on some construction contracts at the airport. I think they accused him of racketeering. They were never able to prove anything. For what my two cents are worth, I think the charges were bogus. He's here every Sunday with his grandchildren."

I don't respond.

"Look," he says, "I'd like to help you. I've heard the rumors. I hold my breath every time I hear his name on the news. If he gets into trouble, so do we—he's one of our largest donors. I have a vested interest in keeping his soul clean."

"Fair enough." I ask if he has any evidence of any hanky-panky in his dealings with the church.

He gives me the response I expect. "He donates money to us through a reputable charitable foundation. If there's any funny business going on, I'm not aware of it."

"Thanks, Ramon. Sorry to ask some uncomfortable questions."

"You're just doing your job."

I'm back in my office and staring at my own computer. I'm looking at the Boys of the Bay Area Web site. I'm thinking about the meeting with Hillary Payne earlier today. All roads lead to Skipper. Two prostitutes: one male and one female. Both crossed paths with Skipper. Both were in his bookmarked Web sites. I have a gut feeling that Donald Martinez is involved in some manner—I just don't know how. The only people who could have connected all the dots were Andy Holton and Johnny Garcia. I decide to take a flier and call the only other person we know of who had a significant relationship with Johnny Garcia: Kevin Anderson. I wonder how much he really knew about Johnny's activities. Or Skipper's, for that matter.

I'm surprised when he picks up his cell phone on the second ring. "I've been following Skipper's case in the papers," he says after I greet him.

"Looks like we're heading to trial," I say.

"If there's anything I can do to help you—"

"Maybe there is," I say. It's time to call his bluff—or at least go on a fishing expedition. "Have you ever heard of a Web site called Boys of the Bay Area?"

There's an almost imperceptible pause before he says, "No."

"Were you aware that Johnny Garcia's photograph appeared on that Web site?"

"No."

I ask him whether Andy Holton was involved in a pornographic Web site. He says again he doesn't know.

Stalemate. "Do you know anybody else who was working for Andy Holton?" I ask.

I know the answer before he says it. "No," he replies.

I decide to move to another line of questioning. "Have you ever met a man named Donald Martinez?"

A second's pause, then, "I've met him."

I ask what he knows about him.

"Not much. He's a well-known businessman in the Mission. My dad bought a building from him a few years ago. We've talked about doing some deals together."

"Is he reputable? I've seen some stuff in the papers about him from time to time. Investigations. Grand-jury indictments. That sort of thing."

"He has an excellent reputation. He has donated a lot of time and money to various charities in the Mission."

"It's been suggested that Andy Holton may have approached Donald Martinez in connection with a business transaction. Do you know anything about it?"

I can hear the disdain in his voice as he says, "People like Donald Martinez don't associate with guys like Andy Holton."

28

NICK THE DICK

"Things were a little different when I started working as a PI. Nobody got bent out of shape if you roughed somebody up a little bit. Nowadays, if you touch someone, they'll haul you into court."
— PRIVATE INVESTIGATOR NICK HANSON. SAN FRANCISCO CHRONICLE. WEDNESDAY, OCTOBER 6.

The North Beach Restaurant has been a neighborhood hangout in the heart of the old Italian enclave for decades. Although it was refurbished a few years ago, it hasn't changed much. You won't find it written up in trendy food magazines. What it lacks in chic it makes up for in reliability. The long bar, paneling and heavy tables give the place the feel of a traditional men's club. As I look around the packed dining room at noon the next day, I see only two women. Some things never change.

Molinari and I are sitting across the table from Nick Hanson, the diminutive octogenarian PI who has been working in this neighborhood since the days when Joe DiMaggio used to play baseball in an empty lot on Bay Street. If you believe Nick, he used to toss a ball around with the Yankee Clipper and his brothers. You have to take everything Nick says with a grain of salt. The tales tend to get taller as the years wear on.

Ed is attacking a sixteen-ounce porterhouse steak. I have no idea how he remains as thin as a rail. He eats constantly.

Nick is chewing on a piece of french bread. At the age of eighty-five, he can still engage in what consultants like to call "multitasking." He can chew his bread, drink water and talk at the same time. Although he's only four foot ten, his double-breasted suit and the fresh rose in his lapel give him a dignified air. His new toupee is reasonably convincing. He tells me that his latest mystery novel is going to hit the shelves right after the first of the year. "It's a Mystery Guild featured selection," he says. I tell him I'll watch for it in my bookstore. He promises to give me an autographed copy.

If you want to talk to Nick the Dick, you have to observe several protocols. You have to take him out to lunch in North Beach. He never conducts business on an empty stomach. You can't rush him. He says it's bad for his digestion. You have to give him a chance to hawk his latest literary triumph. He's very proud of the fact that he's a published author. Most important, you have to let him wax about the good old days for at least twenty minutes. He loves to talk about his old neighbors, the DiMaggios. An audience with Nick is often an all-afternoon affair. It's usually worth the effort, and it's entertaining, too.

We spend almost an hour shooting the breeze. Nick reminds us he used to be the investigator for Ed's father. He says he still has lunch from time to time at the deli on Columbus that Ed's cousin has run for years. He says he and his childhood friends still attend mass at St. Peter and Paul's on Washington Square. He always calls Molinari "Eddie."

He shoves his plate across the table toward me. "You want to try some of my petrale?" he asks. "I like it broiled with just a little bit of butter."

I take a small piece of fish. I figure if I try it, he may not insist that I eat some of the stewed tomatoes that they made up just for him. Then I take another bite out of my club sandwich.

"You know," he says, "you should eat better. Your body needs protein. Next time you're here, I want you to order some real food. Get yourself a nice piece of fish."

I promise him that I'll observe the Nick the Dick diet next time.

"So," he says, "you guys are getting down to the wire on Skipper's case, eh?"

"Yep."

"I talked to the cops about it." He speaks out the side of his mouth. "They said you might be called as a witness at the trial."

"So they tell me." He takes a long drink of water. "We were following your client all over town for a few months. A guy from Leslie Sherman's campaign hired us." He explains that he and his two sons and four grandchildren work in shifts. There was a set of Hanson eyes on Skipper at every moment from the Fourth of July until he was arrested. "By the way," he continues, "if you see Dan Morris, remind him he still hasn't paid my bill."

Molinari smiles. "I promise," he says. "Did you find anything on Skipper?"

A knowing grin. "Indeed we did."

"And what might you have found?" I ask. Whenever I'm with Nick, it doesn't take long before I start talking like him.

He wipes his mouth with his napkin. "You know those two hookers who appeared on the Jade Warner show?" We get a funny look from the two men sitting at the table next to us. Nick lowers his voice and says, "I found them."

"And?"

"They were telling the truth." He glances around. He smiles toward the owner. "I've got the pictures to prove it." He reaches into his pocket and pulls out photos of the two prostitutes. These must have been the shots McBride and Parnelli told me about. Molinari and I study them. "I figure they'll call me as a witness to confirm that the two whores were telling the truth."

Nick Hanson. A veritable temple of political correctness.

"Of course," he says, "the fact that Skipper was sleeping around isn't news to anybody. On the other hand, the fact that he was sleeping around with two female hookers doesn't have anything to do with the death of a male prostitute."

I can't disagree with anything he's saying. "If that's all you found," I say, "I'm not sure there's anything else to discuss."

He calls the waiter over and orders a bowl of mixed berries for dessert. He asks for a cappuccino. Molinari orders the chocolate truffle. I order plain coffee. "Unfortunately," he says, "that isn't the end of the story. I found out a few more things that might be of interest to the cops."

Uh-oh. "Things?"

"Yeah. Things."

"Like what?"

The waiter brings Nick's berries. "I was just talking to Roosevelt Johnson and Elaine McBride about it this morning. I was at the Fairmont that night."

Come again? "You were there?" I ask.

"Yeah."

"Where?"

"The fifteenth floor of the tower."

Jesus Christ. "Where on the fifteenth floor?"

"In the room across the hall from where they found Garcia's body."

Unbelievable. "What the hell were you doing there?" My voice goes up as I say this.

He's indignant. "What do you think I was doing there? I was keeping Skipper's room under surveillance. We had a tip that he was going to be meeting with one of his hookers that night. For what Morris was paying me, I would have gotten right inside his underwear if he'd asked me."

He's the very embodiment of what people refer to as a professional demeanor.

Molinari asks him how he got upstairs.

"The service elevator."

"Why didn't your name appear on any of the police reports?" I say.

"Nobody saw me. As far as they knew, I wasn't there." He pauses. "I try not to advertise the fact when I'm watching somebody."

"How did the cops find out you were there?"

"I don't know. Maybe Dan Morris told them. I admitted it when they called to ask about it." He fingers his rose. "I don't lie to the cops, Mike. It's bad for business."

"Were you by yourself?"

"Nope. My son Rick was with me."

Just when you think you've heard it all, you find out that Nick the Dick has a son named Rick. Say that fast three times. "How did you get out of there without anybody seeing you?"

He sets down his spoon and says, "I'm a professional, Mike. I've been doing this for sixty-seven years. When I watch somebody, I'm invisible. You won't find me in the security tapes. I'm careful about stuff like that."

I'm sure he is. "So you were in the room across the hall?"

"Yeah. We kept the door closed. We were watching the door to Skipper's room through the peephole."

Here goes. "Did you see Johnny Garcia enter Skipper's room?"

He allows himself a small grin. "Indeed I did."

"At what time?"

"One minute after one o'clock in the morning."

"And did he enter the room voluntarily?"

"So it appeared. He was walking."

"Was he alone?"

"Yeah."

I ask whether Skipper answered the door and let him in.

"Yep."

"Did you see anybody else come or go?"

"Nope. We packed up and left as soon as we had the goods on Garcia."

"So you can't confirm whether anybody else entered the room after Garcia?"

"Like I said, we left right away."

"You didn't catch any of this on tape, did you?"

"Indeed we did. We have a miniature camera." He pulls out a videocassette from his briefcase and slides it over to me. "You guys might want to take a look at this," he says.

It keeps getting worse. "And you're prepared to testify to this?"

"Indeed I am."

Molinari and I return to the office after lunch. "We have a big problem," I say to Rosie. I describe our conversation with Nick the Dick.

She frowns. "Do you have any reason to believe he isn't telling the truth?"

"He's eighty-five years old. He's an institution in this town. He hasn't the slightest incentive to lie."

"Even for an extra fee?" she asks.

"Not a chance," Molinari says. "Nick doesn't care about money. He's in it for the love of the chase. And the publicity. And to sell books. I don't think he can be bought."

"Neither do I," I say. A moment later, the three of us are staring at the TV in the martial arts studio. Nick's tape is less than a minute long. It's grainy black-and-white footage of the door to Skipper's room. I can see the peephole and the room number on the door. At precisely one minute after one, a man walks up to the door and knocks. We can see only his back. The door opens, but we can't see who opened it. The man walks inside. The door closes. The tape ends.

Rosie scowls. "You can't tell it was Garcia," she says.

"You can't tell who opened the door, either," I say.

Molinari says what I'm thinking. "There's no way Nick Hanson would phony up a videotape, is there?"

"Nope. But that won't keep me from suggesting to the jury that he did."

Skipper is incredulous. "Well, now the setup is complete," he insists.

Molinari and I sit in the consultation room at the Hall later that afternoon. Ann's here, too. She insisted on being present when we told her father about my meeting with Nick the Dick. She remains stoic as I give Skipper the details of Nick's escapades in the room across the hall.

Skipper says, "So they're paying off Nick Hanson, too?" There is a tone of desperation to his voice.

"How do you explain the tape?" Molinari asks.

"It's a fraud."

"And you think the cops are in on this?" Molinari snaps.

"It wouldn't surprise me."

He's losing it. He's seeing conspiracies everywhere. "Why would Johnson and McBride pay somebody off?" I ask. "Why would they set you up? What's their motive?"

"The cops hate me."

"Where would they get the money to pay off Nick Hanson? And why would Hanson take it?"

I get an icy stare. "*You're* supposed to figure that out," he says. "You're my lawyers. You have to come up with a reason why they want to get me."

I toss my pen onto the table. "Give me something," I say. "Dan Morris hired Nick the Dick. Do you think Morris is paying him off?"

"Maybe," Skipper says.

"But *why*?" I ask again. "Once they placed Garcia in your room, they had you. Why would Morris go to all the trouble to set you up for murder?"

"Maybe Garcia was prepared to admit it was a setup. Maybe he wasn't cooperating."

"You think Morris killed him?"

He throws up his hands. "It wouldn't surprise me."

For the first time since this case started, he's acting panic-stricken. He's just accused his daughter's boyfriend and campaign manager of murder. Skipper looks at her. She's standing in the corner, her face impassive. Then he turns back to me. "He was mad at me," he explains. "And he was thinking of running for governor in two years."

This doesn't qualify as a convincing explanation. "So?" I ask.

"So was I."

I dart a glance at Molinari. "And you think he set you up for murder to get you out of the way so he could run for governor two years from now?" I ask.

"That's one scenario I've considered."

That's one scenario I hope we won't have to try to sell to the jury.

Molinari scowls. "You've got to come up with something better than that," he says. "It's preposterous."

"Look at it this way," Skipper says. "If he can pin Garcia's murder on me, he wins twice. His candidate wins the AG race and he has a clear shot at the governor's seat in two years."

It's still preposterous.

Molinari turns to Ann. "He's your campaign manager," he says. "Was he planning to run for governor?"

She glares at her father. "Maybe. And for the record, if you're suggesting that Dan had anything to do with the death of Johnny Garcia, you're wrong."

We sit in silence for a moment, avoiding eye contact. Then I say, "Skipper, do you know anything about a man named Donald Martinez?"

"I know a lot about Donald Martinez. We've been trying to nail him as long as I've been in office. The feds have been after him for tax evasion and racketeering. They think he's been taking payoffs on con- struction projects for years. We've never been able to prove anything."

Ann rolls her eyes. "Come on, Father," she says, "they've been making those charges for as long as I can remember. There's nothing to them. Besides, what makes you think Donald Martinez has anything to do with this case?"

"We have reason to believe that Martinez may have been approached by Andy Holton," I say.

"Wouldn't surprise me," Skipper says. "If somebody is involved in drugs, prostitution or gambling, Donald Martinez has a hand in it. Anything for money." He pauses and adds, "You might check with Turner."

"Why is that?"

"He's Martinez's lawyer."

I get the expected indignant response when I call Turner from my cell phone on my way back to the office. "Donald Martinez is a respected businessman in the Mission District," he says. "All of his business activities are legal and aboveboard. I will not comment further because of client confidentiality."

This doesn't stop me. "Was he involved with Andy Holton?"

"Of course not."

"Are you sure?"

"I'm sure."

Something stinks. I don't believe him. I don't trust him about this or anything else now. And it stinks even more when the guy's your client's old buddy. Whose side is Turner on, anyway?

29

THE DONALD

"We are very pleased to present this citation for community service to Donald Martinez."

—THE MAYOR OF SAN FRANCISCO.

Donald Martinez has given us a nine o'clock appointment the next morning. Rosie and I are sitting in the leather chairs in his office in an old department store at Twentieth and Mission. The building houses his produce distribution business as well as the offices of the Mission Redevelopment Fund and the Donald Martinez Charitable Foundation. Martinez could run his empire out of a high-rise downtown, but he's chosen to stay in the neighborhood. He's a tanned, charismatic man in his late fifties who looks and talks a little bit like Ricardo Montalban. He's only about five ten, but his erect bearing gives the impression that he is taller. His presence leaves no doubt that he is a man who gets what he wants.

The office is full of pictures. He's got his life on display. There's one of his wife, adult children and four grandchildren on his credenza. On one wall there is an enlarged photo of an old delivery truck bearing the logo of Martinez Wholesale Produce. Martinez tells us proudly that he started his business thirty years ago with that single truck. There are pictures of several low-income housing developments on the opposite wall. I can see citations from the mayor, the Mission Youth Center, St. Peter's and various other community agencies. We exchange polite, labored conversation for a few minutes. Then we get down to business.

We've agreed that Rosie will start. "Mr. Martinez," she says, "we understand that you provide start-up financing for local businesses." Her tone is mild.

"That's true, Ms. Fernandez. I have personally funded several new businesses in the area." He names two restaurants and three dot-coms. "I think it is important to provide economic opportunities to members of our community. Traditional sources of funding such as bank loans often are unavailable." He gives us a half-smile and adds, "In the current vernacular, I'm called an 'angel' investor."

Perhaps, but he is no angel. Rosie pushes on and asks if he ever met Andy Holton.

His response is businesslike. "I believe I met him once, Ms. Fernandez," he says. "He lived in the neighborhood. For a while, he lived at the youth center." Smooth as silk.

I sense Martinez is already trying to distance himself from Holton. I ask, "Did Mr. Holton ever approach you regarding a potential business deal?"

"Mr. Daley, people approach us all the time. As you may know, in addition to my other interests, I am the founder and the president of the Mission Redevelopment Fund, which provides subsidies to local businesses to encourage them to hire young people from the neighborhood. The fund is also involved in the development of low-income housing in the community."

All very tidy, but he hasn't quite answered my question, so I try again. "Mr. Martinez, did he ask you for money?"

His tone remains forthright. "Yes, he did. I remember receiving an inquiry from him about a year ago. I don't recall the details, although I believe it involved a new Internet software venture."

He isn't being openly evasive, but he isn't particularly forthcoming, either. Rosie asks if Holton ever demonstrated the software for him.

"No. We never saw a prototype."

There probably never was a prototype. "Did you meet with Mr. Holton about the project?"

"I believe so. The fund has very specific procedures. We asked him to provide a written proposal and a business plan, which he did." He adds, "We did not provide funding."

"Why not?"

"As I recall, his business plan was inadequate and we did not believe he had the experience or expertise to operate a start-up company."

"Mr. Martinez," I say, "did you do any checking into his background?"

"Yes. Our procedures require it. He was very young and had no experience running a business."

He judiciously leaves out the fact that Holton was a drug dealer and a pimp. "Mr. Martinez," I say, "we understand that Mr. Holton may have been involved in prostitution and drug dealing. We also have reason to believe that he was involved in the creation of a pornographic Web site. We've seen the pictures, and they are quite graphic and disturbing. We're trying to determine who may have provided the funding. Do you have any idea?"

He becomes self-righteous. "The fund does not invest in businesses that engage in pornography. There will always be people like Mr. Holton who try to make a fast buck off the weaknesses of others. I find it appalling. I can assure you that we had nothing to do with it."

He's a little too sanctimonious for my taste. "I wasn't suggesting that you were involved. Do you know who might have been?"

"I have no idea. We would never condone any such activities. It's against my principles." He pauses and adds, "We would never associate with a hoodlum like Mr. Holton."

He certainly wants to put as much space as he can between himself and Andy Holton. I'm sure he's left no tracks.

The clock continues to tick. Jury selection begins on Monday. When we get back from Martinez's office, I spend a couple of hours with our jury consultant. She gives me the conventional wisdom that we should try to load up the jury with idiots. I have worked with dozens of jury consultants over the years, with mixed results. She's fairly typical in that I find her advice useful and her attitude condescending.

After she leaves, Carolyn and I go over our witness list. You can get in trouble if you try to call somebody who isn't listed. California law doesn't like surprise witnesses. As a result, we have loaded up ours with everybody under the sun who might conceivably be called at trial, and many who won't. We lawyers tend to be pretty underhanded about the whole thing. By law, we have provided ours to the prosecution, and they've provided theirs to us. Ours includes the names of everybody who attended Skipper's rally and the entire security force at the Fairmont. We've even included McNasty and Payne; they were there that night. We're tweaking them—they know it. Judge Kelly will never let them testify. I ask Carolyn whether anybody was especially upset at receiving our subpoenas.

"Sure. Morris, Parnelli and Anderson weren't real excited about it. Donald Martinez was furious."

Interesting. He certainly gave us no indication of it earlier today. "And Ann and Natalie, too?"

"They weren't happy about it, either," she says, "but they're ready if we need them."

I hope we won't. I ask her about the prosecution's list.

"They've included most of the people you'd expect." She reads off the names of Tom Murphy, the first officer at the scene, Elaine McBride and Roosevelt Johnson, Rod Beckert and Sandra Wilson. "They've included a few of the evidence technicians and the lab guys," she says.

"And Dan Morris and Turner Stanford?"

"Yup. Along with Jason Parnelli and Kevin Anderson." She notes that everybody from the meeting in Skipper's room also appears on the prosecution's list.

"What about Nick the Dick?" I ask.

"Are you kidding? Absolutely. If they didn't put him on their list, he'd be down there begging."

At three o'clock, I gather the troops in the martial arts studio, which is beginning to look like the backstage area of a theater. We're laying out our props. We've set up easels around the room. We're trying to anticipate the prosecution's case. This is necessary, but by and large, it's an exercise in pure speculation. You never get used to the uncertainty of it.

Pete is the master of ceremonies when we talk about the physical evidence. He's been through this drill many times. He stands at the first easel and reads off the list of everything that was found at the Fairmont. "Handcuffs and the roll of duct tape with Skipper's fingerprints," he recites. "The key in the toilet. Skipper said it didn't work."

"But when the police tested it," I interject, "it did, in fact, open the handcuffs found on Johnny Garcia." When I asked Skipper about it, he had no answer.

Pete ticks off the other items found at the scene. Garcia's naked body. The champagne flutes and the duct tape that covered Garcia's eyes, nose and mouth. Then he goes through the other items relating to the events at the hotel. Garcia's fingerprints on the phone and the doorknob. The phone records. Nick Hanson's videotape. The traces of GHB found in the champagne flutes.

"There is something about the champagne flutes that's bothered me since we got the police reports," I say. "Why did they find GHB in both flutes? Doesn't that seem strange to you? I can see why they might claim that Skipper spiked Garcia's drink, but why would he spike his own? Do they think he knocked himself out?"

"We need to hammer on that," Rosie says.

Damn right. Pete runs through the evidence found at Skipper's house and in his storage locker. The magazines. The Web sites. The photos of the prostitutes. "They're going to try to show he was a pervert," Pete concludes.

The room goes silent. "They're going to put the two prostitutes on the stand," I say. "We'll need to discredit them without attacking them." A delicate dance, indeed.

We discuss Beckert's autopsy report. I explain that our medical expert will testify that Garcia died of something other than suffocation. "At the least, we'll give the jury something to think about," I say. Of course, the jury may still decide Skipper is guilty if they conclude he gave Garcia the GHB. Then again, if we can convince them that he died of a heroin overdose, we all get to go home.

Carolyn asks, "What about the urine and the semen found on the bed?"

"We're supposed to get the DNA reports next week," I say. I don't say it aloud, but if there's a match to Skipper's DNA, we're going to have a very tough time arguing that he wasn't engaged in sex with Johnny Garcia that night. I face a room full of silent stares. Everybody is thinking the same thing.

I ask Carolyn whether she found anything about the ownership of the Boys of the Bay Area Web site.

"The domain name of the Boys of the Bay Area Web site is registered in the name of El Camino Holdings, a California corporation," she says. "The only address shown in the corporate paperwork is a filing service downtown, which wouldn't provide any additional information. The company has not filed a list of officers and directors with the secretary of state, and the names of the shareholders are not a matter of public record for a privately held concern."

"Somebody is paying the bills to maintain the corporation and the Web site," I say.

"That's true. The problem is that somebody could be anywhere in the world with a computer modem."

I ask her what she's found on the Donald Martinez Charitable Foundation or the Mission Redevelopment Fund.

"They're legit. Their corporate filings seem to be in order. Martinez and members of his family make up the boards of directors of both entities, and they're both in good standing with the secretary of state and the attorney general."

"Keep digging."

"I am."

"What about other suspects?" Rosie says. "Let's see where we might be able to deflect blame."

We have gone through this exercise on many occasions. We discuss the various motives that Dan Morris, Jason Parnelli, Turner Stanford and Kevin Anderson might have had. We dismiss Nick the Dick, McNasty and Hillary, though they were all in the building at least until midnight.

Molinari leans back in his chair and says, "Natalie and Ann were there that night."

"Ed," I reply, "I just can't see it. Neither of them ever even heard of Johnny Garcia. There is no way Natalie could have managed it, planned it, even putting aside for the moment how emotionally frail she is. As for Ann, sure, she's tough and hot-tempered—but to set up her own father? And don't forget how the scandal smears the Gates name—it's tabloid heaven. Apart from the risk of being caught, there's the effect on her own political aspirations. *Mayor* Ann Gates? Daughter of the notorious pervert DA?"

Molinari sighs and says grudgingly, "Your points are well taken. Nevertheless, we shouldn't rule anything out. We may need to give the jury some alternatives. Who's your favorite? Who would you blame?"

I look around me at the silent faces. "If we have to pick somebody," I say, "then I would go with Holton. He's the most viable option. We know he was there that night." I leave out the fact that there isn't a shred of physical evidence placing him in Skipper's room. "Moreover, he can't defend himself. It's a perfectly legitimate and tried-and-true defense."

Molinari asks, "What defense is that?"

"When in doubt, blame it on the dead guy."

"Lawyers for the prosecution and District Attorney Gates will meet with Judge Joanne Kelly today to discuss evidentiary issues. The trial is scheduled to begin on Monday. Sources familiar with the case believe the defense is fighting an uphill battle."

—CNN's *Burden of Proof*. Friday, October 8.

"You can't be serious about calling Bill and me as witnesses at the trial," Hillary Payne says. It's Friday, October eighth. Monday is D-Day. Molinari, Rosie and I are meeting with the Princess of Darkness in her office first thing in the morning. As always, she tries to put us back on our heels before we get started. Hillary wakes up every morning in attack mode. For that matter, she isn't much for civility, either. She hasn't even asked us to sit down. "Judge Kelly will never allow it," she says. "You know it as well as I do."

We were invited here on the pretense of trying to narrow the evidentiary issues to be addressed at our pretrial hearing later this morning. In reality, I think Hillary wants to see if she can elicit a preview of our defense. I accepted for the same reason—perhaps we can glean a little about her strategy. My guard is up. In addition, as with any meeting with Hillary, we are giving her a free opportunity to snipe at us. I suspect she's been up all night looking forward to this. I decide to use similar tactics. "You were there that night," I say, pointing a finger at her. "You were in the room where Garcia died. You know what happened. You should tell your story."

"We left at midnight. We didn't see a thing."

"And you both went straight home?"

"Yes."

"And somebody can corroborate your story?"

She's indignant. "Of course." McNasty dropped her off at twelve-fifteen at her apartment on Russian Hill and he went straight to his apartment a few blocks away.

"How do you know where he went?" Rosie asks. I know the answer.

"He told me."

Figures. "What were you doing in Skipper's room?"

"We were showing some face time for our boss. You have to make nice-nice sometimes." She makes little quotation marks with her hands as she says this. "I hate this stuff. So does Bill."

So do I. "We're still going to raise the issue with Judge Kelly, Hillary. I don't think it's appropriate for you to try this case if you were there that night."

"She'll never go for it."

This is true. For almost an hour, we argue about the admissibility of various items of evidence. We have a particularly heated discussion about Nick's videotape and the photos of the prostitutes. Hillary doesn't give an inch. Neither do I.

We go to war.

Eleven o'clock. Rosie, Molinari, McNasty, Payne and I are sitting in the well-worn chairs in Judge Joanne Kelly's airless chambers. We are about to begin a catfight about the witnesses to be called and the evidence to be shown to the jury. We'll also get a preview of what the judge thinks about this case. Her decisions today will have a substantial impact on the course of the trial.

Judge Kelly is a large woman in her early sixties with a gruff bearing and a no-nonsense manner. She has broken a lot of new ground for women in the San Francisco legal community. She was one of the first women to make partner at a large San Francisco law firm, and she was appointed to the bench twenty years ago. She's very funny when she's telling war stories at bar association functions. When she's on the bench, however, she's all business, and when she's in chambers, she can be a terror. "Mr. Daley," she says before I can open my mouth, "have you and the prosecutors huddled to see if there's any chance that we can dispose of this case?"

"We have discussed the possibility of a plea bargain," I say. "We have not reached any common ground."

She rolls her eyes. I expect to see a lot of this expression in the weeks ahead. "Let's start looking a little harder," she says. "Are you ready to proceed?"

Five heads nod.

"Scheduling first," she says. She puts on her reading glasses. "We're set to begin jury selection on Monday. Mr. Daley, your client hasn't reconsidered his decision on the timing of this trial, has he?"

"No, Your Honor. He will not waive time."

She's annoyed. "Fine." She turns to Payne and asks her how many trial days she'll need.

"No more than five," she says.

"Perhaps somewhat shorter," McNasty interjects.

Judge Kelly glares at McNasty. "Mr. McNulty," she says, "I am assuming that Ms. Payne will act as your spokesperson today."

"Yes, Your Honor," McNulty replies docilely.

She turns to me and I tell her that we'll need no more than five trial days. She seems pleased. "All right," she says, "what are we doing here this morning?"

"Witness lists and evidentiary issues," I reply.

Another eye roll. "I've read your papers, Mr. Daley. Do you wish to add anything?"

"Yes, Your Honor," I say. "The first issue relates to the question of whether we can call Mr. McNulty and Ms. Payne as witnesses at the trial."

We've just started and I see I've already hit a nerve.

"As Your Honor is aware," I continue, "Mr. McNulty and Ms. Payne were present at the gathering in the very room where the victim, Johnny Garcia, was found dead the next morning. It is critical to our case that we be given an opportunity to cross-examine them at the trial."

She cuts right to it. "Forget it, Mr. Daley," she says. "I've reviewed their affidavits. I'm not going to allow any of the attorneys in the case to testify at the trial."

"But, Your Honor—"

She cuts me off with a wave of her hand. "No way. I'm not going to allow any of the attorneys in this case to testify at the trial," she repeats.

"Your Honor—"

"I've ruled, Mr. Daley."

I catch the hint of a grin from Payne out of the corner of my eye.

At times like this, you have to approach your job in the same manner that you attack standardized tests like the SATs. If you miss a question, you move on. Nick the Dick's videotape is up next. "Admission of this videotape would be highly prejudicial," I say. "We have no basis to authenticate it other than the word of the man who claims he shot it. It may have been edited or fabricated. We simply don't know. We have no way to verify that it was taken that night and at the times alleged by Mr. Hanson."

"Mr. Daley," the judge says, "isn't it true that the tape shows the time and date it was taken?"

"The tape purports to show that information, but you can reset the timer. If we were videotaping this meeting today, I could manipulate the timer to show any date I'd like."

She ponders for a moment and says, "Mr. Daley, we have no evidence that Mr. Hanson attempted to manipulate the timing device."

"Your Honor," I say, "we cannot verify that either the victim or the defendant appears on the tape."

Judge Kelly's irritation turns to full-blown anger. "Come on, Mr. Daley," she snaps. "It's a videotape. That's why our rules allow for cross-examination. You can ask Mr. Hanson about the circumstances surrounding the taping. You can bring in expert witnesses to show that it may have been altered. You can let the jury decide whether the defendant and the victim appear in the tape. The tape comes in."

I try again. "But, Your Honor," I say, "this tape is highly inflammatory."

She holds up her hand. "The tape comes in, Mr. Daley."

We argue for another hour. We fight about which crime-scene photos will be shown to the jury. The judge agrees to let the prosecution show only two pictures of Garcia's body. We discuss whether the prosecution should be able to introduce the photos found in Skipper's study and his storage locker. I claim that the pictures relate only to Skipper's character and should not be shown to the jury. Judge Kelly doesn't buy it. She rules that the prosecution may use the dirty pictures. For good measure, she says they can introduce Skipper's bookmarked Web sites.

We break for lunch. As we're leaving, Ed Molinari leans over and whispers helpfully, "You're getting annihilated."

The afternoon session doesn't go any better. We challenge the admissibility of the handcuff key found in the toilet on the grounds that it was taken from its plastic packaging and tested. We lose that fight. Our attempts to exclude other evidence on chain-of-custody grounds fall on deaf ears. We fight at length as to whether the prosecution will be permitted to call the two prostitutes who appeared on the Jade Warner show. I argue that Skipper's past sexual encounters are irrelevant. Payne says that Skipper's association with prostitutes is relevant to show his propensity for rough sex. Ultimately, Judge Kelly rules against me. I'm disappointed but not surprised.

Finally, we get to a discussion of whether the trial will be televised on Court TV. "Your Honor," I say, "for obvious reasons, I'm against this. It is difficult enough to empanel an impartial jury and to maintain some sense of decorum without having the entire proceeding beamed live to a worldwide audience."

Payne disagrees. "Your Honor," she implores, "this is an important case. The people deserve the opportunity to observe the criminal justice system at work."

Although Judge Kelly might like some free publicity, her better judgment prevails. "I'll make this simple," she says. "No TV."

Payne argues with her for a moment.

"I've ruled, Ms. Payne," she says. "Unless there's anything else on your plates, we're done. See you next week."

Not exactly a day filled with great victories for the good guys.

There's a message from Rosie's brother when I get back to the office. I punch in the number of the produce market.

"Hector Ramirez stopped by," Tony tells me.

"Did he find something?"

I hear Tony sigh. "No. He got fired."

Hell. "Did he say why?"

"It doesn't take a rocket scientist to figure it out. Martinez is connected in the neighborhood. He wasn't happy about some of the questions you guys were asking. He must have found out that Hector was talking to me. Hector is a smart guy who probably knows a lot more about Martinez's operation than he lets on. He gave me the information about Johnny Garcia because we're friends. If I had known Martinez was going to haul off and fire him, I never would have asked him about it. This is Martinez's way of telling Hector to mind his own business."

Rosie wanders in a minute later. I explain that I have now managed to get a good man fired from his job because he tried to help us.

She scowls. "A little message from Donald Martinez," she says.

"Is there anything we can do?"

"Know anybody who needs a good driver?" she asks.

It gets worse. My phone rings at eleven-thirty that night. Rosie's voice is cracking. "Tony was robbed," she says. "Somebody came by the shop as he was closing and slugged him on the head."

Jesus. I'm afraid to ask. "Is he going to be okay?"

"I think so."

"Where are you?"

"At home."

"Where's Tony?"

"My mom's house. He called from there."

"Call Ron Morales," I tell her. "I'll be there in a minute."

31

IT'S A MESSAGE

"Donald Martinez is a pillar of our community."
—ERNESTO CLEMENTE, DEDICATION OF NEW DORM
AT THE MISSION YOUTH CENTER.

Rosie, I and a sleepy Grace speed across the Golden Gate Bridge. It's after midnight when we arrive at Sylvia's house. She greets us at the door. Ron Morales is right behind her. "He's going to be okay," she says, "but somebody hit him hard."

"We'll take him over to San Francisco General to check him out," Rosie says.

Sylvia shakes her head. "He says no. See if you can talk him into it."

"I just talked to the uniforms at the market," Morales says. "They said it looks like it was a robbery. They took all the money and ran. They smashed up the place. It's a mess."

Tony is lying on the sofa, holding an ice pack to the back of his head, when we walk into the living room. The TV is tuned to ESPN. Rolanda is sitting next to him on the old leather chair that was re-served for Rosie's dad for years.

Rosie gives him a hug. "How're you feeling?" she asks.

"I'm fine."

"Why don't we take you over to the hospital? Somebody should take a look at that."

"I'm fine," he repeats.

Rosie persuades him to let a neighbor who is a doctor come over and examine him. Tony grudgingly agrees. "Is the market okay?" he asks. "How much did they get?"

"The uniforms said the register was empty," Morales says.

"We'll have things cleaned up right away," Rosie adds.

Tony sighs. Rolanda gives him a gentle hug. Rosie, Sylvia and I glance at each other. Morales asks him whether he saw the guy.

"He hit me before I could get a look at him."

"Any guess who might be trying to tell you something?"

"I have a pretty good idea," Tony says. "It's the way Donald Martinez tells people to mind their own business."

We camp out for the night at Sylvia's. I lie on the sofa but can't sleep. At five o'clock in the morning, I'm drinking coffee in the kitchen when Rosie walks in. She rubs my cheek. "What are you thinking about?" she whispers.

I swallow. "Nothing. I couldn't sleep."

"Come on."

"Oh, Rosie, everything stinks," I say at last. "We keep getting people hurt—Tony got slugged, Hector got fired, and just because they were trying to help us. And look at us. We're beat up ourselves. I've already spent one night in the hospital. We're spending twelve, fourteen hours a day on the case, nothing but the case. I get up every morning and take three aspirin and two Pepto-Bismols and see whether my head or my stomach starts hurting first. What kind of life is that? Zilch."

"I don't argue that," Rosie says, "but we have to do what we have to do. It'll be over soon. We committed to the case, Mike—you can't stop now. Wait till it's finished and I promise: We'll take a hard look at ourselves."

I'm not buying it. There's too much misery, too much sleaze, no pleasure in it, much less any joy. I push at her again. "We're all screwed up," I say. "Look at Grace. Our only kid—how much time do we really spend with her? We shuttle her from your house to your mom's so we can work on the trial. Here she is, growing up before our eyes, and we're able to fit in what? An hour or two max. When was the last time we spent an entire Saturday or Sunday together?"

"A couple of months ago," she says almost in a whisper. "But, Mike, listen, we can't stop for this now, we've got a murder trial on Monday."

"I'm aware of that," I say, interrupting her. "You don't have to worry; I promised to take it to the finish line, and I will. But, Rosie, we've got to change things when it's done. This is no way to live. I have to have more time for Grace. For me. For what you and I do together."

She takes my hand. "I agree with you, okay? But now isn't the time. Let it wait until the trial's over—there's too much to do now."

"There's *never* a good time. There's always another case, something else to do. I'm tired of spending my entire life taking on everybody else's problems. I've been doing it for twenty years and look at the scoreboard. We blew our marriage. We blew our pleasure in each other. Here we are, both of us single and still hopelessly dependent on each other, and we've got a daughter we love whom we can't make time for. Grace is spending the night here—again. She should be at home. We should be at home. We're missing it, Rosie. We're missing a lot of things."

She chews on her lower lip. There are tears in her eyes. Finally she says, "I think you're right. I know you are. But it'll take us time to work it out. We can't do it tonight."

"As long as we make the time—okay. But the minute this case is over, I want to talk about it."

She holds out her arms. "We will," she says. "Mike, we're going to get through this." And as I come to her, I realize I'm saying to myself I hope so.

32

LET THE GAMES BEGIN

"Jury selection in Gates trial begins today."
— *San Francisco Examiner.* Monday, October 11.

Show time. It's overcast when Rosie and I arrive at Natalie's house at eight o'clock Monday morning. Ann's face is grim when she answers the door. We've decided to go to court together today. It's a show of support for Skipper. Besides, I want to be sure Ann and Natalie don't get cold feet.

Ann is dressed in her corporate-lawyer costume: a gray suit, her blond hair pulled back, a faint blush of rouge on her cheeks. Natalie makes an appearance a moment later. "Do I look all right, Michael?" she asks.

"You look perfect, Natalie." She does.

"Is there anything you want me to do in court?"

I'm far more concerned about your daughter. "Just act natural. It's okay to show a little emotion here and there, but you don't want to distract the judge or the jury." I don't tell her that she's supposed to play the role of the dedicated wife. I kind of want her to be a little like Nancy Reagan.

"It's time for court," Rosie says.

We get to the entrance to the Hall a few minutes before nine. Molinari walks up a moment later. I ask Natalie and Ann to wait inside and I turn and face the reporters. Rosie stands to my left, Molinari to my right. Everybody will get some footage from the front steps of the Hall today. I look into the nearest camera. A dozen microphones are held up to my face, and I utter the usual platitudes. Reporters shout questions to my back as I walk into the building.

We regroup with Natalie and Ann just inside the door and walk through the metal detectors toward the elevator. The Hall is swarming with cops. Security is tight.

We enter Judge Kelly's windowless courtroom, where the gallery is packed. Her bailiff surveys the scene from in front of the bench. It's noisy. Skipper is already sitting at the defense table. Ann and Natalie greet him and then take their seats in the first row of the gallery, just behind the defense table. Although they are on our witness list, we persuaded Judge Kelly to let them sit inside. A moment later, I see Turner strolling down the center aisle. He greets Natalie warmly and shakes hands politely with Ann, then he shakes my hand and gives me a perfunctory smile. He pats Skipper on the back and gives him a thumbs-up. He, too, is on the witness list, so the judge won't let him stay in the courtroom. As he wishes us luck and leaves, I can't help thinking that I don't trust the arrogant son of a bitch. We're going to watch every move he makes, I decide. I'm going to find out what he and his client, Donald Martinez, are up to. I've assigned Pete to keep an eye on Martinez. I'm tired of getting pushed around—we're going to start pushing back.

I take the seat closest to the center aisle. Skipper will sit between Molinari and me. Rosie is sitting at the end of the table. In all likelihood, neither she nor Molinari will say a word during the trial. Molinari has placed a fresh pad of paper on the table in front of him.

Hillary Payne and Bill McNulty are at the prosecution table to my right, closest to the jury. A young ADA has joined them. Presumably, she will help Hillary present the evidence. Neither Payne nor McNasty glances in my direction. Let the games begin.

The bailiff orders us to stand. Judge Kelly walks quickly to her tall leather chair on the bench. She pounds her gavel once and tells us we may be seated. She calls for order. The courtroom becomes silent. "Any last-minute issues?" she asks.

"No, Your Honor," Payne and I say.

"Let's pick a jury."

Three days later, we're still at it. The crowds have dwindled. The press coverage is minimal. Jury selection isn't great theater. In California, the judge has the authority to ask the jury panel questions during the voir dire. While it speeds up the process, it gives the attorneys more heartburn and less wiggle room. Judge Kelly is putting the same questions to dozens of potential jurors, who may or may not answer them honestly. I'm a firm believer that most trials are won or lost during jury selection. The tricky part is that you never know whether the potential jurors are telling the truth. The odds of getting a jury you like are a little better than winning at roulette, but not much.

We haven't made as much progress as I'd like, though my jury consultant keeps telling me that we're doing fine. She claims she can pick a sympathetic jury by looking at the jurors' body language. I have my doubts. Nevertheless, you don't want to go into a major trial without a jury consultant whom you trust. She keeps reminding me that I should try to fill the jury with women and uneducated men. The women will tend to be more open-minded, she says. The men might be easier to confuse.

Slow though it seemed, by the end of the day on Thursday we've picked our twelve jurors and six alternates. It isn't a dream jury. Nine women and three men. Six of the women and two of the men went to college. So much for the theory that we should be trying to pick idiots. Three of the women are Asian, one is African American and one is Hispanic. One of the men is African American. There are four homemakers, three retirees, a waiter, a woman who works for a telecommunications company, a BART supervisor, an investment banker and a lawyer. Of those who were picked, all but one tried to give some excuse to get out of serving.

After the last alternate is seated, Judge Kelly turns to Hillary Payne and asks her if she'll be ready to give her opening statement tomorrow morning.

"Yes, Your Honor."

The best thing about hiring consultants is that they tell you what they think you want to hear. "You picked a great jury, Mike," ours assures me back at the office later that evening.

"Thanks, Barbara," I say without enthusiasm. "They'll be all right." In reality, I'm not so sure. Many expressed a great deal of animosity toward politicians and lawyers. One of the retired women expressed venom toward anybody who had ever run for office but then backed off. Judge Kelly wouldn't let me excuse her for cause.

"It will be okay," Molinari assures me. "You never know with juries."

Rosie agrees.

We speculate for a few moments about which jurors appear to be favorably disposed toward our case. "Anybody you didn't like?" I ask.

"The investment banker," Rosie and Ed say almost in unison.

I have the same instinct.

That Thursday night, I'm sitting with Pete and Tony in Tony's market. We finished cleaning the place up while Tony was staying at his mom's house. He reopened yesterday. The bump on his head has gotten much smaller. He's trying to act as if it's business as usual. There are two changes, however. The gun that he used to keep below the counter and out of sight is now tucked into his belt. He wears a light windbreaker to hide it. Technically, this violates California's law against carrying concealed weapons, but I'm not inclined to make it an issue. In addition, he has decided that he won't work alone anymore. He's hired a temporary security guard who attends State at night. He used to be the starting middle linebacker on the Mission High football team.

I ask Pete if Donald Martinez had any visitors today.

"Just one," he says. "Kevin Anderson."

Now, that's interesting. Pete's going to see if he can find out more.

On Friday morning, Judge Kelly addresses Hillary: "Are you prepared to deliver your opening statement, Ms. Payne?"

"Yes, Your Honor." Hillary is dressed in navy blue today, with an open collar and tiny gold earrings. She walks to the lectern. She's holding a stack of note cards but doesn't look at them. She gives the jury a quick smile. She's sizing them up. They're doing the same to her. She approaches the jury box. She's going to get intimate with them right away. The jurors shift in their seats. I can hear myself breathing.

"Ladies and gentlemen," she begins, "my name is Hillary Payne. I am an assistant district attorney for the City and County of San Francisco. I'm here to ask you for your help. I need you to find the truth in a very serious matter. If we work together, I know we'll be able to do so."

The jurors' eyes are focused on her. Skipper keeps his eyes straight ahead.

Payne walks toward an enlarged color photo of a smiling Johnny Garcia that she has placed on an easel in front of the jury. She points to the picture and says, "This young man was a tragic victim. His name is Johnny Garcia. He was only seventeen years old when he died in the early morning on September seventh of this year." She pauses. "Just seventeen years old," she repeats.

She scans the faces of the jurors. Her melodramatic tone doesn't seem to impress them, at least not yet. "Johnny Garcia cannot be here to tell us what happened, so we must find out for ourselves. It is our solemn duty."

I'm tempted to object on the grounds that she's supposed to stick to the facts in her opening. I remain quiet. There will be plenty of time to try to break up her flow.

She points at Skipper. "The man sitting over there at the defense table is Mr. Prentice Marshall Gates the Third. He is the defendant. He's the reason we're all here today. He murdered Johnny Garcia."

"Objection," I hear myself say in a measured, almost apologetic tone. "The determination of whether Mr. Gates murdered Mr. Garcia is a factual decision to be made by the jury. I would ask Your Honor to remind Ms. Payne to stick to the facts in her opening statement."

Judge Kelly correctly sustains my objection. "Ms. Payne," she says, "please limit your remarks during your opening to the evidence at hand."

The hint of a grin from Payne. "Yes, Your Honor," she says. She turns back to the jury. "We are going to show you that the defendant was at the Fairmont Hotel on the night Johnny Garcia was killed. He was, in fact, staying in the very room where Mr. Garcia died. We will demonstrate that the defendant hired Mr. Garcia to provide sexual favors. We will show that those activities got out of hand. And we will prove that the defendant covered Mr. Garcia's eyes, nose and mouth with tape. Finally, we will demonstrate that Mr. Garcia suffocated."

That covers it. I glance quickly at Natalie. Her eyes are shut.

Payne spends an hour summarizing the physical evidence. She doesn't leave out any of the sordid details. The jury is entranced. She's very engaging when she wants to be. They'll never know that she's an attack dog outside the courtroom. She takes a step back from the jury box. "It's no secret that Johnny Garcia was a prostitute," she says. "His short life was a sad combination of drugs, homelessness and prostitution. His life was a tragedy, but his death was a greater one. He had a job at last. He had a place to live. He was getting his life together"— she turns and points at Skipper—"until this man, a respected law enforcement officer and member of the community, took advantage of Johnny Garcia. He used his money and position of authority and committed the most heinous of crimes. He bound Johnny Garcia to a bed in the Fairmont Hotel. He covered his eyes, nose and mouth with duct tape. And he watched him die."

Skipper doesn't move.

Payne studies Johnny Garcia's picture for a few seconds. She turns back to the jury. "Ladies and gentlemen," she says, "the people of the City and County of San Francisco put their trust and faith in the defendant. He is the chief law enforcement officer of this city. That's what makes this all the more tragic."

I'll look defensive if I object.

"The defendant breached that faith," Payne continues. "He took advantage of his position and his wealth. He paid Johnny Garcia for sex. He drugged him. And then he killed him." She sighs. "We are going to be reviewing some very disturbing evidence in this case, and I realize that you may be tempted to punish the defendant just because he's a lawyer and a politician. That's not your job. All I ask is that you consider the evidence. I want you to do your part in our system to make sure that justice is served. Johnny Garcia can't find justice for himself, so it is our responsibility to find justice for him. We can't bring him back, but we can do everything in our power to ensure that the person responsible for his death is brought to justice."

She looks at each of the jurors. She glances at Skipper and shakes her head. She returns to the lectern and collects her note cards. She casts a final glance at Johnny Garcia's picture, then sits down.

Skipper whispers, "That was a good opening."

Judge Kelly looks at me and asks, "Mr. Daley, will you be making an opening statement today?" We have the option of waiting until after the prosecution has completed its case. Sometimes, it's good to delay your opening if you want to rebut specific parts of the prosecution's case. On the other hand, if you wait, the jury won't hear much from you for weeks.

"We'll be making our opening statement today," I reply. I stand and button my jacket. I walk toward the jury and look them each in the eye. Hillary started close to them. So will I.

"Ladies and gentlemen," I begin in a conversational tone, "my name is Michael Daley. I represent Prentice Gates, who has been unjustly accused of a terrible crime that he didn't commit."

It's my standard opening. Payne could stand up right now and demand that I stick to the evidence. She elects to sit tight. It doesn't play well to the jury to interrupt thirty seconds into somebody's opening.

"Prentice Gates was at the Fairmont Hotel on the night of September sixth of this year. He attended a campaign rally." I explain that the rally ended around eleven-thirty that night and that certain members of Skipper's campaign team adjourned to a room in the Fairmont tower to discuss the scheduling for his upcoming debates with Leslie Sherman. I tell them that the meeting broke up around twelve-thirty in the morning.

"Sometime between twelve-thirty and seven o'clock in the morning, something terrible happened. A young man named Johnny Garcia was found dead in Mr. Gates's room. The chief medical examiner believes the young man was suffocated, although we will demonstrate that he may have died of a drug overdose." I look at the investment banker. "There is no doubt that the death of Johnny Garcia is a tragedy. And there is no doubt that a horrible event occurred at the Fairmont Hotel that night. On the other hand, Ms. Payne's attempts to blame this entire episode on Mr. Gates are wrong."

I tell them that Skipper was fifteen points ahead in the polls. I explain that he was going to win the election. I note that he is a bright man and an astute politician. "Bringing a known prostitute to a crowded hotel after a big political rally involved a tremendous risk," I say. "Mr. Gates's wife and daughter were at the hotel that night. It makes no sense."

I remind them that reasonable doubt is a very tough standard. I tell them that the prosecution has asked for the death penalty, which makes this a matter of life and death. I ask them for their help. "I need you to help me find the truth," I say. "I need you to work through the evidence with an open mind. After you hear the evidence, you will agree with me that the prosecution cannot prove its case beyond a reasonable doubt."

I get very little reaction from the jurors. Some lawyers believe you win cases in opening statements. I'm not one of them. Although you try to deliver your carefully rehearsed speech in a particular way, you never know if the jurors are with you. A million things are racing through your mind as you're talking. You look for reactions. You worry about the length of your opening. You try to anticipate what will happen during the trial. I give a quick look at Rosie. She closes her eyes. It's time to finish up.

I give them my standard closing that I won't try to mislead or confuse them. It's a lie. I'd confuse them up the kazoo if I thought it would get Skipper off the hook. For better or for worse, that's my job. I ask them for their assistance in making the justice system work. I ask them to keep an open mind. "When we're done," I say, "I'm sure you will agree with me that Prentice Gates is not guilty of these terrible crimes."

I return to the lectern. I gather my notes. I walk to my chair and sit down.

The judge decides to adjourn for the weekend.

Skipper is lukewarm in the consultation room a few minutes later. "It wasn't a great opening," he says.

Thanks.

"I think it got the job done," Molinari says mildly.

Ann has joined us. She says, "I was watching the jurors. I think they liked Hillary better."

I'm beginning to understand how politicians must feel when the pundits offer instantaneous critiques of everything they say and do.

"Who's on their list for Monday?" Skipper asks.

"They're going to start with Tom Murphy, the first officer on the scene. Then they'll call Joseph Wong and some of the security people from the Fairmont. Next are Rod Beckert and some of the technical people."

Ann looks at me and says, "Well, I hope you'll be able to elevate your performance to the next level."

Thanks, Ann.

It's Saturday morning. We've come to see Kevin Anderson, and we're sitting in the kitchen of his remodeled flat on Guerrero Street. The building predates the 1906 earthquake. The living room and dining room have been remodeled with pieces from the Victorian era. Kevin's place has been written up in one of those fancy architectural magazines that you see in the reception areas of big law firms.

Rosie and I are drinking espressos from tiny porcelain cups. Kevin is dressed in a light blue polo shirt and khaki pants. Classical music plays on the stereo. The smell of croissants wafts from the kitchen. He's one of the most eligible bachelors in the Bay Area. Life is good, though he wasn't notably pleased when I called to say we wanted to see him.

"Kevin," I say, "we understand that you may be working on a deal with Donald Martinez."

He freezes for just an instant. "That's true. It's a low-income housing project. We're trying to get the approvals. The project has been delayed—temporarily."

"How is Martinez involved?"

"He has a lot of experience in the real estate business. He has good connections at City Hall. He's helping us get entitled."

"Entitled?" I ask.

"Yes. He's helping us get the building permits we need."

There is undoubtedly more to this than Kevin is telling us. The permit procurement process in San Francisco may be the most byzantine political construct in the western hemisphere. There are severe limits on development, and everything must be approved by the planning commission, which is supposed to be a group of independent experts but in reality is often populated by political cronies of the mayor. Most major development projects include competing proposals that are submitted in a "beauty contest" to the planning commission. Each contestant hires a juice lawyer and one or more consultants who can bring political muscle to bear. Martinez has as much muscle as anybody in the city.

"Who's funding the project?" I ask.

"That's confidential."

Rosie sighs. "Kevin," she says, "we can go downtown and pull the permit applications. Is your father funding this deal?"

"No. We're trying to fund it ourselves. My dad wasn't real excited about it." He explains that his father thinks the returns on low-income housing projects are marginal.

"I take it Turner is representing you?"

"Yes. He's the best."

I ask him what's holding up the process.

"Funding. We need to raise about five million dollars to start predevelopment. It's going a little more slowly than we had hoped. We have to raise the money by the end of the year or the option we have to purchase the property will expire."

"Do you have any funding sources lined up?"

"We're working on it."

"Did you also go to Donald Martinez for cash?"

He hesitates and says, "Yes."

"What did he say?"

"He's thinking about it."

Pete calls Sunday night. He says Turner was at Martinez's office today. I tell him about my conversation with Anderson and suggest that perhaps they were discussing the low-income housing deal. I ask Pete if he saw anything unusual.

"Maybe. They went for a walk late in the day."

"So?"

"They walked around the corner to a residential hotel on Valencia Street. They stayed there for just a few minutes."

"Maybe they're thinking about buying it."

"I doubt it. It's a dive."

"What's it called?"

"The Curtis Hotel."

I'll add it to my list. The Jerry, the Royan and now the Curtis. What would Donald Martinez and Turner Stanford be doing at a joint like that?

33
THE LEADOFF HITTER

"The prosecution will call the first officer at the scene and the San Francisco
medical examiner today."
— NewsCenter 4 Legal Analyst Mort Goldberg.
Monday, October 18.

"Please state your name and occupation for the record," Hillary Payne
begins on Monday morning.

"Officer Thomas Murphy. I've been a patrolman with the San
Francisco Police Department for almost twenty-five years."

Tom Murphy was the first officer at the scene. Not the sharpest
tool in the shed, but a hardworking street cop. He's mid-forties and still
looks as though he just stepped off the boat from Dublin. His uniform
is pressed. He's likable—a good opening act. Payne is going to build
her case slowly. First, she'll show that Skipper was there that night and
that he had motive and opportunity. Then she'll demonstrate that he
had direct contact with the materials used to suffocate Garcia. I expect
her to make all the pieces fit. That's what good prosecutors do.

"What time did you arrive at the Fairmont?" Hillary asks.

"Seven-fourteen A.M. I responded to a 911 call." He explains that
Dave Evans, the head of security at the Fairmont, met him at the front
desk and escorted him to Skipper's room. That's where he found

Skipper, Joseph Wong and other members of the Fairmont's security staff.

The first score goes to Payne. She's placed Skipper at the scene. "What did you do when you arrived at Room 1504?" She's letting Murphy and the jury settle in.

"I called for assistance. I cordoned off the area." He describes the SFPD's procedures for securing a crime scene. He says that reinforcements began to arrive within five minutes.

Payne asks the judge to allow her to introduce a schematic drawing of the fifteenth floor of the tower into evidence.

"No objection," I say.

Payne asks Murphy to describe the scene in Skipper's room.

He walks to the diagram and gestures with his index finger. "We found the victim in Room 1504," he says. He explains that Garcia's body was lying on the bed. He points to the chair in front of the TV, where Skipper was sitting. He shows the locations of the bathroom and the doorway leading to Room 1502.

"Officer Murphy," Payne continues, "was anybody else staying on the fifteenth floor that night?"

"Objection. Foundation. Officer Murphy has testified that he arrived at seven-fourteen. He doesn't have any personal knowledge of who was staying on the fifteenth floor that night." It's a minor point. I just want the jury to know I'm paying attention.

"Sustained."

Payne is undaunted. "I'll rephrase. Did you find any other guests staying on the fifteenth floor that night?"

"No." He explains that they checked the hotel records later on and determined that there were no other registered guests staying on the fifteenth floor that night.

"Thank you," she says, sounding pleased. "Did you have an opportunity to interview the defendant when you arrived?" She isn't going to mention Skipper by name.

"Yes."

"Could you describe his demeanor?"

"Objection. Speculation."

"Your Honor," Payne says, "I wasn't asking Officer Murphy to speculate about how the defendant felt. I'm asking him to describe how the defendant looked and acted."

"Overruled."

Murphy turns toward the jury. "He was uncooperative. He appeared tired and confused."

"How was he dressed?"

"He was in pajamas and a bathrobe."

"Was he belligerent?"

"No. Just uncooperative."

Payne stops. Not the answer she wanted. "What else did you observe in Room 1504?"

"The victim was handcuffed to the bed."

"And there was duct tape on the victim's face, wasn't there?"

"Objection. Leading." Might as well let Hillary know we're listening.

"Sustained."

She tries again. "Did you find duct tape on the victim's face, Officer?"

"Objection. Leading."

"Overruled."

"No. Mr. Gates indicated that he had removed tape from the victim's face. Mr. Joseph Wong, the room service waiter, also indicated that the duct tape had been used to cover the victim's eyes, nose and mouth." He explains that he found a wadded-up ball of used duct tape on the nightstand and an unused roll, along with a telephone. He describes the handcuffs, the champagne glasses and the champagne bottle. He says all of the items were catalogued into evidence.

"Did the defendant offer any explanation for how the victim got into his room?"

"No, ma'am."

"Did he open the door and let him in?"

"He didn't explain, ma'am," he says again.

"Did the victim have his own key?"

"I don't know, ma'am."

"Did someone bring him into the room?"

Enough. "Objection. I'm sure Ms. Payne can list at least a hundred other ways that the victim *didn't* get into Mr. Gates's room."

"Sustained. Move along, Ms. Payne."

"Officer Murphy, did Mr. Gates have any explanation, plausible or otherwise, for how the victim got into his room?"

"No, ma'am."

"And how he died?"

"No, ma'am."

"No further questions."

I approach the witness box. "Officer Murphy," I say, "you've testified that Mr. Gates was uncooperative and confused when you arrived."

"That's true."

"Did it occur to you that Mr. Gates may have been drugged?"

"Objection. Speculative."

"Your Honor," I say, "I'm not asking Officer Murphy to speculate as to whether Mr. Gates may have been drugged. I'm asking him whether he considered the possibility."

"Overruled."

Murphy pauses. "That went through my mind," he says.

"But you didn't insist that Mr. Gates take any sort of blood or alcohol test to determine whether there were any substances in his system?"

"No."

It's the answer I wanted, although he was under no legal duty to require Skipper to take such tests. You try to make small points early in the case. "And neither did any of your colleagues, including the homicide inspectors."

"Not as far as I know."

So far, so good. "Officer," I continue, "did you see the tape on the victim's face?"

"No. The tape had already been removed."

"I see. So you have no firsthand knowledge of how the tape was removed from the victim's face, or whether it was ever on his face at all."

"Objection. Speculative."

"Overruled."

"That's true," Murphy acknowledges.

"And therefore, by the same token, isn't it also true that you have no firsthand knowledge of how the tape found its way onto the victim's face in the first place, right?"

He glances at Payne. "That's also true," he says.

"In fact, except for the descriptions provided by Mr. Gates and Mr. Wong, you have no personal knowledge of whether the wadded-up tape was ever on Johnny Garcia's face. Isn't that correct, Officer?"

"That's correct."

It's all I can do. Murphy is here to set the scene, not to win their case. "No further questions."

Joseph Wong sits in the witness box. He looks at the jury when he explains that he has been a room service waiter at the Fairmont for almost forty years. Payne asks him to describe what happened when he arrived at Skipper's room.

"There was no answer when I knocked on the door," he says. He explains that he is supposed to knock twice. If there's still no answer, he's supposed to open the door and leave the tray.

"And that's when you discovered the defendant and the body of the victim?"

"Yes."

"Where was the victim?"

Wong takes a deep breath. "He was lying on his stomach on the bed. He was naked. He was handcuffed to the bed. His eyes, nose and mouth were covered with tape."

Another score for the prosecution. They've shown Garcia's face was covered with tape. Payne decides to clarify one point. "If he was lying on his stomach, how could you tell that his face was covered with tape?"

"His head was turned to the side. I could see the tape covering his eyes, nose and mouth."

"Could you tell whether the victim was dead?"

"Objection. Mr. Wong isn't qualified to make a medical determination."

"Sustained."

Payne shows the hint of irritation. "Mr. Wong," she says, "was the victim moving?"

"No."

"Was he breathing?"

"Not as far as I could tell."

Payne is pleased. She's making small points now, and they'll do. We know Garcia was dead. She doesn't need Wong to confirm the time of death. Rod Beckert will take care of that. "What was the defendant doing when you walked in?"

"He was sleeping. I woke him up and he called security."

"And what was the defendant's reaction to all of this?"

"He was confused."

"Confused?"

"Yes. He was disoriented. He told me to leave. He said he would take care of everything."

"Did you leave?"

"No. I waited for the security people to arrive."

"And what did you do while you were waiting?"

He looks at Skipper. "I observed Mr. Gates remove the tape from Mr. Garcia's face."

"Did you touch the body?"

"I don't think so."

"Did you remove any of the tape?"

"No. Mr. Gates did."

"Mr. Wong," Payne continues, "you've testified that the victim was handcuffed to the bedposts."

"Yes."

"Did you attempt to remove the handcuffs?"

"Mr. Gates did. He had a key. He tried to release them, but he wasn't able to do so."

"Do you know what happened to the handcuff key?"

"No."

"Would it surprise you to find out that the key was found in the toilet?"

"Objection. Speculation."

"Sustained."

Hillary keeps Wong on the stand for a few more minutes. Over my objections, he repeats that Skipper was confused and says at times he was belligerent. Hillary sits down. She's gotten all that she needs from Wong, and he's connected with the jury.

I walk toward Wong and stand near the jury box. I don't want to crowd him, but I don't want him to become too comfortable, either. "Just so we understand the situation when you arrived," I say, "the victim, Mr. Garcia, was in the bed, naked."

"Yes."

"And he was handcuffed to the bedposts and his face was covered with tape."

"Objection. Asked and answered, Your Honor." Hillary is getting a little jumpy.

"Overruled." Judge Kelly turns to me. "Let's keep moving forward, Mr. Daley."

"Understood." I repeat the question. Wong acknowledges that Garcia was, in fact, handcuffed to the bed and his face was covered with duct tape.

"Mr. Wong," I say, "when you arrived in the room, isn't it true that Mr. Gates called security right away?"

"Yes."

"And he removed the tape from the victim's face and attempted to release the handcuffs, right?"

"Yes."

"So although you described him as confused, he was, in fact, coherent enough to attempt to assist the victim, right?"

Wong has no choice. "That's true."

"And he made no attempt to leave the room or to flee before the police arrived, did he?"

"No."

"And he answered their questions as soon as they arrived?"

"Yes."

One more. "So although Mr. Gates had just woken up, it would be fair to characterize his behavior as helpful, wouldn't it?"

Hillary has heard enough. "Objection. State of mind."

"Overruled."

Wong nods and acknowledges, "I guess you could say that was true."

"Mr. Wong," I continue, "you don't know how the victim got into Mr. Gates's room, do you? You didn't see him arrive in Mr. Gates's room, did you?"

"No."

"And you didn't see Mr. Gates, or anyone else for that matter, handcuff the victim to the bedposts, did you?"

"No."

"And you didn't see Mr. Gates or anyone else cover the victim's face with duct tape, did you?"

Payne objects. "Speculative," she says.

"Overruled."

Wong acknowledges that he didn't see Garcia enter the room. And he didn't see anyone cover his face with duct tape.

"So," I conclude, "you don't know what happened in that room that night, do you?"

He hesitates for an instant and says, "No."

"And it's possible that somebody other than Mr. Gates could have brought Mr. Garcia's body to Room 1504 at the Fairmont, handcuffed Mr. Garcia to the bed and taped his face."

"Objection. Speculative. Argumentative."

True and true.

"Overruled."

Wong is perplexed. "I don't think that's what happened," he says.

I tell him that's not what I'm asking him. I reiterate that I'm asking whether it's possible that somebody else might have done it.

"I suppose when you put it that way," he says, "the answer is yes."

"No further questions."

Payne spends the afternoon questioning Dave Evans and members of the Fairmont's security staff. They introduce the portions of the videos that show Skipper and his entourage heading for the elevators. Evans confirms that there were no other guests staying on the fifteenth floor that night. He tries to demonstrate that it would have been very difficult for anybody to get up there without being caught on camera. On cross-exam, I get him to admit that there are parts of the building that are not captured on camera.

The security tapes provide no clear-cut winners and no big losers. I get Evans to acknowledge that there were many other people in the building. Among others, I have him point out Dan Morris, Jason Parnelli and Turner Stanford in the videos. Turner's appearance after three o'clock in the morning raises a few eyebrows in the jury box. We volley for most of the afternoon. Finally, I run the portion of the videos that were taken at three A.M., point to Andy Holton and ask, "Mr. Evans, were you able to identify this man?"

He looks troubled. "Yes. His name is Andrew Holton."

"And he arrived at the hotel at approximately three A.M. and left a short time thereafter?"

"Yes."

"And did you know that Mr. Holton and the victim, Mr. Garcia, had a relationship?"

Evans pauses. "Yes. We understand that they were roommates."

"That's right. And do you have any idea why Mr. Holton may have come to the hotel in the middle of the night?"

"I don't know."

Bullshit. "Do you know if Mr. Holton and Mr. Garcia were getting along?"

"I don't know."

Fair enough. "Did you know that they were also business associates?"

"No."

"In fact, Mr. Garcia was a male prostitute and Mr. Holton was, for lack of a better term, his pimp, right, Mr. Evans?"

"Objection. Foundation. Mr. Evans knows nothing about this, Your Honor."

"Sustained."

I'll try to plant one more seed. "Mr. Evans, assuming, for the moment, that Mr. Holton was, in fact, Mr. Garcia's pimp, doesn't it strike you as odd that Mr. Holton showed up at the hotel in the middle of the night?"

"Objection. Assumes facts that are not in evidence."

She's right. "Sustained." The judge instructs me to move to another line of questioning.

"No further questions, Your Honor." We'll get back to this when it's our turn.

34
"IT'S ALL DESCRIBED IN DETAIL IN MY AUTOPSY REPORT"

"The prosecution is upping the stakes today. They're going to call Dr. Roderick Beckert, the highly respected chief medical examiner."

—KGO RADIO. TUESDAY, OCTOBER 19.

☀

"The people call Dr. Roderick Beckert," Hillary Payne says.

The following morning, the chief medical examiner of the City and County of San Francisco strides to the front of the courtroom. Beckert's wearing his "going-to-court" uniform: a charcoal business suit with a white shirt and a burgundy tie. The white coat is back in his office. His beard has been recently trimmed. He's been assigned to play the role of the voice of medical wisdom. The battle is now fully engaged.

Payne has Beckert state his name and occupation for the record. She asks him how long he's been the chief medical examiner.

He turns toward the jury and says, "Twenty-nine years."

Nods from the jury box. Beckert sounds good when he's just introducing himself.

Payne begins the process of having him recite his credentials. I stipulate to his expertise right away. His qualifications aren't at issue. Payne walks to the evidence cart and picks up Beckert's autopsy report on Johnny Garcia. She asks Judge Kelly for permission to introduce it into evidence.

"No objection, Your Honor," I say. I try to act as if the autopsy report has about the same significance as the sports section in this morning's *Chronicle*. The jury won't buy it, of course, but it can't hurt to try. Every nuance in court has meaning.

Payne hands the report to Beckert and returns to the lectern. She wants to give him plenty of room to present his findings in all of his glory. It's a smart move.

Skipper leans over and whispers, "Is there anything you can do to slow him down?"

"Not much," I reply. We're going to take our lumps for a while.

Payne has Beckert identify his autopsy report. He holds it as if it were the Holy Grail. "I prepared this report," he confirms.

"And did you perform the autopsy on the victim, John Paul Garcia, on September seventh?"

"Yes, I did."

"Could you please summarize your findings?" Payne asks.

"Of course, Ms. Payne." Beckert takes his glasses out of his breast pocket and puts them on. He pretends to shuffle through his report. "The victim, John Paul Garcia, died of asphyxiation between the hours of one and four A.M. on Tuesday, September seventh." He confirms that Garcia had been handcuffed to the bed. "His eyes, nose and mouth had been covered with duct tape. We were able to confirm this because we found traces of adhesive chemicals on the victim's face. The chemicals were identical to those on a used wad of duct tape that was found on the nightstand in the defendant's room that night." He explains in medical and layman's terms that the victim lost consciousness when his air passages were blocked. "He died within minutes after the tape was placed on his face."

The courtroom is silent. Payne pretends she's studying her notes. In reality, she is giving the jury a little time to digest Beckert's testimony. Finally, she says, "How did you determine the time of death, Dr. Beckert?"

On cue, McNasty puts a poster-size version of one of the crime-scene photos on an easel just in front of the jury box. It shows a naked Johnny Garcia, handcuffed to the bed, lying on his stomach, his head turned to the right. Beckert asks Judge Kelly if he can stand to point to the photo. She agrees.

"It's all described in detail in my autopsy report," Beckert says. He points to the discoloration on the side of Garcia's stomach and the other areas of his body that are touching the bed. He explains that when the heart stops beating, gravity causes the victim's blood to flow to the lowest points of the body. "This discoloration," he says, "is called lividity. In my best medical judgment, the victim, John Paul Garcia, died on this bed while he was lying on his stomach, his hands and feet handcuffed to the bedposts." He looks triumphant. It's almost as if he's daring me to question his conclusion. He drones on for a few minutes about body temperature and the food in Garcia's stomach. I steal a glance at the investment banker on the jury. He's nodding. Sounds good to him.

Skipper leans over and whispers, "Can't you object to any of this?"

I whisper back, "We have to wait till cross."

Payne leads Beckert through another half hour of testimony on the finer points of his craft and his determination of the cause of Johnny Garcia's death. I object from time to time, without consequence. Beckert is a terrific witness. Payne is a good prosecutor. She should score points with Beckert on the stand.

I think Payne is about to wrap up when she asks Beckert to turn to page seventeen of the autopsy report. "That's the section entitled 'Chemical and Other Substances Found in the Victim's Bloodstream,' isn't it, Doctor?"

"Yes."

Hell. They're making a preemptive strike to undercut our argument that Johnny Garcia didn't suffocate but died of a drug overdose. I expected this.

"Could you please tell us what chemical substances were found in the victim's bloodstream?"

Skipper nudges me to object. I can't. I have no grounds.

Beckert puts his glasses on and pretends to study a couple of pages of his report. "We found three chemical substances in the victim's bloodstream," he says. "Alcohol, heroin and gamma hydroxy butyrate, commonly known as GHB." He explains to the jury that GHB is a date-rape drug that causes unconsciousness when it is ingested.

Two of the women in the front row of the jury lean forward.

Beckert says there was a small amount of alcohol in Garcia's bloodstream when he died. When Payne asks him how much alcohol, he says, "Well below the threshold for being convicted of driving under the influence."

"And the heroin?" Payne asks.

"A tiny amount." He goes into detail in both medical and layman's terms to describe the level of heroin in Garcia's bloodstream. "It appears that the victim injected heroin at some point within the last few hours of his life."

Payne hones in. "Was there enough heroin in the victim's bloodstream to cause an overdose?"

"In my best medical judgment, no." They go through the same analysis for the GHB. He concludes that there was not enough GHB in Garcia's bloodstream to have caused his death.

"Is it possible that a combination of heroin, alcohol and GHB caused a reaction or imbalance that could have led to Mr. Garcia's death?"

"Objection. Speculative."

"Your Honor," Payne says, "I'm asking for Dr. Beckert's medical judgment on this issue. Mr. Daley has already stipulated to his expertise."

She's right.

"Overruled."

"No," Beckert says with Walter Cronkite-like authority. "The victim died of suffocation."

"One final question, Dr. Beckert. Isn't it true that you found traces of the victim's semen on his body and on the bed?"

"Objection. Leading."

"Overruled."

"Yes," Beckert says. "We found traces of the victim's semen."

Payne asks him what he concluded from the discovery of the semen.

Beckert exhales and says, "I concluded that the victim engaged in sex shortly before he died."

"No further questions."

I'm up right away. I don't want Judge Kelly to call a recess and give the jury a chance to let Beckert's testimony sink in. "Dr. Beckert," I begin, "you concluded that Johnny Garcia died in the stomach-down position in Room 1504 based upon the discoloration of his body, which is known as lividity, correct?"

"Yes."

I'm going to lead him shamelessly. I want yes-or-no answers. If he starts to explain things, my goose is cooked. "And you indicated that you estimated that time of death was between one and four in the morning."

"Yes."

"Dr. Beckert," I say, "you have testified that the victim, Johnny Garcia, died of suffocation."

"Yes."

"Yet you have also testified that Mr. Garcia's bloodstream contained alcohol, heroin and a potent sleep-inducing narcotic called GHB."

"Yes."

"And both heroin and GHB are very strong chemical substances, aren't they, Doctor?"

"Of course."

I ask him to turn to the pages in his report that deal with the chemical substances found in Garcia's bloodstream. He does so. Then he takes off his glasses and puts them back in his breast pocket.

"Doctor," I say, "isn't it possible that Mr. Garcia injected so much heroin into his bloodstream that he died of an overdose?"

He's indignant. "No, Mr. Daley. I have already testified to the fact that there was only a tiny amount of heroin in his bloodstream. He died of asphyxiation."

"But isn't it theoretically possible that he died of an overdose?"

"Objection. Speculative."

"Overruled."

"It isn't possible," Beckert replies.

"No chance at all?"

"No chance at all."

"Heroin's pretty potent stuff, Doctor."

"No chance at all," he says again.

Well, if the heroin didn't do it, maybe the GHB did. "Doctor," I say, "GHB is pretty potent stuff, too, isn't it?"

"Yes."

"And if you take enough GHB, it could kill you, right?"

"That's true."

"In fact, there have been some recent cases where individuals who took large amounts of GHB have died, right?"

He has no choice. "Yes."

"In a couple of those cases, the individuals who provided the GHB were charged with murder, weren't they?"

He grudgingly acknowledges that this is true.

"Is it possible, Doctor, that the victim in this case might have died from an overdose or adverse reaction to GHB?"

"No. There wasn't enough GHB in his system to cause such a serious reaction."

Not so fast. "Doctor, when did you perform the autopsy?"

"At approximately three o'clock on September seventh."

Perfect. "Doctor, GHB remains active in your system for only a few hours, right?"

He reflects and says, "That's correct."

"In fact, it metabolizes within four to six hours, doesn't it? And as a result, by the time you did your autopsy, there was no way you could have known how much GHB was consumed by the victim, could you?"

Beckert swallows. "In my best medical judgment," he says, "there were only traces of GHB in the victim's system at the time of his death. There is no evidence that he died of an overdose or any cause relating to the consumption of GHB."

It's all I can get. I didn't figure he'd budge. "Doctor," I continue, "isn't it possible that the combination of heroin, alcohol and GHB caused a reaction that killed Mr. Garcia?"

"Objection. Asked and answered."

"Overruled."

"No, Mr. Daley," Beckert says. "It isn't possible. While there were traces of each of those chemicals found in the victim's bloodstream, there wasn't any evidence that Mr. Garcia overdosed or that the combination of chemicals had any bearing on the cause of Mr. Garcia's death."

Our expert will have a different take on this subject. We volley for the next thirty minutes. I try to get Beckert to admit that GHB is a toxin that could kill you if it is combined with other drugs. He argues that there wasn't a shred of evidence that there were enough chemicals in Garcia's system to cause any material adverse reaction. Payne objects every two or three questions. Judge Kelly is getting annoyed.

It's almost noon when I ask Beckert my final questions. "Dr. Beckert," I say, "did your autopsy reveal any preexisting medical conditions that may have contributed to Mr. Garcia's death?"

"No."

"Isn't it true, Dr. Beckert, that Johnny Garcia had been addicted to heroin?"

"Objection. Foundation."

"Sustained."

I introduce a medical history provided by Ernie Clemente at the time Garcia moved out of the Mission Youth Center. Beckert acknowledges that he has read the history and confirms that Garcia had been addicted to heroin.

"And isn't it true that Garcia was clean at the time of his death, except for the heroin that you found in his bloodstream?"

"That's what we understand from his medical history, Mr. Daley. I have no way of corroborating whether he was still clean."

"And isn't it true that recovering addicts are sometimes more susceptible to overdoses with relatively small amounts of heroin or other substances?"

Beckert glances at Payne. "There is some current medical thinking to that effect, Mr. Daley."

"If that is the case, Doctor, isn't it possible that Johnny Garcia may have had an adverse reaction to even a small amount of heroin? Perhaps a reaction that might have killed him?"

Beckert is unimpressed. "No, Mr. Daley," he says. "It may happen from time to time, but it isn't what happened here."

"Doctor, are you also aware that Johnny Garcia had a heart condition?"

"Yes. The same medical history indicated that he had a coronary arrhythmia, an irregular heartbeat."

"Isn't it possible, Doctor, that Johnny Garcia's heart may have given out as a result of ingesting a lethal combination of alcohol, heroin and GHB?"

Beckert pauses. I catch a glimpse of Natalie in the gallery. She is staring straight ahead.

"No, Mr. Daley. That isn't what happened in this situation. Mr. Garcia's heart did not fail."

It's the best I can do. "No further questions, Your Honor."

35
A PARADE OF EXPERTS

"Daley won't be able to shake them. They're the best evidence techs on the SFPD."

— NEWSCENTER 4 LEGAL ANALYST MORT GOLDBERG. TUESDAY, OCTOBER 19.

Hillary Payne is running a beautifully choreographed show. She keeps promising Judge Kelly that she'll have her case wrapped up by the end of the week. First up on this afternoon's dance card is Sandra Wilson, the FET who gathered the evidence at the Fairmont. She's sworn in. She looks uncomfortable in the stuffy courtroom. In her loose-fitting maternity clothes, she appears as if she could give birth in the witness box. One of the women on the jury gives her a thumbs-up. Sandra hasn't said a word, but she's already bonding. I won't object to anything she says unless I must. I want her off the stand as fast as possible.

Payne starts to run her through her impressive credentials, and I stipulate to her expertise before they get to her college education. Like Rod Beckert, there's no point in giving Sandra a chance to read her résumé to the jury. She confirms that she was the lead evidence technician at the Fairmont. She describes the scene. She explains the procedures for collecting and tagging the evidence. She and Payne walk though a rehearsed description of how each piece of evidence was catalogued.

Skipper whispers, "We're getting killed."

Payne spends about twenty minutes standing next to the exhibit cart. She has Sandra identify every piece of evidence from Skipper's room: the handcuffs, the key, the champagne bottle and glasses, the duct tape, the telephone. I object when they introduce the handcuff key. It's overruled.

They go through a similar exercise for the evidence found at Skipper's house. "We followed standard police procedure there, too," Sandra says. She identifies the handcuffs found in Skipper's study, as well as the dirty pictures and the storage locker key. Finally, they go through the same ritual for the items found in the storage locker. Sandra has done her job. She's off the stand in less than thirty minutes. My cross-exam is short. We won't win any arguments on chain-of-custody issues.

Payne gathers further momentum when she calls Sergeant Kathleen Jacobsen to the stand. "I am an evidence technician with the SFPD," Jacobsen says. "I've held the position for twenty-four years." Jacobsen is a calm, gray-haired woman in her early sixties. She's a national authority on evidentiary matters. They've put the first team on this case.

Payne walks to the evidence cart and picks up four sets of handcuffs that are neatly wrapped in clear plastic. "Are you familiar with these?" she asks.

"Yes." She identifies each set. "Those are the handcuffs that were found on the wrists and ankles of the victim, Johnny Garcia. He was handcuffed to the bedposts in Room 1504 of the Fairmont tower."

Payne is pleased. "Did you find any fingerprints on the handcuffs?"

"Yes. The defendant's." There is no doubt.

"And these handcuffs are standard issue for law enforcement officers in San Francisco?"

"Yes."

They go through a similar exercise for the handcuff key, except that she says the key is too small to find identifiable fingerprints.

"And this key was tested to determine whether it fit the handcuffs we just discussed, right?"

"Objection. Leading."

"Sustained."

"I'll rephrase." She turns back to Jacobsen. "Did you test this key to determine whether it would open the handcuffs we just looked at?"

"Yes."

"And did it fit?"

"Yes." She adds, "All four sets of handcuffs."

Payne is very pleased now. "Sergeant," she continues, "do you have any explanation as to how the handcuff key found its way into the toilet in the defendant's bathroom?"

"Objection. Speculative."

"Sustained."

Payne is trying to remind the jury that Skipper tried to get rid of the key. She picks up the champagne glasses from the evidence cart and has Jacobsen identify them. "Sergeant," she says, "did you find any fingerprints on these champagne glasses?"

"Yes." She points to the first glass. "We found the defendant's fingerprints on that one." She points to the second glass. "We found the defendant's and the victim's fingerprints on that one."

Payne studies the glasses for a moment. "And what did you conclude from that?" she asks.

Everyone in the room knows the answer. Jacobsen confirms that Skipper touched both glasses and Garcia touched one of them.

Payne takes the unused roll of duct tape from the evidence cart. She has Jacobsen confirm that Skipper's fingerprints were found on the roll of tape. Likewise, she takes the strips of used duct tape that are packed in plastic and shows them to Jacobsen. She confirms that Skipper's fingerprints were found on the used tape, too.

Skipper leans over to Molinari and whispers, "Isn't there anything we can do to stop this?"

Ed shakes his head. I hear him whisper, "Nope."

Payne leads Jacobsen through a similar analysis of the handcuffs, magazines and photos found at Skipper's house and in the storage locker. His fingerprints were on all of them. The local law schools should bring their students down here to watch a textbook direct exam of an excellent witness by a well-prepared prosecutor. We take a pounding for an hour and a half before Payne sits down.

I approach Jacobsen. If I try to embarrass her, I'll look like an imbecile. From the cart I take the four sets of handcuffs that were used to bind Garcia and hand them to her. "Sergeant," I say in my most respectful tone, "did you find any fingerprints on these handcuffs besides those of the defendant?"

"No."

"Are you aware that Mr. Gates attempted to remove the handcuffs from the victim?"

"That's what I understand."

"And it is therefore possible that the defendant may have gotten his fingerprints on these handcuffs when he tried to remove them, isn't it?"

She has no choice. "Yes," she responds.

"And even though you have testified that you found Mr. Gates's fingerprints on these handcuffs, you cannot, in fact, tell us whether he got his fingerprints on these handcuffs while he was trying to take them off or when he was putting them on. Isn't that a fact, Sergeant?"

"Objection. Asked and answered."

"Overruled."

Jacobsen has no choice. "That's true, Mr. Daley. It would be impossible to determine precisely when he got his fingerprints on these handcuffs."

I glance back toward Skipper.

"Sergeant," I continue, "let's talk about the handcuff key for a moment." I ask her to confirm that she did not find any fingerprints on the key. She acknowledges that this is true. I hand her the strips of used duct tape in their plastic wrappers and ask, "You testified that you found Mr. Gates's fingerprints on these strips of tape, didn't you?"

"Yes."

"In fact, it is certain that Mr. Gates may have gotten his fingerprints on these strips of tape when he removed them from the victim's face, isn't it?"

She glances at Payne and says, "It's possible."

Juries hate games of semantics, but I have to push the point. "It isn't just possible, Sergeant. It is an absolute certainty that Mr. Gates may have gotten his fingerprints on the tape when he removed it, isn't it?"

I've framed the question in a manner that she has only one possible response. "Yes," she says.

Thank you. "So, in other words, Sergeant, isn't it fair to say that even though you found Mr. Gates's fingerprints on the handcuffs and the duct tape, you have no conclusive evidence that Mr. Gates put the handcuffs or the duct tape *on* the victim, Johnny Garcia?"

"Objection. Asked and answered."

It's a legitimate objection.

"Sustained."

I've made my point. "No further questions."

Payne finishes the afternoon with Roosevelt Johnson, who goes through every dirty picture and magazine found in Skipper's study and storage locker. The testimony about the copies of *Hustler* and the pictures of the naked prostitutes seem to offend several members of the jury. There is very little I can do about it. The searches were legal.

Payne leads Johnson through a tour of Skipper's bookmarked Web sites, complete with graphics and projections. We spend an hour looking at pictures of naked men and women, many of whom are bound and gagged. At ten to five, they focus on the Boys of the Bay Area Web site. A copy of the site's home page flashes on the screen. Payne directs Johnson to a photo on the screen. "Do you recognize this young man, Inspector?" she asks.

"Yes," he replies. "That's a picture of the victim, Johnny Garcia."

We adjourn for the day.

That night, Rosie, Pete and I are at Tony's produce market. You can't tell it was trashed just a few days ago. Tony stands by the cash register, his arms folded. Ernie Clemente is standing by the door, eating an apple. Pete has just handed me a copy of a printout of the home page of the Boys of the Bay Area Web site. There's a handwritten street address on Valencia in the corner and the words *Room 204*.

"Where did you get this?" I ask Pete.

"I gave it to him," Ernie says.

"How did *you* get it?"

"A couple of months ago, Andy Holton asked one of my kids if he wanted a job doing some modeling. Turns out he meant nude modeling. The kid was supposed to meet Andy at this address on Valencia. He chickened out and didn't show up."

"How old is the kid?"

"Seventeen."

"Is he willing to testify?"

"I doubt it."

Then again, we may not need him. "Where is this address?"

Pete says, "It's the Curtis Hotel on Valencia. It's the building where Martinez and Stanford went a couple of days ago." He hands me another piece of paper. "This is a certified copy of the deed of the building located at the same address on Valencia Street. I got it from the county recorder's office."

I scan the legal document. The owner of the building is listed as the Mission Redevelopment Fund. Bingo. It's the connection we've been looking for between Andy Holton and Donald Martinez.

Rosie looks at Pete and asks, "Have you gone up there and checked out Room 204?"

"Sure, but it was locked. Nobody answered when I knocked. And I wouldn't think of breaking the door down. Breaking and entering is illegal," he says primly.

"So what do you propose we do?" I ask.

"What every good citizen would do—call the cops."

We call Ron Morales at home and meet with him at Mission Station. Pete tells him that he's received an anonymous tip that there are illegal activities going on in Room 204 of the Curtis Hotel. Morales is cautious. He legitimately points out that the information is still too sparse to justify a search warrant. He suggests that Pete keep the room under surveillance for a couple of days. "Maybe we'll spot somebody who is involved in running the operation," he says. He offers backup if necessary—Mission Station is just down the block.

I ask, "What if we don't find anything?"

"Then we'll pull a warrant and go in."

36
A CHANGE OF PACE

"Things are going to liven up considerably this morning."
—NewsCenter 4 Legal Analyst Mort Goldberg. Wednesday,
October 20.

Mort the Sport is all excited as he gushes, "Today should be a big one. The prosecution is going to call a known prostitute to describe her sexual escapades with District Attorney Gates. If you think this trial has been sordid so far, just wait. We're going to start wallowing in the mud now."

They cut to the pretty young woman who reads the traffic reports.

Hillary Payne stands and says, "The people call Roberta Hall." There's murmuring in the courtroom. The petite prostitute who appeared on the Jade Warner show walks up the center aisle. She's wearing a pantsuit with a plain white blouse this morning. She's left off any makeup and her short hair is simply set. Payne has told her not to dress like a prostitute.

She's sworn in. She takes her seat in the witness box, pours herself a glass of water and drinks it. Then she pours herself another one. She adjusts the microphone.

Hillary picks up the cue. She moves toward her and says in a comforting voice, "Would you please state your name for the record?"

"Roberta Hall." She tugs at her blouse.

"And what is your occupation?"

She clears her throat and says, "I'm a prostitute."

"Ms. Hall," Hillary begins, "you've met the defendant, Mr. Gates, haven't you?"

"Objection. Leading." No sense letting anybody get too comfortable here.

"Sustained."

Payne is annoyed. "I'll rephrase. Ms. Hall, have you ever met the defendant, Mr. Gates?"

"Yes."

"When did you first meet him?"

"About a year ago. I was working the street near the Fairmont." She looks over at him. "He drove by in his car. He stopped and asked me what I could do for him."

"Objection," I say. "Move to strike. Hearsay. Furthermore, this entire subject matter is irrelevant to this case."

We've been down this path in chambers. I've lost. Judge Kelly is going to let Roberta testify as to her sexual encounters with Skipper. I'm objecting to make a record for our appeal.

"Overruled," says Judge Kelly.

Skipper stares straight ahead as he whispers, "You have to stop this."

I don't respond. I glance at Natalie. She doesn't move.

Payne asks, "How long were you providing services for Mr. Gates?"

"Objection. No foundation."

"Overruled."

"About six months."

Payne asks Roberta what types of services she provided for Skipper.

"At first," she says, "we had sex in the conventional way."

"In other words," Payne says, "you engaged in consensual sex in which Mr. Gates penetrated your vagina with his penis."

"Objection, Your Honor. I think everybody in this courtroom understood what the witness meant."

"Sustained." Judge Kelly casts a scornful eye at Hillary, who looks contrite. She turns back to Roberta and asks whether Skipper's demands changed after their first few appointments.

"Yes," she says in a voice that is barely above a whisper. She takes a deep breath. "On our third date, he asked me if we could try something a little more exotic."

Payne tries to look inquisitive. "Exotic?"

"Yes."

"When he used the word *exotic*, what did you think he meant?"

"I thought he meant he wanted me to perform oral sex on him."

"And is that, in fact, what Mr. Gates had in mind?"

"Objection. Irrelevant."

"Overruled."

"No, Ms. Payne," Roberta replies. "He didn't want me to perform oral sex on him."

"I see. What did he want?"

"He wanted to tie me up."

Murmurs. Judge Kelly pounds her gavel. The courtroom becomes silent. Payne asks Roberta to finish her story.

"He said he liked to handcuff women to his bed. He called it a harmless fetish. He promised he'd never hurt me. He said it was a turn-on for him."

There are tears in Roberta's eyes. Skipper doesn't move.

"So you agreed to let Mr. Gates handcuff you?"

"Yes. He was paying me five hundred dollars a night. I've had drug problems. I have a child to support. I didn't think I had any choice."

Skipper glares at me. If I interrupt her, I'll only give the jury more reasons to be sympathetic toward her.

"So," Payne continues, "you let Mr. Gates handcuff you to the bed and have sex with you."

"Yes."

"And did this satisfy Mr. Gates?"

"Objection. State of mind."

"Sustained."

Payne doesn't pause. "Ms. Hall, did Mr. Gates ask you to engage in any other unconventional sexual acts?"

"Objection. Move to strike the use of the term *unconventional*."

"Sustained."

Payne tees it up once more. "Did Mr. Gates ask you to engage in any other sexual acts?"

"Yes." She's crying now. "He used to like to cover my eyes and mouth with tape."

Payne glances at the jury. The women in the front row look sympathetic. "And what did he do while you were blindfolded and gagged?"

She wipes her eyes with a tissue. "He used to do it to me."

"In other words, Ms. Hall, he used to penetrate you while you were handcuffed to the bed and your eyes and mouth were covered with tape."

Natalie closes her eyes.

"Yes," Roberta says.

Judge Kelly asks her if she would like to take a short break. She takes a deep breath and declines. She wants to get off the stand as fast as she can.

"Ms. Hall," Hillary says, "did Mr. Gates ask you to engage in any other sexual acts?"

"Yes. After a few weeks, the handcuffs and the tape weren't good enough for him. He said he wanted something more."

"And what was that?"

"One night, while I was handcuffed to the bed and there was tape covering my eyes and mouth, he decided to cover my nose with tape, too."

"He tried to suffocate you?"

"Yes. I couldn't breathe."

"And what happened while your eyes, nose and mouth were covered with tape?"

"He came."

The gallery buzzes. Judge Kelly pounds her gavel.

"You mean he penetrated you at that time?"

"Yes. He told me it was a big turn-on for him."

Skipper stares straight ahead. Natalie's eyes are still closed. Ann glares at me.

"And did he remove the tape after that?"

"Yes."

Payne walks back to the lectern. "Ms. Hall, did you ever tell Mr. Gates that you didn't want to do these acts?"

"Yes. I told him I was willing to let him handcuff me to the bed, but I wouldn't allow him to suffocate me."

"And what was his response?"

"Objection. Hearsay."

"Overruled."

"He hit me in the face. He broke my cheekbone. He told me that I had to do what he wanted or he would have me prosecuted and sent to jail. He said I'd lose my daughter."

"When did you break off the relationship, Ms. Hall?"

"After he broke my cheekbone. I told him I didn't care if he prosecuted me or not. I couldn't take the physical and emotional abuse anymore."

"No further questions, Your Honor."

Judge Kelly decides it's a good time to call a short break.

I approach Roberta. "Ms. Hall," I begin, "would you like another glass of water?" I'm not being a nice guy. I want her to drink a lot of water. It will make her look nervous.

"No, thank you."

"Okay." I glance at the jury. "Ms. Hall, before we talk about your relationship with Mr. Gates, I'd like to ask you a few questions about yourself. For example, where did you get that nice outfit you're wearing?"

Her eyes dart toward Hillary. "Ms. Payne got it for me."

"And did you pay for it?"

"No. I presume Ms. Payne's office paid for it."

"I see. Is that because you couldn't afford it?"

"Objection. Relevance."

"Your Honor," I say, "we intend to demonstrate that this witness has been provided with special treatment in order to obtain her testimony. Her economic situation is relevant to this discussion." It's an old ploy. If I can't punch holes in her message, I can attack the messenger.

Judge Kelly overrules the objection but tells me that I'll have to show relevance in a hurry.

"Ms. Hall," I repeat, "did Ms. Payne's office buy you that outfit because you couldn't afford it?"

"Yes."

"And you have a child to support, don't you?"

"Yes."

"And a drug habit?"

She glances at Payne, who nods. "Yes."

"And isn't it a fact, Ms. Hall, that you were paid the sum of twenty-five thousand dollars to appear on a local TV show a few weeks ago?"

She looks down. "Yes," she whispers.

"And who paid you that large sum of money?"

"I'm not sure."

"Your Honor," I say, "I would ask you to instruct the witness to answer the question."

Judge Kelly tells Hall that she has to reply.

"The money came from Mr. Parnelli."

"Jason Parnelli? The man who works for Dan Morris, the campaign manager for Mr. Gates's opponent, Leslie Sherman?"

"Yes."

"And did Mr. Parnelli instruct you what to say on that show?"

"No."

"Isn't it a fact, Ms. Hall, that Mr. Parnelli told you that you wouldn't get the money unless you implicated Mr. Gates?"

"No."

"Isn't it a fact that they told you to lie?"

"No." She's crying.

"Objection. Argumentative."

"Ms. Hall," I continue, "did Mr. Parnelli pay you to appear at this trial?"

"No."

"And did he tell you what to say here today?"

"Objection. Ms. Hall has already indicated that she has not been paid to appear at this trial."

"Sustained."

"Just a few more questions, Your Honor," I say. I turn back to Hall. "Isn't it true, Ms. Hall, that you have negotiated a deal with Ms. Payne whereby you would agree to testify today in exchange for which the DA's office agreed not to prosecute you for prostitution?"

She looks at Payne but doesn't respond.

"Isn't that true, Ms. Hall?" I repeat.

She's silent.

"Your Honor," I say, "would you please instruct the witness to answer the question?"

She does.

"It's true," Hall says. "Ms. Payne agreed to give me immunity if I agreed to testify." She turns and looks at the jury. "But I'm telling the truth about my relationship with Mr. Gates."

"Move to strike, Your Honor."

"The jury will disregard Ms. Hall's last comment."

"No further questions, Your Honor."

"The jury thinks I'm a pervert," Skipper says as he chews on a turkey sandwich during the lunch break.

Yes, they do. "At least we were able to show that she accepted money. Payne took a calculated risk by putting her on the stand. She knew we'd raise the issue that Parnelli paid her to appear on Jade Warner's show. At least we were able to mitigate the damage to a degree," I reply.

"Not by much," he says.

"Look, Skipper, it's not going to get better. You know the evidence they're going to bring up. I'll do everything I can to cast doubt on it, but add it all up and it's going to have an effect on the jury."

All I get is a glare. He isn't giving an inch. I remind him that Nick the Dick is their next witness. "He's going to show his videotape and testify that you let Garcia into the room," I warn.

"It's a crock."

"We'll see."

37

NICK THE DICK REDUX

"When we were kids, Joe DiMaggio played shortstop. I played second. His brothers were in the outfield. We used to play in an empty lot on Bay Street. I taught Joe how to slide. He taught me how to hit. He was better at sliding than I was at hitting."

—NICK HANSON. SAN FRANCISCO EXAMINER. WEDNESDAY, OCTOBER 20.

The trial resumes at one o'clock. "The people call Nicholas Hanson," Payne says.

On cue, the door to the courtroom opens and there's Nick the Dick, standing as tall as he can. He takes his own sweet time strolling down the center aisle. He nods to the reporters. He works the room. He shakes hands with the gossip columnist from the *Chronicle*, who is sitting in the second row. The only thing that's missing is a small band to play "Hail to the Chief."

He stops in front of the bench and says, "It's always a pleasure to see you, Your Honor."

I catch the tiniest smile in the corner of Judge Kelly's mouth. "Nice to see you again, Mr. Hanson," she says.

The bailiff tells Nick to raise his right hand and asks him if he swears to tell the truth.

"Indeed I do," he replies. He struts up the steps and climbs into the witness box. He adjusts the microphone and pours himself a drink of water. He offers a drink to the judge, who declines. He gives the jury a quick salute, then he looks at Payne, who has been taking all of this in at the lectern. There are giggles throughout the courtroom.

After a moment, Judge Kelly decides she's seen enough of this spectacle. She calls for order and pounds her gavel.

Skipper leans over and whispers, "I don't like it."

I'm with him on that.

Payne stands at the lectern and smiles. Having a witness like Nick the Dick on your side is like winning the lottery. She's going to play this for all it's worth. "Good afternoon, Mr. Hanson," she sings out like a camp counselor. She asks him to state his occupation for the record.

"I'm a private eye," he says. He looks at the jury when he speaks. His left eye twitches. "I've been doing this for about sixty-eight years."

"How old are you, Mr. Hanson?"

I could object on grounds of relevance. I'd tick off the retirees on the jury if I did.

"Eighty-five."

"And you still work full-time?"

"Indeed I do. I've lived and worked in North Beach my entire life. My office is on Columbus Avenue. My children and a couple of my grandchildren work for me."

Grins in the jury box.

Payne turns serious. "Mr. Hanson, were you hired to observe the defendant?"

"Indeed I was."

"Why were you hired?"

"The defendant was running for attorney general. His opponent's campaign manager, Mr. Dan Morris, hired me in June of this year to keep the defendant under surveillance."

"Why?"

He gives her a sideways look. "Come on, Ms. Payne. You've been around the block a few times. Politics is a nasty business. They wanted me to dig up some dirt on him."

"In other words, Mr. Hanson, they wanted you to follow the defendant and see if you could find him in a compromising position?"

Enough. "Objection. Leading."

"Overruled."

"That's right, Ms. Payne," Nick says. "They wanted me to see if I could find him in a compromising position."

Payne is pleased. "Mr. Hanson," she continues, "did you keep Mr. Gates under surveillance in June, July and August of this year?"

"Indeed I did." He explains that he and his sons and grandsons work in shifts. "We had a set of eyes on him at all times," he says. "We were paid a thousand dollars a day to see what we could dig up."

"And were you able to dig up anything on the defendant, Mr. Hanson?"

He's triumphant. "Indeed we did, Ms. Payne. For that kind of money, I couldn't disappoint Mr. Morris and his campaign staff."

"Objection," I hear myself say. "Move to strike Mr. Hanson's editorial comments."

"Sustained." Judge Kelly instructs Nick to limit his answers to the questions asked by Payne. The chances that he will do so are one in a million.

Payne asks Nick what he found.

"We found the defendant had an ongoing relationship with a prostitute named Roberta Hall. We saw them together on several occasions. I took pictures of a few of their meetings. Mr. Morris was very pleased with our work."

Skipper stares straight ahead. Natalie doesn't move.

Payne introduces photos taken by Nick and his sons showing meetings between Skipper and Hall. I object on the grounds that Skipper's relationship with Hall is irrelevant to the case at hand. Judge Kelly overrules my objections. She seems intent on punishing Skipper. They project the photos onto a large screen in the front of the courtroom. Skipper wasn't very discreet.

"Mr. Hanson," Payne asks, "were you at the Fairmont Hotel on the night of September sixth and the early morning of September seventh of this year?"

"Indeed I was."

"Would you mind telling us where you were?"

"I was in Room 1503 in the tower. It's the room across the hall from where the defendant was staying."

"What were you doing there?"

"I was keeping the defendant's room under surveillance."

"And how were you doing that?"

"We removed the peephole and we mounted a miniature video camera in the opening. We aimed the camera toward the door to the defendant's room. Then we sat and waited."

The jury is entranced.

"What time did you arrive at the Fairmont that night, Mr. Hanson?"

"A few minutes before eleven."

"Was anybody with you?"

"My son, Rick."

"And did you go straight to Room 1503?"

"Yes. We had to be careful, though. We didn't want anybody to see us setting up our equipment. So we came in through a back door and we went up to the tower by the service elevator. We had studied the layout of the hotel. We were dressed as maintenance people."

"How long were you in the room across the hall from Mr. Gates?"

"Until a few minutes after one o'clock."

Payne pauses to gather her notes. "Mr. Hanson, did you observe the victim, Johnny Garcia, enter Room 1504 that night?"

He doesn't hesitate. "Indeed I did."

"At what time?"

"One o'clock in the morning."

"And did he enter the room voluntarily?"

"Yes. He was walking."

"Was anybody else with Mr. Garcia?"

"No."

"So nobody pushed him, carried him or otherwise assisted him when he entered the defendant's room?"

"That's correct."

"And Mr. Garcia was conscious at the time?"

"Objection," I say. "Asked and answered. Mr. Hanson has testified that Mr. Garcia was walking. Presumably, he was conscious when he was doing so."

"Sustained."

Payne doesn't slow down. "Did the defendant open the door to let Mr. Garcia in?"

"Yes."

"And did the defendant close the door after he let Mr. Garcia in?"

"Yes."

Payne gives a glance to the jury. Skipper is chewing on his lip. "Mr. Hanson, did you happen to get this encounter on videotape?"

"Indeed we did."

"And how did you get your videotaping equipment upstairs without it being noticed?"

"Our equipment is very small. It fit in a toolbox."

Payne asks Judge Kelly if she can introduce Nick's videotape into evidence. I renew my objections. She overrules me. McNasty pulls a TV and VCR in front of the jury. He pops a cartridge into the VCR. They play the video three times. It's only about fifteen seconds long. First they play it at regular speed, then in slow motion, then at regular speed again. The jury is spellbound. It's always good to give them something to watch. Nick sounds like a TV announcer as he points out the highlights. He shows a man walking up to the door. The door opens. The man goes in.

"Mr. Hanson," Payne says, "is it clear to you that the victim, Johnny Garcia, entered Mr. Gates's room in the early morning of September sixth?"

"Yes."

"No further questions, Your Honor."

It's late in the afternoon. Judge Kelly asks me how long my cross-exam will last. I don't want her to adjourn until morning. I don't want to give the jury the chance to spend the night thinking about Nick's testimony. "Just a few questions," I say.

I approach Hanson and stand right in front of him. "Mr. Hanson," I begin, "what did you do after you allegedly observed someone enter Room 1504?"

"We packed up our gear and headed out. We were on our way down the hall, when we saw Mr. Morris and his associate, Mr. Parnelli, in the doorway to Room 1502. We stopped and left the videotape with them." He smiles. "Needless to say, they were ecstatic."

"So, Mr. Morris and Mr. Parnelli were still in Room 1502 when you left?"

"That's correct."

"Do you know when they left?"

"No."

It isn't exactly a smoking pistol, but at least he's placed Morris and Parnelli in the room next door after everybody else left. "Mr. Hanson," I say, "let's take another look at your videotape."

"Of course, Mr. Daley."

I cue the video machine. I run the tape in slow motion. The courtroom is silent as we observe the man Nick says was Johnny Garcia approach Skipper's door. "Mr. Hanson," I say, "would you agree that you can see only the back of this man's head?"

"I'd have to look at the tape again."

I rerun it. The grainy tape shows only the back of the man's head.

"It was Garcia," Nick says.

"But you would agree that you see only the back of his head, right?"

"It was Garcia," he repeats.

"And you would agree that it was dark and this was taken through a small peephole."

He repeats it was Garcia.

Let's try something else. I run the video one more time in slow motion. "Mr. Hanson," I say, "you can't see who opened the door, can you?"

"It was the defendant."

I rerun the tape one more time. "You can see the door open, Mr. Hanson. But you can't see who opened it. You can't see a face behind the door."

He's adamant. "It was Mr. Gates," he says.

"Did you hear Mr. Gates say anything?"

"No."

"Did you record any sound from this incident?"

"No."

I give the jury an incredulous look. "This videotape shows nothing more than the back of a man's head. It shows a door opening. It doesn't show Johnny Garcia. And it doesn't show Prentice Gates opening the door."

"Objection. Mr. Daley is making a speech."

Indeed I am.

"No further questions of this witness, Your Honor."

Judge Kelly adjourns for the day.

Outside the courtroom, Nick the Dick is surrounded by reporters. "Tough cross-exam today," he tells nobody in particular. "I still think we made our points."

I tell Molinari and Rosie that I'll catch up with them at the office. I wait for the media horde to break up. I catch Hanson. "Nick, can I talk to you for a few minutes?"

"Of course."

We stroll to the side of the long corridor, not far from the elevators.

"Nice work on cross today," he says.

"Thanks. I didn't mean to beat you up."

"You were just doing your job."

So were you.

"It was Garcia," he says. "And I'm sure it was Skipper who let him in."

"Nick," I say, "I want to ask you something. And I don't know how to do this without being direct, so here goes—"

"I didn't dummy up the tape, Mike," he says. "I'm eighty-five years old. I don't need to do that kind of stuff. It would be beneath my dignity."

I think he's telling the truth. "I thought so."

"So why did you want to talk to me?"

"Are you busy the next week or so?"

"I'm always busy. Why?"

"Can I hire you to watch somebody for a few days?"

"A thousand dollars a day."

"Deal."

He asks me who I want him to watch.

"Turner Stanford."

"It's a deal," he says.

38
"SEEN ANYBODY YOU RECOGNIZE?"

"Prosecutors Promise New Evidence Tomorrow."
— SAN FRANCISCO EXAMINER. WEDNESDAY, OCTOBER 20.

That night, Rosie, Tony and I are sitting by the front window at the Pancho Villa, across the street from the Jerry Hotel. Tony has been coming here every night after he closes his shop. He has a regular spot by the window. He brings a book and tries to look like he's reading. In reality, he's looking out the window in a last-ditch effort to try to find my attacker. We're going to have to do something very nice for him after all of this is over.

I've checked in with Pete. He's still sitting in his Plymouth across the street from the Curtis Hotel. Nobody has come or gone from Room 204 in the last two days. He's getting impatient. I'm getting frustrated. I've told him that if nothing happens in the next day or so, we'll ask Ron Morales to pull the warrant he promised and find out what's up there.

I take a bite out of a steak burrito. "How's your head?" I ask Tony.

"Fine. How's yours?"

"Okay." I ask him whether the police have any leads on the man who robbed him.

"Nope. They won't find him."

Probably not. "You don't have to come here every night, you know."

"I know."

Rosie asks, "Seen anybody you recognize?"

"I recognize everybody." He acknowledges, however, that he hasn't seen anybody who resembles the man who hit me or the man who robbed him. He asks how the trial is going.

"Not great." I ask him how he's getting along.

He takes a drink of soda. "I'm okay," he says. "It's a little lonely. I don't get to see enough of Rolanda. She's busy with school and the job." A halfhearted shrug. "It could be worse."

I ask him if he ever called his friend's sister.

"No. Not my type. Are you still interested?"

"Maybe next time," I say. Then I add, "You just need to give it some time. You need to make some new memories for yourself."

He finishes his burrito and nods to the young man working behind the counter. "One more soda," he says.

An attractive young woman enters the restaurant by herself and smiles at Tony. His eyes light up. He smiles back. "Hi, Louisa," he says.

He introduces us to her and she goes up to the counter and places an order. "She's Hector's sister," Tony explains. He adds in a whisper, "And she's single. We're going to a movie next week."

Rosie grins. "That's great, Tony."

He grins back. "I haven't been on a date in twenty-five years. I'm a little out of practice."

"It's like riding a bike," I say.

"Things have changed since I was young. Will she be offended if I don't ask her to sleep with me on the first date?"

I wink at Rosie. She gives me a surreptitious thumbs-up. "I think you'll be safe if you take things a little more slowly," I say. "Besides, if you ask her, Hector will beat the living daylights out of you. You can play it by ear. And don't stay here all night."

To my surprise, the lights are on when Rosie and I return to the office. We find Carolyn sitting behind Rosie's desk, studying an official-looking document. She's startled when we walk in. She takes off her glasses. "We have a real problem," she says.

"What now?" I ask.

"The DNA reports came back," she says.

"So? We already knew that Johnny Garcia had sex shortly before he died."

"That's true," she says. "Now it's been confirmed. The semen on the bed matches."

"And?"

"Page three," she says.

She hands me the report and I flip to page three. It says that they found Skipper's semen on the bed, too.

I call Ann to let her know and ask her to tell Natalie. She says she's coming right over. We're huddling in Rosie's office when she arrives. "This isn't happening," she says. She reports that her mother took the news of the DNA results badly.

"Is somebody with your mother tonight?" I ask.

"Yes. I asked Turner to come." She pauses. "But she may not make it to court tomorrow. I'm worried."

"What are our options?" Molinari asks.

"None that are good," I say. "We can't argue that Skipper's semen was planted. That's absurd. We can't challenge the validity of the DNA tests; everyone knows they are reliable."

"Maybe he can deny it," Ann suggests.

There's a great idea. Let's just say the problem doesn't exist and hope it goes away. "You know that won't work," I snap. "We'll lose what little credibility we have left if we do so."

She doesn't respond.

I hold my hand up and say, "We have no choice. We have to admit that Skipper engaged in sex in that bed that night."

Molinari asks, "And how would that help us?"

Rosie interjects, "That's irrelevant. Mike's right. If we come up with some absurd argument or look like we're trying to hide it, the jury will turn on us. We'll have to find other ways to get to reasonable doubt."

I look at Ann, who says, "Father will never admit that he had sex with another man."

"Maybe he's going to have to," I reply.

It's almost two in the morning as we drive across the Golden Gate Bridge toward Marin County. "Do you think Skipper really had sex with Garcia?" I ask Rosie. The fog is heavy. The radio is turned to jazz.

"Do you have any other remotely plausible explanation?"

"Nope."

"Neither do I. Is there anything we could have done to have avoided this disaster?"

"Probably not," I say. I recall Ed Molinari's observation that Skipper will admit the truth only when he's caught in a bald-faced lie. Then again, human nature being what it is, it doesn't surprise me that he waited to see if the DNA tests would implicate him. Who knows? Maybe he used a condom and thought nothing would turn up.

"I'm exhausted," Rosie says.

"So am I."

As we pass through the Waldo Tunnel, she observes, "This case makes no sense. I can understand why they think Skipper put the GHB in Garcia's glass, but there is no plausible explanation for the GHB in Skipper's. I can't believe he spiked his own drink."

"There were a lot of people who had the opportunity."

"Yes, but it would have been very risky. The people who were there aren't reckless idiots. They're very calculating."

"Maybe it was an act of opportunity. It wouldn't have been that difficult to put a few drops of GHB into the glasses."

"Maybe, but it would have been impossible for somebody to have orchestrated everything else that happened. If Skipper really was set up, somebody would have had to have gotten Garcia upstairs or known he was coming, spiked the drinks, bound Garcia to the bed, planted semen from both of them and left the building without being caught—all in a crowded hotel right after a big campaign rally. It just doesn't add up."

"You're assuming, of course, that the same person orchestrated everything. Maybe more than one person was involved."

"I've thought about it," she says. "If you start considering conspiracy theories, the permutations are endless." She yawns and adds, "I'm too tired to try to work them out tonight."

"So am I. Would you do me a favor in the morning? My God, that's only six hours from now. Would you stop at Natalie's house on your way in? I think she's going to need a lot of support in the next few days. I'm not sure Ann is up to it."

She says of course she will.

39

THE DAY OF RECKONING

"It is the policy of the district attorney's office to treat all employees with dignity and respect regardless of their gender, race, religion or sexual orientation."

— STANDARD CLAUSE IN LETTER FROM SAN FRANCISCO DISTRICT
ATTORNEY'S OFFICE TO NEW EMPLOYEES.

Molinari, Ann and I have just told Skipper about the DNA report. We're in the consultation room behind Judge Kelly's courtroom, and his initial reaction is stony silence. Then he says, "What are our options?"

"We can challenge the validity of the report's findings," I say. "I must tell you, however, that these tests are very reliable. You know that."

He doesn't respond.

"We can argue that the evidence was tampered with or planted," Ed adds.

Skipper sighs. "That won't work," he says. "They won't buy it."

I'm glad he's realistic about that. I tell him we can agree to stipulate that the semen found on the bed was, in fact, his.

Skipper puts his elbow on the table and rests his chin in his hand.

Ann breaks the silence. "Father," she begins, then stops. "Daddy," she says, "is there something we need to talk about?"

Skipper sits up at last and looks her in the eye. "Yes, honey," he says. "I'm afraid there is."

His explanation takes only a few minutes and he never takes his eyes off Ann. He says he and Natalie had stopped sleeping together over twenty years ago. They agreed that they would not divorce, but that they were both free to see other people. Skipper did so. Natalie didn't. He says he had affairs from time to time but mostly sought gratification from prostitutes. About ten years ago, he developed a bondage fetish. With the advent of the Internet, he was able to satisfy most of his needs.

Ann is looking down as she asks, "What does all of this have to do with a male prostitute?"

"About six months ago, I began an experimental phase. I became interested in young men. I started turning to male prostitutes."

"And that's how you found Johnny Garcia?"

"That's how I found Andy Holton. He posted pictures of male prostitutes on his Web site, Boys of the Bay Area. Johnny Garcia was the second one he provided. I had a private phone number that I would call. He took care of everything."

Molinari and I glance at each other. "Does Natalie know about this?" I ask.

"Yes."

"Does anyone else?"

"No."

Ann is grim. She swallows and struggles to find the correct words. "Daddy," she says, "were you . . . safe? Did you . . . use protection?" She finally blurts out, "Did you use a condom, for God's sake?"

Skipper nods. He says he flushed it down the toilet.

Ann heaves a sigh of relief.

Molinari says, "You realize that this is now going to become a matter of public record?"

"I understand."

"And you're prepared for that?"

"No." He pauses. "But I have no choice."

He looks at Molinari, then turns to me. "I never hurt anybody," he says. "I'm prepared to withdraw from the attorney general's race. But I didn't kill that kid. I hired him to come to my room. I had sex with him. I handcuffed him to the bed. I taped his eyes and mouth. But I didn't drug him and I didn't put the tape over his nose. No way."

"What do you want us to do, Skipper?" I ask.

"Stipulate to the fact that I had consensual sex with Garcia."

"I'll go talk to Payne."

Molinari and I sit in Payne's office a few minutes later. "I trust you received the DNA reports last night?" she says.

"Yes, Hillary," I reply.

"Is your client willing to reconsider a guilty plea?"

Keep the tone measured. "He didn't do it, Hillary," I say.

She lowers her voice and tries to sound conciliatory. "Come on, Mike. Let's stop the posturing. Let's put all the cards on the table. Notwithstanding your attempts to discredit Nick Hanson, the jury has already accepted the fact that Skipper invited Garcia into his room. His fingerprints are all over the handcuffs and the tape. His fingerprints are on the champagne flutes."

"But, Hillary—"

"Be reasonable, Mike."

"Hillary, he is now prepared to admit that he had consensual sex with Garcia. He's humiliated and his life is in ruins. He has nothing left to hide. If he killed Johnny Garcia, I'd be in here begging you to cut a deal. He didn't do it."

Her green eyes gleam. She looks like a panther. "Oh, come on," she says. "His sexual escapades got out of hand. He handcuffed him. He taped his face. He killed him."

So much for the conciliatory tone.

"It doesn't make sense," I say.

"How do you figure?"

"If he hired Garcia to have consensual sex, why would he have needed to drug him?"

"Maybe Garcia changed his mind."

"So you think Skipper poured a glass of GHB-laced champagne down his throat?"

"Who knows what turned him on? Maybe he liked to have sex with people who were unconscious."

"Why was there GHB in the other flute? Do you think Skipper drugged himself?"

"I don't know. Maybe he made a mistake and put it in both of them."

"That's bullshit."

"Then prove it—put him on the stand to explain it."

I don't respond.

I reach Rosie on her cell phone a little while later. She's gone to Natalie's house. "Natalie won't be coming to court today," she says. "She isn't feeling well."

"Can you talk?" I ask.

"No," she replies flatly.

"Is she there with you?"

"Yes."

"I have to go see Judge Kelly in a few minutes," I say. "Can you stay with Natalie? She shouldn't be alone."

"Sure."

"We're going to stipulate to the fact that Skipper had sex with Garcia."

"Got it."

"I'll call you later."

We're meeting in Judge Kelly's chambers. She delayed the proceedings when I requested a conference before the jury was brought in. "I've seen the DNA report," the judge says. "Do you plan to contest it?"

"No."

She raises an eyebrow. "You're going to stipulate that your client had sex with Johnny Garcia that night?"

"Yes. And we want to do it as quickly as possible."

We discuss the logistics of having a stipulation read into the record. We agree to have the DNA report entered into evidence.

Judge Kelly glares at me and says, "I would encourage you to discuss a plea bargain with the prosecution."

"Judge Kelly," Payne interjects, "we have attempted to do so."

I say, "The prosecution has not offered anything that would be acceptable to Mr. Gates, Your Honor."

Payne feigns exasperation. "We've told the defense from the beginning that we would agree to second degree with a recommendation of a lenient sentence," she says. "It's a very good deal."

Judge Kelly looks thoughtful. "I may be speaking out of turn here, Mr. Daley, but if I were to persuade Ms. Payne to offer you a plea bargain for voluntary manslaughter, would you be prepared to recommend it to your client?"

Tough call. "I'm prepared to deliver such a proposal to my client," I say.

"You have to deliver the proposal to your client," Judge Kelly says. "The critical question is whether you are prepared to recommend it."

I stop to consider for what seems like a long time. The chambers are completely silent. The minimum sentence for first-degree murder is twenty-five years to life; second degree is fifteen to life. The minimum sentence for voluntary manslaughter can be as short as three years but could be as long as eleven. In any event, it's a far better deal than I ever thought we might get. I look at Molinari, who purses his lips. "I will deliver it to my client," I say, "but I won't recommend it."

Payne's narrow shoulders droop.

Judge Kelly sighs. "You seem determined to proceed with this trial, Mr. Daley. I guess we'll see you in court at one o'clock. I'll expect to see a draft of your stipulation by noon."

Molinari pulls me aside in the corridor. "What were you thinking in there?" he asks.

"About what?"

"About the plea bargain. Why won't you recommend voluntary manslaughter? He could be out in three years."

I look into his eyes. "I don't think he did it, Ed."

He takes a half-step back. "You believe him?"

"Yes."

"Are you out of your mind?"

"He's already lost everything, Ed. He's been confronted with the truth about his relationship with Garcia. He's given up on the election. If he killed him, he would be trying to cut a deal for a plea bargain now."

"Do you really think you can win this case?"

"I do."

"Are you serious?"

"Yes, I am. There was far too much at stake. He took a huge risk to invite Garcia to the hotel. It would have been suicidal for him to have drugged Garcia and killed him. There were too many other people around. And we know that Morris, Parnelli, Holton, Anderson and Turner were at the hotel after Garcia arrived. It isn't a big leap for the jury to blame somebody else, or at least get to reasonable doubt."

"That's it?"

"That's it."

"I hope to hell you're right."

Natalie is sitting in the armchair in her living room, a faraway look in her eyes. Rosie leans forward as she says to her, "So you knew about Skipper's relationships with the male prostitutes?"

"Yes. I tried to get him to agree to counseling. He refused."

"How long have you known?"

"About female prostitutes, at least ten years. He started seeing males only a short time ago, however. He used to make all the arrangements from pay phones. He never used the phone in the house or his cellular. He was very concerned about privacy."

I'll bet.

"I didn't know what to do," she says. "I couldn't leave him. For all of his faults, I still love him very much—I simply could not destroy him or what's left of our family." She turns back to me and asks, "What would you have done?"

I look at Rosie and I say, "I don't know, Natalie." I can't begin to imagine the magnitude of the pain she has suffered.

Rosie asks who else knew about this.

Her lips quiver. "As far as I know, just Prentice and me." She pauses for a moment. "And Andy Holton, who made the arrangements, and of course Johnny Garcia. He was Prentice's choice."

"What about Turner?" I ask.

"No," she says. Then she adds quickly, "Why should he?"

Indeed. It's none of his business and Skipper said he didn't know, yet I sense she's defensive. That's strange. Turner has been close to her, but why would she protect him? "Did you know that Skipper was going to invite Garcia up to his room that night?" I ask.

"Not until I saw the bottle of champagne. Then I knew. He always started with a bottle of champagne."

This is curious, too. When I asked Turner who had ordered the champagne, he said he did. And he also said that room service was supposed to bring more glasses but had made a mistake. "Did he ever drug any of the prostitutes with whom he had relations?"

"Not as far as I know."

Rosie asks, "Do you know how the handcuffs and dirty magazines got into his study?"

"He brought them, I presume."

"And you knew they were there?"

"Yes."

Great.

"Did you know about the materials they found in the storage locker?"

She hesitates before she says, "I didn't know."

Rosie folds her hands. "Mike has to be in court now, Natalie, but I'd like to stay here with you. It's been a rough day."

"Thank you," she says.

The afternoon session doesn't take long. Judge Kelly explains to the jury that DNA tests have been conducted on the semen found on the bed in Room 1504 at the Fairmont. She asks Payne to read the stipulation into the record. It says that the defense stipulates that it will not challenge the results of the tests, which concluded that Skipper's semen was found, as well as Garcia's. It also says that the defense does not contest the prosecution's contention that Skipper engaged in consensual sex with Johnny Garcia.

After Payne finishes reading the stipulation, the courtroom becomes silent. The jurors turn their eyes to Judge Kelly. "I'm going to adjourn for the day," she says. "I have some other matters that I must attend to this afternoon." She turns to Payne. "How many more witnesses, Ms. Payne?"

"Just one, Your Honor."

She's going to call Elaine McBride to pull their entire case together.

"We'll be done by the end of the day tomorrow," Hillary says.

Perfect. They're going to put on their strongest witness on a Friday. Unless I miss my guess, she'll finish up late in the afternoon. Just in time to give the jury the entire weekend to think about what she's said.

40

INSPECTOR MCBRIDE

"I've always had an aggressive philosophy about law enforcement. The criminals need to know you're serious."

— INSPECTOR ELAINE MCBRIDE. SAN FRANCISCO CHRONICLE. FRIDAY,
OCTOBER 22.

"My name is Elaine McBride. I'm a homicide inspector with the San
Francisco Police Department."

It's nine A.M. Hillary Payne has conducted a tight prosecution:
short, sweet and to the point. She has kept her promise to Judge Kelly
that she would finish her case in just one week. The jury is still interested. Bill McNulty should be proud. His protégée has put on a textbook performance.

Payne walks McBride through her credentials. I interrupt from
time to time. Finally, Payne asks her what time she arrived at the Fairmont on Tuesday, September seventh.

"Seven-twenty A.M." She says she was escorted to Room 1504 by
the Fairmont's security personnel. Roosevelt Johnson joined her a few
minutes later.

"Would you please describe what you found at the scene?"

They've rehearsed their presentation. "The uniformed officers had
secured the scene," she says. "The body was still on the bed. The coro-

ner's unit had been called." She points to a chart of the fifteenth-floor room on an easel in front of the jury. She shows where the body was found. She points to the nightstand. "Here's where we found the duct tape that the defendant used to suffocate the victim, Johnny Garcia."

"Objection. Move to strike. There is no foundation for Inspector McBride's conclusion that the duct tape was used to suffocate the victim." It's a legitimate objection. It's also an attempt to break up their rhythm.

"Sustained. The jury will disregard Inspector McBride's conclusion that this duct tape was used to suffocate the victim."

Sure they will. Payne rephrases the question. McBride restates her answer, leaving out the conclusion this time.

Payne asks what happened next.

McBride describes her interviews with Joseph Wong, the police at the scene and the paramedics and the technicians from the coroner's office. She says that Garcia was pronounced dead at the scene at seven twenty-five. "We talked to the building security guards. We prepared lists of everyone who had been present on the fifteenth floor that night."

"Did you interview the defendant?"

"Yes."

"Could you describe his demeanor?"

"Agitated and confused."

"Was he belligerent?"

"Objection. Leading."

"Overruled."

"Yes, he was. The defendant was very upset."

I steal a glance at Skipper, who nods to himself.

"When did the defendant become a suspect?"

"Immediately. He was at the scene. He had no explanation as to how the victim got into his room. He had no explanation for how the victim died. He was uncooperative."

"Move to strike. Inspector McBride is commenting on the defendant's state of mind."

Judge Kelly is unimpressed. "Overruled."

Payne walks toward the evidence cart and turns to McBride. "Inspector," she says, "I'd like to take a few minutes to ask for your assistance in identifying some of the physical evidence found in Room 1504 of the Fairmont that night."

"Of course, Ms. Payne."

Molinari whispers into Skipper's ear. I can make out the words "Stay calm."

Payne starts with the first set of handcuffs, wrapped in plastic. She hands them to McBride and asks her to identify them.

"These are the handcuffs found on Johnny Garcia's right wrist," she says, "which was handcuffed to the bedpost." They go through a similar exercise for the three other sets of handcuffs that were used to bind him. Then Payne leads her through an identification of every piece of evidence found in Room 1504: the duct tape, the handcuff key, the champagne flutes, the champagne bottle, the fingerprints on the phone and the doorknob. They go through the telephone records from Room 1504. I object from time to time. I remind Judge Kelly that all of this evidence has already been introduced. It's an exercise in futility.

At a quarter to twelve, Skipper leans over to me and says, "We're getting killed."

"Be quiet," I say.

At noon, Judge Kelly asks Payne if she'd like to take a break.

"Yes, Your Honor," she says. "We're almost done. We should finish early this afternoon."

"All rise." Judge Kelly's courtroom is called to order after lunch. The shuffling in the gallery stops. The A-list reporters are here. They're waiting for Hillary's wrap-up.

McBride returns to the stand. Judge Kelly reminds her she's still under oath. Then she nods to Payne, who is standing at the lectern.

"Inspector McBride," Payne begins, "were you present at the Pacific Heights residence of the defendant when it was searched on Tuesday, September seventh?"

"Yes."

"Would you mind describing what was found?"

"Objection," I say. "All of the materials found at Mr. Gates's home have already been introduced into evidence."

"Overruled." Judge Kelly glances at Payne. "Let's keep things moving, Ms. Payne."

Hillary nods. She leads McBride through a brief description of everything found in the study: the handcuffs, the pictures of the bound prostitutes, the copies of *Hustler*, the bookmarked Web sites. For good measure, she takes her through a detailed inventory of the photos and magazines found in Skipper's storage locker. Although they have heard most of this before, the jurors look very troubled.

The afternoon session wears on. Payne keeps lobbing softball questions to her and McBride keeps slamming home runs. She describes her interviews with the people who attended the summit conference. They go into further detail on the items found in Skipper's storage locker. They paint a portrait of Skipper as a pervert. Finally, at a quarter to three, Payne steps back to the lectern and asks McBride to summarize her conclusions for the jury. I object on the grounds that the question is speculative. Judge Kelly overrules my objection.

McBride looks at the jury and says, "I believe the defendant lured Johnny Garcia, a seventeen-year-old male prostitute, into his room at the Fairmont. I believe he drugged him, handcuffed him to the bedposts and covered his eyes, nose and mouth with duct tape. I believe he engaged in sex with the victim while the victim's eyes, nose and mouth were covered with tape. The victim died of suffocation in that room that night."

Then Payne turns to Judge Kelly. "No further questions, Your Honor."

I stand up immediately. The last thing I need right now is for the judge to decide to recess until Monday. I don't want the jury to have two days to think about McBride's testimony. I walk past the lectern and position myself in front of her. I want to get right in her face.

"Inspector McBride," I begin, "you said you arrived at the Fairmont at seven-twenty A.M. on September seventh, and you said Mr. Gates was agitated and confused."

"That's correct."

"Yet he answered all of your questions, didn't he?"

She hesitates and says, "Grudgingly."

"And if he answered all of your questions, Inspector, it's fair to say that your characterization earlier of Mr. Gates as uncooperative and belligerent was not entirely accurate, right?"

She sighs. "Mr. Gates answered our questions only after he concluded that he had no other choice."

"Move to strike. State of mind."

The judge tells the jury to disregard McBride's statement. McBride then acknowledges that Skipper did, in fact, remain in the room and provide the police with a full description of the events of that night. It's not a huge point, but it helps. "And did it occur to you that Mr. Gates may have appeared agitated and confused, and perhaps even belligerent, because he had been drugged?"

McBride is indignant. "It did not appear to me that the defendant's demeanor was consistent with that of an individual who had been drugged."

It's the answer I expect, but it still gives the jury something to think about. I get her to say that she did not request that Skipper take a drug test after he was arrested. "Inspector McBride," I continue, "you have testified that you found his fingerprints on the handcuffs and the duct tape used to bind Johnny Garcia."

"That's also correct." She acknowledges that nobody saw Skipper put the handcuffs on Garcia, and that he may have gotten his fingerprints on them when he tried to remove them. It's a small victory and I don't belabor it—the jury has heard a lot about the handcuffs already.

We volley for about an hour about the evidence found in Skipper's room. For the most part, McBride doesn't give an inch. We argue about the handcuff key. She insists that the champagne glasses show that Garcia sipped champagne spiked with GHB.

"Inspector," I say, "you have concluded that Mr. Garcia was unconscious, right?"

"Yes."

"And Mr. Gates drugged him in order to induce him to have sex."

"That's true."

"Yet we know that Mr. Garcia entered Mr. Gates's room voluntarily and Mr. Gates had made arrangements to have sex with him."

"That's true, too."

I give her a puzzled look. "Inspector, if the victim, Johnny Garcia, had come to Mr. Gates's room and they had already agreed to have sex, why in the world would Mr. Gates have needed to drug him?"

"Objection. Speculative."

"Sustained."

It's a legitimate objection. I decide to go just one step further. "If they had agreed to engage in voluntary sex, Inspector, why would Mr. Gates have given him a narcotic that causes unconsciousness?"

"Objection. Speculative."

"Sustained."

I glance toward the defense table. Skipper is nodding. Molinari remains stoic. Rosie scratches her left ear. It's time to move on.

We pound on each other for the rest of the afternoon. I challenge the handling of the evidence. I ask whether McBride had seriously considered any other suspects.

"All of the evidence pointed toward Mr. Gates," she insists.

"Did you consider any of the other people who attended the meeting in his room that night? Perhaps Mr. Morris or even Mr. Parnelli?"

"There wasn't a shred of evidence pointing in their direction."

"Are you familiar with a man named Andrew Holton?"

"Yes."

"And what was his relationship to Mr. Garcia?"

"He was his roommate."

Not so fast. I lead her through a discussion of Andy Holton's background and history with Johnny Garcia. Finally, I ask, "Mr. Holton was Mr. Garcia's pimp, right?"

"Yes."

"Why didn't you consider Mr. Holton as a suspect? He was seen in the security videos."

"Objection. Speculative."

"Overruled."

"There was no evidence indicating that Mr. Holton was involved."

"No evidence?" I say, my voice rising. "He was Johnny Garcia's pimp, for God's sake."

"Objection. Move to strike Mr. Daley's editorial comments."

"Sustained." Judge Kelly points her gavel at me but speaks to the jury. "The jury will disregard Mr. Daley's outburst," she says.

No they won't. "You had already decided that Mr. Gates was your man, hadn't you? You didn't consider Andrew Holton because he didn't fit within your theory of the case, right?"

"Objection. Mr. Daley is badgering this witness."

"Sustained."

That isn't going to stop me. "What about Mr. Stanford? He came back to the hotel at three twenty-five. He was seen in the security videos as well. Did you ever consider him as a suspect?"

"There wasn't any evidence placing him in the room, Mr. Daley." She's indignant now.

All right, enough smoke. "Inspector," I say, "didn't you think it was odd that Mr. Gates was still in the room when Mr. Wong arrived the following morning?"

McBride gives me an inquisitive look. "I'm not sure I understand the question."

"If Mr. Gates had, in fact, killed Johnny Garcia, don't you think he would have left the building?"

"Objection. Speculative."

"Sustained."

I decide to try it another way. "Inspector, in your many years of experience as a police officer, isn't it usually the case that an individual who has committed a crime tries to flee?"

"Objection. Speculative."

"Your Honor," I say, "I'm not asking Inspector McBride to speculate. I'm asking for an expert opinion based on her experience as a police officer and homicide inspector."

"Overruled."

McBride has no choice. "Yes, Mr. Daley," she says. "It is usually the case that an individual who has committed a crime tries to flee."

"And that didn't happen in this case, did it?"

"No."

"In fact, Mr. Gates was in the very room with Johnny Garcia's body when Mr. Wong arrived, wasn't he?"

"Yes."

"And he answered all your questions?"

"Grudgingly."

Good enough. "How do you account for the fact that Mr. Gates didn't try to flee?"

"Objection. Speculative. State of mind."

Right on both counts.

"Sustained."

"If you had just committed a murder, Inspector, don't you think that you would have left the room right away?"

The judge sustains Payne's objection. I've planted the seed. "No further questions, Your Honor."

"Redirect, Ms. Payne?"

"No, Your Honor."

"Any other witnesses, Ms. Payne?"

"No, Your Honor. The prosecution rests."

Judge Kelly turns to me and says, "I take it you would like to make a motion."

"Yes, Your Honor." I make the customary motion to have all charges dismissed.

"Objection," Payne says. "There's no basis for this."

Judge Kelly waves her back into her chair. "Sit down, Ms. Payne," she says. She turns to me. "The motion is denied. I presume, Mr. Daley, that you'll be ready to call your first witness on Monday morning?"

"Yes, Your Honor."

41

THE BALL IS IN OUR COURT

"Michael Daley was unable to discredit the compelling testimony of re-spected homicide inspector Elaine McBride."
—NEWSCENTER 4 LEGAL ANALYST MORT GOLDBERG. SATURDAY,
OCTOBER 23.

Rosie and I head over to the martial arts studio to meet Carolyn and Ed and recap our defense tactics. I tell them I'm going to cast doubt on the physical evidence and then call our medical expert. "He's coming over in a little while so Ed and I can prepare him," I say. "He's going to testify that Garcia may have died of a heroin or GHB overdose, or from an irregular heartbeat from a combination of drugs and alcohol."

"If Skipper gave him the GHB and he died as a result of a chemical reaction," Rosie points out, "Skipper still might have caused his death."

"I realize that. Ed and I are going to spend a lot of today working with him," I say. Ted Raffel is a full professor at Stanford. He's a chatty fellow who makes the rounds on the pathology circuit. I've met with him three times already. He tells me about the hole in one he got thirty years ago every time I see him. At least he's engaging, and he has the right degrees from the right schools. "I'll talk to him about it."

We break up into smaller groups. Molinari and I spend the morning and part of the afternoon working with Dr. Raffel on his testimony. Carolyn and Rosie work on exhibits and our computer-generated graphics. It's not enough to show the jury pictures anymore. You have to dazzle them with special effects.

At eight o'clock that evening, I'm at Rosie's house. Grace has lined up all her Beanie Babies for roll call. She's told me that I have to read them a story tonight. Her new favorite book is called *The Adventures of Captain Underpants*, by a good-hearted anarchist named Dav Pilkey. It's very funny. I'm willing to read anything she wants, within reason. Tonight, I'm reading chapters four and five. The Beanie Babies appear to be more interested in this story than the jurors are in Skipper's trial. I read them the story. As usual, I'm reading the words though my mind is on other things. I'd like to do this every night.

We finish chapter five. Grace looks up and says, "Daddy, can we watch the *Cats* video?" It warms my heart to know she'd rather watch a video of a Broadway musical than a cartoon.

"Sorry, sweetie," I say. "It's bedtime. And Daddy and Uncle Pete and Uncle Tony have to do some work tonight."

"On a Saturday night?"

Busted. "Yeah, sweetie. The trial is almost over. Then we're going to take a little break for a while."

"How long?"

Good question. How about the rest of my life? "I'm not sure."

"Daddy, did Mr. Gates kill that prostitute?"

Jesus. When I was eight years old, I didn't know what the word *prostitute* meant. "No, sweetie," I say. "I don't think so."

"Then you'll be able to get him off, right?"

"That's right."

We gather the Beanie Babies and find room for them on her bed. She kisses each of them in turn and then she kisses me. "I love you, Daddy," she says.

"I love you, too."

"Don't get yourself whacked on the head again, okay, Daddy?"

I see Rosie standing just outside the door, smiling. I kiss Grace and say, "I'll be careful."

———

Rosie says the same thing a few minutes later.

"I'll be careful," I assure her, too. "I've got the troops with me this time. Ron Morales and a couple of uniforms from Mission Station are going in. Want to come? You'll get to ride in a squad car."

"I think I'll pass. I had more than enough fun when you decided to storm the Jerry." She turns serious. "I trust you'll be waiting outside in the police car this time?"

"Absolutely."

"Listen, cowboy," she says, "remember what happened last time you tried a stunt like this. I don't want to spend another night at San Francisco General. This time, you leave the cops-and-robbers stuff to the pros."

"I promise."

She smiles. "And you'll call me just as soon as you know something?"

"You bet."

She hugs me.

At ten-thirty, Pete, Tony and I are sitting in the squad room in Mission Station. Ron Morales and three of his cohorts have a handmade diagram of the floor plan of the Curtis Hotel. "The appliance store on the ground floor is closed," Morales is saying. "John and I will go in the main entrance." He points at the other two uniforms. "You guys will go up the back stairs."

"What about us?" Tony asks.

"You guys will wait in the squad car until we come and get you. Leave the police work to us. We don't know if anybody is up there."

"Got it."

Eleven o'clock. Pete, Tony and I are in the backseat of Morales's squad car as we pull out of Mission Station and head up the block toward the Curtis. Morales and one of his colleagues are in the front. A second squad car with the other two officers follows behind us. We stop in front of a beat-up three-story building with a small sign on the front that says Curtis Hotel. Morales and John walk inside the front door, their guns drawn. The other two uniforms jog down the gangway next to the building and disappear.

We sit in silence. Cars are whizzing by us on Valencia. The blinking red lights on the top of our squad car cast flashing reflections off the buildings across the street. We look at the second floor and see a light in the Boys of the Bay Area room. A moment later, Morales leans out the window, holding up his hand to signal us to stay where we are. His head pops back inside.

"You think they found something?" Tony asks me.

"Can't tell."

A moment later, two more squad cars pull up behind us, their lights flashing. Four cops leap out and head straight up the main stairway. They ignore us.

"What's happening?" Tony asks.

"They found something," Pete says.

The flashing lights make it look like Rockefeller Center at Christmas. A few minutes later, Morales walks out the front door and motions us to come in. "I'm going to take you guys upstairs," he says. "Be careful not to touch anything."

We climb up to the second floor. The hallway of the Curtis is like those of the Jerry and the Royan—drab, gloomy, grungy, smelly, ominous. The lights are dim, but at least they're working. People are milling around in the corridor on the second floor. A young Hispanic man in a T-shirt and shorts is talking to the police. A woman holding an infant peers out her door. She appears frightened. I pause to consider how difficult it must be to try to raise a child here.

As Morales leads us to Room 204, he instructs us to follow the exact path that he takes. The police have already cordoned it off with yellow tape. "Don't touch anything," he reminds us again.

Two police officers who came with us are standing in the middle of the room. One of them is talking on his cellular phone. He nods toward us when we walk in. There is a double bed pushed up against one wall but little other furniture. I see a laptop computer, a printer and a fax machine on a table against the wall near the bathroom, and a small bookcase packed with dozens of videotapes.

There is a door with a broken padlock propped against the wall next to the bathroom. The cops have forced the door open with a crowbar and taken it off its hinges. It led into a big closet, and inside I can see more bookcases tightly packed with videos and binders and a metal file cabinet.

Morales is wearing plastic gloves. He shows me a black binder marked Boys of the Bay Area. It contains photos of naked men. He flips through it until he spots a familiar face: Johnny Garcia's.

Morales pries open the top drawer of the file cabinet. He reaches inside and pulls out two large clear plastic bags containing white powder.

"I presume that's not sugar," I say.

"Yeah," he says. "This must be a distribution center. It looks like you could buy anything from them over the Internet—sex, drugs, porn. Somebody's been running a high-tech shopping center. This heroin is probably worth about a quarter of a million bucks on the street."

I observe that an operation of that size requires considerably more funding than Andy Holton would have been able to provide. "And you know this building is owned by the Mission Redevelopment Fund," I add.

Morales gives me a sarcastic grin. "We're aware of that. As usual, it looks like all roads lead back to the same place we always end up— Donald Martinez. If past history is any indication, I'll bet you anything he has a perfectly legitimate explanation for everything."

By the time I finally get home on Sunday morning, the sun is coming up. I'm getting too old to pull all-nighters. I have only one day to finalize our exhibits and line up our defense, which will be short. We'll take potshots at the evidence and try to shift the blame on some of the other people who were there that night. Then we'll sit the hell down and let the jury decide. A friend of mine who is a prosecutor in San Diego tells me that juries usually end up making the right decision.

They don't always have the correct reasons, but they get to the right place. We'll see.

I walk into my kitchen, think about making a pot of coffee, then decide to pull a Diet Dr Pepper from the fridge. I must look like hell. At nine o'clock tomorrow morning, I'm supposed to take a leading role in Skipper's defense. I close my eyes, then open them again. The blinking red light on my answering machine has caught my eye. I have only one message. I hit the play button.

"*Beep. Saturday. Eleven-thirty p.m. Mike, it's Nick Hanson. Please call me as soon as you can. I found some stuff that you may find very interesting. Beep.*"

I pick up the phone and punch the number he gave me. I get an answering service. They tell me that Mr. Hanson is working, but he'll call back right away.

I ask for one of his sons.

"They're all working, too," the cheerful voice replies.

That figures.

42
SMOKE AND MIRRORS

"Gates defense begins today."
— SAN FRANCISCO EXAMINER. MONDAY, OCTOBER 25.

Monday morning comes too soon. It's overcast when Ed Molinari and I push our way through the throng of reporters at the front of the Hall. Rosie and Natalie are already inside. Rosie has managed to convince her that it would be helpful for her to be seen in the courtroom today. I hope she's up to it.

The reporters assault us. "We're very pleased with the way the trial has progressed thus far," I say. "We are very confident. We have no further comment at this time."

And by the way, my head feels like somebody hit me with a two-by-four.

"All rise," says the bailiff.

Judge Kelly strides to the bench. She's ready to roll. She turns to the jury and says, "The defense will begin its presentation today." She looks at me and says, "You may call your first witness."

"The defense calls Douglas Kaplan," I say.

A lifelong "white coat," Doug Kaplan is a fifty-year-old civilian scientist who does chemical analyses in the bowels of the Hall. Black-framed bifocals surround his droopy eyes. He isn't a charismatic guy, but he's very good at what he does. I run him through his résumé, then show him the two champagne flutes found in Skipper's room. "Mr. Kaplan," I say, "do you recognize these?"

Kaplan moves his glasses to the top of his bald head and studies the tags. "Yes," he decides. "They're the champagne flutes found in the defendant's room at the Fairmont Hotel."

I hand him the first flute and ask him if he is familiar with the fingerprint analysis prepared by Sergeant Jacobsen.

"Yes."

"And she found only Mr. Gates's fingerprints on this flute, right?"

"Yes."

"And no fingerprints of the victim, Johnny Garcia?"

"That's true."

"So it's logical to conclude that Mr. Gates handled this flute, right?"

"Objection. Speculative."

"Overruled."

"Yes," Kaplan replies. "It is logical to conclude that Mr. Gates handled this flute."

"And it is logical to conclude that the victim, Mr. Garcia, did not handle it."

He acknowledges that there is no evidence proving that Garcia touched it.

"Mr. Kaplan," I say, "did you inspect this flute for traces of fluids or other chemicals?"

"Yes."

"Did you find anything?"

"Yes."

"Which fluids or chemicals did you identify?"

"Two. We identified champagne and traces of gamma hydroxy butyrate, or GHB."

"And what did you conclude from this?"

"Champagne and GHB were in this glass at some point on the night in question."

Good. "Mr. Kaplan, do you have any way of knowing who ingested the contents of this flute?"

"Objection. Speculative. Foundation."

"Overruled."

"No."

I walk right up to him. "Mr. Kaplan," I say, "were you able to determine whether the victim, Johnny Garcia, consumed any of the champagne and GHB in this glass?"

"Objection. Foundation."

"Overruled."

I'm pleased. I know the line of questioning I'm launching is out of Kaplan's territory, but I want the jurors to start wondering about the whole premise of Skipper's guilt. If I can make some points before the judge shuts me down—and she will—it'll plant the seed and perhaps start easing them in the direction of reasonable doubt. So far so good.

Kaplan answers my question. "No, sir," he says, "I was simply asked to identify any fluids in the glass. I have no way of knowing who drank from it."

"And by the same token, were you able to determine whether Mr. Gates may have consumed the contents of this glass?"

"No."

"But you were able to determine that Mr. Gates—and only Mr. Gates—handled this glass."

"I was able to determine that Mr. Gates's fingerprints were found on it and that there were traces of alcohol and GHB in it."

Nice deflection. "Mr. Kaplan, if there was GHB in this flute, and Mr. Gates drank from it, he would have been rendered unconscious when he drank from it, wouldn't he?"

Payne reacts as I expect. "Objection. Mr. Kaplan is not an expert on that subject."

"Sustained."

I'm not about to give up. "Doesn't it seem odd to you, Mr. Kaplan, that Mr. Gates would have put the toxic date-rape drug GHB into his own flute?"

"Objection. Speculative."

"Sustained."

I've just begun speculating. "Do you think Mr. Gates intended to drug himself? Given the fact that it doesn't make one iota of sense that Mr. Gates spiked his own drink and knocked himself out, isn't it far more likely that somebody else came to his room and put the GHB in both flutes?"

"Objection. Speculative."

"Sustained."

One more time. "Mr. Kaplan, in light of the fact that GHB was found in Mr. Gates's champagne flute, doesn't it make more sense to conclude that somebody else spiked the drinks and then proceeded to kill Johnny Garcia when both were unconscious?"

"Objection. Move to strike. Mr. Daley is testifying."

Yes, I am.

"Sustained. Enough, Mr. Daley."

"No further questions, Your Honor." I've had a much better run than I expected.

Payne tries to undo the damage in a brief cross-exam that falls flat. To my relief, she offers no new explanation for the presence of the GHB in both flutes. She sits down.

For the first time since the trial started, there are signs of cautious optimism in the consultation room during the mid-morning break. "Nice work with Kaplan," Skipper says.

"It never made any sense that they found GHB in both flutes," I say. "Did they think you drugged yourself?"

"Evidently."

Molinari eyes him warily. "Do you have any idea how the GHB got into the champagne flutes?" '

"No," he says flatly.

"The defense calls Dr. Theodore Raffel."

Our medical expert, Ted Raffel, is in his late fifties, with wiggly jowls, a bald head and a chatty manner. He may be a Stanford professor, but he looks like he could be tending bar at Harrington's. His delivery is folksy. I wish I had found him a few years ago. Ed Molinari uses him for his class-action cases all the time. Raffel acknowledges the jurors with a warm smile as he takes his place in the witness box. According to Ed, he's great if you need somebody to charm the pants off a jury.

He states his name for the record. He adds, "I'm a full professor in the departments of pathology and trauma surgery at Stanford Medical School." He nods as he says it. He is very good at nodding. In fact, he was doing so with great authority during our rehearsals, even when he was spouting unadulterated bullshit.

I ask him to recite his credentials. Payne interrupts him right after he says he got his undergraduate degree at Stanford and his medical degree at Johns Hopkins. "We'll stipulate that Dr. Raffel is an expert in his field," she says.

Raffel is pleased. I hand him a copy of the autopsy report. "Dr. Raffel," I begin, "have you had a chance to review Dr. Beckert's autopsy report on Johnny Garcia?"

"Yes."

"And do you agree with Dr. Beckert's conclusions?"

Payne begins to object, then reconsiders. She's already stipulated to his expertise.

"I'm afraid I don't," he says. He turns to the jury. "I have a great deal of respect for Dr. Beckert," he says. "However, in this particular case, I believe that he came to the wrong conclusion."

I ask him to explain.

He addresses the jury, his tone solemn. "Dr. Beckert concluded that the victim, Johnny Garcia, died of asphyxiation. I have no doubt that there was duct tape placed over the victim's eyes, nose and mouth. On the other hand, I believe there were other factors involved in Johnny Garcia's death. Unfortunately, Dr. Beckert chose to ignore them."

I'm still at the lectern. "What were those factors, Doctor?"

He picks up the cue. "It is a documented fact that Johnny Garcia was a recovering heroin addict. It was also documented that he had a history of coronary arrhythmia—an irregular heartbeat. At the time of his death, he had a substantial amount of heroin in his bloodstream." He explains in medical and then layman's terms that Garcia had enough heroin in his system to render him unconscious and to kill him. "It is clear to me that he had a serious adverse reaction to the drug."

"And what was the result, Doctor?"

"He overdosed. It caused his heart to beat too fast. The increase in his heart rate caused a fatal coronary arrhythmia. He died within seconds."

He's better today than he was in rehearsals. "And you're convinced that Johnny Garcia died of an arrhythmia caused by a heroin overdose?"

He juts out his lower lip. "Absolutely." He nods for good measure. "It is also possible," he continues, "that the arrhythmia was caused by a combination of heroin, GHB and alcohol."

We discuss the possible effects of heroin, GHB and alcohol. He points out that the GHB alone could have caused Garcia's death if he had consumed enough of it. "There are dozens of documented cases of deaths caused by GHB poisoning," he says. "It's a very dangerous substance."

I don't want to get into a detailed discussion of the possibility that the GHB alone might have killed Garcia, because Skipper's fingerprints were, in fact, found on the champagne flutes. It wouldn't be a huge leap for the jury to decide that Skipper caused Garcia's death by giving him the GHB. On the other hand, the possibility of GHB poisoning may help us to demonstrate that Rod Beckert's conclusion was flawed. I decide to ask one more question. "Could you tell how much GHB Johnny Garcia had taken?" I ask.

"No. GHB metabolizes into other substances very quickly. It's essentially gone within four to six hours. The fact that there were traces of GHB in the victim's system at the time of the autopsy more than eight hours after the body was discovered leads me to conclude that the victim may have consumed a substantial amount of GHB as well as heroin."

It's enough. The jury seems interested but not fascinated. I say, "No further questions, Your Honor."

Payne is out of her seat before I sit down. "Dr. Raffel," she says, "you testified that the victim had a substantial amount of heroin in his bloodstream when he died."

"Yes."

"Yet Dr. Beckert characterized the amount of heroin in his system as a trace, didn't he?"

"That's true. However, you must take into account the fact that Dr. Beckert did not examine the body until more than eight hours after it was discovered. Heroin remains active within the system for only a few hours. Then it breaks down into other substances, including morphine. If you still find a little heroin in a corpse eight hours after the body is discovered, it means that there was a much larger amount of heroin in the party's system several hours earlier."

"Even so, isn't it generally accepted that a minute amount of heroin could not cause an overdose in a healthy young male?"

"Not necessarily. In my experience, a fatal overdose can be caused by a very small amount of heroin, especially in the case of an individual who was a recovering addict. It depends upon the age and health of the individual, his size and weight, the amount of heroin injected, the severity of the addiction and the possible combination of the heroin with other drugs and toxic substances. I have seen cases where very small amounts of heroin have proved fatal. In this case, in my opinion, the amount of heroin found in the victim's bloodstream not only could have caused an overdose, it did so."

Nice parry.

Payne is frustrated. "How much experience do you have working with drug overdose patients?"

"A lot. I worked at the emergency room at San Francisco General for five years before I began my teaching career at Stanford."

From her expression, it seems Payne didn't know this. She regroups and asks, "You didn't examine the body, did you?"

"No. The body was cremated."

"And you didn't have an opportunity to question Dr. Beckert, did you?"

"No. I did, however, have an opportunity to study his report in detail. And I did have an opportunity to discuss the toxicology results with the technician who performed the tests."

Good answer.

Payne searches for a tone of measured incredulity. "And based upon your review of the autopsy report and the interview with one lab technician, you concluded that an experienced, respected coroner such as Dr. Roderick Beckert simply got it wrong?"

That's about the gist of it, Hillary.

"Yes, Ms. Payne," Raffel replies.

They joust for another thirty minutes. Payne pounds on Raffel, who holds his ground. I object only once. He doesn't need any help from me. He keeps saying that based on his best medical judgment, he believes Johnny Garcia died of a severe irregular heartbeat brought on by an overdose. It's just the way I wrote it for him. At this juncture, he's persuasive enough to read the phone book to the jury and they would believe him. Hillary doesn't pursue the possibility that Garcia may have died from an overdose of GHB—it won't help her case to suggest that Beckert got the cause of death wrong.

Finally, Hillary decides to go to a standard ploy. "Dr. Raffel," she says, "how much are you being paid to testify today?"

I could object to this question on grounds of relevance, but I elect not to do so. Raffel is an impressive guy. The jurors seem to like him. I don't think the fact that he's getting paid a lot will cause them to turn on him. Besides, they may be even more impressed when they hear his hourly rate.

"My standard rate," Raffel says, "is four hundred seventy-five dollars an hour. My fee for this consultation is fifteen thousand dollars."

"So Mr. Daley was able to buy your opinion for fifteen grand?"

Now she's crossed the line. "Objection. Argumentative."

"Sustained."

"And you would have said pretty much anything he asked you to say, right?"

"Objection. Argumentative."

"Sustained."

Payne shakes her head in mock disbelief. "No further questions, Your Honor."

Skipper gives me a quick nod. He seems pleased. When I turn around to look at Natalie, I see her being hurriedly escorted out of the courtroom by Ann.

We spend the afternoon parading our evidence experts to the stand. We've found a Ph.D. from Berkeley who swears that their fingerprint analysis on the handcuffs was questionable. Payne lights into her with little success. We get a chemical expert to argue that the adhesive found on Johnny Garcia's face wasn't a perfect match for the duct tape on the nightstand. Smoke and mirrors. In a particularly creative trip through the looking glass, we trot out an expert on heroin addiction to testify that sexual drive is diminished when you're high. As a result, we argue, it is inconceivable that Johnny Garcia engaged in sex that night and that his semen must somehow have been planted on the bed. I wouldn't bet a penny on it, but the jury seemed to like the little guy with the long beard and the tiny glasses.

Judge Kelly decides to call it a day at a quarter to five. "How many more witnesses, Mr. Daley?" she asks.

"Just a couple, Your Honor." I glance toward Skipper.

I'm dining upscale with Nick Hanson at Moose's on Washington Square, just down the block from Ed Molinari's office. Nick's a regular. He nods to the proprietor and then dips his bread into a plate of olive oil and chews it heartily. The jazz combo in the middle of the crowded room is banging out Duke Ellington's "Satin Doll."

"I've been trying to talk to you for the last two days," I say.

"I've been working."

I'll bet. "What did you find?"

Nick takes a sip of his martini and holds up his hand, indicating that it isn't yet time to talk about business. Then he launches into a twenty-minute discussion of the marketing plan for his new mystery. I nod and smile at appropriate times. The waiter brings Nick's calamari and my petrale. We eat. We schmooze. Forty-five minutes later, I ask him again what he found.

He holds up the index finger. "I've been watching your pal, Turner Stanford."

That was the whole idea. "And?"

"I found something."

You have to let him tell the story. At the rate things are going, we could be here until midnight. I try once more. "What did you find, Nick?"

He wipes his hands on his napkin and reaches into his breast pocket. He takes out a small white envelope and hands it to me. I look at the photos as he does the play-by-play.

"Here's Stanford walking out the back door of his house."

No big deal so far.

"Here's Stanford entering the back door of Skipper's house."

Still no big deal. "When did you take these pictures?"

"Saturday night."

"Could you tell who answered the door?"

"Mrs. Gates."

I shuffle through several more pictures of the back door of the Gates mansion. Finally, I get to a picture of Turner coming out the back door. "When did you take this one?" I ask.

Nick finishes his calamari. "It was about seven o'clock the next morning."

"He spent the night at Natalie's?"

"Indeed he did."

Indeed I am stunned. "Natalie and Turner are having an affair?"

He gives me a sideways grin. "I don't know for sure," he says. "I couldn't see inside the house." He drinks his wine. "That would appear to be a logical conclusion, however."

Christ. I close my eyes. Moose's is a very noisy restaurant. At the moment, I don't hear a thing. My mind races. I see freeze-frames of Natalie and Ann. I see Skipper's smiling face. The room spins. Who is protecting whom? Who is setting up whom? Did Turner set up his best friend? Did Natalie set up her husband? I can't put it together. There is a whole array of unanswered questions, of trails I can't connect.

I open my eyes. I see Nick Hanson sitting in front of me, looking serious. "Thanks, Nick," I say. "You did your job." I ask him if he's prepared to testify if we need him.

"Indeed I am," he says.

I head right to Rosie's after Nick and I part. "What are you going to tell Skipper about Natalie and Turner?" she asks.

"The truth," I say. "We have no choice. It gives both of them a motive to have framed Skipper. They were both there that night. They both had a chance to plant the GHB."

"And what do you propose to tell Natalie?"

"For the moment, nothing. I want to talk to Skipper first."

"And Ann?"

"Nothing there yet, either."

"And Turner?"

"Not a word," I say. "We need to think this through. If we tell Natalie, she'll tell Turner. We don't want him to find out anything. We may need to ambush him in court."

43
"I'M A POLITICAL CONSULTANT"

"Gates defense ponders whether to let defendant take the stand."
—SAN FRANCISCO DAILY LEGAL JOURNAL. TUESDAY, OCTOBER 26.

Skipper explodes Tuesday morning. "That son of a bitch!" he shouts. "I'll rip him apart." He throws a paper coffee cup against the wall in the consultation room and says, "Turner had no right. That bastard."

"You didn't know?" Molinari asks.

"Of course I didn't know. I had no idea. Natalie and I have been married for almost forty years. He was best man at my wedding. Who the hell does he think he is?"

We sit in silence for a few minutes. Skipper chews on his fingernail. His face is red.

It's time to lay all the cards faceup. I strain to find my best priest-voice. "Skipper," I whisper, "it's possible they may have been involved in what happened at the Fairmont."

I get an icy glare. He says emphatically, "Natalie would never get involved in something like that."

I struggle to keep my tone measured. "That may be true," I say, "but she is very unhappy and her relationship with Turner may have some bearing on your case. I need to know what was going on with you and Natalie and Turner."

Skipper eyes me with disdain. "Look," he says, "Natalie and I made a deal a long time ago. I already told you about it. We agreed to remain married for the sake of appearance. We were each allowed to have other relationships as long as we were discreet about it. It isn't a perfect arrangement, but it was the best we could come up with."

Why am I not surprised that his marriage evolved into a business deal? "And her relationship with Turner?" ·

"Technically, if she wanted to have an affair with him, it fell within the parameters of our agreement, although it strikes me as—as inappropriate. He's our neighbor. He's my best friend. He is Ann's god-father, for God's sake. At least I kept my affairs discreet."

Right up until the time you got arrested when they found a dead male prostitute in your room, you bastard. I realize I'm furious. I can't contain it. "So it was one thing for you to sleep with prostitutes but an-other thing for Natalie to sleep with Turner?" The back of my neck is red hot.

"I didn't mean that."

"You just said that." I am leaning forward in my chair.

"It's not what I meant."

My face is about eight inches from his. "I think it's exactly what you meant."

We stare each other down. After a moment, Molinari stands and pushes us apart. "This is a serious issue," he says, "but we have to keep our eye on the ball here. This is material new information that may have a significant bearing on this case."

That's for damn sure. "We're going to have to put Natalie on the stand," I say. "She and Turner were both at the Fairmont. Either of them could have spiked the drinks. She had access to your study and the storage locker. She knew about everything."

Skipper folds his hands in front of his face, deep in thought. Fi-nally, he says in a measured tone, "Natalie has been protecting me for four decades. She is the mother of my child and one of the most caring members of our community. She respects human life more than any-body else I know. She would never get involved with anything like this.

She would never do something that might cause her such embarrassment and humiliation. And she would never—ever—kill anybody."

His raw emotions are exposed. I don't think there's a chance that he's lying. Nor do I think he's trying to cover for her.

"What about Turner?" Ed asks.

His expression changes instantaneously to one of scorn. "That's an entirely different story," he says. "We've been friends since we were kids, and we always will be. But that doesn't mean I don't know the kind of man he is. He's the consummate user. He always has been. He'll do anything to get what he wants. That's why he's such a successful political consultant. That's why he's the best juice lawyer in town. If people are hurt along the way, so be it."

I get a quick glance from Molinari that suggests he's thinking exactly the same thing that I am: This is also a self-portrait of Skipper. "Do you think he set you up?" I ask.

He ponders for a moment and says, "After all these years, nothing would surprise me about Turner. On the other hand, I can't see any motive he would have."

"Except Natalie."

Skipper swallows and says, "He seems to have had that already."

True enough. "Did Turner know about your arrangements with Andy Holton and Johnny Garcia?" I ask.

"Of course. He put me in touch with Holton in the first place."

So Turner lied. He really did know what was going on with Skipper. I stop to think for a moment. How would he have known a pimp like Holton? Then the answer becomes obvious. "He represents Martinez and Anderson," I say. "There must be a connection."

"Maybe, but if Martinez is involved, you'll never find any hard evidence that leads to him."

We stare at the walls for a few minutes. I'm certain there are more pieces to the puzzle, but I can't find them. Finally, Molinari says to Skipper, "It would help our case if we could call Natalie and Turner as witnesses and deflect suspicion over to them."

Skipper is indignant. "I realize that you are just doing your job," he says with an edge in his voice. "And I appreciate the fact that the correct legal strategy is to put Natalie on the stand. Nevertheless, I want to make something absolutely clear to you: Natalie didn't do any-thing and I will not let her testify. She's suffered enough humiliation."

"Can we talk about this for a moment?" I ask.

He sits up ramrod straight. "I'm the client. Natalie will not testify. That's final." Molinari and I exchange glances, and Skipper adds, "Do whatever you want with Turner. Take him apart on the stand if you have to. But I don't want Natalie in the courtroom."

Sensitive guy. "What do you want me to tell Natalie?"

"The truth. That we know about their relationship."

"She'll tell Turner."

He ponders this. "Don't say anything to her yet," he decides, "and be sure to get her out of the courtroom before Turner takes the stand. Then she can be told."

"How?"

"You figure out a way."

The deputy knocks on the door to take Skipper to the courtroom. Molinari and I stay behind for a moment. After the door closes, he asks, "How do we handle this?"

"Rosie?" I say. Who else?

When I huddle with her moments later just outside the court-room, she asks me in a whisper what she's supposed to do. "Take Natalie home when we break for lunch," I say.

"And tell her what?"

"The truth. That we know about her affair with Turner. It won't be easy and I don't know how she'll take it, but we have to get it over with. I guess you'd better tell Ann, too—she's got to know."

"Christ—that'll make my day complete," Rosie says.

"My name is Jason Parnelli. I'm a political consultant."

The reporters in the gallery are settling in. The courtroom artists are holding their sketch pads. This morning, we've decided to put Jason Parnelli, Dan Morris's little toad, on the stand before his boss so Morris won't have a chance to brief Parnelli on what he testified. I'm sure they've already compared notes on how to proceed.

Parnelli has abandoned the business-casual look in favor of a tradi-tional pin-striped suit. He looks uncomfortable in the witness chair.

He's never done this before. People with his connections are generally not subjected to this sort of thing. He looks toward Payne for moral support.

I stand at the lectern for a few extra moments and shuffle paper. I want to give him plenty of time to sweat. "Mr. Parnelli," I begin, "you were at a meeting in Room 1504 in the Fairmont tower on the night of September sixth of this year, weren't you?" I try for a tone that gives the jury the impression that he's committed a felony just by being in the hotel that night.

"Yes," he replies.

"And the meeting ended at twelve-thirty in the morning on Tuesday, September seventh, correct?"

"Yes."

I walk toward him and point my index finger at him. "But you didn't leave the hotel at twelve-thirty, did you, Mr. Parnelli?"

"No." He's been told to keep his answers short.

"In fact, Mr. Parnelli, you stayed for quite some time after the meeting ended, didn't you?"

"I stayed until about one-thirty."

"One-thirty?" I say. I'm tempted to ask him why he stayed for so long, but that would be a mistake. I don't want to ask open-ended questions. I want to keep him on the defensive by eliciting brief answers. "Who was with you until one-thirty?"

He glances around the courtroom. "I was with my boss, Mr. Dan Morris, in Room 1502."

"Anybody else?"

"No."

I go back to the lectern and leaf through my notes. It's an act. I'm trying to make him nervous. It's sort of like calling a time-out right before a basketball player is about to shoot a free throw. "Mr. Parnelli," I say, "you met someone in the hallway around one o'clock in the morning, didn't you?"

His eyes dart. "Yes. As we were leaving, we saw Mr. Nicholas Hanson in the hallway." He acknowledges that Nick the Dick gave them the videotape, after which they returned to the room.

"In fact," I say, "you hired Mr. Hanson to try to dig up some dirt on the defendant, didn't you?"

"Yes."

"And Mr. Hanson did just that, didn't he?"

"Yes."

"And did you and Mr. Morris have an opportunity to view the videotape in Room 1502 that night?"

"Mr. Hanson left as soon as he delivered the information and the tape."

Not exactly responsive. I ask him again whether he and Morris watched the videotape in Room 1502 that night.

He gulps water. "Yes."

Good. "There was a problem with the tape, wasn't there, Mr. Parnelli?"

"Objection. The witness is not qualified as an expert on videotaping techniques."

"Your Honor," I say, "I am not attempting to elicit a film review. I'm trying to determine whether the videotape contained the information that Mr. Parnelli and Mr. Morris hoped it would."

Judge Kelly gives me some leeway. "Perhaps you could rephrase the question?"

"Of course." I ask him whether the tape contained uncontroverted evidence that a prostitute had entered Skipper's room that night.

"There was a problem with the tape, Mr. Daley," he says.

Yes.

"The problem," he continues, "is that the tape did not clearly show who opened the door."

"You mean you couldn't tell whether it was Mr. Gates?"

"That's correct."

He's far too honest for his own good. He keeps letting the truth get in the way of an effective story. He'll never work for Dan Morris again. "And you couldn't see the face of the individual who entered the room, could you?"

"It was the victim, Johnny Garcia."

"But you couldn't tell that for sure from the tape, could you?"

"We were sure."

I try once more. "But you couldn't see his face, could you, Mr. Parnelli?"

"Objection. Asked and answered."

"Sustained."

"You knew Mr. Gates was going to see a male prostitute that night, didn't you?"

"No."

"You must have been pretty sure."

"We didn't know."

"Then why did you hire Mr. Hanson to spy on him?"

He's flustered. "It's standard procedure in our line of work to hire a private investigator to keep your opponent under surveillance."

"And you would have had an even better story to tell if somebody found Mr. Gates in a room with an unconscious prostitute, right? And you didn't want to take a chance that the videotape might be inconclusive, right?"

"Objection. Argumentative."

"Sustained."

"Come on, Mr. Parnelli. You're under oath. Maybe it was your idea. Maybe Mr. Morris told you to do it. You found a way to spike the two glasses of champagne during the meeting in his room, didn't you?"

"Objection. Argumentative."

"Sustained."

It's the right call. I'm testifying again. I say with disdain, "No further questions, Your Honor."

Dan Morris is next. He smiles at the jury as he adjusts the microphone. He states his name for the record. "I'm a political consultant," he says. He confirms that he and Parnelli left around one-thirty A.M.

I move right in front of him. "Mr. Morris," I say, "you met with Nick Hanson at around one o'clock that morning, didn't you?"

"Yes." He describes the handoff of the tape. He confirms that he and Parnelli viewed it. So far, his story jibes with Parnelli's testimony.

"There was a problem with the videotape, wasn't there, Mr. Morris?"

"Objection," Payne says. "This issue has been addressed."

"On the contrary, Your Honor," I say, "Mr. Morris's analysis of this evidence is critical."

"Overruled."

I repeat the question.

"There was no problem with the videotape."

Wrong answer. You just contradicted your flunky. If you had said there was a problem with the tape, I would have asked you to describe it and you could have spun it any way you wanted. Now you're going to have to do a more intricate tap dance. "Would it surprise you, Mr. Morris, to find out that your colleague, Mr. Parnelli, has testified that there was, in fact, a problem with the tape?"

He's adamant. "There was no problem with the tape."

"Well, that's not what your colleague said."

"My colleague must have been mistaken."

Perfect. He's just undercut Parnelli's credibility. At the same time, he's undercutting his own. "Mr. Morris," I say, "Mr. Parnelli was quite certain that there was a problem." I tell him Parnelli said that they could not identify the person entering the room or the person who opened the door.

Payne objects to my shameless recasting of Parnelli's testimony. Judge Kelly overrules her.

"You had a serious problem, didn't you, Mr. Morris?"

"I don't know what you're talking about."

"You had a tape that was supposed to show the defendant inviting a prostitute into his room. However, the tape didn't show the defendant or the prostitute."

"That's not true."

"And you couldn't have Nick Hanson testify that he was in the room across the hall, because he wasn't supposed to be there in the first place, right?"

"Objection. Argumentative."

"Overruled."

"We hired Mr. Hanson to observe Mr. Gates."

"I understand. But if the world found out that you hired a PI to sit in the room across the hall and spy on him, there would have been serious fallout, right, Mr. Morris? Spying on your opponent is bad politics, isn't it? It looks bad to the voters, doesn't it? Maybe you could have just planted a hidden camera in the defendant's room."

"Objection. Argumentative."

"Sustained."

"In fact, Mr. Morris, you had nothing to show for that night, did you? You had an inconclusive videotape and the testimony of a private investigator who wasn't even supposed to be there. Isn't that about it, Mr. Morris?"

"Objection."

"Sustained." Judge Kelly points her gavel at me. "Wrap it up, Mr. Daley."

Okay. Let's plant one final seed. "Mr. Morris, you had access to Mr. Gates's room during the entire summit conference, didn't you?"

"Yes."

"And you saw the waiter prepare a bottle of champagne and two flutes in Mr. Gates's room, didn't you?"

"Yes."

"Mr. Morris, you were among the very last people to leave Room 1504, weren't you?"

"That's true."

"In fact, you and Mr. Parnelli were the last people to leave other than Mr. Stanford, right? And you then moved next door to Room 1502, correct?"

"I believe that's right."

"Mr. Morris, it's possible that Mr. Gates and Mr. Stanford were not watching you at every instant that evening, right? Especially after everyone had left. Perhaps one or both of them went to the bathroom at one time or another."

"Objection. Speculative."

"Sustained."

"Mr. Morris, you had reason to believe that Mr. Gates might be meeting a prostitute that night, didn't you?"

"No."

"Then why did you hire a private investigator to sit in the room across the hall and spy on him? You must have known something was going on."

Gotcha. He stops. "It is true that we had been told that Mr. Gates might be engaging in some extracurricular activities that night."

"Mr. Morris, it certainly would have helped your candidate's campaign if an unconscious prostitute was found in Mr. Gates's room, right? In fact, you wanted to embarrass Mr. Gates so that your client would have a clear path to election as attorney general, didn't you?"

"That's preposterous."

"And you had plenty of opportunity to slip some GHB into the champagne glasses that night, didn't you?"

"Absolutely not."

I pause and glance at the jury. No discernible reaction.

"Anything further for this witness?" asks Judge Kelly.

It's as far as I can go short of accusing him of murder. That would strain credibility with the jury. "No, Your Honor."

After a brief consultation with McNasty, Hillary decides not to cross-examine Morris.

Carolyn stops me in the hallway as we leave the courtroom for the lunch break. She hands me a thin manila envelope and says, "Remember El Camino Holdings—the owner of the domain name? This is a certified copy of the articles of incorporation."

"I trust that you obtained this information legally?"

"Absolutely. I got it from the secretary of state. It's a matter of public record. I didn't even need to pull any strings."

"That's great. Who signed the articles of incorporation?"

She smiles. "Turner."

"Really? Did you get any other information?"

"Not yet. There's nothing else in the public records. It looks like he filed the papers with the secretary of state and has done nothing since then. The corporation is required to file a list of officers and directors but hasn't done so yet."

"It's a start."

"I want to testify," Skipper says at the lunch break. "The jury expects me to testify."

Molinari, Ann and I exchange glances. "We've been through this," I say. "It's a bad idea. I know you want to tell your story, but it's too damn risky."

"The jury wants to hear me," he says.

"The jury doesn't need to hear you," I reply. I leave out the obvious argument that he's already been caught spinning a web of lies. Payne will tear him apart if we give her the chance. "Let's see how things go with Turner. Then we'll decide."

"I'm not going to change my mind."

There's a knock on the door. The deputy lets Rosie in. "Ann," she says, "your mother isn't feeling well. I'm going to take her home. Will you come with us? I think she'd like that." As always, Rosie is playing her part in this ballet to perfection. They leave together.

Skipper looks at me and says, "We haven't finished our discussion of my testimony."

"They'll tie you in knots," I say.

"No, they won't."

Molinari points a finger right into Skipper's face and says, "Yes, they will. Let me tell you something as your lawyer and as your friend. They absolutely, positively, one-hundred-percent *will* tie you in knots. And if you get up on that stand, you're not just an idiot—you're a stupid fucking asshole."

I couldn't have said it any better myself.

44
"GOOD AFTERNOON, MR. STANFORD"

"Defense attorneys for District Attorney Gates are expected to call their final
witnesses this afternoon."
> —SAN FRANCISCO DAILY LEGAL JOURNAL. TUESDAY, OCTOBER 26.

Molinari and I walk past Turner Stanford in the corridor just outside
the courtroom. If he's nervous about his testimony this afternoon, he
isn't showing it.

We take our seats at the defense table. Skipper is brought in. The
seats in the gallery where Natalie and Ann were sitting are now occupied by reporters. The society columnist from the *Chronicle* is sitting
in the next to last row. Somebody must have told her that the residents
of Pacific Heights may be airing some dirty laundry this afternoon.
Judge Kelly bangs her gavel once and calls for order. The bailiff brings
in the jury.

"Are you ready to call your next witness?" Judge Kelly asks.

"Yes, Your Honor," I reply. "The defense calls Turner Hamilton
Stanford the Fourth."

Turner glides to the front of the courtroom. He glances at the jury
as he's sworn in. I'm not sure, but I think I see him wink at the investment banker.

"Good afternoon, Mr. Stanford," I say. When I ask him to describe his occupation, he says he's an attorney, political consultant, private investor and restaurateur. Four careers running at full throttle. Two of the jurors in the back row nod at each other as if to say "Not bad."

I stand at the lectern and start with an easy one. "Mr. Stanford, you were a partner of Mr. Gates's at the Simpson and Gates firm, weren't you?"

"Yes."

"And you've been neighbors for many years?"

Payne is already jumpy. "Objection," she says. "Relevance."

I try to keep my tone subdued. "I'm trying to show that Mr. Stanford and Mr. Gates are friends and former colleagues, Your Honor. I promise to show the relevance in a moment."

"Overruled. Let's keep moving, Mr. Daley."

I look contrite. "Yes, Your Honor." I turn back to Turner and get him to acknowledge that he and Skipper are friends and neighbors as well as former law partners. "And you are his campaign manager, aren't you, Mr. Stanford?"

"Yes."

I approach him. "You were at the Fairmont on the night of September sixth, weren't you?"

He confirms that he was at the campaign rally and the summit conference. He says he left around twelve-thirty A.M.

So far, so good. I move in closer. "Mr. Stanford," I say, "did you go straight home?"

"Yes."

"And did you remain at home the rest of the night?"

He looks at Skipper, then at Payne. "No," he says. "I returned to the hotel for a few minutes at approximately three twenty-five in the morning. Mr. Gates called me at home and said that he had a problem. He said there was an unconscious prostitute in his bed and he needed my help."

So far, this squares with Skipper's account. "Until you received that phone call, were you aware that Mr. Gates had made arrangements to procure the services of a prostitute that night?"

"No. Mr. Gates's personal life is none of my business."

Bullshit. "You knew nothing about it?"

"That's correct."

He's lying, but I have no way to prove it. "So you returned to help Mr. Gates?"

"Yes."

"What happened when you arrived at the hotel?"

"I went to his room. I couldn't see any signs of activity, and there was no answer at his door. I couldn't get in, so I left."

I try to act unimpressed. "So you decided to let Mr. Gates fend for himself?"

He doesn't show the slightest hint of emotion when he says, "What else could I do, Mr. Daley? I couldn't very well go down to the front desk and ask them to let me into his room because he might be in there with a prostitute."

A smattering of laughter in the gallery. Judge Kelly pounds her gavel.

He's holding his own. I need to try to knock him off balance. "Mr. Stanford," I say, "you have an ongoing social relationship with Mrs. Gates, don't you?"

Murmuring in the back. Judge Kelly silences the gallery with a frown.

"We're friends."

"Isn't it a fact that you and Mrs. Gates are more than just friends?"

He holds his hands in front of him with the palms up and says with just the tiniest edge of irritation, "I don't know what you're talking about."

I move right in front of him. "I thought you might say that. I'm going to give you one more chance. Isn't it a fact that you and Mrs. Gates are more than just friends?"

"Objection. Asked and answered."

"The witness hasn't answered truthfully, Your Honor," I say.

Before Judge Kelly can rule on the objection, Turner blurts out, "If you're suggesting that we are involved romantically, you are badly mistaken."

If you think you can get away with lying on this one, *you* are badly mistaken.

Judge Kelly overrules the objection. Turner issues another adamant denial. I turn to the judge and say, "We would like to interrupt Mr. Stanford's testimony for a few moments while we recall another witness."

Judge Kelly's impatience is starting to show. "Very well," she says. "The defense calls Nicholas Hanson."

Payne and McNasty look at each other in disbelief. Payne's objection is overruled. Nick the Dick was supposed to be *their* witness. I overhear an exasperated McNasty whisper to Payne, "Whose side is he on?"

It takes Nick the Dick longer to walk down the center aisle than it does for him to testify. We introduce his photos of Turner entering and exiting Natalie's house. He confirms that Turner was there the entire night. I sit down.

Payne is flustered. She exacerbates the situation when she challenges Nick's stamina and eyesight. She suggests that he may have fallen asleep while Turner left Natalie's house. Nick assures her that he hasn't fallen asleep on a job in sixty years. She tries to get him to admit that it was dark outside when he took the pictures. Nick says his state-of-the-art telephoto equipment works just as well at night as it does in the daytime. Turner is outside the courtroom while Nick the Dick shreds his credibility in front of the jury. After just a few minutes of cross-exam, Payne throws in the towel. I notice a reporter from the *Chronicle* looking inquisitively at the seat where Natalie had been sitting. McNulty is at the prosecution table, his eyes closed.

Turner returns to the witness box a few minutes later. The fact that the jury now has conclusive evidence that he's a liar doesn't seem to have the slightest bearing on his demeanor. He continues to try to charm them. "Mrs. Gates and I have been involved for some time," he acknowledges. He says he lied about it just fifteen minutes ago to protect Natalie's reputation. He turns toward the jury and adds, "I'm sure everyone in this courtroom can understand."

Not everyone, Turner.

I move in closer. "Mr. Stanford," I say, "you went back to the Fairmont that night because you knew Mr. Gates was in trouble, didn't you?"

"As I told you, I was concerned."

"And you claim you wanted to protect him?"

"Yes."

"In fact, Mr. Stanford, you knew that Mr. Gates had made arrangements to obtain the services of the victim that night, didn't you? In fact, you knew all about the operation that provided the prostitutes, didn't you?"

"No, I didn't."

"Are you lying again, Mr. Stanford?"

"Objection. Argumentative."

"Sustained."

I take a step back to the lectern. It's time to start fitting some of the pieces together. If we are to have any hope of convincing the jury of Skipper's innocence—or at least get them to reasonable doubt—I'm going to have to do this in a manner they will understand. I turn on a computer projector. The first thing that appears on the screen in the front of the courtroom is the home page of the Boys of the Bay Area Web site. It all starts there.

I approach Turner and ask, "Are you familiar with an Internet Web site called Boys of the Bay Area?"

He glances at the screen. "No."

"I thought you might say that," I say. "We've talked about it earlier in this trial." As a reminder to the jury, I explain to him that Johnny Garcia's picture appeared in the site and that the prosecution has asserted that Skipper obtained prostitutes through that site. None of this should be news to him, although he feigns ignorance. "It's a pretty nasty business, Mr. Stanford. It's a bodies-for-sale business—boys' and young men's bodies. A boy like Johnny Garcia. Are you sure you've never heard of it?"

He holds up his hands. "Doesn't ring a bell," he says.

Okay. I introduce a written affidavit from a company called Network Solutions, the major registrar of Internet domain names in the United States. It states that the domain name for the Boys of the Bay Area Web site is owned by a corporation called El Camino Holdings. I show the affidavit to Turner and ask, "Does the name El Camino Holdings ring any bells?"

A brief pause, then, "No."

"Really?" I say. I look at the jury for a moment and then turn back to Turner. "Didn't you file incorporation papers for that entity?"

"I don't recall," Turner says. "I'm called upon to form many new entities. It's a perfectly routine process."

"But not all new entities own the domain names to pornographic Web sites," I say. "And not all Web sites provide the services of male prostitutes, one of whom happened to be the victim in this case. In fact, it was this Web site that provided the services of Johnny Garcia to Mr. Gates. Are you still saying you had nothing to do with that?"

"That's exactly what I'm saying."

It's exactly the answer I expect. I introduce the certified copy of the articles of incorporation of El Camino Holdings. I have already provided it to Payne, who doesn't object. I distribute copies to the jury. A moment later I hand a copy to Turner and ask him, "Is your memory of El Camino Holdings getting any better?"

"No."

"That's your signature on the articles of incorporation, isn't it?"

"Yes."

"And you're an astute and experienced attorney, right? It's hard to believe you would have signed your name to something you knew nothing about."

For the first time in the years I've known Turner, he shows a hint of concern. "Now that you mention it," he says, "I do recall the entity. A client asked me to file the incorporation papers."

"A client asked you to form an entity that was engaged in pornography and prostitution?"

He swallows. "A client asked me to file the papers. I had no idea what the entity would be used for."

Right. "Which client?"

"That's confidential."

I ask the judge to compel Turner to answer.

Judge Kelly considers the issue for just a moment. "The witness will answer."

Turner looks up at the ceiling and says, "My client was Mr. Donald Martinez."

"I see. And you and Mr. Martinez were business partners on this deal, weren't you?"

"No."

"And you helped form a profitable pornography and prostitution business and now you're trying to protect its main investor, Mr. Martinez."

"Objection. Argumentative."

"Overruled."

"No. Mr. Martinez asked me to file the papers because he and an associate wanted a corporation in place for a potential new deal. I didn't have anything to do with the business. I just filed the articles of incorporation. And I can assure you that Mr. Martinez is not involved in pornography or prostitution."

When in doubt, deny. For the moment, however, it's all I can get. It will serve no useful purpose to accuse Turner of putting the GHB in the drinks or the duct tape on Garcia's nose. There is no evidence suggesting that he did, and we'll lose credibility with the jury if we do. I'm going to try to raise questions in the minds of the jurors. Payne doesn't cross-examine Turner. We'll see what Martinez has to say about all of this in a moment. He's up next.

Donald Martinez's gold cuff links gleam as he sits in the witness box a few minutes later. The jury seems appropriately impressed when he says he owns a major produce business, a construction firm and several car dealerships. I see the BART supervisor nod when Martinez says that he is the president of the Mission Redevelopment Fund.

The home page of the Boys of the Bay Area Web site is still projected on the screen at the front of the courtroom when I approach him. "Mr. Martinez," I say, "we understand that you asked your attorney, Mr. Stanford, to form an entity called El Camino Holdings."

"That's correct."

"Would you mind telling us the purpose of the entity?"

"Of course. I have no secrets. It was formed as an investment vehicle for one of my business associates. It was going to take title to a property on Valencia Street. It is very common to form a separate entity in such circumstances in order to minimize potential liabilities."

"Would you please identify your business associate?"

"Kevin Anderson."

The ball is bouncing from Turner Stanford to Donald Martinez to

Kevin Anderson. We'll see where it bounces next. I ask him if he has any ownership interest in the business.

"None."

"Are you an officer or a director?"

"No."

"Mr. Martinez," I say, "Mr. Anderson is a sophisticated business-man. He has his own lawyers. Why did he ask you to form the new en-tity?"

"We had discussed the possibility of being coinvestors in the deal. And we use the same lawyer on certain matters, Mr. Stanford."

He has a tidy answer for everything. "And did you complete the deal?"

"No. The property acquisition never moved forward. We never used the corporation."

I point to the screen and say, "Are you familiar with a porno-graphic Web site called Boys of the Bay Area?"

"I've heard the name. I have nothing to do with it."

It's the answer I expect. I show him the domain name affidavit and ask, "Do you have any idea how the corporation that you formed hap-pened to acquire the domain name of an entity that engages in pornography and prostitution?"

He shakes his head. "I have no idea."

"And is it your testimony that you had no involvement in the setup or operation of this Web site?"

"That's correct."

That figures. "Mr. Martinez," I continue, "you are the president of a nonprofit corporation called the Mission Redevelopment Fund, aren't you?"

"Yes."

"And one of the properties that the fund owns is the Curtis resi-dential hotel located on Valencia Street, isn't it?"

"That's true."

I ask him if he is aware that a police action took place at Room 204 of the Curtis on Saturday night. He acknowledges that he was told about it. "In fact," I say, "the police found all sorts of drugs and porno-graphic materials in Room 204, didn't they?"

"I can't comment on the details, Mr. Daley."

"Well, maybe I can help you with that. It was reported that Room 204 was the location where the Boys of the Bay Area Web site was produced, wasn't it, Mr. Martinez?"

"Yes."

"And they found something else up there, didn't they?"

He frowns. "They found drugs."

"A substantial amount of drugs, right, Mr. Martinez?"

"Yes."

"In fact, Mr. Martinez, they found heroin in that room with a street value of over a quarter of a million dollars, didn't they?"

He exhales loudly. "So I'm told."

"Mr. Martinez," I say, "were you aware that the Boys of the Bay Area Web site was maintained in a room at the Curtis?"

"That was brought to my attention this week. I was very disturbed by this information."

"Do you know the name of the tenant who signed the lease with your agency?"

He pauses and says, "My property manager informed me that there was no lease on that room."

I stop to give the jury a chance to think about his answer, then I say, "Isn't that unusual, Mr. Martinez? Isn't it customary for your agency to sign a lease with each tenant?"

He has no choice. "Yes."

"Yet there was no lease in this case."

"That's correct."

"Can you explain why?"

He shakes his head and says, "No."

"Who had access to the room?"

He exhales loudly and says, "I don't know."

How convenient. "And neither you nor your colleague, Mr. Anderson, had anything to do with this business?"

"That's correct."

Not so fast. "Yet it was operating out of one of your rooms."

"We own a lot of properties, Mr. Daley. We can't possibly keep track of the activities in every room."

Sure. "Mr. Martinez," I say, "do you spend any time at the properties owned by the redevelopment fund?"

"Yes."

"Did you spend any time at the Curtis?"

"From time to time."

"In fact, it's just around the corner from your office, isn't it?"

"That's correct."

"Did you ever check out what was going on in Room 204?"

"Mr. Daley," he says, "we don't enter the rooms unless we have a compelling legal reason to do so. We had no idea what was going on behind its doors. We had no reason to investigate."

"So the fact that one of your rooms was being used to run a pornography and prostitution ring in a building just around the corner from your office never found its way onto your radar screen, did it?"

"That's correct."

"That's absurd, Mr. Martinez."

"Objection."

"Sustained."

It's as far as I can go with Martinez. Payne asks him just a couple of questions. He issues yet another denial of any involvement in the Boys of the Bay Area Web site. The connections between Turner, Martinez, Anderson and the events at the Fairmont are still too tenuous to make a credible case to the jury that any of them might have been involved in Garcia's death.

It's almost four o'clock when I call Kevin Anderson to the stand. This is our last chance to put everything together for the jury. The jurors are still staring at the home page to the Boys of the Bay Area Web site. I get Anderson to confirm that he asked Martinez for help forming an entity called El Camino Holdings for the purpose of buying a piece of property on Valencia Street. Turner filed the incorporation papers. "We never bought the property," he says. "We never used the corporation."

"Do you have any idea how the corporation came to own the domain name for the Boys of the Bay Area Web site?" I ask.

Anderson remains confident. "I'm not entirely sure, Mr. Daley," he says. "A young man in the neighborhood named Andrew Holton approached me about starting a business. He wanted to incorporate and he asked for my help. I told him he could save the time and money if he used the existing corporate shell that we had put together for the Valencia Street deal, so I gave him the incorporation papers for El Camino Holdings. I presume he registered the domain name."

He's more forthcoming than I would have thought. Then again, he doesn't want to be the last one holding the El Camino Holdings documents when the music stops. Like Stanford and Martinez before him, he's trying to distance himself from El Camino Holdings. El Camino Holdings has now been lateraled over to Andy Holton. He won't be able to pass it to anybody else. "How did you happen to meet Mr. Holton?"

Anderson pauses and says, "I was his roommate's social worker."

"And who was his roommate?"

"The victim, Johnny Garcia."

Good. At least we have a connection running from Turner, Martinez and Anderson to Holton and Garcia. Other than that, I'm still shooting in the dark.

"Mr. Anderson," I say, "did you have anything to do with the creation of the Boys of the Bay Area Web site?"

"No sir. I don't know anything about a pornographic Web site. I had no idea the domain name was registered in the name of that entity."

"Was anybody other than Mr. Holton involved?"

"Not that I'm aware of."

"What can you tell us about Mr. Holton?"

"He's dead."

"What else?"

"Not much. I didn't know him well. He used to work at a restaurant on Sixteenth Street called the Pancho Villa. He and the victim lived at the Jerry Hotel across the street."

"Are you aware that he was a drug dealer?"

"That's what I understand."

"And are you aware that he was a pimp?"

"So I'm told."

"And are you aware that Johnny Garcia, the individual for whom you were a social worker, was a prostitute?"

"Yes."

"And you must have been aware that Mr. Garcia was working for Mr. Holton."

"I am aware of that now. I thought they were just roommates. I had no idea they had a business relationship."

Bullshit. "It seems to me that you didn't keep a very close eye on Johnny Garcia."

"Objection," Payne says. "Is there a question there?"

"Sustained."

Let's take this in another direction. "Mr. Anderson," I say, "I understand that Johnny Garcia called you the night he died. Twice, in fact."

"That's correct."

"And you've told the police that Mr. Garcia left messages for you that he needed help."

"Yes. I didn't get the messages until the following morning."

"Right. And he wanted you to go over to the Fairmont to help him, right?"

He looks appropriately contrite. "Yes. If I had gotten the message a little earlier, I might have been able to help him."

Sure. "Mr. Anderson," I say, "who was Mr. Garcia working for that night?"

"Mr. Gates."

"No. I'm not asking who procured his services. I want to know the name of his pimp."

Anderson looks toward the judge for help. She instructs him to answer the question. He says, "I believe he was working for Andy Holton that night."

I feign incredulity. "The same Andy Holton who started the Boys of the Bay Area Web site?"

"Yes."

"The same Andy Holton who was found dead a few weeks later at the Hotel Royan on Valencia Street?"

"Yes."

"Yet it is your testimony that neither you nor Mr. Holton had anything to do with Mr. Garcia's death."

"That's correct."

One more connection. I cue the video player and run a portion of the security videos from the Fairmont. I turn to Anderson and ask, "Do you recognize the person in that video?"

"Yes. It looks like Andy Holton."

"It is. And would it surprise you to find out that he returned to the Fairmont the night Johnny Garcia died?"

He pauses. "I was told that was the case."

"Did you talk to Andy Holton that night?"

"No."

"Did he try to contact you?"

"No."

"Do you have any idea why he may have gone to the Fairmont that night?"

"No."

"Is it possible that he may have gone there to pick up Johnny Garcia?"

"It's possible."

"And isn't it a fact that you told the police that Mr. Garcia and Mr. Holton were fighting shortly before Mr. Garcia died?"

"That's true, but it doesn't have anything to do with Mr. Garcia's death."

"How do you know? What were they fighting about?"

He remains calm. "The usual stuff, Mr. Daley. The rent. The bills. They were roommates. They also had a business relationship. They didn't get along very well."

"Mr. Anderson," I say, "explain this to me. We have a corporation set up by Mr. Stanford at the instruction of you and Mr. Martinez. Out of the goodness of your heart, you gave the corporation to a known prostitute and pimp named Andrew Holton, who ran a pornographic Web site and prostitution service out of a room at the Curtis, which, coincidentally, was owned by the nonprofit corporation controlled by Mr. Martinez. Mr. Holton's roommate turned out to be a male prostitute who was found dead in my client's hotel room. Coincidentally, both Mr. Stanford and Mr. Holton were at the Fairmont right around the very same time that Mr. Garcia died. In fact, you were there that night, too. You have also told us that Mr. Holton and Mr. Garcia were fighting. To top it off, you claim that neither you nor Mr. Martinez nor Mr. Stanford is in any way involved in any of this. Is that about the gist of it?"

"Objection. Mr. Daley is starting his closing argument a little early."

"Is there a question there, Mr. Daley?"

"Yes there is, Your Honor. My question is this: How are Mr. Anderson, Mr. Stanford, Mr. Martinez and Mr. Holton connected to the Boys of the Bay Area Web site and Johnny Garcia?"

The judge says, "I'll allow the witness to answer."

Anderson sums it all up by saying, "Mr. Martinez, Mr. Stanford and I were involved only to the extent that we arranged to have incorporation papers filed with the secretary of state for the entity that owned the domain name. We had nothing to do with its operation and we certainly had nothing to do with the events that took place at the Fairmont Hotel in the early morning of September seventh."

I give him an incredulous look and he adds, "I know how it must look, Mr. Daley."

"So does everybody in this courtroom, Mr. Anderson."

"Objection."

"Sustained."

"No further questions."

He's given a forceful denial. Payne has no reason to cross-examine him.

"How is Natalie?" I ask Rosie, who is still at Natalie's house. I've called her from my cell phone from the corridor in the Hall.

"Not well. She must be in dreadful pain. She's withdrawn. She won't talk to me. One of the servants told me she hasn't slept in weeks."

"Is Ann with her?"

"Yes, but she won't talk to Ann, either. Her doctor is here. He's prescribing sleeping pills."

Damn.

She asks me how things went at court.

I tell her about El Camino Holdings and say, "I think I was able to show that Turner, Martinez and Anderson were all connected to the Boys of the Bay Area Web site."

She pauses to consider for a moment. "That's great, except all it shows is that they were involved in the porn business," she says. "It doesn't prove that any of them killed Garcia."

"I was also able to connect them all to Holton and Garcia. But you're right. Let's face it: There's no smoking gun. We know Turner and Holton were there that night, but we have nothing solid that can let us blame Garcia's death on either of them. All we can do is hope the jury gets to reasonable doubt."

She sighs. "We're supposed to wrap up the case tomorrow. What now?"

"Time for one more trip down to the Mission," I say. I ask her to meet me there.

"What do you propose to do down there?"

"Hold a summit conference."

45

"DO WHAT YOUR HEART TELLS YOU IS RIGHT"

"Gates defense team attempts to discredit respected Mission businessman."
—SAN FRANCISCO CHRONICLE. WEDNESDAY, OCTOBER 27.

The defense team regroups at eight o'clock that night in the corner of the squad room at Mission Station. Ron Morales is sitting on his desk, a grim look on his face. Pete, Rosie, Molinari and I huddle around him. A moment later, Tony walks in with Hector Ramirez.

"You wanted to see me?" Hector asks.

"We need your help," I say.

He eyes me warily. "Why me?"

"You're our only contact who knows anything about Martinez's operation. We were hoping you might be able to give us some additional information." And we're desperate.

He scowls. "What do you want to know?"

"We think Donald Martinez, Turner Stanford and Kevin Anderson are all somehow involved in the business that operates the Boys of the Bay Area Web site, which has been run out of the Curtis Hotel. We can't figure out how the pieces fit together."

"What does this have to do with me?"

"Maybe nothing," Rosie says. "Maybe you've told us everything you know. Maybe this is all just a dead end. But you're the only person who might be able to help us connect the dots. Is there anything you haven't told us about Donald Martinez?"

Hector glances at Tony and asks me, "What sort of things?"

"His involvement with the Boys of the Bay Area Web site and Andy Holton," I reply. "Anything unusual or suspicious in his activities. Do you know anything?"

"I can't help you," he says.

"Let me ask you this," Rosie says. "Is there stuff that you know that you can't tell us? Maybe you can at least point us in the right direction."

I've seen Rosie use this line before. It works.

"There are some things I haven't told you," he says. "Things that I *can't* tell you."

"Hector," Tony says, "what you tell us tonight won't leave this room. I promise." He looks at me and then at Rosie.

"I can do even better than that," Rosie says. "As of this moment, you are now a client of Fernandez and Daley's. Everything you say to us is confidential." She gestures toward Tony, Pete and Morales and adds, "You guys aren't here." It's a slightly strained interpretation of the attorney-client privilege rules, but it will have to do in the circumstances.

Hector turns to Tony and asks, "Why are you so interested in helping out Skipper Gates?"

Tony says, "I'm not. I'm interested in helping out Rosie. And I'm interested in finding out what happened to Johnny Garcia." He thinks for a moment and then adds, "Though in all honesty, I wouldn't mind nailing Donald Martinez's ass to the wall for sending that goon to my store."

Hector scowls. "I can't do it," he says. "I have a wife and kids. I've already lost my job."

Tony looks at him and says, "I'm going to fix that right now. I need help at the market. Effective immediately, you're working for me—full-time."

Hector ponders and says, "It isn't that I'm ungrateful, but next time they could beat me up like they did you—or worse."

Morales says, "There won't be a next time."

INCRIMINATING EVIDENCE

INCRIMINATING EVIDENCE   353

"How can you be so sure?"

"We will protect you and your family. Guaranteed."

"There are no guarantees. If you're wrong, I'll end up dead."

Morales raises his index finger and says in a tone that leaves no doubt, "That will not happen."

"Ron," I say, "Hector needs more than a promise. He needs assurances."

"That's right," Hector says. "Assurances."

"What kind?" Morales asks.

Rosie says, "Guaranteed, full-time, round-the-clock protection from the SFPD. We need a police car sitting in front of his house—twenty-four hours a day—at least until this blows over."

"You know we don't have the resources," Morales says.

"Then find them," Rosie replies.

Morales drums his fingers on his desk. "I haven't even heard his testimony yet—it better be awfully good."

Hector stares him down and says emphatically, "Oh, it's good."

Morales's eyes open wide. "How good?" he asks.

"Real good."

Morales is now fully engaged. "Like what?"

"I've delivered envelopes containing large amounts of cash from Room 204 at the Curtis Hotel to various destinations in the neighborhood." Hector looks at Morales as if to say "Is that good enough for you?"

"I'll need to know the details," Morales says.

I interject, "We'll have to work out arrangements for Hector first."

Morales is irritated. "What arrangements?" he asks.

"We need to find him a decent apartment in the neighborhood for his wife and kids. He can't stay in the projects."

Morales throws up his hands. "Be reasonable," he says. "We're cops—we're not in the housing business. You know I can't promise him a new apartment."

I say, "Call Ernie Clemente. Call Ramon Aguirre. They know everybody in the neighborhood. They have connections. They can find a new place for him."

Rosie adds, "And we'll need complete immunity for Hector. I don't want you guys to arrest him for a traffic ticket after he testifies."

I add the final touch. "We want all of this in writing tonight."

Morales swallows. "Why tonight?"

"Because we're supposed to finish up our case in the morning. We need Hector to testify."

Hector's eyes dart in my direction. He's afraid.

Morales is exasperated. This is more than he had bargained for. "We're the SFPD, not the CIA, for God's sake. Do you think this is the federal witness protection program? These things take time. I don't have the authority to do this on my own."

I hand him my cell phone. "Then find somebody who does. This may be the best chance you'll ever have to get Donald Martinez. You can start by calling your captain and Elaine McBride and Roosevelt Johnson. And call Hillary Payne and tell her she's more than welcome to come down here and join us."

And then Hector finally talks.

Ten o'clock. The crowd now includes Payne, McNulty, the captain at Mission Station, an assistant chief, McBride and Johnson. If we pooled the resources of everybody present, we could bring down a small third-world country.

Payne stands with her arms folded. "This had better be good," she says.

"It is," I promise.

"Then, what *is* it?"

I glance at Hector, who is sitting in Morales's chair. I introduce him and explain that he used to work for Martinez until he was unceremoniously fired. "Mr. Ramirez," I say, "is prepared to testify that he was called upon three times a week to deliver thick manila envelopes from Room 204 of the Curtis Hotel to various places."

"So?"

"The envelopes contained large amounts of cash."

Payne is intrigued. "How much cash?" she asks.

"Thousands of dollars," I say.

Payne glances at McNasty. "Were the envelopes sealed?" she asks.

"Yes," I say.

"How did he know they contained cash?"

Hector says, "I know."

"You're prepared to testify that there was money in the envelopes?"

"Yes."

Payne turns back to me. "Explain to me what Mr. Ramirez would ask in return for this information."

"Full immunity, a new place to live and round-the-clock police protection—guaranteed."

"You're asking for a lot," McNulty says.

"He's giving a lot," I reply. "Donald Martinez is an influential man."

"Martinez already fired him," Morales adds. "And we think Martinez was responsible for a robbery and attack at Tony Fernandez's store. I'm not going to let that happen again. We can't let that happen again."

"There's a serious problem," McNulty says.

"What's that?" I ask.

"It isn't against the law to transport cash. We have no evidence that it was stolen. We have no evidence that it was obtained through illegal means or in connection with illegal activities. For all we know, it was just the daily receipts from Martinez's produce business."

"Come on, Bill," I say. "They found the headquarters of a prostitution ring and a quarter of a million dollars of heroin in Room 204 at the Curtis Hotel. That's not where he ran his produce business. You guys should be able to put the pieces together."

McNulty looks at Payne and says, "It may be enough to consider opening an investigation, but it's not enough to file charges. And it certainly isn't enough to make any charges stick. No deal."

Hell.

We sit in silence. I can hear the buzz from the lightbulb above us. Hector looks down at the floor.

Rosie says, "Would you make the deal if we could prove that the money was obtained illegally?"

McNasty doesn't hesitate. "Absolutely. But I don't see how you're going to be able to do that." He looks at Hector and says, "I presume your involvement in this matter was limited to delivering the envelopes. I take it you were not involved in obtaining the funds."

I leap in. "You don't need to answer that, Hector." All we need right now is for Hector to get his ass arrested by admitting that he was involved in drug deals or prostitution.

Hector holds up his hands and says, "It's all right, Mike. I can assure you I didn't have any involvement in the activities in Room 204 of the Curtis."

McNulty nods. "That's fine," he says, "but it still leaves us with a hole. I can't make a deal unless you can show the money was obtained illegally."

Stalemate. The assembled group is completely silent. McNulty stands with his arms folded. Morales's disappointment shows in his body language. Payne picks up her briefcase. She and McNulty begin to head toward the door. My mind races. I need to buy time. I turn to Hector and ask, "Where did you deliver the money?"

Payne and McNulty turn around.

Hector thinks for a moment, then says, "The places you'd expect: the bank, supermarkets, restaurants, suppliers."

Still no smoking gun. "Anyplace else? Anywhere out of the ordinary?" I ask. I'm hoping he's delivered bribe money to half the Board of Supervisors. It isn't likely—Martinez is far too careful to be caught red-handed.

"Not really," he says. "I made my deliveries mostly to people in the produce business."

Shit.

He stops. Then he says, "And I made a few deliveries to the office of Mr. Kevin Anderson."

There it is! The connection between the Web site and Martinez and Anderson. "How many deliveries?" I ask.

"Two or three."

"Did the deliveries involve substantial sums?"

"I think so. The envelopes were fat."

I look at Payne and ask, "Is that enough?"

She shrugs and says, "It still isn't enough to charge anybody with anything. Martinez and Anderson will both claim the money was delivered for perfectly legitimate purposes."

Damn. I ask Hector if he took cash anyplace else.

He ponders for a moment and says, "I did make some deliveries to Father Aguirre at St. Peter's every once in a while."

Seems innocuous enough—even commendable, I suppose. "How often?"

"Every couple of weeks."

"Was it a lot of money?"

"Well, the envelopes were pretty thick."

I scan the faces of McNulty, Payne, Johnson and McBride. McNulty asks, "Did you get a receipt from Father Aguirre?"

"No."

Payne remains unimpressed. "It isn't illegal to make charitable contributions to your church."

Roosevelt tries to help us. "No," he says, "but it would be very interesting to see if the cash had been reported by Martinez as taxable income. Tax evasion is illegal even if the funds are donated to a church. And it's also illegal for the church to accept donations without reporting them—a case can be made for fraud on the part of the donor *and* the church. The attorney general's office is in charge of monitoring the activities of charitable and religious organizations. I have a couple of friends in the AG's office who might be willing to open an investigation."

"It's a huge stretch," Payne says. "Think about what you're suggesting. You want to try to get Martinez for tax evasion and fraud for donating money to St. Peter's. That's insane. You may even be suggesting that Father Aguirre did something wrong. St. Peter's is the most prominent social institution in this community. Father Aguirre may be the most influential clergyman in the Bay Area. Donald Martinez is a highly regarded businessman. Think of the fallout when you try to nail Martinez for donating money to the church. Think of the backlash when you go after Father Aguirre. You'll look like a fool. We'll *all* look like fools!"

Roosevelt folds his arms. He brings to bear the authority of all forty-two years of his experience on the SFPD when he says without raising his voice, "This is the best chance we've had in twenty years to get Donald Martinez and you won't even open an investigation. You have a chance to show some courage and make your mark as a prosecutor, and you're going to play politics and worry about your image in the newspapers. This is a sad day for law enforcement in this city."

Payne responds, "There isn't enough evidence, Roosevelt. You know that. There's nothing we can do."

Silence. Then I say to her, "You're saying you won't go after

Martinez even though everybody here knows he's running a drug and prostitution ring across the street from Mission Station."

"You can't prove it."

"And you won't investigate the fact that we now have documented proof that he's using drug and prostitution money to make fraudulent contributions to St. Peter's."

Payne takes in my diatribe without showing emotion. "You can't prove that, either," she says. "I'd like to nail him as much as you would, but I can't open an investigation or file charges unless I have evidence. Right now, I don't."

I can feel my hands start to shake. I raise my voice. "Christ, Hillary!" I shout. "Don't you give a damn about *justice?*"

Payne glares at me and says in a measured tone, "As a matter of fact, I do. And I believe in the rule of law, which says that I have to have sufficient evidence to open an investigation or file charges." She nods to McNulty and says, "This meeting is over. We'll see you in court in the morning." She and McNulty start for the door.

I'm desperate. "Hillary," I shout to her back, "what *would* it take to get you to open an investigation? What corroboration do you need?"

She looks at McNulty and then turns slowly and faces me. She thinks for a moment and says, "I'll agree to your deal for Mr. Ramirez and I will open an investigation of Mr. Martinez if, and only if, you get me corroboration that St. Peter's accepted cash donations from Martinez that the church did not report."

My mind races. "Wait here, please," I say. "I'll be back in a little while."

"Where are you going?" Payne asks.

"To church."

"What is it, Mike?" Ramon Aguirre asks. "You said it was urgent."

It's midnight. He was asleep when I called him, but he's gotten here fast. We're sitting in the front row at St. Peter's. The church is still. A single votive candle flickers near the altar.

"I need your help."

He says after a pause, "I hope this doesn't have anything to do with Donald Martinez."

"It does."

"I can't."

"Ramon, we need somebody to corroborate the fact that Martinez was moving money through a corporation called El Camino Holdings. The corporation was funneling money from a prostitution and pornography Web site."

"I don't know anything about it."

"They were selling heroin, Ramon. They were destroying lives."

He doesn't respond.

"Listen, Ramon, one of Martinez's former employees has told us that Martinez made substantial cash donations to St. Peter's. He told us he delivered thousands of dollars in cash from the Curtis Hotel to the church. It is our presumption that the church never reported these donations. If that's correct, the attorney general may be willing to open an investigation if we can get corroboration of this. I know it's difficult, but please, Ramon. They're selling young men. One is already dead. They're distributing millions of dollars' worth of heroin. Somebody almost killed Rosie's brother. You can make this stop. You can end it."

"I can't, Mike."

"Ramon, you have to."

"You don't understand. It's complicated."

"You won't be implicated. We'll get you full immunity."

"I'll lose my job. It's the only job I've ever wanted. The church will never back me up."

"The church will think you're a hero if you blow the whistle on the drugs and prostitution."

He looks at the altar and says, "Maybe. Maybe not. But this isn't about me. The extra money we get from Martinez goes straight to the neediest members of our parish. Innocent people will be hurt. They use the money to buy food. This is about people who can't fend for themselves."

"They shouldn't be using blood money from prostitutes and drug dealers to do so."

"Easy for you to say. You don't live on the street. You aren't trying to make ends meet on a monthly welfare check. You aren't trying to feed Grace on a minimum-wage job. You don't wake up every day without hope. I have no idea where the money comes from. I don't want to know. It's delivered to my office at the rectory, no questions asked."

I walk to the altar and make the sign of the cross. Then I turn back to him and say, "This isn't easy for me, either. I'm on your side. I know the hardships you face. I know you have a tough job. But I'm going to call you as a witness tomorrow. I want you to do what we were taught in our first week at the seminary—I want you to put your faith in God and do what your heart tells you is right."

I'm back at Mission Station at one-thirty. Pete has taken Hector home. Rosie, Molinari and I are sitting with Payne and McNulty to pound out Hector's immunity agreement on Rosie's laptop. I've promised that Ramon Aguirre will testify tomorrow that the church did not report substantial cash contributions from Donald Martinez. I hope he'll come through.

"There's something else we should discuss tonight," I say.

"What?" Payne asks.

"Seeing as how we're going to prove that Martinez and Anderson were involved in the porn business, it seems to me that you should drop the charges against Skipper."

"Mike," Payne says, "Hector's testimony is going to show that they may be involved in drugs and prostitution. We won't fight you when you introduce his testimony. But that's all. You haven't demonstrated that they had anything to do with the murder of Johnny Garcia."

"Stanford and Anderson were both there that night," I insist. "They both had opportunity. They both had motive."

"You can save yourself the embarrassment of losing this case," Rosie says. "You'll make up for it by prosecuting Donald Martinez."

McNasty shakes his head. "Not so fast," he says. "We've got a murder case in trial. You guys have shown that Martinez and Anderson were in the porn business and that Stanford set up the corporation that owned the pornographic Web site. So what? The porn business may be unsavory, but it isn't illegal. You still haven't shown that they were involved in the murder of Johnny Garcia. And you haven't cleared Gates. You're the ones who have to make the pieces fit. For the reasons we've discussed, I'm willing to let Hector Ramirez testify and give him immunity, but I will not drop the charges against Skipper. The case against him remains."

"See you in court in the morning," Payne says.

Wednesday is a blur. First off, I inform Judge Kelly that we plan to call Hector and Ramon as witnesses and that the prosecution knows this. Hector takes the stand at nine o'clock and tells the jury that he delivered cash from Room 204 of the Curtis Hotel to Anderson. He says that he also delivered cash to Father Ramon Aguirre at St. Peter's. He is not only remarkably collected, he's almost serene. I am less surprised by this than I would have been if Rosie hadn't told me on our way to court that he has a very personal reason for wanting to nail Martinez. It turns out Johnny Garcia was his godson. He had promised Johnny's mother that he would help take care of him, he confided to Rosie, and he hadn't done a very good job. I lead him shamelessly. Hillary does not object. Nor does she cross-examine him.

I call Ramon Aguirre to the stand and ask him whether a representative of Donald Martinez ever delivered cash to him at the church.

He doesn't hesitate. "Yes."

"And were those donations substantial?"

"Yes. Thousands of dollars."

"Were those donations documented in the church's standard manner?"

He tugs at his collar and says, "No. The donations were not recorded on the books of the church."

"Why not?"

"Mr. Martinez asked us to keep them confidential."

I ask him how the funds were used.

"They were redistributed to needy members of the community."

"And do you know the source of the cash?"

He looks straight at me and says, "I have recently been told the cash came from the Curtis Hotel. I have also been told that there may have been illegal prostitution and drug-related activities going on there."

"No further questions."

Payne does not cross-examine him.

I recall Donald Martinez, who says that it is common in the produce business for large amounts of cash to change hands. He says that all donations to St. Peter's were reported in the appropriate manner and that deliveries to Kevin Anderson's office were for legitimate business purposes relating to a project they were developing together. I think I see a couple of jurors shaking their heads. Payne doesn't cross-examine him.

Finally, I put Anderson back on the stand to explain the cash deliveries to his office. He insists that they were all made for legitimate business purposes. He acknowledges that although it is uncommon for him to deal in large amounts of cash, it is not unheard of. I look at the jury, but I can't tell what impact, if any, all this testimony has had. Payne doesn't cross-examine him, either.

"Any further witnesses?" Judge Kelly asks me after Anderson steps down.

I glance at Skipper and say, "No, Your Honor. The defense rests." She pounds her gavel.

Hillary begins her closing argument at ten o'clock. We lawyers like to think that if our closings are eloquent enough, we might be able to persuade the jury to do what we want. I've never bought it. Most jurors that I've talked to have said they've made up their minds well before the lawyers begin their closings. A juror in a murder trial a few years ago summarized things succinctly. "I didn't believe a word you guys said," he told me.

After weeks of playing the role of the aggressive prosecutor, Hillary tries for a folksy approach. After she finishes, I opt for a conversational tone. I feel myself walking around the courtroom. I see the jurors' faces when I try to punch holes in each piece of evidence. I suggest to them that the relationship among Martinez, Stanford and Anderson, and their respective connections to the Boys of the Bay Area Web site and Andy Holton, leaves them with ample cause to find reasonable doubt. A lot goes through your mind when you're in the middle of a closing. You watch for signals in the jurors' eyes. You monitor the time. You pace yourself. Suddenly, the clock on the wall says it's almost noon. I glance at Rosie, who closes her eyes. I give the jury one last look. "I want you to look at the facts when you go back to the jury room," I say. "I want you to deliberate. We have very serious issues in this case. And Prentice Gates's very life will be decided in that jury room."

I thank them for their attention. If the jury bought any of my closing, they aren't showing it. I can't tell. I'm exhausted.

Judge Kelly charges the jury right before lunch. She promised them a short trial. She is remaining true to her word. There's nothing we can do now except wait.

Reporters surround me as I leave the Hall. Microphones are jammed toward my face. I offer the usual platitudes about the strength of our case. A reporter from Channel 5 asks me whether we plan to appeal. I tell her it's customary to wait until the verdict comes down before we start thinking about appeals. The silver-haired sage from Channel 7 asks me how Skipper is holding up.

"Just fine," I reply. He's in better shape than I am.

"What are you thinking about?" Rosie asks me as we drive back to the office.

"Nothing."

"Come on."

"My closing."

She tells me I did fine.

"Thanks. I'm not so sure."

"The jury was with you."

I hope so. We head east on Bryant and turn left at Third. I replay the trial in my head. I think of everything I would have done differently. I berate myself for agreeing to let Skipper rush into an early trial before we had the results of the DNA tests.

I feel Rosie's hand on my cheek. "Don't beat yourself up on this one," she says.

"I can't help it. It's the way I'm drawn."

"Maybe you should get redrawn."

"Maybe." I swallow hard.

"What is it?" Rosie asks.

"I was just thinking about Ramon."

"What about him?"

"How tough his job is."

"You should know."

"I do. We just made it a lot tougher—if he still has a job."

Rosie sighs. "You can't blame yourself for that. Dirty money is— dirty. Donating it to the church is wrong, even if it goes for a good cause."

"A lot of people are going to get hurt."

"A few prostitutes and some kids on heroin may catch a break."

"The prostitutes will still be there tomorrow. The kids on heroin will find their fix from somebody else."

"You're trying to take a drug dealer off the street, Mike. That's a victory, even if he was a big benefactor of St. Peter's. Why can't you accept the fact that there's no such thing as a perfect world?"

She's right, of course. It doesn't make me feel any better. We drive the rest of the way to the office in silence.

That night, we're in Rosie's office, watching the local news on Bay TV. In what might best be described as the legal profession's equivalent of harmonic convergence, Mort the Sport Goldberg is interviewing Nick the Dick Hanson. The discourse is conducted at a highly professional level. "In especially riveting testimony," Mort says, "prominent local businessman Donald Martinez was accused of funding a prostitution and pornography business in the Mission District. It was also suggested that some of the proceeds of the business were funneled to the historic St. Peter's Catholic Church. The attorney general's office says it will open an investigation. In a hastily convened press conference outside of the courtroom, Mr. Martinez denied all the accusations and referred the matter to his attorney. A spokesman for the archdiocese said the matter was being investigated and had no further comment at this time."

Rosie turns off the TV and says, "This case has certainly touched some raw nerves."

I agree. I ask her if she's spoken to Ann.

"Yes. Natalie's doctor has put her on stronger medication," she tells me. "I'm worried about her. Ann's going to stay with her tonight." She looks at me and asks, "Are *you* going to be all right?"

"I hope so."

She puts her hand on my cheek. "Would you like to stay with me tonight? Grace is staying at my mom's."

My stomach churns. "I'd like that." I need it.

Rosie's phone rings. She picks up and looks surprised. "That's awfully quick," she says. "What time?" She hangs up. "The jury's back," she says. "They'd decided to deliberate into the evening. They're going to read the verdict at nine o'clock tomorrow."

Wow. They've been out for only six hours. They certainly didn't waste any time, but I remind myself that short deliberations don't necessarily cut either way. It is almost impossible to predict which way a jury will go. "Do me a favor," I say. "Tomorrow's going to be very rough for Natalie. Would you go out to the house and come with her and Ann to court? I have a feeling she'll need you."

"Sure."

I spend a sleepless, stomach-churning night staring at the whirling ceiling fan in Rosie's bedroom. My demons always come out at night. I barely slept during our divorce and custody hearings. Every time I close my eyes, I see all the faces: Skipper's once charismatic glow reduced to a hollow pallor; Natalie's once brilliant eyes, now virtually lifeless; Turner's self-righteous smirk; Martinez's confident facade; Anderson's complacent grin; Ann's icy stare. I see the pain on Ernie Clemente's face and the resignation on Ramon Aguirre's. I see fear and desperation in the eyes of Johnny Garcia and Andy Holton.

At four A.M., I look at Rosie. Even with all the trauma in our lives, she manages to sleep at night. I don't know how she does it. I've always loved the way she smiles when she sleeps. She looks so content. Somehow, she senses that I'm looking at her and her eyes flutter open. She looks at me and says, "Go to sleep, Mike. Things will look better in the morning. They always do." She rubs my back for a moment and then rolls over and goes back to sleep.

"I love you, Rosita Fernandez," I whisper to her back.

46

"WE HAVE A SITUATION, YOUR HONOR"

"Prominent local businessman Donald Martinez denies accusations of funding a porn business and tax evasion."
— *San Francsico Chronicle.* Thursday, October 28.

Skipper, Molinari and I sit at the defense table. I look around for Rosie, but there's no sign of her yet. She went to pick up Natalie and Ann. Payne and McNulty are talking quietly at the prosecution table.

Judge Kelly takes her place on the bench and studies her notes.

Skipper leans over and whispers, "What do you think?"

Beats the hell out of me. "Innocent," I say.

Judge Kelly turns to me and asks, "Any last-minute issues?"

"No, Your Honor."

As I'm saying this, I hear voices behind me and I turn around. A uniformed police officer is coming down the center aisle. "Excuse me, Your Honor," he says.

Judge Kelly asks, "What is it, Officer Nevins?"

The uniform approaches the bench and says, "Your Honor, I apologize for the interruption. Mr. Daley has an emergency phone call."

My heart pounds. I glance at Skipper, who gives me a puzzled look. Did something happen to Grace? To Rosie? "From whom?" I ask.

"Ms. Fernandez."

I turn to the judge and say, "Your Honor, if I could ask your indulgence for just a moment."

"Yes, Mr. Daley."

I motion Skipper to stay put. My heart is pounding as the officer escorts me outside the courtroom. He opens a cell phone and punches a button. "Ms. Fernandez, it's Officer Nevins. Mr. Daley is with me." He hands me the phone.

"Rosie?"

"Yes."

"Are you okay? What's going on? They're about to read the verdict."

"Go back inside and ask the judge for a recess." Her voice is shaking.

"Why? What happened?"

"It's Natalie. She committed suicide last night."

Dear God.

"It looks as though she swallowed a bottle of sleeping pills."

My mind races. "Where are you?"

"At the house. Ann and I found her. The police are here."

"I'll be there as soon as I can."

"Mike?"

"Yes?"

"There's something else you need to know." I hear her gulp. "There's a suicide note. Natalie wrote that she put the GHB in the champagne flutes. Mike, Skipper didn't drug Johnny Garcia—Natalie did."

Jesus Christ. I hand the phone back to Officer Nevins and take a deep breath. Then he escorts me back into the courtroom. As soon as I walk inside, Skipper stands and looks right at me. I hurry down the aisle and put my arm on his shoulder. I whisper, "I have some very sad news. Natalie decided to take her own life last night." He slumps into my arms as I whisper, "I'm so very sorry, Skipper."

The courtroom is spinning. I hear the buzz of the gallery, the banging of Judge Kelly's gavel. Skipper is sobbing into my shoulder. Above the roar, I hear the judge's voice saying, "Mr. Daley? Mr. Daley?"

Skipper falls back into his chair. I see Turner coming toward us down the aisle. I realize Ed Molinari is standing next to me. I look at Judge Kelly and say, "May it please the court, we would respectfully request a brief recess. We have a situation, Your Honor."

47

"MY VERY DEAR PRENTICE"

"The wife of San Francisco district attorney Prentice Marshall Gates the Third was found dead in her Pacific Heights mansion this morning, the victim of an apparent suicide. Her husband's murder trial has been delayed while police investigate."

—KGO RADIO. THURSDAY, OCTOBER 28. TEN A.M.

A caravan of police cars leaves the Hall of Justice and heads for Skipper's house. Judge Kelly, Hillary Payne and Bill McNulty are riding together in an unmarked car. I'm jammed between Skipper and Turner in the backseat of a squad car. Ed Molinari is behind us in his Jaguar. The judge agreed to delay any further proceedings. For the moment, the trial is in limbo.

I hear the barking of the police radio. Two uniforms sit in the front seat. Skipper is staring straight ahead. He hasn't said a word since we got in the car. Turner's eyes are closed. He swallows every few seconds.

I fold my hands in my lap. I listen to the police band. I watch the cars stream by on Van Ness and then Broadway. It's hot outside and the car is stuffy. I can smell Turner's cologne. Time creeps.

There are a half dozen black-and-whites parked in front of the house. Skipper gets out first. Ann is waiting at the door and she hugs her father. I see Rosie standing behind her.

Elaine McBride and Roosevelt Johnson meet us in the foyer and express their condolences to Skipper. The judge, Payne and McNulty join us. McBride tells us that Rod Beckert and a team from the coroner's office are in the bedroom.

Skipper asks Ann what happened. She says Rosie arrived at eight. Natalie hadn't gotten up yet, so they went to wake her. The door to her room was locked, and they knocked but got no answer. They kicked in the door and found her.

"Sleeping pills?" Turner asks.

Ann nods. "There was an empty bottle next to the bed."

We stand in silence. Then Skipper takes Ann by the hand and they go into the atrium. I whisper to the assembled group, "We should give them a moment." We can hear their sobs as we stand there. I look at Roosevelt and ask, "Was it a suicide?"

He glances at Judge Kelly and says, "I'm not allowed to make any official determinations on cause of death."

"I know. Was it a suicide?"

He shrugs and says, "It seems to be. It looks like she swallowed an entire bottle of sleeping pills."

Turner is visibly distraught. "Did she feel any pain?" he asks.

Roosevelt shakes his head and says, "Probably not."

We're all silent for a moment, then I say, "I understand she left a note."

Roosevelt nods. "Yes." He asks us to wait in the hallway. He returns a moment later with two clear plastic bags. There's a sheet of paper in each. I read it through the plastic. Turner and the judge are reading over my shoulder. The handwriting is steady and very clear.

My very dear Prentice,

By the time you read this, I will be gone. I am completely spent. I have no energy left to protect you. I can no longer lie for you and I cannot bear to watch you suffer. Nor can I stand my own pain. I cannot continue the charade that our marriage became more than twenty years ago. I cannot live with the daily humiliation of watching my husband parade all over town with female and now male prostitutes. You need help, my love. You have for a long time. I am too weary to keep telling you this anymore.

I have never stopped loving you, Prentice, but I cannot live with the emptiness any longer. I went to Turner for comfort. Be kind to him. He has helped me through some very difficult times.

You took away my dignity, Prentice, and you would not seek help, so I decided to take away your political dreams. The only way I could think of doing this was to show you that I had the power to expose you.

But it went terribly wrong, my dear, and I cannot live with the consequences. I knew you had set up the assignation when the champagne was delivered to the room. I had been waiting for such an opportunity, because it was the last resort I could think of to compel you to seek help. I wanted you to wake up and find yourself with an unconscious prostitute in your room. I planned ahead. I obtained GHB over the Internet. I have become quite proficient at obtaining medication for my depression over the Internet and it was not difficult to obtain the GHB. I kept the vial with me always, waiting for the right time. It seemed so simple: to put a drop or two in the flutes when no one was looking, so that when you poured the champagne, you would both be sedated and sleep through the night. When you woke up, you would have found him there with you, and you would have faced a difficult if not impossible situation—not unlike my own. My plan was to confront you when you came home—to show you that I knew everything that had happened and demonstrate to you once and for all that I had the power to humiliate you and end your political career if you did not get help immediately. If you refused or argued with me, I was going to show you the materials I had planted in your storage locker. I knew you kept the photos of those prostitutes at your desk. I had them copied. This would have been a final confirmation that I could—and would—bring you down.

But instead of your waking up with the prostitute still in your bed, the waiter found you and the Garcia boy was dead. I was appalled when I learned this and that you had been arrested for his murder. The weeks since then have been unendurable, and when I heard in court that the GHB might have been the cause of death, I could no longer face myself. I never intended to kill anyone, Prentice. I cannot live with the possibility that I am responsible for it. I hope somehow you will understand.

I will miss you very much, my beloved. I hope you will be able to remember and cherish the good times. And please look in on Ann. She loves you.

Natalie

I swallow hard. Judge Kelly bites her lip. Turner looks away. Payne and McNulty read the letter after us and hand it back to Roosevelt. I say to him, "I'd like to show this to Skipper."

He looks at Judge Kelly, who nods. I take it to Skipper. I am with him and Ann as he reads it. Tears stream down their faces.

Then Skipper turns to me and says, "We'd like to see Natalie."

"Let me see what I can do." I go back to the foyer. "Your Honor," I say, "under the circumstances, I would ask you to permit Mr. Gates and his daughter to have a few moments alone with Mrs. Gates. You have my word that they won't touch anything or otherwise disturb the evidence."

Judge Kelly reflects for a moment. She casts a glance at McBride, who says, "Given the circumstances, it's okay with me." Payne nods. Roosevelt says he'll ask the people from the coroner's office to step out of the room for a moment.

I return to Skipper and tell him they've agreed. "I'll come with you if you'd like," I say.

"I'd appreciate that." He looks at Ann and says, "Come on, honey. Let's go say good-bye."

48

"I NEVER MEANT TO HURT HER"

"My charitable work brings me great joy and satisfaction. If you touch just one life, it's worth it."

—NATALIE GATES.

"She looks so peaceful," Ann says.

She's holding Skipper's hand as they gaze at Natalie, her head resting against the pillow, her eyes closed, the blanket smooth over her body. Death has erased the lines of tension that were so palpable these last weeks; peaceful is indeed the word for what we see before us. The sunlight cascades across her face. I don't know for sure, but I suspect the team from the coroner's office tidied up the scene before Roosevelt escorted them out to the hallway. It was a kind gesture.

"She could be asleep," Skipper says at last, his voice breaking. She's as—as lovely as the first time I saw her. All those years . . . I don't know why everything went so wrong." He sighs and Ann turns to him.

"Don't, Daddy. We can't change it," she says gently. "She's left us. Now it's time for us to leave her."

As she eases him away from the bed, he looks at Natalie one last time, and as we leave the room, I hear him say under his breath, "I never meant to hurt her."

Later that afternoon, we're all in the living room—Skipper, Ann, Turner and I. Judge Kelly and the prosecutors have returned to the Hall of Justice, but the judge agreed to let Skipper remain at the house for the day so that he and Ann could take care of the funeral arrangements. They're done at last, and as we sit quietly in that gracious room, I realize we're all aware of the empty armchair that was Natalie's. It's a melancholy time.

And then, abruptly, I see Skipper sit erect and take charge of himself, as if he's had enough of regrets. It's a different Skipper all of a sudden; even his stance looks focused, determined. Turner sees it, too, though I'm not sure from his expression that he's happy about it.

"I need to tell you what happened that night," Skipper says to Ann. "I should have told you long ago. I can't explain it all—I only know what I did, and saw, but you need to know I didn't kill the Garcia boy. I can't tell you when he died. I can only tell you that up to the time he passed out, he was alive. He was breathing. He'd passed out right after we"—he struggles to find the right words; Ann may be an adult, but still she's his daughter and this is hard for him—"we had sex, but he was okay. And when I came to in the morning, when the waiter woke me up, he wasn't—he was dead." It's almost as if he's seeing Garcia's body all over again, he looks so anguished, but I can also sense he's glad to get this off his chest.

Ann is silent, but she reaches for his hand and strokes it. I ask Skipper whether Johnny had been his usual self when he came to the room.

"Not really," he says. "There was nothing different about the arrangements—I set it up with Andy Holton the way I always did; Garcia was to come to my room at one o'clock. But he was really high when he got there, frantic to the point of panic. I guess heroin can have that effect sometimes. I tried to talk him down, and when that didn't work, I poured him a glass of champagne—I figured the alcohol would calm him. He must still have been panicky, though, because there were those calls to Anderson. I never even knew he made them—I guess it was when I was in the bathroom."

Still, they went through the usual routine, he tells us; and it was only after Garcia passed out that he realized there was trouble. "I couldn't wake him. He was out cold, and I couldn't get the cuffs off. I was scared. I tried to reach Holton, but I couldn't, so I called Turner for help. And I drank a glass of champagne to calm myself while I was waiting for you," he says to Turner, "and that's the last I remember. I must have passed out, too."

"Before that, when you were trying to get the cuffs off," I ask, "was his face still covered with tape?"

"Yes. But only his eyes and mouth—not his nose. I didn't tape his nose. I could hear him breathing. In fact, I listened for it because I was worried about his passing out like that. But it sounded perfectly normal. And that must mean," he says to us, "that somebody else did it. Came into the room when I was out and . . . *suffocated* him. And I keep trying to figure out who—and why."

It's interesting. For the first time in ages, I perceive signs of lawyer-thinking in Skipper. It's been impossible to discern amid all the bombast of the politician in action. In fact, it wasn't easy to find back in the old law firm where we were uneasy partners. Even then, he was too busy working all the angles, promoting himself.

I pick up on what he's just said. "Let's look at the possibilities," I say. "First, of course, is why? Who'd have had it in for you to the point of setting you up for murder? You've got plenty of enemies—politicians do, and as the DA you made still more of them. But *murder*—that's a stretch."

Ann's been following all this quietly, but now she speaks up. "Why are you so sure Daddy was the object of the plot—if it was a plot?" she asks. "Look, we can forget about the GHB. We know Mother did that, but even if it's what knocked them both out, it isn't what killed Garcia. He didn't die accidentally, he was suffocated. Somebody deliberately covered his nose with tape. Maybe killing *him* was the point. Let's concentrate on him for a moment. Let's assume your being there was a coincidence—convenient, to take advantage of, but that's all. In that case, who could have wanted Garcia dead?"

Well. This is a different Ann. She's dropped all that attitude, the abrasiveness and vitriol, as if the death of her mother has stripped away a veneer. There's a tenderness in her voice as she talks to her father, and something else as well. She's thinking like a lawyer, too, and maybe she's right. Maybe Johnny Garcia was the point all along.

I take myself back to the crime scene and consider the hours between his arrival and Wong's waking Skipper at seven o'clock. If he died between one and four A.M., as Beckert estimated he did, who were the people we've identified around the Fairmont? In fact, we can move ahead an hour or so, because from what Skipper's said, Garcia passed out after they had sex. That lets out guys like Parnelli and Morris, because they left too early. So I turn to the guy who's at hand and say, "Fill us in, Turner. You knew Garcia was coming—you arranged for the champagne setup. You got those calls from Skipper and Kevin Anderson. And you came back to the hotel. There's more to it than your just knocking on Skipper's door, isn't there?"

Ann and Skipper listen with me as Turner speaks up at last. I wish we'd known what he had to say before now—it would have saved all of us a lot of pain. I think about Natalie and imagine they're doing this, too. Would it have made a difference? We'll never know.

"I went to the hotel because Anderson said I had to," he tells us. "The first time he called was after he got Garcia's messages on his answering machine—he told me there was a problem at the Fairmont and that he was warning Holton. The second call was really urgent. He said Holton had gone to the hotel and gotten no answer when he knocked on your door, and that there was big trouble and I was the one who'd have to deal with it. This was around three o'clock, and I got over there fast. I got no answer to my knock, either, but I still had a key to the hospitality room next door, so I went in and found the connecting door was open."

He stops. I register the fact that Kevin had lied when he told the police and me he didn't get the messages until the next morning, but that's not news. What really gets me is Turner. It's as if he doesn't know how to continue—or doesn't want to. When he finally goes on, I realize why. He's feeling guilty. Turner, the cold fish, the guy who never gives an inch, is feeling guilty. That's a switch. It takes a lot to have cracked that facade.

"I found you passed out in the chair," he says to Skipper, "and Garcia handcuffed to the bed. I fiddled with the handcuffs, but I couldn't release them and I couldn't wake you up, so I . . . I left. I just got the hell out of there." He feels our eyes upon him and adds in protest, "What else could I have done?"

I see Ann wince at this, but Skipper lets it pass. "What about Garcia?" he asks. "Was he still alive when you left?"

"Yes."

"If you didn't put the tape over his nose and I was dead to the world, who did? It means someone must have come in after that."

We watch Turner's face as he says, "I can't tell you for sure. But I do know that other than me, there was only one person besides Holton who knew about you and Garcia, and Holton had already come and gone before I got there. Kevin Anderson knew."

Is he fingering Anderson? That doesn't make sense and I tell him so. "What possible motive could Kevin have for killing Garcia?" I ask. "He was a big earner for the porn operation. He was bringing in a load of cash. Why wipe out a moneymaker?"

"I didn't say he did," Turner answers. "I don't know that he did. But Garcia was big-time trouble—that I do know. Anderson told me this when I was setting up sessions with Garcia for Skipper. He was very worried about it. He said that some of his 'service providers'—his term—were unreliable, and Johnny most of all—a real troublemaker. He was pressing for a bigger cut of the action and he was a major threat. He knew a lot about the whole operation—that Kevin had set up the Web site and that Martinez had funded it. I gathered he was becoming unmanageable."

"Unmanageable" indeed. I like to believe that I'm not naive, but even so, the callousness stuns me. It's as if Garcia were an *object*, not a manipulative, screwed-up, destroyed kid, and setting up sessions, procuring him for Skipper, was a straightforward business deal. Once Skipper stopped seeking out streetwalkers when he wanted sex and shifted to young male prostitutes, he just asked his old friend Turner to take care of it. To hear Turner describe it, you'd think buying Johnny's services was no different from doing your holiday shopping at Macy's. Business is business. What could be simpler? I can tell from Skipper's face that he's hearing it that way, too. And he must be seeing himself in the transaction as well; he looks shaken.

And does it make any sense? Even allowing that Kevin had reason to want Garcia out of the way, how could he have brought it off? "Let's say he had a motive," I say to Turner. "How'd he have gotten into the room? And how come he didn't show up on the security videos?"

"I don't know. Maybe he had a key. Maybe I left the door un-locked—when I left, I left fast. Whichever, he's a shrewd guy—there's nothing here he couldn't have managed. And I'm sure he knew how to beat the cameras—Garcia didn't show up on the tapes, either."

That's plausible enough, and sure, Anderson had to find out what was going on with Johnny after those phone calls, but I'm still having a hard time moving from that to murder. "Okay," I say, "I can see why he needed to check out Garcia. But he didn't have to kill him. There are plenty of other ways Garcia could have been silenced—look at Martinez and his goons. Why would a man like Anderson take that kind of risk in a public place like a hotel? It's foolhardy."

Turner has an answer for this, too. "Oh, I suspect he didn't plan to," he says matter-of-factly. "I imagine it was simply a crime of oppor-tunity. After all, consider what he found when he got there. Skipper was out cold. So was Garcia, his nemesis, the guy who was threatening to expose him for running a male prostitution ring—and not only him but his bankroll, Martinez. They're prominent citizens. They've got reputations to uphold. It would ruin them both. And there are the other businesses, too, the heroin trade and all the money that was bringing in. I can see very easily why he'd take advantage of the mo-ment. It all adds up."

If you're Turner, I guess it does. Christ—talk about cold-blooded.

I ask him whether there's a way to prove any of this, and he shakes his head. "Not that I can think of," he says in that same detached voice. "He's too smart to have left any traces. And there weren't any—we know that."

So we do. And there were no traces to Holton's death, either. Turner professes no knowledge about this or about the guy who slugged me at the Royan. But he points out that Holton, too, was a danger to Martinez and Anderson. "After all, he was the only other person who knew about the entire operation," he says. "It wouldn't surprise me if Anderson took care of him as well—got him some extra-strong heroin and set it up for somebody else to find his body."

That somebody else was me. And it makes perfect sense. In fact, everything Turner's said makes sense. He's put it all together so clinically. He's worked it all out—the dispassionate observer, unmarked by compunction, responsible for nothing.

And of course he'll deny this conversation ever took place. "Where do you fit into this?" I ask him.

"I was just the lawyer, Mike," he says.

Just the lawyer. He procured male prostitutes for Skipper, he set up the entity for the Web site, he helped Anderson and Martinez cover their tracks—and all it makes him is a *functionary*.

"I take it Martinez did fund the Boys of the Bay Area operation," I say to him.

This time he allows himself a sardonic grin. "Absolutely," he replies. "But no one will be able to prove it. I know how he operated. He always used cash. That's untraceable. There won't be any records." He shakes his head as he says this, and adds, "There's no way to know for sure what happened at the Fairmont that night, but I do know they'll never catch Donald Martinez. Not a chance."

Skipper is appalled. "You're telling me the son of a bitch is going to get off again? That's hideous!"

I feel the bile rising at the back of my throat and I want to protest, too, but I know Turner's probably right.

"But you knew about what they were doing all along," Skipper insists. "There must be *something* you can do."

"My job was to try to keep everybody out of trouble," Turner says bluntly. "That was it. I wasn't involved in the operation of the business. I don't condone their activities."

Skipper gives him an incredulous look. "You're telling me you're clean?"

Turner says tersely, "Yes."

"That may literally be true," I retort, "but it's horrendously self-serving. You have just managed to deflect the entire blame to Kevin Anderson and Donald Martinez."

"It's the truth, Mike."

"But you represent both of them."

He nods.

"And you made the arrangements for Skipper to meet Andy Holton."

"That's true, too. I had no choice. We had an election to win."

Skipper looks at his old friend and says bitterly, "I'm not a puppet, you know, there for you to pull the strings as you choose."

Turner shrugs and says, "You were becoming reckless. You were going to get caught in a compromising position." He turns to me and adds as if Skipper weren't there, "Among other reasons, I took on the position of his campaign manager so that we could control the flow of information."

I say, "And in your capacity as his campaign manager, you decided to make arrangements to help him fulfill his needs?"

"Yes. I made certain everything was done in confidence."

"And when Garcia threatened that confidentiality, you played no part in arranging for his death?"

"No."

No, no, no. He's responsible for nothing—including the plight of his decades-long friend who sat in a jail cell charged with the murder of the prostitute Turner had secured for him.

Ann reaches for Skipper's hand. She's as angry as he is. "You've destroyed my father and you talk of being clean," she charges. "You manipulate lives and assert your innocence. My mother is dead and all you talk of is how you controlled the flow of information. How *dare* you? How can you even speak to us now?"

"I felt it was the right thing to do," Turner says blandly. "Your mother was a kind and generous woman. She left a legacy of good works. She didn't kill that boy, and I thought you ought to know that."

I can't restrain myself any longer. "You sanctimonious ass!" I shout. "You talk of kindness as if you are fit to sit in judgment of Natalie or anyone else. You insult her memory and you insult us all—you, who could have prevented this living hell if you had chosen to speak up, to tell the truth."

He sits there in silence, his face impassive.

I hope you burn for all eternity, Turner.

49
A FITTING TESTIMONIAL

"Mistrial declared in Gates murder case."
— *SAN FRANCISCO CHRONICLE. SUNDAY, OCTOBER 31.*

Natalie's funeral is held at Grace Cathedral the following Tuesday, election day. The dignified structure looks like Nôtre-Dame in Paris, except that the San Francisco version is in better shape. The stained-glass rose window above the main entrance always gives me chills when I walk in.

It is the saddest of occasions. The Pacific Heights crowd has turned out to say good-bye; there must be a thousand people.

Rosie and I go up to the front and express our condolences to Skipper, who is wearing dark glasses. He thanks us for coming and for defending him. His voice is barely audible. We offer our sympathy to Ann, who is next to him, her hands in her lap. She acknowledges our words with a faint smile, but her eyes are far away.

The minister delivers an eloquent eulogy to the silent gathering. He speaks of Natalie's generosity and kindness. Her dignity. Her innate elegance. "She was an example for us," he says. "She represented all that we should aspire to become." Skipper begins to sob. Tears are streaming down Rosie's cheeks.

Ann walks to the podium. She thanks everyone for coming and for their tribute to her mother. "I want to announce to you today that my father and I are establishing a charitable fund called the Natalie Gates Memorial Fund, which will be used for the purpose of assisting inner-city youth," she tells us. "We are each donating one million dollars to build the Natalie Gates Memorial Wing at the Mission Youth Center. When it is completed in two years, it will have the capacity to house at least forty young men who would otherwise be living on the streets of the city." She looks around the vast cathedral. "It won't solve all of the city's problems," she says, "but it's a start."

It is a fitting testimonial.

Ernie Clemente comes up to the podium to escort her back to her seat. As he embraces her, we hear her break into sobs.

At the end of the service, I turn and hug Rosie. We don't say anything. We don't need to.

After the service, we stand on the cathedral steps and watch the mourners file past us into the heavy fog. Elaine McBride is with Roosevelt Johnson and Ron Morales. They pause to say hello. McBride tells us the prospective attorney general has indicated that she intends to conduct a full investigation of the activities of the Mission Redevelopment Fund and the Donald Martinez Charitable Foundation.

It is ironic that Skipper's opponent will handle the investigation of Donald Martinez. Word of the investigation received a great deal of attention in the papers. It's all supposition at this point—the skeletons are probably buried by now. We'll see.

"And Kevin Anderson?" I ask.

"We have him under investigation for running a prostitution ring," McBride says. "The evidence is pretty skimpy at this point. We're trying to persuade Stanford and Martinez to testify against him."

Seems unlikely. Unless they're both given full immunity, it would be impossible for them to testify without implicating themselves.

They head down the steps, and Rosie whispers to me, "They're all going to get away with everything, aren't they?"

"Maybe not," I say without the slightest conviction.

Judge Kelly comes out a few minutes later and greets us. She declared a mistrial on Saturday. "You did a nice job," she says. "You had terrible cards and you played them well." She pauses and looks me in the eye. "Do you want to know?"

"Know what?"

"How the jury decided?"

"It doesn't matter anymore."

"I know. But I asked the foreman. I was curious."

"No. It isn't important," I say.

The judge nods and says again, "You did a good job, Mike."

It's drizzling as we head north on the Golden Gate Bridge. Rosie leans over and pecks me on the cheek as we reach the Paradise Drive exit.

"What was that for?" I ask.

"For coming to funerals with me."

"You're one in a million, Rosita Carmela Fernandez," I tell her.

"So are you, Michael Joseph Daley," she says, but I hear her voice crack and realize she's crying.

I reach over and hold her hand tightly. "Rosie, what is it?" I ask. "Is it Natalie?"

"It's everything," she tells me. "This has all been so sad. So unnecessary. I'm tired, Mike and I feel so—so *hopeless*."

I'm shaken. Rosie's my bulwark. She's always been the tough one in the family; she keeps me on course. I've seen her in every kind of mood: feisty, hardheaded, tender, angry, sardonic, but never before have I seen her ready to give up.

"You can't lose heart, Rosie," I plead.

"Why not?"

"Because you're a fighter. Because you have a brave heart. Because you try to do what's right." I reflect for a moment and add, "And if you lose heart, I will, too. I'll be a basket case again, the way I was when we got divorced. Except it will be worse this time."

This brings a grin. "Not that again," she says. "That I can't take. It was bad enough the first time." I feel her straighten up as she adds in a stronger voice, "Okay, I'll work on it. But you've got to work on it, too. Like it or not, we seem to be a duet—neither of us is any good dancing alone. So it's all right to drive me crazy, but you can't give up. Besides, you make a lousy basket case."

She's right on both scores, and I tell her it's a deal. I'll try.

Then she reminds me of the night I nearly crashed. "Remember when you said we needed to take a break?" she asks. "You were right—this has been no way to live, not for us and not for our kid. How about starting now? Can we take it easy for a little while?"

It's a great idea. We could go somewhere warm. Do something fun. "What do you think about Hawaii?" I ask.

She likes that. "Yes!" she says. "Let's do it right away. We can pull Grace out of school for a week. She's never seen Hawaii. For that matter, we haven't, either."

I smile and say, "She confessed to me the other day that third grade isn't really that hard."

"Do we have any money left?"

"Probably not," I reply. "We spent most of the Asshole Premium already."

She chuckles. "Of all the lawyers in the world out there, I have to be partners with an Irish Seinfeld."

"You wouldn't want it any other way," I tell her as we pull into the driveway of her house. Grace and Sylvia are standing on the porch, waiting for us. I wave to them and say to Rosie, "We can call the travel agent in the morning. Grace looks hungry. What do you say the four of us go out for some burgers and shakes?"

Rosie's eyes light up. She tells Grace, who beams.

ACKNOWLEDGMENTS

In the last couple of years, I have learned that it takes a lot of effort and hard work by a dedicated team to publish a novel. I'm lucky. I get a lot of help from many kind and generous people. I can't possibly thank all of you, but I'm going to try.

To Ann Harris, my thoughtful, tireless and exceedingly patient editor, collaborator, mentor and friend. I cannot imagine trying to write my stories without you. And thanks for letting me write long acknowledgments.

To Irwyn Applebaum, Nita Taublib, Barb Burg, Susan Corcoran, Betsy Hulsebosch, Gina Wachtel, Carolyn Schwartz and the rest of the team at Bantam. Thanks also to the wonderful sales force for being so enthusiastic.

To the bookstores, mail order clubs and online services and your hardworking staffs who play a huge role in helping me get my stories to my readers.

To my agent, Margret McBride, and to Kris Wallace, Donna DeGutis, Sangeeta Mehta and Jessica Clark at the Margret McBride Literary Agency. I appreciate your professionalism, wise counsel and good humor. You're the best.

To my generous writing instructors, Katherine V. Forrest and Michael Nava, who write wonderful books and who helped me get started.

To the Every Other Thursday Night Writers' Group: Bonnie DeClark, Gerry Klor, Meg Stiefvater, Kris Brandenburger, Anne Maczulak, Liz Hartka, Janet Wallace and Priscilla Royal. Thanks for getting me to the finish line again. I can't do this without you.

To my board of advisers, who (thankfully) know so much more about murders and trials than I do: Inspector Sergeant Thomas Eisenmann, Officer Jeff Roth and Inspector Phil Dito of the San Francisco Police Department, criminal defense attorney David

Nickerson and Dr. Gary Goldstein. If I got anything wrong in this book, it's all my fault.

To my friends and colleagues at Sheppard, Mullin, Richter & Hampton (and your spouses and significant others), who have contributed continuing expertise, support and encouragement. You are the finest professionals I've ever met and you're the best friends a person could have. In particular, my thanks to Randy and Mary Short, Cheryl Holmes, Chris and Debbie Neils, Bob Thompson, Joan Story and Robert Kidd, Lori Wider and Tim Mangan, Becky and Steve Hlebasko, Donna Andrews, Phil and Wendy Atkins-Pattenson, Julie and Jim Ebert, Geri Freeman and David Nickerson, Kristen Jensen and Allen Carr, Bill and Barbara Manierre, Betsy McDaniel, Ted and Vicki Lindquist, John and Joanne Murphy, Tom and Beth Nevins, Joe Petrillo, Maria Pracher, Ted and Sydney Russell, Rick and Chick Runkel, Chris and Karen Jaenike, Ron and Rita Ryland, Kathleen Shugar, John and Judy Sears, Mathilde Kapuano, Jerry Slaby, Dick Brunette, Aline Pearl, Terry Meeker, Bob and Elizabeth Stumpf, Steve Winick, Judy Hathorne-Waters, Bill Wyatt, Greta Love, Maria Sariano, Nina Porcella, Avital Elad, Chuck MacNab, Sue Lenzi and Bob Zuber. Thanks also to my very understanding clients, who have been kind enough to rearrange their legal problems so that they occur when I'm not on deadline.

To my friends who patiently read my drafts and provide kind and helpful input: Rex and Fran Beach, Jerry and Dena Wald, Gary and Marla Goldstein, Ron and Betsy Rooth, Rich and Debby Skobel, Dolly and John Skobel, Alvin and Charlene Saper, Doug and JoAnn Nopar, Dick and Dorothy Nopar, Angele and George Nagy, Polly Dinkel and David Baer, Jean Ryan, Sally Rau, Bill and Chris Mandel, Dave and Evie Duncan, Jill Hutchinson and Chuck Odenthal, Joan Lubamersky and Jeff Greendorfer, Tom Bearrows and Holly Hirst, Melinda and Randy Ebelhar, Chuck and Ann Ehrlich, Chris and Audrey Geannopoulos, Julie Hart, Jim and Kathy Janz, Denise and Tom McCarthy, Raoul and Pat Kennedy, Eric Chen and Kathleen Schwallie, Jan Klohonatz, Marv Leon, Christie Musser, Erica Peresman and David Jaffe, Kathleen Vanden Heuvel, Bob and Leslie Berring, Louise Epstein, David Rubin, David and Petrita Lipkin, Pamela Swartz, Cori

Stockman, Allan and Nancy Zackler, Ted George, Nevins McBride, Marcia Shainsky, Maurice and Sandy Ash, Elaine and Bill Petrocelli, Penny and Tom Warner, and Sheila, Alan, and Leslie Gordon.

To my extended family: Charlotte, Ben, Michelle and Margaret Siegel, Ilene Garber, Joe, Jan and Julia Garber, Terry Garber, Roger and Sharon Fineberg, Jan Harris Sandler and Matz Sandler, Scott, Michelle, Stephanie and Kim Harris, Cathy, Richard and Matthew Falco and Julie Harris. As always, family matters.

To my twin sons, Alan and Stephen, who think it's very neat that Daddy writes stories, and who go to bed on time every night so Daddy can work on his books.

To my wife, Linda, who has been my love, support, best friend and lucky charm since we met in a parking lot in Berkeley in 1982. Thanks for editing my stories—and me. And thanks for putting together my Web site. Everybody thinks it's really cool. It's nice to be married to an electrical engineer.

Finally, thanks to my wonderful readers, who have been so supportive, especially those of you who have taken the time to write or e-mail. I appreciate your enthusiastic feedback.

ABOUT THE AUTHOR

Sheldon Siegel, a graduate of the University of California/Berkeley's Boalt Law School, has been in private practice in San Francisco for over seventeen years, and specializes in corporate and securities law with the firm of Sheppard, Mullin, Richter & Hampton. His first novel was the critically acclaimed national best-seller *Special Circumstances*. He lives in Marin County with his wife, Linda, and their twin sons. He is working on his third Mike Daley story. He can be reached by e-mail at sheldon@sheldonsiegel.com and on the Web at www.sheldonsiegel.com.